Linda

Hope you enjoy! Sweetie ♡

DERAILED

Love changes everything.

by

RENEE LEE FISHER

Love-
Renee

Credits

Dedication

For all the times in my own life that I have come to a cross road, I am grateful for the distractions that steered me in a different direction. I would never have taken some of the paths and met so many incredible people if I stayed straight on my course. I am glad that, often, I too have been **derailed**.

For all those who have met me along the way, I am glad you were a part of my life, my journey. This book I dedicate to all of you, even those not in the forefront, who have waved and cheered from the sidelines in my life.

Prelude

We are born into this world with no direction. Choices overwhelm us, molding us into one type of person or another. Our personalities grown, distinguishing us from our neighbor and helping us connect on certain levels with others. Unique characteristics set us apart. What we doubt within ourselves, another may love.

Sometimes, life leads us in different directions. It pulls us into the unknown and unfamiliar. It is a journey we travel on an unforeseen course. As we progress through our years, often moments stop us in our tracks, and we decide what to do next or think on it just one more day. Where the heart is involved, it may take a much longer period of intense thought.

It could be only a one-time occurrence or, for some lucky people, more than just once, but when you get hit with it, you will know. You can't see it, but it takes your breath away. It makes you tingle, lose time, and forget everything that surrounds you. In that moment, **love changes everything**.

Chapter One

THE SUN BARELY SKIMMED THE top of the crowded metal floral basket hanging outside her door, full of blooming Abutilon (Red Bells of Summer) and crisp white Begonias, preparing to burn away the fog visiting off the ocean. Aubrey glanced out before turning the sign on the bakery door to *open*. Every morning, seven days a week, she completed the same ritual while hoping income would increase and make her dreams for *Sweet Treats* as fruitful as her pies.

Turning, she observed her business with the same contentment she'd felt looking at the sun rising over her quaint beach town. From the white wrought iron café tables with vases of fresh flowers in the center to the simple crème walls that framed the colorful, painted floral canvases, she'd created a setting designed to welcome the local residents and tourists alike. However, the bakery display cases filled with fresh baked delights and the counter top brimming with baskets loaded with fresh muffins lured them in. The scent of sliced lemons and ripe blueberries lingering probably didn't hurt, either.

Even though the revenue came from the tourist season, which was about five months of the year, most of her enjoyment occurred with the steady flow of the town locals. She had the opportunity off-season to talk with them more and engage in what was happening with the town. They stopped in often to share their stories, talk of the weather, and also mention their opinions for her love life. Most assured her she was quite attractive and her baking skills were a plus to any man's heart. Problem was she knew most of the men in the town, and many were already taken. Those not taken yet simply hadn't let their eyes cast her way.

Smoothing her floured hands on her apron, she licked her lips slowly and tasted the remnants of the red velvet frosting, today's special cupcake flavor. One more light wipe around the baskets on the counter top with her dish cloth, and she was ready to begin this new day.

Her first patrons were cheerful and friendly. Pete and Levi popped in for their morning brew, a kiss to her cheek, and sprinkled donuts; they favored the red, white, and blue, as they were police officers. As per normal, and cutting into her profits, she packaged them each a brownie and a huge chocolate chip cookie for the remainder of their shift. She never wanted to charge them as they often checked in on her, knowing she worked alone except on delivery days when a local teenager helped out.

"Aubrey, you're such a beautiful sight to see first thing in the morning," Levi complimented. She smiled. He said this to her every day he stopped in before work. Aubrey was still finishing the last of the to-go bags for them, folding the top down tightly to keep the contents fresh as Pete reached across the counter and put a twenty dollar bill in front of her. She'd learned not to dispute his actions and took it, placed it into the register, and nodded to him as her thank you.

Aubrey never thought of herself as beautiful. Her simple brown hair framed her face and landed just past her shoulders, easy for her to manage. Light makeup and a swift application of a gloss to her already pink lips and she was ready for the day with the bakery crowd.

Despite the dark brown of her eyes, a brightness always shined through. Her body was petite but well-endowed. She had to tone it down in the bakery, wearing a tee shirt with a crew neckline under her apron. She didn't need anything low cut to flaunt that her chest was a great asset.

As nice as it was to hear men tell her endearing comments, the only compliments she wanted to hear were those about her baked goods. For a moment, she played with the icing that dripped over the edge of the one pastry. Her fingertip was smoothing it out, making it perfect, yet she was remembering how she couldn't fix her recent relationship. Aubrey thought how hard it was not hearing compliments from Emerson, her ex-boyfriend she'd let go a short time back. His life and what he sought to do were too extreme for hers. He seemed to wander into doing things that were against the law. Also, as many times as she could recall, she had to keep trying to please him, and no one should have to constantly work so hard at doing that. Love should be a give and take and definitely working together.

Emerson had placed himself in the mix of some bad guys and that did not work with Aubrey at all. His one friend, Damon, gave her chills when he was around. Something about him didn't seem legit. He didn't seem like a worker on the construction site with Emerson at all. He appeared rough and had that don't mess with me attitude. He would be a fine fit as a bouncer at the local bar. Damon never said much, just observed. He trailed along side of Emerson any place he went. Thinking again of why she and Emerson parted, she licked her finger of the excess sweet, sugary icing and recalled it soured when Emerson had become too involved in drugs. She didn't want to lose her home and the bakery because of his stupidity. Cutting him loose from her life was tough but seemed the right thing to do.

The front door bells rang, and other locals came in, breaking her thoughts. The customers browsed her cases, and their eyes opened to the edible wonders she created. When she turned to assist the new customers, the officers were leaving to start their shift and sent her a friendly wave as they took bites of their breakfast. She smiled at the crumbs that left a trail behind their heavy shoes.

Aubrey went from the empty case of the pastries out front to the backroom. There she cut generous slices of her homemade pies and plated them and spent time filling the empty spaces of the ones purchased. Today she was busier than normal, but she knew that since she made enough of her treats for two days of sales that she could relax this evening. She planned to catch up with her roommate, Tessa, but for the next week, Tessa was meeting some friends in the city. She had begged Aubrey to come, but Aubrey had to run the bakery and passed on the invitation. One day, maybe, she would venture in the city for some nighttime fun. Even though Tessa seemed to want her to come along, Aubrey sensed she was just being pleasant as a roommate. It wasn't her scene in the city, and Tessa knew that. Each time she left for a few nights, Aubrey welcomed the peace and quiet of her home and a hot bath after being on her feet all day, sometimes fourteen hours.

Now Tessa, she need not work. She was the daughter of the mayor, and her father had a lot of real estate that brought in a good chunk of money. She was his only child now as he had lost his son some time ago. The town talk was that he had been shot and killed through mistaken identity. Tessa and her father rarely commented on their loss, and most didn't pry as it probably still was an open wound. The mayor, a widower who never remarried or had a current love interest, focused all his attentions on his daughter. She didn't mind that her daddy spoiled her, but she wanted some independence so she up and told her father that she was planning to move down the beach and live with Aubrey.

Despite her father's argument that the area wasn't as favorable to the eye as the homes and condos right off the streets and water's edge in the main part of town, Tessa moved in with Aubrey in the house her grandmother had left her when she passed away. The grand, Victorian style beach home with six bedrooms, five bathrooms, a wraparound porch, and a spacious second floor balcony facing the beach sounded more impressive than it looked. Mostly, the value was due to the large lot it sat on and the location. Every rainstorm, Aubrey dodged between all the rooms putting vases and buckets to catch the many leaks.

For Tessa, it gave her freedom away from her father. For Aubrey, it was the roof over her head, and the bakery and the money Tessa paid in rent kept it there. The place had a major perk, though. It was located on the beach, which had a priceless view, and Aubrey knew she wanted to keep it in her family. She was grateful that a property was hers.

Time to time, Aubrey would ask if Tessa wanted to help her out at her bakery, but it never happened. Though Tessa always fussed over herself, her makeup, her hair, and her newest, secret boy toy–never realizing a world existed beyond herself—she and Aubrey really hit it off. They both met when Tessa couldn't rid herself of a local named Wade that continuously asked her out. One day she simply told him she couldn't go out with him because she knew Aubrey had a thing for him. Begging Aubrey to go along with it, they laughed together long after the date Aubrey and Wade had was a total flop. He backed off from coming around. Occasionally, she saw him across the street, but rarely did he enter the bakery.

The afternoon slowed to a quiet one. Aubrey sat on top of the counter and swung her legs, giving them a good stretch. She kept promising to buy herself a pair of decent work shoes to relieve her aching feet, but for now, her beaten and food-spotted sneakers were all she could afford. She rested her head on the side of the commercial coffee maker, one that she shut down earlier but remained warm, and closed her eyes for what seemed to be a second.

The bells sounded on the front entrance. The noise often awoke her senses as hearing them ring alerted her to new patrons. They were nautical pieces strung together that she picked up at one of the stores in town. The long strand of shells and bells twined together gave off a delicate ring with each customer who entered.

Jumping down off the counter and straightening out her apron, she apologized to the patron before she even regarded his or her face. As she glanced up, she hesitated. A sudden awareness touched her neck, as if a strand of her hair had fallen loosely from being pinned up and swept across her skin. The feeling lingered, definitely something out of the ordinary.

"Hey, no apologies. Just wanted some coffee," the rough voice stated.

"Good morning. I am Aubrey. Your coffee is coming right up. Are you from the area?" She tried to lighten up the mood, knowing he was definitely not a local.

"No, not from here. I'm just waiting on a friend from the train station. I was feeling a bit tired so I thought the coffee would do me good." His voice was wary and reluctant.

Although he seemed polite, she watched as his eyes shifted around the place, checking it out. In that moment, she took in his large build, the few tattoos, and a definite shadow on his cheeks from not shaving. His features were chiseled, and although he appeared rough, he was handsome with a slight kindness to his face. Politeness rose from the depths of his deep voice. She was staring at him but then kept glancing away. He had that rugged sexiness that none of the locals displayed.

"Would you like cream or sugar?" Politely asking, she poured the hot coffee.

"Both," he simply stated.

"Anything else I can bring you?" She slid the coffee across the counter to him. She suggested the Red Velvet iced cupcakes, as only a few remained.

"Thank you, but no thank you," he replied in his deep voice, deliberately skimming his hand against hers when he grabbed the cup. At first it felt like their skin connected, and oddly enough, their hands remained touching for what was only a second. That brief moment, he felt an intense sensation of warmth from *her*. Tate contemplated the cupcakes because he was certain they were good, but when he eye-balled them, he caught the thick red icing. They made his stomach turn instantly.

Aubrey pulled back nervously from his intrusive touch as he took his cup of coffee. Although in that brief skin-on-skin moment, she experienced that sensation once again. He left a couple singles on the counter. When she didn't reach back out to take them from his hand, she could see disappointment in his eyes. Aubrey counted the money. She intended to tell him he'd left too much, but he was already out the door. She watched as he sat on the bench across the street and two doors down. Remembering the heaviness of his boots on his exit, she'd recognize if he came back to cause problems.

Her work day was coming to a close. Aubrey broke off a

corner from a crumbled cookie that came off her tray earlier. Placing the sugary piece on her tongue, it soothed her inside. Her fingers reached up and unpinned her hair that was piled in a loose-swept pony tail. A tug on the bow around her neck released her apron, and it was scrunched and tossed into the laundry basket to take home and clean. Aubrey was heading to close up the bakery and turn the *open* sign around. As she approached the door and spun the wooden sign, the door pushed open, and he stepped in and kept her from locking up.

"Oh, please say you're not closing just yet?"

She looked at the customer and smiled pleasantly. Jackson, Tessa's cousin, was the town's best real estate agent. In fact, he had worked with her to finalize the deal on this commercial space. It needed a lot of work, but he worked a price with the lessor to fit her budget. Plus, Jackson was always helpful in the business sense. Why he had not found a lovely local to settle with was a question all the single women asked.

"No, I have a few minutes to grab you whatever you need," Aubrey courteously offered. She headed back around the front counter. Jackson scanned the displays and what pastries remained.

"I don't see any of those pecan twirls in the case. Do you have any in the back?"

"Jackson, I always have extra for you. Let me put a box together."

Aubrey went to the rear of the bakery. Boxing up the sweets for him, she started to hum. The day was over, and he was her last customer and a kind one, not like the out-of-towner from earlier that put her senses on alert.

There had been something distinctive about the stranger. She'd even thought about his facial features and how handsome he was a few times during the day. Her eyes hadn't pored over a guy that striking in a long time. She supposed he caught the train or met who he was waiting on as she hadn't seen him on the bench the last time she peered out the front window. As she placed the last gooey twirl in the box and was about to tape it shut, her hum was muffled and, in seconds, her breath taken from her.

A hand forcefully grabbed her from behind. Frantically, her arms wheeled in the air. She hit and tossed bowls filled with flour and icing, anything she could reach on the back counter. Her attacker pushed her over the butcher block, unzipping her skirt until it fell to the floor and exposed her pale thighs.

"Aubrey, I don't want to hurt you. Just don't fight me. If you fight me…" Something sharp brushed against the skin of her neck, and her eyes automatically explored where the knife that she'd cut the pies with earlier had been. Gone. Worse, she realized that no one would hear her if she did scream. The bakery was closed, and the streets outside had been deserted. And Jackson was going to rape her. "This is going to be sweet, baby girl. You might even like it." The sound of his zipper was louder than his words, a moment before he pushed her panties down.

Squeezing her eyes shut, Aubrey imagined the faint sound of bells as she prayed someone would help her. Instead, though, she felt Jackson move his hand from her mouth to her throat and then lower. She let out a light crying whimper. His hardness pressed between her legs, and she knew he was about to enter her before he hastily pulled away.

His weight lifted off her. Long moments passed as her senses returned. The sound of flesh pounding flesh filled her ears. When she opened her eyes, the stranger with the heavy boots was delivering punch after punch into precise areas of Jackson's body.

Her shaking hands pulled up her panties, and she nervously moved away from the two men. Her legs quivered, causing her to stumble as she moved toward the door. Even with her attacker lying bloodied and moaning on the floor, she could barely gather her thoughts to decide what she needed to do next.

"Are you okay?" the stranger asked. Aubrey was too frightened to answer. "I said, 'are you okay?'" She nodded, stepping back as the man approached her. Instead of taking advantage, he handed her the skirt she'd left behind, looking away for the moment to give her a bit of privacy.

Aubrey repositioned her skirt, her fingers still trembling. He waited, he opened and closed, and flexed his throbbing fists, as she smoothed the front of her skirt, apprehensively wiping her hands back and forth over the fabric several times. His movement broke her concentration on her clothing as he handed her the phone that was now covered with his bloody fingerprints and a towel. "You need to call the police and have them take this piece of trash out of here. First, though, wipe my prints off this phone. Can you do that for me?" Audrey nodded her head at his words. "Good. I'm going to leave here, but I'll wait across the street until they arrive."

He reached toward her face, his thumb set to brush her cheek. She jerked back, and he paused. When he tried again, she didn't move, and he tenderly swept his thumb across her face to erase her tears. The moist drops that formed from her eyes now coated his bloody finger.

"Aubrey, you are going to be alright." She heard her name spoken with sincerity in his voice. She was surprised he had remembered it from when she greeted him earlier in the day. Even him saying her name felt safe and reassuring coming from his mouth.

As quickly as he came in and saved her, he left. All she heard was the thump of each step of his boots until that quieted and the sound of the sirens became louder. Across the street, he remained true to his word, and as the police car promptly arrived in front of the bakery, he began his walk down past the store fronts and the few locals gathered to watch the bakery. As he crossed the street, he bent down to remove the pink icing that was embedded on the sole of his left boot from the bakery floor. He grabbed a leaf and wiped it off. Then he continued to walk far from the commotion of the street.

TATE MANNING HAD JUST SAVED this beautiful girl that he knew nothing about. He had been in the right place today to prevent a brutal act. The meeting at the train station never took place; the person he was waiting on never arrived. Tate had nothing to keep him here in Cape May, New Jersey. It was a quaint town with an initial inviting sweetness about it, but his journey took him town to town. Rarely did he stay more than one night.

He saw her face as she stood near the ambulance that arrived, and he watched her shake her head to signal that she didn't want to be taken away. Again, his heart felt funny in his chest, just as it had when his fingers touched hers around his cup of coffee earlier. Tate watched, also, as they removed the scumbag that he just roughed up. He knew one more punch in the right area would have taken him out, but Tate had learned a while back to reel it in. If he didn't pull back, he'd have left a long list of dead men across the states. After all, his only mission was to travel and take down the person or individuals that were involved in his wife's murder. Too many demons played in his head because of his loss. They would never be silenced until he found closure.

Today, as much as he wanted to stay and help Aubrey with the authorities, that was not his task. He didn't want the local police department finding out that he was a cop, as that would raise a lot of flags with him just happening to be there and beating the guy near death. He wanted to walk away and continue onto the next lead in the unsolved murder that caused him to never sleep. He headed farther away from the bakery and crossed the next intersection to the bus depot. Seemed like all the traffic in this town was in front of *Sweet Treats* now. He didn't have to check for cars coming...nor would he have as he walked across the main street.

A bus pulled away just as he arrived. Tate was in no rush to head anywhere, so he bought a ticket and sat himself down to wait for the next bus. He could sit again. Hell, he had waited on the bench at the train station all day long. It wasn't too long before the bright blue and white bus rolled in. Tate stood with others to board. When the bus was filled with the passengers, it rolled out. As it left the parking lot, Tate took a quick last glimpse down the street. He was still standing at the curb, his feet reluctant to board the bus. Appeared like Tate was going to have to find a room to sleep in tonight.

He had watched the bakery the entire day, waiting on his contact, but when they never showed, he still observed *Sweet Treats* and the activity that came and went. Something kept him on the bench. A few times, he walked down the block to stretch his legs. When he came back to sit at the bench, his glance across the street caught her eyes from the bakery. Was she looking at him or for him?

He thought a few times of leaving, but decided to stick it out till late in the afternoon. He knew the bakery would be closing, and he hoped to get one last glance at her. He observed a sleek black Mercedes quickly whip into the front parking space next to her parked car. He watched her greet the man with a smile and turn the bakery sign to *closed*. Tate wasn't sure if it was her boyfriend, but he picked up on the guy seconds earlier was looking up and down the street just before she let him in. Something here was off.

Tate sensed that more than the obvious was going on. Maybe the bakery was a front, a cover-up. His days on the force pursuing drug dealers had him on high alert. His mind was stirring, and he decided to go check it out. He walked toward the front door, his head almost connecting with the red flowers that brimmed closely along the doorframe. The air was still until he detected loud banging sounds, something crashing to the floor.

There was no evidence of the guy in the front area where customers should be. He tried the door, and it was unlocked. As he approached the back, he could see the pastries scattered across the floor. He thought he heard someone cry softly. He stood and listened in the hallway. Next, all he had to hear was the words, "This is going to be sweet, baby girl. You may even like it." Fury rushed through him, pulsing blood in the veins of his powerful arms. He thought of Callie's throat cut, and he pictured this pretty woman in a situation that sounded horribly bad.

When he entered the back room, the assailant had no clue he was there. The guy had his pants down, prepared to violate her. He was focused on nothing else as his fingers deeply gripped her waist and held her painfully as her flesh reddened. He overpowered her petite, delicate frame and was seconds from taking her, entering her, and forcefully hurting her. Tate reacted. Though he wanted to kill her attacker as soon as he yanked him away from her, he paused after several hits to the man's face and chest. He knew just where to aim his vigorous pounding punches that would take him down, leaving him sprawled out motionless but still alive on the tile floor below. Tate knew the scumbag wouldn't be touching her or anyone for a long time or ever again.

Now that was messed up; he had wanted to come to this town and leave, never thinking he would be involved in something like this. Now though, he wanted to enfold her in his arms and comfort her, to stay with her. He'd known he had to leave once he helped her to dress; he knew it was best that he go. As he continued his walk to find a bed to sleep in for the evening, he rung his hands together and wiped them in his pants pockets, trying to remove the blood. He was sure he would have to sign in and register at the place he found to sleep.

Chapter Two

WALKING DOWN THE TOWN'S STREETS, he came to one block lined with inns and hotels. He wasn't selective. He walked toward the first one that caught his eye with the vacancy sign. As soon as he entered, he asked if he could use the restroom. The girl behind the lobby desk pointed to the door just behind him. He kept both his hands deep down in his pockets.

After he thoroughly washed every finger, the water in the sink ran red before it cleared, making its way down the drain. Tate tugged a few towels from the wall dispenser, wet them thoroughly, and pumped out the scented hand soap from the bottle on the corner of the sink. Rigorously he scrubbed his pockets. He removed a folded, cotton guest towel from a pile on a small table next to the sink. Tate dried his hands completely. No blood remained. He stood for a moment and looked in the mirror. His face needed to soften or he would scare the shit out of this innkeeper, if he hadn't already. His chest took a few deep breaths and then he went back to the lobby to check in.

Tate accepted whatever room the innkeeper suggested.

"My name is Lacey, and welcome to the Hamilton Inn." She seemed to be a pleasant host, but hearing her rattle off a detailed history of the property and whichever famous person allegedly stayed there was of no interest to him. He gave her an occasional nod or slight smile, because that's all he could do. He rarely smiled. This world brought out the worst in people, and he had seen that first hand. He wanted to rid his head of the demons that tormented him, keeping him solemn and existing day to day. His hopes, happiness, and any reason for aspiring toward a future vanished long ago.

"I need a room for tonight. Doesn't have to be anything special, just a bed," he stated. His eyes traveled to the tiny camera that was mounted in the corner as a security measure. He didn't want to be photographed or known to be in any particular place. His personal mission was to roam into the town, find out what he needed to, and move onward. How would he react if he found the person that murdered his wife? Often he thought about that scenario, but surely didn't know how it would play out.

Tate handed over a one hundred dollar bill for the room that was only seventy-five dollars. "I will get you some change," Lacey stated. She was very cute. He did take care to notice that. Her dark hair was swept across her face, hiding one eye, but the one that was shown was a beautiful shade of blue. Ocean blue, and here he was by the sea. So appropriate.

"No need. I will square up with you before I leave. I'm pretty tired and just want to rest." He would be gone by morning, and the extra money was a nice tip for her genuine smile as she checked him in.

All Tate thought about with each squeaky wooden step to the second floor was arriving in the room Lacey selected and lying flat out on the bed. He wanted to clear his head from what happened at the bakery.

Lacey attempted to show him the layout of the small accommodations of this room, noting the towels and the remote, but Tate thanked her quickly and just wanted to be alone. As she exited, he closed the door and hit the switch allowing the ceiling fan above to begin to whirl.

His head hit the pillow, and it was too low. Tate took the other pillow and placed it under his head. That felt so much better. The room was airy with big windows. The breeze blew through the open window, bringing just a hint of the sea air smell inside. It was only September so no chilly nights just yet. He remembered that he had been to the beaches that lined the New Jersey coastline when he was younger with his friends, but he didn't recall ever coming to this beach town, which was the last one in the string of many. It actually appeared as though the earth ended when you hit the edge of this town. Now with his head sunk comfortably in the pillows, he stared up and was watching the blades spin round and round. Without removing his boots or his clothes when he lay back, he soon was fast asleep.

TATE HAD BEEN WORKING HARD on a case, putting in long hours. Callie and he hadn't shared a meal together in days. As he left the

station, he thought he would pick up some dinner and flowers before heading home. The dinner choice was easy, some barbeque take out, but he stood and pondered over the floral selection. He remembered she loved the color pink so he grabbed two wrapped bunches of roses, and pink they were.

Tate was an undercover officer in the narcotics division when he first met his soon-to-be wife, Callie. It was at the station. She was coming in to bail out her father for drug possession. Tate stood in the hallway and watched her every move and wanted to meet her but knew he would blow his cover. Shortly after springing her father from the authorities, Tate conveniently ran into Callie at a local coffee shop, and he approached her.

He knew it was conflict of interest with his job, that if he told her his occupation she would think he was using her to secure a position inside to take down her father or those that worked for him. It may have appeared like that but was never the case. Immediately, Callie and Tate connected. The day did come that he told her what he did for a living, and she was glad actually, hoping he would knock sense into her father to halt his involvement with the corrupt drug dealings. When Callie shared with Tate that her mother died from a deal gone bad, he knew he wanted to protect her and be with her forever.

Every day he worried about her if they parted for several hours or if a case kept him working many long and late hours. He was completely devoted to her. He didn't want to overwhelm her with his keeping track of her, not from mistrust, but his love for her had him keeping one eye open where she was concerned. Callie and Tate both agreed to keep his occupation under wraps from her father. He would have never let his only daughter marry someone in law enforcement. Callie told her father that he worked in investments. Her father loved that, hoping he could invest his tainted money one day into big returns. If her father had only known his true identity.

Most of the time when Tate and Callie visited her father, Tate overheard a few words of the conversations while her father was finishing up daily business, and Tate kept his eyes and ears open. They didn't have to be too wide open because Callie's father didn't even try to hide his wrong-doings. He flaunted it often, and Tate knew one day that her father would be caught and put away in jail for a long time or taken down by someone that he once dealt wrongly.

He wanted to move her away someplace more secure, but Callie was stubborn. She loved her father, even though he worked with the most corrupt people. He was all she had. She'd lost her mother so tragically. Drug dealing had built a nice roof on the home for Callie and her father. It had been at the price of losing her mother when one of the deals went totally wrong.

Callie's father dictated all the deals and tried to bring Tate in to his fold. Tate never wavered from his stance to wipe the earth clean of the bad people. He vowed to Callie to find who killed her mother. That justice was carried out by another's hand, but at least Callie had her mind at rest knowing the murderer was dead. He remembered Callie and he visited her mother's grave and placed pink roses near her headstone. Callie said they were her mom's favorite and hers, too. Although he never met her mother he was certain she would have approved of her daughter's choice for her husband.

Tate rolled over in the bed suddenly restless as the bright flowers faded and darkness seeped into his mind.

"Tate, someone is downstairs. I can hear them. Please get here right away. I already pressed the silent alarm to alert the police. It beeped."

Callie's desperate voice was whispering and shaky. Urgency and nervousness peppered each word.

Tate whipped his steel grey pickup truck around, barely checking for oncoming traffic, and accelerated in the direction of his house. "I'm coming now. Hide someplace. Keep the phone open; stay with me. You don't have to speak so they don't hear you. Just know I am right there with you. I am not leaving you."

Tate remained calm in his directions as his foot pounded the gas pedal harder. No street lights hindered him as he blew through the intersections, one after another. Only a few blocks from his home, he heard the sirens.

He was relieved to see the large police presence at his home, knowing they were calming his wife, from whoever was putting her in danger. He vowed to protect her and that he did, knowing that her father was into things that may put her life at risk one day. Tate understood everyday he had to be careful. Having a high end security system installed was assurance, but there was never any peace of mind for Tate. He felt comfortable each night he climbed into their bed and enfolded her into his strong arms, reassuring her that he was there for her always.

Turning his truck swiftly on to his lawn, Tate threw it into park and jumped out. "Babe, I'm here. Coming in the house now!" He didn't hear her speak back but surely she was safe, probably giving details to his fellow officers. As he passed the police presence that was outside on his property, they tried to halt him. "No, where is my wife?" He didn't stop, just pushed passed their extended arms, eagerly questioning her location. He wanted her to take comfort and feel safe in his arms immediately.

"Tate, hold on," Reed, his partner, called out to him.

Tate was on his own mission and took the steps two at a time.

*"Callie? CALLIE? **CALLIE?**" Her name escaped in a loud desperate shout as he passed another policeman on the top landing.*

His senses were on high alert, and he was anxious to reach her. He wanted to shelter her from this upsetting ordeal. He needed to see her face and know she was alright. Seconds before he entered the bedroom, he felt it. Dread washed over him. He foresaw the familiar crime scenes with blood freshly oozing from a victim and the fear of lifelessness. Tate stood only inches in their bedroom doorway and could see the pool of red that surrounded his wife's head. She was on the floor across the room. He fell to the rug, pounding his fists until they bloodied. His own blood dripping from his hands. Tate's body trembled. His lips quivered as they repeated "No" over and over. The officers left him alone in his sorrow.

Tate anxiously tossed on the bed and moaned in his sleep.

Her father stood without emotion at the morgue. He had sold his soul to the wrong side in life long ago. Tate approached him. "You knew this would happen. You knew one day those piece of shit people you hire for the drugs would turn on you. You son of a bitch, haven't you learned from the loss of one woman, your wife? No, you learned nothing! Another sweet woman, my wife, was sacrificed for your drug money. I vow I will find who killed my wife and I will take care of this. I will not stop there. I will arrest each person that works for you one by one so this stops. This has to end. I will find her killer."

Callie's father gave no response to Tate, but his head nodded slowly. His aged face was worked over with remorse. He knew her father was finally dealt his own private hell. When Tate stated his mission to seek justice in Callie's death, he was certain her weakened and defeated father would never halt his pursuit.

Shifting in his sleep, turning onto his side, he sensed his feet were heavy and weighed down. Tate leaned up partially on the mattress, still weary from sleeping, and laughed to himself, noticing his boots were still tied in place. He loosened the top laces enough to jerk them free. They thumped as they landed to the side of the bed. He hoped the sound didn't bother the person in the room below.

With the weight of his boots lifted, he was more comfortable. Falling back into the indentations that remained pressed in his pillow, he remembered why he came to this sleepy beach town. It was for information someone believed was valuable to Tate. If it involved even the slightest hint about his deceased wife, he was all ears.

He had boarded the train nearby where he lived in Maryland bound for New Jersey. He hadn't packed much more than items to carry him for the day and maybe overnight. When he arrived, he was to meet "Lange," and that was the only name he was given. Tate had waited most of the day at the train station across from this small bakery. He sat on the uncomfortable, distressed bench for hours, but the meeting never happened. Lange was a no-show. Seemed fate intervened, as he was still there to save Aubrey from what occurred later in the bakery.

His mind was still restless. He came here to find a tip on the killer of his wife, and he wound up helping a beautiful woman instead. He pictured her in his head again. Aubrey. His mind wandered, and he carried on his own mental conversation of what he planned to say if he saw her again.

She seemed genuine and kind as she introduced herself. She had that sweet, pleasing small town charm, but Tate didn't know what sweet was. That was taken from him long ago.

Another town, another dead end. It was clear he was heading out of this town in the morning. He was tired because he hadn't slept in so long. His brain always tracked a tip. The hope took over and gave him the adrenaline to keep going. Finally after such a long day, his brainwaves calmed, and his eyes closed.

Several leads came to Tate quickly. His friends at the precinct knew he wanted her killer found. Many of them went out on a limb for him with confidential information. Sometimes, he felt like he was close on the trail of her killer, and other times, he felt he was miles off. He had recently received a call. It was from a male. He was clearly trying to alter his real voice. "Is this Tate Manning? I know you don't know me, but I reside in a small beach town, Cape May, New Jersey. I believe I may have some information on who killed your wife."

"Who are you and how did you get my number?" Tate perked up and was rough and coarse in his tone.

"I heard a conversation about how a drug deal went really bad a while back. There was a murder, and a woman was brutally killed in Hagerstown, Maryland. Sad they said, she was beautiful, but her father was also high in the rankings of the drug world. I did some digging since I am from a quiet town and we don't hear that too often. I found a Callie Sana Manning who died, or was murdered, and you were her surviving husband."

"Please tell me more. Do you know who the person was that was talking about it?"

"No, it was in our local bar one evening. Two men who gave the

impression they were from out of town said they were meeting their contact the next day here in our town."

"How recent was this?"

"Quite a while back and I let it rest until it stirred in my head again when I heard rumors of some drugs being sold at the far end of our pleasant town. Then a couple times I saw those same two men in the local bar, and that is when I had to consider making this call."

"Well, I'm glad you did. I would like to speak more in person. Can I come to your town?" Tate's voice sounded unruffled during their talk, but unaware to the caller, he anxiously tapped his thumb pad to the chair arm where he sat.

"Yes, my name is…Lange." There was a pause as he simply stated his name. Perhaps he was nervous phoning Tate out of the blue.

Tate was attentive to his hesitation and didn't want to lose this lead. Willingly, he offered, "You tell me where and when, and I will jump on the next train to meet with you. Thank you…Lange."

Tate knew that was not his real name. They agreed to meet the following week at the train station in Lange's town. Tate would travel in, and Lange would meet him to discuss the matter in person. It had been dry without leads for a bit. Reed, Tate's partner, had a few here and there, but nothing amounted to much. This caller in the night intrigued him. Maryland to New Jersey wasn't too far on the map. A quick train ride.

Lange never showed.

He stirred in his sleep in the middle of the night, fidgeting like when he sat upon that bench at the train station all day. Tate's sleep was a bit restless at first, recapping all the events, but toward the morning hours, he relaxed when his dream state took him to thoughts of Aubrey. His first touch of her hand had jolted him so that he almost spilled the hot liquid over the counter and both their hands.

He hadn't planned to venture across the street; Tate was ready to buy a return ticket for the next train. His eyes searched the schedule, and it was coming in an hour, so he thought he would kill time with a cup of coffee and something to tap down his stomach hunger. The bakery storefront across the street caught his eye and he was so glad he walked over there. In his sleep, his lips pursed a smile, a big smile. He recalled as he dreamt just how pretty she was. His mind took a pleasant mental note that when the sun rose and he awakened he would see her just once more before he headed out of this town.

Chapter Three

THE NEXT MORNING, OPENING *Sweet Treats* felt daunting and upsetting to Aubrey. She turned her head over her shoulder many times while filling up the display cases. Her fingers touched the door lock as she checked and rechecked it was locked until the posted opening time. Her first glance into the back room hit hard. Her hands clung tightly to the wide door molding, bracing herself as she stomached the view. Her breathing hitched, as it did when she was alarmed about something.

Her mind raced over what nearly happened in there. As she replayed yesterday afternoon, she turned her back to the wall for support. Aubrey was stunned at how quickly her life was threatened. One thing for certain, if Tate had not stayed near the bakery all day, or not checked on her, that it all could have ended so horribly. Her head full of doubts and she questioned whether she should have screamed out loud or tried to fight him harder. It angered her that he was able to make her fearful. Aubrey was tired of being a victim: First when her parents were suddenly taken from her as a young child and again when her grandmother passed. Both of those times, she was a victim of what fate had dealt her. Yesterday she was a victim by choice, his choice. Jackson planned to attack her.

Aubrey wondered how long Jackson thought about coming here to harm her. She recalled often she waved to him on the street or stopped and talked pleasantly with him when they passed one another in town. Her body instantly shivered and reminded her what he intended to do when he trapped her against the prep table.

She bit down on her lower lip. Instant pain distracted her in an attempt to silence his words. She sighed and moved slowly as she entered the back room. Each tiny step made her stronger. She felt relief as she regained her composure and took back her space, the place she loved to get lost in for many hours of baking. She stood alongside the prep table, gripping the edge, and mentally reminded herself this was her bakery and he was an intruder.

Her breathing relaxed, and she pushed herself to accomplish something productive this morning. She busied herself as she gathered the hurled dirty mixing bowls lying on the floor to run through the dishwasher. She had them all loaded and reached to press the start button when she was startled by a swift clicking noise that came from directly behind her. Her body instantly tensed. Gradually, she turned around, braced for the unknown. Her face was not frightened, but washed over with sudden relief. She then laughed as she realized it was only the ice machine making new cubes.

Her amusement relieved her momentarily, but as she observed the room, she recalled yesterday what flew in the air as he grabbed her. She'd only concentrated on staying alive.

Icing was smeared across the floor, and the room Aubrey normally kept clean was in total disorder. Trying to block out her thoughts of almost being raped, she began to work. Grabbing a bucket and a cloth soaked in warm sudsy water, she washed away the colorful icing that dried and hardened on the tile floor and the sticky residue left from the cinnamon pastries.

She scrubbed away the untidiness from the day before just like she did each night or following morning, but this she hadn't caused from the fun of her fine baking. It was from a local guy, someone she had felt comfortable around. This was his mess. He caused this. She focused on the wiping of her counters as she tried to keep her mind clear of images of him. If she didn't store the events of the attempted rape deep in the back of her mind, she would never have been able to return here this morning. This bakery was her escape to create sweetness even though her mind often recalled sadness—sadness that her parents, her grandmother never had the opportunity to see her succeed. When she felt sad, Aubrey baked items from her mothers and grandmothers recipes. That made her feel good inside and worked as keeping a part of them alive.

The early morning hours passed quickly. She sponged the entire floor a final time and loaded the hot ovens with her new creations to sell when her doors opened for business. The sweet aroma filled the air and settled her uneasiness just as a child calms as soon as they are handed that piece of candy after having a fit. It was a sudden stillness. She checked her ovens, making sure not to overbake any of the items, and then her eyes shifted to the clock to her right. Perfect, she would be opening in fifteen minutes. As per her daily routine, Aubrey had her fresh baked pastries displayed, and the bakery was open for business.

THE DOOR CHIMES SOUNDED AS Tate walked into the bakery. It was very busy this morning, and Aubrey was juggling the patrons the best she could. He stood away from the door, courteously allowing others to enter. Aubrey smiled and politely greeted each one. Some were regulars that came so often that she turned and had their order ready before they requested it.

She leaned close to the glass of the pastry displays hoping to see her reflection, making certain she wasn't wearing icing on her face or in her hair. She watched him as he moved behind everyone in the line. She was aware he returned again today, which made her very self-conscious of her appearance. Aubrey noticed one woman in line that glanced toward him when he entered. That woman did a complete once over from head to foot.

He seemed a hard man in his ways with his voice and stature, but he sure was easy on any woman's eyes. He'd captured her attention yesterday, and today, she focused simply on the wall in his direction, hoping to catch a stolen peek. Her head played tennis as she turned to take care of each customer and then view him once more.

Her morning had started off difficult as she nervously returned to the bakery. Earlier, her emotions were scattered all over the place like the back room had been with bowls when she arrived. As the morning hours passed, she was pleased with her decision to open her bakery this morning. Her face saddened as she thought not of yesterday but that if she hadn't opened today she may not have seen him again. Her eyes again swept across the room to view him once more. He wasn't facing her direction so she had the chance to watch him more than a quick second.

Finishing up with the last of the morning customers, Aubrey packaged their orders and cashed them out. She caught her breath from the morning rush and rubbed her hands on her apron, taking off sprinkles and sugar that coated them. She pushed back the strands of her hair that came loose from behind her ears as she leaned in and out of the racks, gathering pastries. Tate remained on the far side of the bakery floor in no apparent rush for service this morning.

"Can I take your order?" Aubrey asked loudly.

TATE HADN'T EVEN NOTICED THAT the bakery had emptied of all the patrons and surely many morning treats. He was up next, as the line was gone. His heavy boots sounded on the floor as he approached the front counter. He folded his arms and "Hmmmm"ed while he considered what to select, but he knew he was staling. He tried to gather what to say to her because the moment he got closer, his heart felt her. He sensed something incredible from an arms distance away. In fact, he had awoken this morning in a content mood having slept peacefully after the first few demons caused their nightly disruption of his dreams. He had taken longer in the shower this morning, letting the tepid water rain over him. He'd relaxed and his thoughts soon had him thinking of Aubrey. Again and again, he had replayed her name.

"Aubrey…give me a moment," he replied. He pretended to be checking out the variety of pastries.

Another customer entered, and Aubrey turned to Tate for his order, but he signaled for her to wait on the other gentleman first. "So what can I get you, Harrison?" Obviously, she knew everyone here in town.

Tate was starting to take his mental notes. He usually did this on the drug dealers before he took them down. "Miss Tanner, I need another sweet fix of your pastries." His eyes widened with delight over his options. Pointing to each of his selections, he followed with the quantity, and she quickly filled his request.

Tate realized that Aubrey probably had exact counts of all the items she baked. He knew he was great at counting the steps it would take his feet to reach and apprehend a suspect that stood across from him in a takedown. It was though, effortless times that counted the most like him standing in her bakery as his latent heart all of the sudden pulsed warmly. Her customer, Harrison, remained in conversation with her for a moment. Again, local chatter filled the bakery as it did with every customer she waited on.

The bakery emptied, leaving just Tate and Aubrey standing with the counter separating them. "So what will it be?"

she asked sweetly.

He directed his attention to her instead of the pastries and simply stated the obvious truth. "Your eyes are so beautiful." Tate watched her reaction as her eyes definitely brightened.

"WELL, THAT DOESN'T TELL ME your order. That's more like a line." She pursed her lips playfully. Her first meeting with him made her uncomfortable, but after he saved her, she was thankful to see him again. She thought if he mentioned the previous day's events that she would comment, but if he didn't bring it up, she would let it lie and have the authorities do their job.

It had shaken her up really bad. She didn't crumble but pushed to make it through this day. As she waited for his next response, she returned the glass pot to the coffee station. She placed herself where she caught her reflection in the mirror on the wall. Her cheeks were reddened, and she hadn't applied any makeup. She was blushing at the thought that this extremely handsome stranger who'd appeared in their quiet town seemed to have taken a sudden attraction to her.

At first, she believed her redness was out of embarrassment from yesterday afternoon, but she knew it wasn't that. She felt flushed, heated throughout her body, along with something new, a pinch of excitement. His words that complimented her made her feel so good inside. Not much had been able to make her happy lately unless it was a new recipe that came out perfectly baked.

His deep voice interrupted her thoughts of a freshly baked pie. "That wasn't a line. You're very pretty. It was an observation. I also think I'll let you pick what I should try. There were a lot of people in here this morning so everything has to be great." His gaze dipped to her chest, and he smiled. He pointed his finger toward her.

"What are you aiming at?" She countered uncomfortably as she knew his eyes shifted lower to her chest.

Tate calmed her quickly. "I was thinking something chocolate like the giant lump that is sitting on your apron."

Aubrey looked and laughed at herself as earlier she'd tried to sneak a piece of a chocolate-filled donut and it apparently dripped onto her. It sure had been good, though.

"Sorry for what almost happened here yesterday to you, but glad you're okay. Nothing should ever happen like that to anyone and not someone as pretty and nice as you."

"Thank you for everything and your very kind words. What I'm selecting for you to eat this morning is on me." Aubrey reached for the chocolate-filled donuts first.

Tate leaned on the counter closer toward Aubrey, "You didn't tell me that I was hitting on you when I mentioned again that you were pretty. I meant this purely as my personal observation."

"Well, you appear to be a good person to have come to the back room and saved me." Their eyes met, captured one another's look, as the bakery silenced for the moment.

Aubrey hoped he couldn't hear her heart pounding feverishly. A pleasant sensation filled her body with warmth, like sipping a hot drink on a cold day. Hiding her inner emotions well, she outwardly presented a controlled partial smile. She hoped he didn't notice just how much his words excited her.

SOMETHING ABOUT THIS GIRL HAD turned his head. He didn't want to walk away and give up. He wanted her to know he was sincere as he asked, "Would you be comfortable giving me your number? I know we just met, but I would like to talk to you more outside of here." He hoped she wouldn't reply "no" immediately. He continued without hesitation, "And if you are wondering if this is me hitting on you or a line as you called it, I actually just want to get to know you." He reached for the coffee she set down as he watched her place a second chocolate donut and some other items in her brown bags with her fancy bakery logo on them.

The door chimed, and an elderly couple entered. Aubrey shouted her standard welcome to the bakery greeting. She knew the only relationship she was in was a working one with her bakery. Aubrey leaned on the counter on her elbows and quietly spoke to Tate, "I am in a relationship that requires all my time. All my time. I have no free time, so I can't have you call me nor can I date you. I am thankful to you, though, for what you did for me."

Aubrey slid her baked items in his direction and never rang it up. Tate was satisfied with the warm cup of morning coffee that was made exactly like yesterday's cup. She remembered. He walked over to the wall counter and leaned on it, momentarily watching what was happening outside on the street. Tate waited, and the couple finished their order with Aubrey as he heard the register close. When they exited, he returned to the counter and again asked her, "Just your phone number? If not, I will be forced to come here every day till I receive a yes, but hopefully, it will be soon be-cause—as good as these pastries are—I will be huge if you delay."

AUBREY FELT HIM STANDING FIRM, despite her trying to tell him she was already committed. He had made her laugh as he patiently waited for her to answer. He wanted to see her write down her number as her fingers reached toward the napkin dispenser. Tate's lips parted cheerfully. Her eyes traveled from his eyes to the napkin she held. Her fingers trailed alongside the register where she located a pen im-printed with the *Sweet Treats* logo. The bakery door sounded, announcing an incoming customer. Aubrey was ready to nicely deliver her welcome greeting as Tate respectfully stepped to the side of the register. Her voice halted. No words escaped, the pen slipped from her hold, rolling underneath the front counter.

In walked a pretty boy. Well-built but carrying himself in a cocky manner, he had dark hair with dark eyes to match; a good guess was that pure Italian blood ran through his veins.

Emerson walked right up to the counter and kissed her on the cheek. "How's my girl today?" She wasn't his girl, and she'd made that clear. Her two years with "one of the town's hottest catches" had been more than enough. For so long, she'd thought he was the greatest, appreciative when he spent time with her or gave her his attention. She'd felt lucky to have him as her boyfriend, knowing a lot of the other women in town envied her. Even her roommate reminded her how awesome Emerson was, though Tessa did concede that he got a great girl in Aubrey, too.

When Aubrey had opened the bakery, he told her to help fund some ideas he had. He came from family money, but he didn't want to ask his family for more. Aubrey didn't have much. She just managed what she had the best she could. She knew his ideas were fast track measures for money. Quick pot scores, selling pills to others, and such, but she turned her cheek to his actions. When he progressed into the heavier dealing, claiming it was for her and his future, she naively believed him at first.

It fell apart after a full day at the bakery, a busy day before a holiday. Her feet were tired, and she wanted nothing but to fall into a massage by Emerson's hands after a warm soak in her tub. None of her wishes for relaxation ever evolved as she walked in to Emerson seated on the floor in only his blue jeans, his zipper almost completely open. He seemed drunk. No, he wasn't drunk…he was high. She had even stayed late to make him a chocolate-strawberry tart that he often requested.

When she entered the kitchen, she dropped the glass plate that held the luscious tart. It broke apart, shattering across the ceramic tile flooring. Emerson had tried to stop her before she made the turn to the kitchen, which held the makings of a drug lab. Not only was that bad enough, it also had a half-dressed girl seated on the barstool snorting a line. "Aubrey, this isn't what you think. I mean her and me, she just stopped by. All this, the drugs, this is money for us, for you and I. When I sell this, we can go away together."

Aubrey wasn't stupid; it had to end here. She took all the drugs and dumped them into the sink when Emerson went to grab a shirt as the girl followed him. When they came back, they freaked. "Aubrey, what did you do?" Emerson screamed at her.

"Oh no, don't put this on me. What did *you* do?" Aubrey pointed to the girl first. "GET OUT!" Then she'd told Emerson to remove everything he owned and leave her home as well. He tried to plea with her, but Aubrey shut down inside. Finally, after two years of trying to be perfect for Emerson, she had realized she could take no more.

Initially after their breakup, when she attempted to avoid Emerson, she coincidentally found a broken bakery storefront window and a theft from her register. If she acted kind to him, things ran smoother, and she had no more reports to her insurance company. Aubrey heard the door chimes sound and focused away from Emerson. She only saw the back of her rescuer's head, and she'd still never learned his name. He did leave her money that he laid across the plain white napkin she had set down. She breathed in and seconds later exhaled slowly from deep inside. *I survived that close call yesterday with Jackson and previously being with a drug supplier. I don't think my life will bring me anything good. As long as I have this bakery, I am content and my tiny life is sweet.*

TATE EXITED THE BAKERY AND paced down a few small streets off the main beach block, rethinking how close he was to acquiring her phone number. He veered into an alley way that circled him back in the direction he traveled yesterday when he left the bakery. This time, he was determined to be out of this area and miles away by daybreak. With his head down, searching the ground below, he would have missed what was happening if not for someone calling out a name. He thought he heard someone holler "Callie." The next time he heard the name yelled, it was actually Mally.

He lifted his head and something immediately caught his attention on the far corner. There he saw a car with the guy he thought was Aubrey's boyfriend, exchanging money and drugs with others. Tate had a radar for that shit. He watched the entire transaction. That was the shit he thrived on taking down. He was a good cop, got heated sometimes but followed the law. His tough build intimidated most people at first. Beyond his initial appearance, he was sweet inside just like one of Aubrey treats. He paused on the street, filled with distaste, and observed several more vehicles as they stopped and greeted that guy, her guy. More dealings unfolded.

As he headed back to the room he was staying at for just the one night, his thoughts were that he was ready to leave this town. It hadn't provided him any new tips. He didn't need to get involved in what was going down on these streets. His dedication to the law, however, focused him on the drugs that were openly dealt during the daylight hours. He was irritated by what he witnessed and made his decision to walk away or get involved. He stood at the desk, and Lacey again greeted him pleasantly. "Are you leaving us so soon?"

"Actually, I wanted to tell you the room was fine, and I slept well, but I wanted to extend my stay for rest of the week." Lacey handed him some extra towels and told him maid service would come midweek. Something was definitely keeping him remaining here in Cape May. Was it what he felt twice in his chest while around Aubrey or was it a drug deal he witnessed that could be so much more?

Tate returned to his room and fell back on the bed. His hand still firmly clenched the brown bag that was loaded with items Aubrey gave to him earlier. He set them on the side table. He needed to think more on how sweet Aubrey could be with a man who dealt drugs. Maybe she didn't know. Instinctively, his fingers reached over and grabbed at one of her pastries, consuming it without paying attention. All the gears in his mind continued to spin. This town was so far removed from street drug dealings and anything like that. It was a polite, pleasant place. A wonderful tourist town. At the present time, it was the perfect month where the extreme wave of tourists had passed and the locals could catch their breath.

He had heard a few conversations at the inn he where he roomed and also in the bakery that the locals loved the sudden calm that swept over their town at this time of year. Tate felt unrest here, though, replaying the night he answered his phone to the male caller who claimed to reside here. It was one call he wouldn't forget, informing him that the dealings in this town may have a connection to his wife's death. Tate knew he had to at least remain another few days to see what was happening or what he could find out. Tate hadn't traveled too far on his most recent trip. His train pass carried him only two states away from where he lived. Actually, he lived more on the road than at his home.

Despite the sugar from her baked treat, he fought to keep his eyes open. Slowly, he lost the battle.

TATE STOOD TALL, OVERSHADOWING THE doorframe of the lawyer's office. He dreaded moving farther into the office. It would make it so final. The impassive lawyer requested several times that he take a seat, but Tate remained standing. The lawyer paged through a stack of standardized documents. "Your wife had a life insurance policy of one million dollars. She left you as the sole beneficiary."

His first thought was that it wasn't odd for a wife to leave her husband her life policy. *But why so much money?* Then the lawyer continued. "She wrote that she believed that you would do something amazing with the funds." Tate blew out his pent up breath.

He remembered he and Callie wishfully discussing that they both wanted to rid areas of bad influence in the neighborhoods. Her father, his father-in-law, was a main contributor, but he knew that man would be taken out someday. Thus far, the drug life that his father-in-law had chosen took the lives of his wife and now his own daughter. Tate knew that was the final blow, and he had heard that his father-in-law was lying low, out of the dealings, and the narcotics division had him currently off their radar.

Tate stood with his hands deep in his jean pockets. "Mr. Manning, did you hear the terms of her policy?"

Tate nodded. He had to take this all in. One million dollars. He lived a simple, wonderful life when Callie was alive. They would take a vacation here and there, but nothing extravagant. He had left his job when he couldn't focus on any other cases, just his own vengeance for locating who killed his wife. It became his obsession. He hadn't wanted to jeopardize his partner, as Tate lacked concentration of all other police matters.

His unit had been sad to see a fine narcotics officer leave, but they all believed he would sort it out and return in time. He had used most of his savings and saved pension the past two years just to pay bills and live. Although once Callie died, he stopped living inside, only functioning on the outside. He put his home, their home, up for sale immediately, as he never could even bring himself to walk back in there after the day his wife lay bloody and lifeless on their bedroom floor. The money from the sale of the house was in his bank account, just sitting there. He hadn't needed to remove any yet.

"You need to come over here and execute these documents," the lawyer instructed him. Tate walked from the threshold, and his boots he dragged lazily across the wooden office floor. To sign off and receive money from his wife's death gave him a feeling of selling out. He hadn't found her killer or killers yet.

"I'm out of here. Just deposit the funds into my personal account." Tate scribbled the numbers of his account across the legal paper and left.

"Tate, Tate," the lawyer called after him, but he never turned back, never went near the street he lived on, never returned to the life he had. Tate went full throttle forward to find her killer.

Tate tossed in the bed, and uneasiness slipped through his mind. Initially, a pleasant thought formed. He imagined Aubrey displaying her gentle smile, and he pictured her with just a dusting of powdered sugar delicately laying across her cheek. Then he mulled over the guy that kissed her today on the cheek, close to her lips. Tate was uneasy and concerned with that man. Combining that with witnessing his dealing drugs made Tate more unraveled, and he could feel his upset building.

He rose with a sudden jerking motion. He was confused at first, but then he examined the room, noticing his surroundings and remembering where he was. His thoughts couldn't keep him in a peaceful rest. It was only the middle of the afternoon. After the events of yesterday, he thought he would go back down the street, just pass her bakery one time to make certain she was okay. He didn't pass it once. Constantly, he strode up and back on the sidewalk, repeatedly until he locked eyes with hers through the front glass when she finished with a customer.

Her smile was warm, but Tate turned away quickly. He wasn't good at this shit. He'd tried to ask her out. That went wrong, so he wasn't sure what to do next or if he should do anything further. On his final turn to pass the bakery one more time, he watched the shiny black truck pull in and park opposite of the parking lines. This driver definitely thought he was entitled to be above the law. The door opened, and out jumped the guy who was there earlier. Tate knew this was surely her man.

"WHAT ARE YOU DOING BACK in here?" Aubrey questioned after Emerson made it a few steps into the bakery.

"Well, I am happy to see you, too, Sugar."

"Emerson, you don't need to keep coming in here. We aren't together anymore, and although I haven't broadcasted it in the towns' headlines, you need to just go your own way."

"The way I see it, you haven't told anyone because you still want me. So I think it best that you smarten back up and we return to the happy couple we were before. I am done with the drugs and wouldn't want you caught up in that anyway. I care about you. My brother assigned me to a construction team for a job just one town over. That contract should carry me the rest of the fall and into the winter. At least, if we pour all the foundations before the extreme cold weather, we can work inside the rest of the time."

"Emerson, I know your ways. I lived with you. I loved you, but you blew it. You took advantage of me in my own home."

"That will never happen again." Emerson came behind the counter and placed his hand on the back of her neck. "I care about you. Come here." He pulled her closer.

Aubrey had loved him for the past few years. She hadn't told the town that they broke up because she felt when she did she would have lost the best thing that ever came to her. This town wasn't full of handsome, available men like Emerson, and it may sound odd, but it made her feel special to be the one he wanted to be with. Many times, he let her down, and many times, she cried, but there were the good times that she also recalled. Their relationship hadn't been all that bad.

His persuasive pull brought her closer, closer, and soon her lips were one bite from his. "See, Aubrey, this is where I want you and me. We are good together." Emerson brought his lips over hers and held her neck firm with his hand. Aubrey only hesitated for a moment and then fell into the rhythm of his convincing, powerful kisses.

TATE PAUSED FOR A MOMENT on the sidewalk to reply to the local police officer who introduced himself. "Hey, I'm Levi. I saw you walking on our main street yesterday. How is your visit going?"

"Good, thank you. I'm Tate Manning, and work brought me here."

"What type of business are you in?"

Tate said the first thing he could and the same lie he'd long ago told Callie's father. "I manage investments. Real estate." Tate was actually investing all his time into trying to track down a murderer/drug dealer. Adding the description covered his lie nicely. Many stopped in this town for real estate ventures. There was an abundance of charming hotels, B & B's, family-owned to fine dining restaurants, unique to exclusive retail shops, and a spectacular beach line giving plenty of bang for the buck in the warmer months of the year.

"Well, we always welcome investors to our lovely town. If I can help you with any of the history or questions you think of, let me know. I will add that this is a very safe and historical town, and we pride ourselves on that."

"Levi, I can see that, and that is exactly what led me here." They separated as Levi returned to his squad car.

"What a fine couple they make." Tate questioned him. "Who?" Before Levi responded, Tate saw Aubrey through the bakery glass, kissing the drug dealer behind the counter, and more than on the cheek. Internally, Tate angered, but he never displayed that as he calmly asked Levi, "If you don't mind me asking, who is the guy? What's he do in this town?"

"That's Emerson DeLuca. His family owes a large construction company that is awarded most of the real estate contracts here in town and the surrounding areas. Their company is very well known. It's been around for many generations. He is also known as the most eligible bachelor here in the cape if you ask the local ladies."

Tate finally knew his name and was eager to contact his old partner to use the police database to run a thorough check on this guy. Something about Emerson bugged him more and more. He couldn't stop viewing Aubrey through the decorated window glass. Painted cupcakes and pie pieces and coffee cups swirled all over the panes of glass was not what was making him hungry. It was a deep hunger for her. Her lips were on Emerson's, but for a brief moment, Tate wondered what her lips would feel like on his. *Soft but oh so sweet.* Aubrey was sweet.

Aubrey and Emerson's lips parted, and Tate noticed she didn't smile back toward her man. That was a minor detail that Tate had observed in people. If someone truly loved another, their smile would never diminish. Aubrey restacked the napkins on the counter neatly as Emerson now reached for a chocolate éclair. Her eyes shifted to the store front to see if any patron would be coming in. He locked eyes with her. Her smile warmed instantly. Tate's did, too. Separated by glass, they still shared a few tender seconds together. Instantly, Tate reflected on their chance meeting. *I only traveled 224 miles by train, but it is the closest to happiness my heart has felt in a long, long time.*

Levi came back and tapped him on the shoulder, breaking his moment. "Hey, Tate. If you want, some of the guys from the station go for wings and brew on Wednesday nights. You are welcome to come if you're still in town."

"Yeah, that would be real nice… I mean cool." Tate was still focused on that vision of her beautiful smile. He saw her lips happily change when she noticed him, and he definitely felt that.

"We go to DeLuca's Den. It's only a few blocks over. And yes, before you ask the next question, it is owned by Emerson's family. You can't get lost in this town. So stop on by." Levi waved and was off.

Tate picked up his feet, started to move forward, and

didn't turn back. He was sure if he glanced quickly one more time into the bakery that Emerson would have his hands all over her or at least be trying to. A tip had brought him to the town, but more than that was keeping him here.

Chapter Four

T IME SEEMED TO STOP IN this town, and every day appeared just like the one before. A beautiful September morning was wakening and so was Tate. He rose and downed a complimentary water supplied to his room and then opened the brown bag and eagerly ate one of the sweet treats Aubrey packed him. Crumbs cascaded onto his cheek as the pastry had hardened. They were much softer when they were freshly baked or right out of the oven. He set the bag down and reminded himself to return for more pastries, creating another excuse to see her.

He walked into the bathroom, and soon his naked body revived as he stood in the shower with the warm water spraying down over him. He remained there for a minute after he turned the faucets off. His body dried as the wet droplets traveled over the defined muscles of his very fit body. He believed in keeping his mind and body in shape. He worked out faithfully, and he was this morning going to inquire if there was a local gym.

After Tate was dressed, he went to the front desk. Lacey was up and greeting the patrons with a sincere, friendly smile, directing them to the east room for breakfast. East or West, he was sure the room was a mere ten steps from the front lobby, but her description sounded impressive.

"Good morning, Tate." Her eyes rose to his enthusiastically. "Sleep well?" Her sandy brown brows lifted.

"Yes, I did, and good morning to you as well. Hey, Lacey, is there a gym in town?"

"Yes, over on First Street, there is JR's. It's not a fitness chain, but a place where some take yoga classes or kick boxing. I know the owners, Jaci and Ryan. They have plenty of weights and all the new machines."

"Thanks."

LACEY WATCHED HIM LEAVE. HE was a complete package. His hair appeared to be a medium brown. He kept it buzzed to his head. His blue, sea water eyes were very captivating. He had an alluring appeal that was effortless. She knew that the local girls working out at the gym this morning would claim his view far better than that of the enticing ocean they gazed upon from their treadmill. He was extremely toned with strong arms and nice build.

She saw no wedding ring adorned his left finger, not even a trace of one being there. With his tee shirt on, she could see his awesome arms and the ink that decorated them. He had startled her the first day with his rugged and tough voice, but there was something smooth in this man. Although he was big and solidly built, when she looked at his eyes, she believed she saw a true gentleman. Lacey didn't waiver from her stare, and Tate turned back. He caught her eyes focused on his ass. Yes, he caught her. She quickly turned to fluff up the basket of towels to busy herself.

TATE CHUCKLED. HE SEEMED TO have a great effect on women, but had lost his heart when the only woman he vowed to love was brutally taken from him. Remembering the past always made Tate feel unrest. He wanted to start the day putting that out of his mind quickly. It would be best if he found the fitness location early this morning, so he could release some of his tension. His first stop, though, was to buy something to wear for his weight training. He had nothing with him but the clothes he rolled into town with. Stepping into a store that boasted they carried *everything* on their window sign's tag line, he found that true. He purchased a few solid colored tee shirts, two pairs of black shorts, muscle tank tops, socks and lastly a pair of inexpensive sneakers. Tate was glad to find sneakers in his size as his heavy boots wouldn't work at all for gym footwear. He felt a bit odd carrying a store bag into the gym instead of his gym bag, but he needed to work out far more than he cared about impressions he made on others.

JR's sat on the corner of First Street and Ocean Avenue. It had a large neon orange colored *JR's Fitness First* sign wrapped across the façade on top of the floor to ceiling windows. He was surprised to see so many people in there already this morning, but there wasn't too much else happening in the town. It was warm enough to hit the beach still, and he thought that would be his next stop after an intense workout. Upon entering, he approached the front desk to inquire on a day pass or, actually, he would need a pass for the entire week. A man greeted him. The man definitely worked out. The guy extended his hand to Tate's. They exchanged an extremely firm handshake.

"Welcome, I'm Ryan. How can I help you?"

"Well, I am staying over at the Hamilton Inn, and Lacey told me where I could find a place to work out."

Ryan examined Tate discretely. His eyes watched some surfers hitting the first morning waves then observed Tate's dedicated, muscular build. "This is probably not what you are used to. Where are you from?"

"Just outside of Hagerstown, Maryland. I belong to a club there, but I'm here for the rest of the week."

Ryan hooked him up with a multiday pass, and in no time, Tate exited the tiny locker room, comfortable in his new clothes and eager to get his blood pumping through his muscles. Lifting weights, the grip of the irons, quickly put his mind and body in control. The place was no fancy fitness club, but a clean modest gym that Tate found comfort in. The owner, Ryan, had a good amount of free weights, and the cardio machines were top of the line. A few girls had sneakily watched him in the wall mirrors as he moved with his heavily loaded weights to the bench to begin his bicep curls. They weren't just glancing. They were staring. Tate mentally dove into each lift of the heavy iron and pumped them in and out. Nothing surrounding him caught his attention. His interest was solely on pumping out a few extra curls, giving his muscles an intense burn. Working out gave him a satisfied rush. His mind cleared.

On his way out the door after rinsing in their gym shower, he was thinking of Aubrey and wanting to spend a day with her at the beach and have the ocean waters rinse over them both when he bumped right into Emerson, who was hurrying through the entrance. Emerson shot him a quick stare and then continued on his way, no friendly greeting shared nor engaging conversation. None needed. He didn't know him, but he knew full well he was watching this man. All the eyes of the ladies transferred suddenly to Emerson, and he heard several of them say, "Good morning, Emerson."

The guy was built extremely well. Seemed he spent his time here working off those sweets he devoured and at her bakery spreading his sweet-laced charm. Standing in the middle of the gym floor, he knew he would be the center of attention as he slowly lifted his hoodie over his head and displayed his well-ripped chest to all. He made sure he paraded in front of the ladies. Tate wished that Aubrey could see this side of him. He knew, though, as long as Emerson was here at the gym she was free. Aubrey was alone at the bakery.

Quickly he returned to his rented room to drop his bag of clothes off that he wore earlier this morning, he didn't want to be carrying that around. Even though he wasn't dressed to impress coming from working out, he pulled a tee shirt over the training tank he was already wearing to appear a little more presentable. Tate didn't linger back in his room, moments later he was making large strides in his steps walking toward the bakery. He wanted to stop there just to satisfy his sweet fix, not of a donut or anything sugary, but of her. All he needed was her soft smile and adoring eyes directed his way. He would be down with that for the entire day.

SWEET TREATS' NUMBER OF CUSTOMERS was slow this morning. A delivery came in, and Aubrey was assisting the few patrons that just placed their order at her counter. The delivery man remained patiently out front, and Tate thought he would jump right in and help. "I can grab these." Tate took two large boxes full of flour and sugar and piled them onto his shoulder, bracing them tightly with his arms. They were heavy and another workout in itself. He walked in the shop with the boxes blocking his face from her view. Aubrey yelled out, "Just put them on the table in the back, and I will be right with you." She waited on her patron. Tate remained in the back. When the delivery guy brought back the next few, Tate handed him a few rolled bills. "Thanks." The delivery man told Aubrey he left the purchase order on top of the delivery and bid her a nice day.

The door chimes sounded over and over. What Tate thought was a quiet morning was a bit busier for a short time. When all the ringing silenced, he knew she would take a break and come toward the back. He didn't want to scare her after her recent encounter with the other guy. In clear view, he positioned himself next to the prep table and waited.

Aubrey hummed as she carried a tray toward the back to grab a water and to refill the front shelves with some more

Danish. This morning, they were the chosen favorite. Her eyes caught Tate's, and she didn't flinch, scream, move back, or appear nervous at all. "What a nice surprise! I didn't know I had a new delivery man. Thank you for my order, but why are you still in my prep kitchen? I don't tip. I will pay the invoice at the end of the month," she teased confidently.

"I wanted to see how you were. I needed to know you were alright. You jumped back into work the day after that asshole came on to you."

"Well, that's over. I only think about the way that you saved me, and I can't share that with anyone or give you that credit because I know you don't want to be involved." Her arms reached for a tray of iced Danish. It was too high for her to grasp. Aubrey passed Tate to retrieve a wooden step stool near her pantry.

"Allow me." Tate pushed himself from resting against the prep table and brought the large metal tray down for her.

Her eyes were pleased with his helpfulness. She was very thankful for his assistance today, and ever so grateful from the time before. "Can I offer you anything…to eat?" She hesitated as she spoke, her confidence wavering.

"First, I think I should offer you my name. I'm Tate, Tate Manning, and very glad to meet you. I wondered if you can answer a question for me, and I don't want you to take this wrong. You are so beautiful and sweet and, well, I guess I am trying to say I can't see you with your guy, that guy I saw with you." Tate just put it out there.

Aubrey smiled at his observant style. He made her heart warm inside each time he told her she was beautiful. A frown edged her lips briefly until she parted them to speak. "It's complicated. I believe he loves me, and we were in a relationship for two years."

Tate jumped in place as if he was shooting hoops and landed the winning basket. He had a huge smile. "Were? As in not together anymore?"

"Honestly, I don't know what we are to one another. I asked him to leave my home a while ago. He upset me, and I didn't want to have him around."

"Well, that means you took a stand. And how do you feel about that?"

"Confused, not sure of whether I want to be with him exclusively or not, but he thinks everything is back to the way it was."

"Can I ask you something else?" Tate didn't want to have any dead air in their conversation.

"Sure." She was interested in his wanting to know about her, and she was already making her mental list of questions to ask him.

"Can you close early today? I'd like to take you for a walk and talk to you outside of here, even if for just an hour. You know I won't hurt you. I just want to talk to you without all the tempting sweets that I keep smelling. Or soon I will embarrass myself with my stomach rumbling."

"I SUPPOSE I COULD CLOSE up. After all, I do own the shop. Let me wipe up a bit and shut the coffee pots off, and then yes. Yes, I would welcome a break from here to take in some fresh air." Aubrey thought she couldn't remember the last time she closed for anyone, not even herself. Even when the attack happened, she didn't shut down. She pulled herself into work the next morning. She remembered that she still had to arrange to go to the police station to fill out some forms, which was going to be very uncomfortable for her.

For now, she didn't want to think about how she was going to handle that. Jackson, she hoped, was just as uncomfortable sitting in his current cell. She was also wondering how her roommate Tessa would feel after hearing all that happened while she was away, especially because she was related to Jackson. Aubrey, putting that aside, was happy that Tate had stopped by. She felt he was still protecting her even though today it was from her sneaking another half of a donut.

Tate moved out to the front of the shop and gathered the glass coffee pots to help her. Aubrey turned the bakery sign to *closed*, noting to herself it was still very early in the day. She felt like she was skipping out early from a high school class to enjoy the great weather, something she long ago liked to do.

Tate not only carried the pots to the back but began to wash and lay them out as she brought several trays of her baked items, and he helped her pack them in her storage containers. Some items, like brownies and cookies, would hold for another day.

"Not too much shelf life for these donuts and croissants so I filled you a bag to take with you later." She smiled, knowing that wasn't much but all she could offer this man that actually saved her. A full brown bag was extended to him.

"Aubrey, they are so good. I ate more this morning, but then had to find the local gym to work them off."

"You don't need to work anything off. You are perfect...I mean, fit." She blushed.

TATE SMILED INSIDE. HE HEARD her and knew she was seeing him. Not having a clue what he intended to talk to her about, he was just content with getting to spend time with her.

He placed the brown bag near the front door and told Aubrey to remind him it was here when they returned. Tate wished he had his truck with him, but he never planned to stay. He had planned to come in and out of the town swiftly.

"So where are we heading?" Aubrey asked. She glanced in both directions of the street awaiting his suggestion.

"Honestly, Aubrey, you decide. I'll follow wherever your lead. Why not start with showing me a part of this town you like?"

"I can do that. I've been here for a long time, and I know just about every street and sand dune." Aubrey turned and her sneakers squeaked as she led him in the opposite direction of the Hamilton Inn. They passed her car parked in front of the bakery. She wasn't concerned or worried that Emerson might come by the bakery because lately he said he would be tied up with his construction job during most of the daylight hours.

Without any second thoughts, she appreciated that Tate came in and suggested a change to her afternoon regimen.

Casually, they both walked and lightly conversed as they passed several long streets. Their feet came to rest on the sandy area just slightly out of town where even the sundries stores had ended a few blocks back. It was a vacant strip of the beach area, a little overgrown with sea grass and piles of sand not flattened out or groomed nicely like the main beach area. Aubrey slipped off her old sneakers and tucked her toes deep into the sand. "That feels so good after standing on my feet all day." She let out a soft moan.

Tate had to catch himself as her low sexy sigh was like a match igniting something within him. He suddenly became heated. "How about we sit here for a while?" he offered as he removed his tee shirt, keeping the muscle tank on, and that instantly cooled him down. Tate didn't look at her but wondered if she thought for a moment, as he lifted his shirt off, if he was going to expose his naked chest. Leaning over he swept his hand across the sand, flattening it and laying his shirt over top so she would be seated comfortably. The spot where they sat was perfect. Plenty of privacy surrounded them by mounds of sand that were piled high. The only thing in front of them was the welcoming ocean and the sun high above, extending rays of warmth on this flawless September day.

At first, they sat in silence and took in the beautiful view. Aubrey felt herself relaxing. She felt at ease and that enabled her to freely ask him some questions. "So, Tate, what brought you to our town and what do you do, business wise?"

"Well, I came to your town to meet a pretty girl, and I

think I have succeeded." They laughed. It gave Tate time, bought him a few moments to think quickly and deliver her an untruth perfectly. "Actually, I am here checking out real estate opportunities. I came in on the train from Hagerstown, Maryland. I will be here a few days to see what this town offers." He was vague and didn't want to stumble with too much information.

"Is that where you are from?" She was already onto her next question.

"Not originally and not planning on staying there too long. As I said, real estate opportunities fuel me." He was pleased with his little white lie. Tate could not begin to tell this girl of his wife being murdered or his occupation working undercover in the narcotics division. She would run. He knew that for sure.

"I don't see you in that field at all," Aubrey stated and caught his eyes.

Suddenly deflated, his ego took a hit. He thought she would accept his phony occupation. She was smart, and he challenged her, "Oh, what field do you see me in?"

"Maybe once a lifeguard, definitely a construction foreman. You have strong arms for sure." Her eyes suddenly shifted from his arms to stare at the sand, and again, the redness filled her cheeks.

"So my arms gave it away. Actually, you are right. I was a life guard on Rehoboth Beach during my college years."

"See, I knew it!" she said with sass. Her hand played in the sand, sifting it through her fingers.

"Well, you don't seem like a bakery owner," he countered.

"Okay, I'll give. Why not?

Tate took a moment. "Aubrey, honestly, I can see you don't eat a lot of your baked items. I would imagine a baker perhaps heavier, sampling all those sweets. I do know the first time I saw you that you absolutely stopped me dead in my boots. Your personality is very warmhearted, and I see you as extremely pretty. The best part is, I don't think you see that in yourself. This town would probably agree with me that you are the sweetest thing in your shop."

Aubrey couldn't remember the last time that Emerson said something nice to her, or even if he had. Tate's words struck her deeply. Her fingers touched her lips to hold back her reaction. Tate touched her neckline lightly, breaking her silent moment. Aubrey jerked. "I didn't mean alarm you. It's just the sun is hitting your shoulders, and your skin is turning pink. I didn't want you to burn."

Aubrey rose up quickly. Tate thought he startled her and blew their casual conversation. Aubrey stood for a moment and then pulled her skirt tight and sat back down with her back facing the sun. She pulled her legs under her skirt. Tate watched everything about her and even noted the pink color of her painted toes that matched the icing his boots stepped in previously at her bakery. He quickly tapped that awful thought from his mind. With her seated next to him here on the beach, it seemed to be their first perfect moment. He didn't want that clouded with what occurred the other day, but he was still curious about something. "So I have to ask you, and you don't have to tell me, but have you talked to your guy about what happened in the back room of your bakery?"

"I did, as he heard from the town talk, but he told me I was probably acting too sweet and led Jackson on. Actually, Jackson is my roommate Tessa's cousin. She is out of town in New York City for a few weeks, but I wonder how that will go over when she returns."

"Wait, you mean to tell me that your guy didn't offer you compassion about what almost happened?"

"He said he could see I was alright, and that was all he needed."

"Aubrey, promise me something. Don't settle for any guy."

"I hear you, Tate. I have to be honest. I felt upset that he didn't comfort me. He still believes in his mind that we are very solid and happily together. This town never received the news flash that we broke up. We were living in the beach home that my grandmother left me on the other end of town until that day I asked him to leave."

"Can I ask you why you asked him to leave?" Tate wondered if Emerson cheated on her or already had another girl on the side.

"I don't want to get into that. I just wasn't happy with something he did. But I do think people deserve second chances."

"Not if it was something that hurt you." Tate was concerned for her as he searched for more information, but didn't press.

"No, he didn't hurt me. It's just...can we not talk about

it?"

Her hand lightly squeezed his forearm with reassurance that she was fine. Her fingertips touched his skin, a stranger to her, and yet she sensed such warmth and not from the weather of the day. She was settling and always had been, but then again, great men didn't up and come to this town and stay. They vacationed and went away. Tate, too, would do the work he came here to do and be on his way.

Tate was deeply troubled, watching her pat down the conversation she and Emerson had. He was convinced this guy was no good. He decided it was a good idea that he extended his week stay at the Hamilton Inn. This would give him more time to hopefully find a way to convince Aubrey not to take Emerson back.

"I came here to this same spot on the beach a lot after my family died. It became my own private area." Aubrey concentrated on the pile of sand in front of her as she spoke. "I built up walls, so angry that my parents were killed and taken from me so early." Her eyes glazed. "I loved them, and I remember hearing there was a car that nose-dived off the bridge. It was years ago, and I was brought to live with my grandmother thereafter. I loved vacationing at her home. We would bake cookies and gooey pies and plant really colorful flowers in pots on her deck. She told me that they wouldn't grow well in the sand. Visiting my grandmother became my permanent residence. I had been told that my parents wouldn't be picking me up from my recent stay because they took a very long detour and arrived in heaven and couldn't come back.

"A young couple plunging into the bay waters was news-worthy. Veering onto the under-construction portion of the bridge in the darkness, they sank to the unfinished concrete below. They were coming to pick me up after they had a week without me. I was all excited with my suitcase packed by the front door and ready to show them all my drawings of flowers on the beach that I drew that entire week with my grandmother." The tears dropped one at a time from Aubrey's cheek. "I guess remembering them really hit me." She tried to wipe her eyes and toughen up.

Tate didn't want her to be embarrassed, and he gave her a moment to compose herself. He knew already she hit him in his heart. He felt it; he could not deny it.

"Tate, sorry. I guess sometimes you think you can get past the pain and loss of someone, and you never really do."

If only she knew how true her words were. Tate often dealt with sadness and pain in his dreams from Callie's murder. He nodded and was choked up inside. He wanted to hug her and remove the pain her parents' death caused her, but he, too, was suffering a sorrow; he didn't want her to share his burden.

Aubrey looked at him, and somehow, she knew that he was keeping something of his past silenced. "Tate, I always wished that they would develop this end of the beach. Level the sand and clean up the beach and maybe put an ice cream vendor down this way. The view of the sun setting from this point on the beach is picture-worthy." She successfully steered their early topic of conversation to something upbeat. "When my parents died and I got older, I thought of putting some money to building a sand park or even put nice benches and such down this way." She smiled. "I put all the money I received from their death and, later, my grand-mother's to making baked goods. At least that would keep me fed, and I can still come here when I need to put my thoughts into perspective." She looked at his eyes. They captivated her. Her thoughts were in check today as they were on him, and he—in her mind—was already pretty amazing. She blushed, but hoped he would see it as the sun's rays coating her light skin.

Tate was impressed with her wishful thoughts and loved her idea. To make this desolate beach area a nice place was definitely a dream of hers that could be accomplished. Perhaps one day, he would see her face light up with the biggest smile if her original concept took the unkempt piles of sand ridden with weeds to a beautifully renovated beach area with freshly raked sand.

Their time here was productive. It was a peaceful after-noon as they established getting to know one another much better. Tate watched the small waves come up closer to where they sat. He thought about what it would be like to go in the water with her. He could wade out pretty far for his height, but would make certain he kept her above the water with him. That would mean she would have to be held tightly in his arms.

He let out a smile. He saw her catch a glimpse of it. A few times, he stretched his long legs. He finally had removed his sneakers and stuffed his socks in them while she told him of her parents passing. The water came in just close enough to skim his toes, and the coolness was refreshing. Their conversation progressed as they shared with one another more about their lives and aspirations. Tate rose and turned his neck in circles, moving his shoulders around. He had sat too long. "Aubrey, I'll be right back."

He walked several feet down the beach. He needed to pace himself. He knew it was unreal that he was already falling for her. Pausing at the water's edge, he checked to see if anyone else was nearby on the beach. Once an officer of the law, inside always one. He glanced down the one strip of the water and out to the street that had become a dead end a half a block back. No one visible and not a sound nor word of any other conversation was heard. He walked back, his footsteps leaving impressions in the soft sand.

He found that even when he gazed out over the water his mind was clearly seeing her. Aubrey was still seated on the beach sifting the sand through her hands playfully. He observed her beautiful features and couldn't stop looking at *her*. His heart was in a good place because with each step away and each on returning from his brief walk, he felt her stare.

"The coast is clear. Seems like it's just us on our own private beach." He approached her commenting.

"Yeah, most locals stay away from this end. Lately, nothing good comes to this area. Sometimes the wrong crowd hangs here, and we really don't want that to enter the town."

"Aubrey, what type of wrong crowd?"

"Drugs, I think mostly. This area is the closest to the parkway entrance, and from there, it's straight routes to all the cities. Not that I know anything about drugs. Just what I hear." Tate felt she knew something or surely someone as she added an underlying defensive tone in her comment. He wanted to not dissect each of her words, but clearly, he was trained to certain key words and mannerisms people said or displayed.

"I wouldn't think such a pretty girl like you would get a mile close to any of that shit. This area seems nice enough."

"Tate, it is during the day, but mostly on the weekends at night, it has been known to have traffic." She knew that was where Emerson met up with others and made their trades. Emerson had told her that much while dating her and that he didn't want her hanging out this way at night. She had laughed to herself that Emerson was showing concern, but it was probably more that he didn't want her caught and ratting him out.

"Aubrey, you want to head back? I have a bag of pastries waiting for me, and please don't let me forget them."

"There are always more where they came from. I know I keep repeating this but am so grateful for you being there at the bakery to save me. I wish I could say that Jackson was drunk and didn't know what he was doing because I thought he was a good man. He knew, though, what he was doing, and he planned it. That is the part that frightens me so." Her arms wrapped around herself, and he saw her sudden nervousness.

"I have to go to the station tomorrow and give a detailed report. I will be sure to just say a random guy was in the right place at the right time. That would be you helping me, but I understand you don't want to be involved."

"Aubrey, I was involved. I beat him pretty bad. I just think my involvement ends there. No need for the locals, or even Jackson, to know about me." Tate didn't want to stir the towns focus on him. He wasn't here for that. "Aubrey, if you need me, though, I give you my word I am here for you."

"Well, Pete just wanted me to fill in some blanks on the initial report. He called me earlier, and Jackson is being charged with assault with a deadly weapon. Pete knew that would make me relieved that Jackson is not out nor able to cause me upset or anyone else harm. He was usually only in town for the summer months, showing properties and rentals, but I heard he will be held in custody here in town till his day before the judge. Hopefully, they will place him far from here in a cell for an extended amount of time after the judge makes a ruling. I can only hope I never have to come close to him again."

"I'm not happy he is still here in this town. At least he is locked up. Mark my word, he won't get to you again or near you ever." Tate was visibly upset by what almost happened to Aubrey combined with what happened to Callie, who he'd once vowed to protect too.

To change the scenery and topic quickly to something more positive, Tate extended his hand and helped her up. He thought they would leave this beach area and yet still walk together some more. After sitting so long, though, her leg had fallen asleep, and she instantly fell back, off balance, into the sand. Tate fell with her. They laughed together, amused with their mishap after he found she was fine. They lay on the ground and viewed one another, each dusted with a light coating of sand.

When her leg felt normal and the pins and needles had vanished, Tate rose and helped her up. They stood close together, and Tate was about to start to sweep the sand from her shoulders, but Aubrey beat him and placed her hands to his chest, freeing the particles to the air. She was on her tip toes, stretching as she reached to free the granules that lay on his shoulders. Her soft touches that patted his clothes were welcomed and appreciated. Her gentleness warmed his veins and would long after the sun set.

Her playful side showed as she beat him to retrieve his shirt on the sand that she sat upon. She was feeling like she won a prize having the advantage of holding onto it. Aubrey then stood with it tucked tightly under her one arm. He reached out to take it from her. She took a tiny step back and dug her feet in the sand.

"Tate, I am one woman you do not mess with." She stated but then bit her lip, which showed her innocence.

"Why is that?"

"Well, because I'm offering to clean this shirt, and if you don't let me, I will cut you off from my bakery goods. This week I'll be making my famous Red Velvet Fudge Pie."

"I have heard of cake. You mean Red Velvet Cake?"

"No, Tate, I clearly said pie. You will have to let me wash this shirt, and when you come by to pick it up, I'll set aside a huge piece of the pie for you."

"You drive a hard bargain there, but deal."

✧ ✧ ✧

ACROSS THE BEACH, JUST WHERE the street ended, Damon sat in his car. It was early for the drop this evening. He sat and listened to the music beating through his headphones. He was caught by surprise when he saw a man walking along the unkempt beach area, but even more surprised when he saw a guy and a girl. As he looked harder...Damn, that was Aubrey. Damon wondered what Aubrey was doing out this end of town with some guy. He was certain Emerson probably had no idea. He watched Aubrey and the guy begin to walk in his direction. He noticed that they didn't show any type of affection.

He always questioned why his friend Emerson choose Aubrey in the town to be his girlfriend when any of the other girls that seemed cooler would have jumped at that title. One day, he asked Emerson, and it was quite simple. Aubrey had a nice place on the beach. She was a nice girl, and the town loved her. With her sad family tragedy, the town embraced her, and if Emerson was her guy, then the town would surely adore him and never suspect he would be into criminal dealings.

Damon knew Aubrey was really a nice girl, and if her staying in her little gingerbread house in town selling sweets kept her busy and not into Emerson's business, that was fine with him. Emerson shared with him that Aubrey caught him with a bunch of stash and kicked him out, but then Emerson could be persuasive, and all he had to do was turn on his charms, and she would be taking him back. Earlier today, Emerson told Damon he would be back in her home and out of his living room by the week's end.

Even though Emerson was crashing at his place all these months, many nights he never came back. Damon wasn't stupid. He knew his buddy was surely spending time with some other town ladies. Damon didn't want to get Emerson all worked up about seeing Aubrey today. They had a big client coming in for a pick up, and his focus had to be on that. The week had been great. They had drop-offs in the city already paying top dollar, and tonight would be yet another fine score. Damon cranked up the next song that played and closed his eyes to feel the music. When he checked again, they had passed him. From where his car was parked, it appeared like he was waiting outside the end beach house. Nothing suspicious at all.

TATE WALKED NEXT TO AUBREY. There was a height difference so he leaned in to her each time she spoke to not miss a word. From the time they left the beach area, he couldn't take his eyes off of her, even if it was just peering down onto the top of her head. Arriving back where they started, Aubrey opened the shop and grabbed his bag of sweets. "I don't want you to forget this, and our walk and talk today, I won't forget. It was nice to take a break."

"My pleasure; thanks for showing me a part of the town that is special to you." Tate felt hesitation between them.

Aubrey went to relock the glass door and fumbled with her keys, and they dropped to the pavement below. Tate reached down at the same time as her to retrieve them. Their hands crossed over the silver metal key dangling from the ring that displayed the cupcake logo of *Sweet Treats*. Neither pulled their hand away.

Aubrey tilted her head down. "Thank you, Tate. I got this."

Tate was caught up in the moment, still touching her finger. "You certainly got me, Aubrey. I have to leave you knowing that." He rose first and didn't want to press her. They'd just had a wonderful time together.

"Tate, have a nice walk back. I hope to see you again soon, that is, if you are staying in town for a while longer." All he needed was her sweet words requesting his stay.

"I'm just up the street at the Hamilton Inn." Tate offered, hopeful that one day his arms would enfold her as they watched the mesmerizing surf roll in and out. Tate already had the view at the inn, just not her. Of course, other thoughts crossed his mind, but he really was falling for her and coming undone. Looking out for her, he made certain she was seated in her car pulling her seat belt across her, and he tapped the door after he shut it. His hand removed the brown bag she gave him that he had set on the hood of the car. Without turning he walked toward the inn. His mind ran through a mental list of everything he needed to do.

First, he needed to return home, well, to his apartment in Maryland and bring his truck back here so he would have wheels. Next, he needed to ask Lacey if there were any rentals for at least the next month. He knew there were, but he was seeking perhaps one that placed him closer to Aubrey's house on the beach. He also wanted to tell his partner Reed, that he was going to stay put here in town for a bit. Even though he left the division, he and Reed kept in touch, and Reed shared with him inside information that kept him on his quest for Callie's murderer. He knew he would stop and hang with Reed for a night and catch him up. It was nice still having the ties to the force without being there.

Tate knew he couldn't legally give his partner or the others in his division support. It had been a tough decision that he'd thought about for a while before requesting to leave the department. The day he left the captain's office, he didn't return. He walked out satisfied with the final decision he stated. He missed seeing everyone that he worked with on so many stake outs for long periods of time. The only one he kept in touch with was Reed. Actually, Reed came looking for him.

Tate had sold the home he and his wife lived in. He took the money from that and her life policy disbursement and put them into a new account under just his name. He closed the joint one they once shared, and he didn't want to have anything linked to Callie that her father may come sniffing for. Her father hadn't a clue the amount of money left to Tate. Even Tate was still at a loss to what he would ever do with it.

His mental list complete, he thought tomorrow night he would head and join the local cops at Deluca's Den. He could inquire with the guys if they had incurred many problems with drug traffic here in their town. After all, he was here to avenge Callie's death. Or was he?

He was done here. Actually, his contact never showed so he should have been back on the next train, but there was something else happening. A tick, if one called it that, kept nagging at him to stay.

Chapter Five

L YING IN THE COMFORTABLE BED in his room at the inn, he replayed the entire afternoon with Aubrey. He had great attention to detail. During their talk, his mind drifted once to Callie as he missed her. Looking ahead and right in front of him and not rethinking the past was Aubrey. He wanted to know her and, for some reason, wanted more than anything to just kiss her, hold her. There was something soothing, comforting to the way Aubrey's eyes looked into his. He didn't want to think more on Callie in that moment; he wanted to escape the demons. Instead, he focused on Aubrey, and he studied her face even more in his mind as he stored her beautiful features in his thoughts.

Folding the pillow in half under his head, he thought back to Aubrey asking him where he was from. He had just come from a simple one bedroom loft apartment that an elderly couple renovated. It worked. They were glad there was a man around to assist once in a while, and he made that tiny space into the cockpit of his detective work.

His leads were posted on one full wall in the living room to enable him to see who was linked to another or if a tip would take him further. Tate was certain that the drug dealer was on the East Coast, and he would find him. He would find the person that stabbed his lovely wife Callie. Tate knew he would probably want that person to suffer the same, but in his sane mind, he wanted the murderer to just be punished and put away for life.

He rolled on his side and glanced at sweetness. Another brown bag of goodies from Aubrey. Reaching in the bag, he selected a chocolate twist, it was drizzled with white and dark chocolate, Tate ate it up. When he headed out again, he would be sure to offer the remaining pastries to Lacey and her ladies that cleaned the rooms. He didn't want to hurt Aubrey's feelings, but bags of these were not what he usually started his day with.

Closing his eyes to take in some beautiful randomness, his thoughts led him to Callie. He could still see himself playing with her lovingly on the beach, picking her up and spinning her. Believing her life was not in danger with him around. Her smile gave him the best present that he could ever have, knowing it was for him and he was a great husband. Then the blood, oh god, all that blood. Her pale face pressed into the carpet. The redness absorbing and expanding in radius. Punching the carpet till both his fists bloodied. He had been in shock and distraught. He felt like he was losing control. He lost sight of those in the room doing their jobs, a job he trained to do. He couldn't hear their voices talking to him, trying to help him, calm him. He only remembered hearing the last words of their conversation that ended suddenly before he reached her.

Tate left his home, went to the station, and wrapped tape around his knuckles so they wouldn't bleed onto his desk. He sat knowing a recent large haul of drugs from a local bust was one room away. He thought of how he could go in there and take it till he didn't feel again. Take enough to never wake up again. Make this awful pain that he was now carrying go away.

He rose from his desk and opened the door with his key. On the table was the confiscated cash and drugs. Tate slit the side of the cocaine with his key. It poured onto the table. He licked his finger and swept it in the pile. He coated his gums with the white powder, numbing his mouth and beginning to take away his pain one sweep at a time. His rolled a dollar bill to the huge line he had cut out, knowing this would take him far away from reality for a short while. He snorted it and had three quarters done. He pulled up his head from the desk, tossing his head back.

The rush hit him, release melting into his system and absorbing his inner pain, as it numbed his entire body. His mind was alert to stop him from finishing the rest of the line of coke before him, his thoughts knowing this wouldn't remove his agony. Tate knew there was something far more powerful that would permanently remove his pain. He moved toward the confiscated firearms. His fingers shook as they skimmed over several pieces. He traced his fingertip along each of their triggers. He wanted to do harm, but somehow he heard in his head not to do it to himself, but to use the law he stood for and take down those that did this. In hurt and anger, he swept all the drugs and money and arms from the table, scattering them to the floor. He exited the room leaving cocaine white footprints along the hallway. He walked so far away that he only returned one day weeks later to clear his desk and turn in his badge.

Jerking from that vision, Tate fisted his pillow, not feeling comfortable, trying to put those past troubled memories at rest. He turned, facing the side table next to the bed, and already it had accumulated brown bags with her bakery name written on the one side. He smiled inside as he pictured her; his thoughts turned pleasant. He no longer had to wrestle the pillow as it now felt comfortable as his head rested upon it. He focused on his lovely vision of Aubrey and his tired eyes calmed. He thought he smelled a sweet aroma probably seeping from the pastry bags, but he grinned because, being close to Aubrey, he had smelled a fragrant scent of chocolate, vanilla, and cinnamon.

On the beach yesterday, he kept thinking he was hungry. He was imagining food when it was probably her clothes releasing the pleasing scents from the bakery aromas. From scents to scenarios, he was now caught up in a reverie of her tender touch when she talked of her parents' death. That touch, though innocent and simple, made him jolt. When she later dusted the sand from his chest, he'd almost exploded. He actually had to hold his breath.

He adored her already. Even when he reached down to pick up his shirt that she sat upon, she pulled it from the ground first playfully and suggested she would wash it. Tate never needed taking care of. He always took care of everyone.

He could use a clean shirt. He was already on the second day of his same clothes. When he was at the gym, he helped himself to a free tee shirt for signing up with the temporary membership, and later today, he planned to walk through some of the town shops to see if there were some other essentials to hold him till the end of the week. At the week's end, he would be heading back to his place to grab some of his own stuff to carry him over for however long he remained in this town. He thought maybe just another few weeks.

The time on the clock couldn't be the real time. It was already almost noon. Tate rarely slept peacefully, and for some reason, this bed with its pillow top mattress cover devoured his strong body and led him to rest. Rising up slowly and stretching, he knew he already missed an earlier coffee excuse to see Aubrey. He decided he didn't need more treats, and he would let the day go and not stop in to bother her. Tate knew, though, he would walk at some point near the bakery for a glimpse of her inside. Nothing creepy, by any means, just that his heart felt something even when he simply said her name in his head.

Dressing in the same clothes he originally showed up in the town with, he knew he had to tackle that first. Buy some other clothes. Tate had already picked up some new workout items but needed to find a regular shirt or two. After a quick shower, he headed out of the inn, but before he left, he found Lacey and asked her opinion of where he should shop. Lacey suggested a few places and mapped them out on the inn's brochure. Not that it was a big town, but he was relying on walking everyplace now. Thanking Lacey, he dropped off a full bag of sweet items for her and her staff to enjoy. "Thank you, Tate. You are going to spoil us." Tate nodded and went out to enjoy this new day with visions of Aubrey still fresh in his mind.

The first few stores he went in were mostly sale items of the summer finds: t-shirts, beach umbrellas, sand buckets, and souvenirs. The next shops were perfect, not what he was familiar with, but he found a few items to hold him over. "Hey, Tate," a man's voice called from the other side of the store. It was Levi.

"Oh hey, Levi. Off your shift already?"

"Yeah, I'm off the next two days. I figured I'd come buy a new shirt for myself. I may have a date with Lacey, the innkeeper where you are staying."

"You may have or you do have?"

"Well, I have been trying to get up enough nerve to ask her, and just this morning, I stopped in to say hello to her, and she offered me a cinnamon bun. I think she likes me."

Tate laughed inside. Those were the buns he gave to Lacey. "Levi, just ask her out. She seems really nice."

"I know, but I think she has her eye on Emerson."

"Wait a minute, you mean the Emerson that..." Tate stopped. He didn't want to elude that he knew Aubrey and Emerson broke up, as others didn't have that news. Plus, he didn't want to share anything Aubrey told to him.

"Yes, Emerson Deluca. For some reason, all the women in this town drool over that man, even Tessa, who is Aubrey's roommate. I have seen her and Emerson real chummy at the diner a few times. I am sure it is nothing. Tessa seems nice. She is from old money passed down, real estate money. I heard she is out of town for the week, but if you are around, you will take a second glance in her direction. I prefer a more down to earth girl, whereas Tessa flaunts all the goods, if you know what I mean."

Tate nodded. He understood. He also wondered why someone with money would be sharing a place with Aubrey. His thoughts saddened that perhaps Aubrey had it tough and wasn't able to make it solely on her own.

"Well, Tate, remember to try to stop for a beer with us guys tomorrow. The tourists are all gone. It's a bunch of us locals hanging."

"I plan to. I want to meet a few as I may stay here in town for a bit longer. Lacey shared with me some listings of rental properties down on the outer beach of town. Not the most popular homes, but they're furnished and Lacey told me the owners are quite welcoming of any rental deal in the off-season."

"Yeah, Aubrey lives down that way. I am keeping an eye on her. There was an incident the other day at her bakery, and I want to make sure she is safe."

Tate knew it was Jackson and his coming onto her. It was nice Levi was keeping a watchful eye, but Tate thought he was far better suited for that. Just in this brief conversation, he was making mental notes about Tessa, Emerson, and little things he picked up on that came from Levi's words.

"Well, enjoy your shopping. I may just walk past the Hamilton Inn in the hopes that Lacey is sitting on the porch rocking in the swing…alone."

"You do that man, and see you tomorrow night." Tate patted Levi's shoulder. This was a good man. He appeared dedicated and a perfect fit for this local town of small crime, but definitely not for the level of the narcotics division, which was challenging and often intense. Tate knew he was once a good cop, too, but when his life changed, it hardened him. He wanted to be that man he was before, the one his friends called "Bear Rug" due to his big and overpowering size and gentle and caring personality. He knew that there was no way he and Levi were on the same playing field in law enforcement, but they shared a common trait of law in their blood.

Tate made certain that he purchased enough items to tide him over a few days, and with his bags in his hands, he walked back to the inn, only he had to pass by her bakery first.

FINALLY, THE AFTERNOON ARRIVED, AND Aubrey had down time. This was when she prepared all the items for the following day. She kept an eye on the door here and there, since the sign was still showing her bakery as open. Usually, the flow of people slowed to a trickle in the afternoons. If there was a special order placed, she made the pickups during that timeframe. Her mornings were sometimes so hectic, especially during the three main summer months.

Aubrey removed all her ingredients to make her special red velvet fudge pie. She had placed the sign in the window that she would have it for a few days. It became a special to the town locals as she didn't offer it during the busy months—too much work involved and there would surely be too much demand.

Turning on the mixer, she watched the deep red cake batter churn. Another mixer sounded, making the dough for the pie crusts. When the dough was in a large ball, she removed it to begin rolling it out for the many pie plates that were lined up on her prep table waiting. She shut off the other mixer and thought she heard the chimes from the front door. Wiping her hands off on her apron, she went to greet a late day customer.

For a moment, her neck tingled just as it did days ago when it was Jackson that came in here. Her morning had been an early one as she stopped at the police station to help them with all the information they requested. One nagging thought was that Officer Pete kept asking her, "So you have no idea who this man was that helped you? No idea where he came from? He just appeared and beat the shit out of Jackson and left?" Aubrey knew Tate didn't want involvement, and for him saving her, she had honored his simple request.

"Well, hey there, Mr. Arms Full of Packages." Her eyes brightened.

"I thought I would stop and see if I can buy what you have left here today as I polished off all the rest." Tate knew she would be happy to hear that. He set his packages down near the counter. He also knew she wouldn't take the money, but he folded some bills and tucked them off the corner of the register. She would find them when she cashed out her drawer.

"Well, I don't have much, but I am in the back making red velvet fudge pie and can whip you up a small loaf of red velvet from the batter." Before heading there, she walked to the front door and turned the sign to *closed*. "Well, I'm glad you stopped in. I wanted to thank you for suggesting we take that walk yesterday." She continued to speak as she walked toward the back.

Tate headed to the back with her and leaned on the far end of the huge butcher block prep table, to keep out of her way. He watched her move around, pouring this and flouring that. He caught himself admiring her, every inch of her. All dusted in flour, she was still incredibly beautiful.

"I was glad to learn more about you…I mean, the town yesterday."

His slip was caught, and she smiled with her head turned from him, finishing a loaf pan and placing it into the oven. "So, Aubrey, show me your goods, how you make the pies."

She laughed at his humor. "Well, I already got it started. Now all I have to do is cut the shells and pour the red velvet into them. I am on the home stretch. Do you want to help?"

He nodded and took hold of the batter that was to be poured in the shells. Aubrey took the sharp knife from the butcher block holder and began to slice the sheet of rolled dough. Tate dipped his finger into her mixing bowl and placed her sweet mixture to his tongue. All the while, Aubrey followed his finger's motions.

"No, don't you do that…OUCH!!!" She dropped her

cutting knife and grabbed her hand. Aubrey had sliced her finger, not watching what she was doing. Blood began to drip.

Tate saw the knife and the blood and froze for a second. He had to rip free of the thoughts that took over his mind. It wasn't Callie. This was a simple cut from a knife, and it was Aubrey. He immediately was at her side, taking her hand over to the sink and ran cold water over it. It wasn't too bad, but he kept insisting she go have it checked.

"I can't leave all these pies out. It will be a waste of money. Let me just get a Band-Aid or two over it and finish this baking. I promise, if it's still bleeding when I finish, I'll get it checked."

Tate knew when he licked the batter from his finger that he accidentally got her sidetracked from what she was cutting with the knife. "I'm so sorry I distracted you." Tate helped her with the simple task of applying double Band-Aids to her skin.

"Oh, Tate, it's not the first time this has happened to me. I have had my share of cuts and burns. There are many tiny scars I carry as reminder wounds that I work in a kitchen environment."

His thoughts were not on her wound, but that this was the first time he had felt incredible in the presence of another female in so long. Not thinking, he took her hand to his lips. He gently kissed her wrist first and then proceeded to place his lips on each delicate finger. There was definitely a moment beginning between them until the timer rung and broke the silence. Tate didn't let that bother him as he lingered a bit longer with her touch captured on his lips.

"Tate, I have to get that." She pulled her hand from his and went to retrieve the loaf pan for him. Once she set it to cool, she busied herself with another mixer for crème cheese icing to top it.

"You sure you're okay?" He leaned in toward her and brushed his fingertip near her bandaged area.

"Yeah, I am fine." She tried to assure him as it wasn't the cut to her finger that she was concerned with. It was his touch, one that that made her heated. She knew that she couldn't remember the last time she felt this hot in her own bakery, and it wasn't coming from the ovens. Tate had truly awakened something in her from the very first day she met him.

SHE ACTUALLY FOUND HERSELF SITTING on her balcony overlooking the beach last night remembering their walk. She eyed his body as he kicked the sand from the beach. He was tall, built solid. His hair was shaved closely to his head, making his appeal even more rugged. Each time his eyes met hers she was breathless.

Her mind recalled watching his every movement while they were beachside, how he turned on the sand and began his slow pace back to where she was sitting. His head had been more focused on the wet waters toppling over his feet. She didn't mind he had taken a brief walk as it allowed her to stare at him, viewing his front and back even more. He towered over her, and she liked tilting her head upward to him in conversation.

She propped her feet up onto her balcony railing making herself comfortable. Anytime she was off her feet, it was like spa time for her. Aubrey watched the reflections scatter the evening tide, and with each breaking wave that glistened from the moon light, she made a wish, hoping that he would walk past her beach house. It was strange that she was thinking this, as when she arrived home there were many phone messages from Emerson asking her when he could move back in. She left them unanswered and pulled a bottle of chilled wine from her refrigerator. She poured a full glass and carried it onto the balcony to toast the close of her wonderful day. Last night, she recalled, was the perfect pairing, the wine she selected and her mind content with thoughts of Tate.

"Aubrey, you want help getting these into the oven?" Tate waited, "Aubrey?"

"Oh, I'm sorry. I was just thinking about us…I mean, no need to fuss…over me." Aubrey attempted to recover from her slipup. She saw his eyes react, and she knew he caught it. She glanced at the clock to change the subject. "Time flies. I forgot my bakery closed an hour ago. I need to go out front and lock up." Aubrey was flushed in her face, and she hadn't been near the oven heat. She walked toward the hall, but Tate stopped her as he questioned, "I think I saw you turn the sign on the door before we came back here." She hesitated. This man had her memory blurred, but her feelings were crystal clear.

"You're right. I seemed to forget I did that already…thank you." She walked to the oven the long way so she didn't have to brush up next to him. Aubrey then loaded all the red velvet pies into the oven on two levels. "The secret to my pies is I top them with chocolate chips immediately when they come out of the oven, and they melt down quickly. Then you see, Tate, it will be my red velvet fudge pie."

His eyes opened wide. "I can't wait. Everything you make is so good." He was also still thinking of how good his heart felt when it pulsed rapidly moments ago as he heard her say she was thinking about them.

The time passed, and they conversed on daily topics of the weather, the ocean waters still being warm enough to swim in, and how good this pie was going to be. When the first few were removed from the oven, Aubrey shook chips over them generously. She tested the chocolate with her touch as it quickly melted away and smoothed. Lifting her finger, she was imprinted with the chocolate. "Oh no, that is not going to waste." Tate stepped over and took her finger to his lips, into his mouth, and slowly removed the chocolate. Aubrey felt the jolt run from her fingertip to her panties in a mega warm rush. She was coming undone by his handsome appearance, his voice, his simple touch, and now his lips tasting her…chocolate.

Tate moaned softly. The chimes of the front door startled them both. Someone had entered out front. She had turned the sign but must not have locked the front door. Aubrey was about to head in that direction when she heard the patron call out. "Bree, Bree, you back there?" Emerson walked straight to the back.

"Yes, I am making pies," and she hurried to the other side of the block table, separating her from Tate. Not that they were still caught up in their moment, but she felt guilty like she was doing something wrong.

"Hey, who are you?" Emerson asked, shifting his attention to Tate's face.

Tate peered down to him. He was easily inches taller than this asshole. "I am…"

"He is the new delivery guy for today. I needed help with some of my deliveries, and he stopped in for some pastries and gladly offered assistance."

"Oh, cool, just didn't want you moving in on my girl, because Aubrey here, all this sweetness, is mine."

Aubrey said a thank you to Tate, but before she could catch another warm glimpse from his eyes, he was heading out, remembering to grab his shopping bags of items he purchased earlier. All she saw was his back to her, and his arms holding his items tightly. She wished he didn't leave and that he held onto her that way.

"So, girlfriend of mine, you never answered my calls last night. When am I bringing my bags back to your bedroom?"

"Emerson, I need to think some more. I was really pissed off that you lied to me about that shit you were dealing or cutting for whomever. I know you said you were done with the drug scene, but I can't have that around me or in my home."

"Bree, you have my word it won't happen ever again. I want nothing in between you and me, not even a bed sheet."

Tate lingered in the front of the store for a moment, hearing just enough to confirm that this guy was a total asshole and certain he was pushing drugs. He knew he couldn't ask Aubrey to not go back with him because he just met her, but he hoped this guy wouldn't sugar coat his way into her heart once more. Tate let himself out. He held the chimes separating them so they wouldn't jingle and then closed the door slowly. He was certain he needed to watch this Emerson dude more closely. What she stated was, in his opinion, was that Emerson was into drugs or some kind of drug situation. He wanted to call Reed back in Maryland and see if they could run a check on this Emerson DeLuca. Tate was upset that he came in and ruined the tender moment he shared with Aubrey, but also, he missed out on his personal red velvet loaf and a piece of that amazing red velvet pie that he excitedly awaited.

Chapter Six

AUBREY AWOKE LYING ON HER side, glancing out to the beach that was the most beautiful view in her home. It was captivating and held her attention. It distracted her from the darkened water stains above on her ceiling and the distressed drywall peeling from her walls that needed repairs. The balcony doors were open, letting the cooler morning air sweep in. The sheer white curtains that hung to the floor were dancing, full of motion. Looking out at the expanse of beach water, it appeared never-ending in her eyes.

She lay there focusing on the water rising up and then fading back. It seemed to be testing its boundaries. She drove her thoughts to Emerson's promises, all of his little ways of making her crack a smile even when she was pissed at him. She rethought how she gave in and let him come home with her when she closed the shop late yesterday. She left her car, and she and Emerson went for a bite to eat at his family's bar. Seated next to him, Emerson turned her stool into his welcoming, open stance. He brought his lips so close to hers. He wanted a scene. He thrived on attention, and he wanted to prove she was his as he openly displayed public affection to her.

The bar sounded loudly with taps against the wood bar. It was like banging a spoon on a glass at a wedding to entice the couple to kiss. Aubrey blushed but went with it. Everyone here thought they were together and had been for the past two years. She still loved Emerson, that was a given, but was that enough? She doubted whether she was still *in love* with him or ever was.

A few times back when they lived together, she had some uncertainties. Too often, she thought he was having a conversation with a woman. He would seem nervous for a little while after she would ask "Who were you just talking to?" Emerson usually answered with "Oh my brother. He needs some money" or "He wants me to come meet him for a beer." In the past, she occasionally glanced at recent callers on his phone. Some were his brother. But most times, they had been someone named TLU. She didn't know anyone by those initials so she shrugged it off.

One time, her insecurities really took over, and she shared with her roommate that she thought Emerson may be seeing someone. Tessa started laughing and walked over to her and shook her. "Are you crazy? That man has nothing but eyeballs popping out of his sockets for you." Remembering those words from Tessa made her feel good. Here at the bar tonight, Aubrey smiled as the locals were clapping and requesting her and Emerson kiss once more. Emerson, without hesitation, moved in toward her lips.

His lips pressed firmly against hers as he prolonged the kiss. Aubrey kissed him back, wanting to have no doubt about him. She had once believed they were heading for the scattered flowers on the beach and a heart carved in the sand to commit themselves for life to one another. Was that still what she hoped for and was it to be with him?

She played with her drink. Still red-faced from that kiss, she licked her lips. A few thoughts ran through her mind as her finger traced along her glass. First, God, she missed Tessa. She'd received a text earlier that she may be home as early as tomorrow. Must be nice to just take off, hang out with other friends, and not have a care in the world. Aubrey never met Tessa's other friends. Odd maybe, but then again all Aubrey did was wake each morning to open her bakery and keep that running in order to keep her beach home a float.

Aubrey returned Tessa's text hoping she would respond. Aubrey even requested that she call her and not text because she really wanted to tell her personally what happened with her cousin Jackson. Tessa liked Jackson; he was well-liked by the town. Since he wasn't successful in forcing himself on Aubrey, holding him at the county jail would keep Jackson from harming anyone else. The occurrence was not broadcasted the other day, which helped to lesson embarrassment for Aubrey. Although she did absolutely nothing wrong to ever hold her head down, she just didn't need this town feeling sorry for her once again.

The second deep thought that took her away was a clear vision of his lips on hers. Not Emerson's, but Tate's. She unconsciously rubbed her finger to her lower lip, and her tongue touched her finger nail. "Bree, where are you? I asked you three times if you want another beer." Emerson was waving in front of her face and landed his hand with a light tap to her nose.

"I was just thinking how I miss Tessa."

"Yeah, you have yourself a great roommate." He smiled and again pointed to her empty beer glass for a response of another or not.

Aubrey hesitated as another beer poured into her glass would carry her past her own personal limit. She was already thinking of Tate. With more alcohol, she wondered what may happen in her thoughts. After a long, dead pause, she conceded. "Sure one more won't hurt me."

Aubrey smiled as the guys to her left said, "That's a girl! One more." After the next round of beers came, she politely excused herself to head to the ladies room. Emerson was in conversation with another guy so he didn't respond. As she walked past the bar and down the hall, two girls were chatting, and she overheard, "Emerson is great. I loved working out with him yesterday, and I would love to have any type of work out with him." She laughed, and Aubrey didn't. Passing them and acting like she hadn't heard a word, she knew there were not two Emerson's in the town, especially after all the tourists had gone. She was certain they were talking about him, her Emerson, and for now, he was trying to reposition himself back into her good graces.

The beer hit her. She thought she had a couple, maybe several, definitely too many. Standing to wash her hands, warm water ran from the faucet. Aubrey held her palm to the steady stream that flowed, and it felt comforting. What was uncomfortable was the way she was thinking of how warm Tate felt in her presence. So many thoughts about him kept entrancing her mind. His incredible eyes, her tilting and stretching her neck upward to take him in, and his muscular, strong arms that she believed would enfold her entire body gently and adoringly.

Her breath seized for a passing moment. Aubrey knew there was nothing there because he would be just passing through the town. She did know that she forgot to cut him a piece of pie and had a separate loaf pan of red velvet cake just for him. Emerson interrupting them sent Tate into an immediate exit. Note to self, tomorrow or Friday, take those desserts for him to the Hamilton Inn if he didn't come for them first. If she went to the Hamilton Inn, it would also be a chance to catch up with Lacey.

Lacey and Aubrey were good friends. Aubrey knew deep down that Lacey was a little put off when Aubrey's first choice was Tessa to room with her at the beach house. She knew that Lacey would have loved the chance. It was just a matter of timing. Aubrey was hanging out more with Tessa when she needed to take on a roommate.

Aubrey and Lacey both worked a lot of hours so it wasn't that their relationship faded. They simply didn't have the time to hang out together especially during the high season. Aubrey had wanted to confide in Lacey about breaking it off with Emerson, but neither could commit to a free night out with their schedules. She knew Lacey was still booked with many reservations filling up at the inn. The end of August through early September were still popular vacation weeks for vacationers. Aubrey was relieved that their scheduled time off didn't line up. She was glad she hadn't wasted her friends limited free time and bent her ear with her Emerson details because Aubrey knew tonight she would be leaving with Tate—Whoops, she meant Emerson—after they finished their drinks.

PUNCHING THE PILLOWS WAS TATE'S release as he had left the bakery feeling like the outcast when Emerson commanded the show and he lost the two incredible things that were there in front of him. First, his stomach had been rumbling from the anticipation of that red velvet fudge pie, and his mind kept rethinking that unforgettable kiss to her finger. Since he only sampled the kiss for a moment, he stopped at the sandwich shop on the corner and asked for a full size turkey sub to satisfy his appetite. After polishing off the entire sandwich, he rested in bed rethinking in his head everything that has occurred lately. He drifted instantly in to a deep and sound sleep, which was unusual for him. As he dreamt, he revisited every thought of her. Aubrey. A smile widened on his tired face while his eyes remained tightly closed.

OPENING HIS EYES TO THE early morning light that filled his room, his initial thought was he would definitely stop in to see her briefly this morning. His night was planned as he was catching beers with the locals and hopefully gathering some news tips on Emerson. He didn't have to stop to see her or check in with her in any way, but he felt he needed to. Something pulled him to her more and more. If Emerson hadn't walked in and interrupted them, Tate knew he would have kissed her lips and enfolded her into his arms. Tate was a complete gentleman, but each time Aubrey was close to him, she had no clue the effect she that she was having on him.

Frustrated last night that Emerson appeared, he pushed that from his mind as he felt too incredible this morning. He awoke content from a full night of dreams that were filled with her lovely face and contagious smile. He lay waking up with a hard-on peeking under the sheet. "Ugh." He let out a moan as it was such a pleasant dream, but no telling how he was going take care of this unpleasantness unless it was his own doing. Time to hit the shower and also relieve himself from his rock hard penis.

He stood and pressed his hands firmly to the tiles on the shower wall as the water from the shower head rinsed over him. As the water sprayed down his neck and over his back, he let it wash away the ruthless thoughts of this guy Emerson. Just thinking about him made Tate twitch in the shower like an intense muscle spasm just occurred. The steady stream of warm water worked well to soothe and remove that guy that pained his mind. He concentrated on a single tile in the shower and recalled walking with Aubrey to the end area of the beach line. It was private with piles of small man-made hills of sand and very secluded. He mentally journeyed from the walls of the shower to losing himself in how deeply he desired her. He was imagining in detail the moment of lying her carefully down on the soft blanket in the sand. Next reaching down and unzipping and lowering his jeans, releasing his hard on. In his mind, he envisioned he was finally taking her. Her eyes shared that she loved him and wanted him. He also knew her need was not to be fulfilled in a quick manner, but slow and long, everlasting...forever.

Tate didn't do forever, though. He tried that with Callie, and it ended too soon. Slowly he rubbed himself and then picked up the pace and began to hold himself tightly. Aubrey's satisfied smile after he would make love to her was what took him over the edge. He squeezed his facial muscles and shook himself vigorously as he exploded all over the shower floor. He was breathing heavily and could only imagine how incredible he would feel the first time they would make love. The moment he would be deep inside of her.

Tate grabbed for the towel that hung on the wall and patted his body dry. He needed to wipe away those thoughts that aroused him or he would be sporting another hard on in no time. The towel didn't succeed as a diversion so he turned the shower dial to cold. Immediately, both his feet lifted up as he jumped in place from the sudden chill. He then stood and braved the extreme coldness that fully awakened him and relieved some of his growing excitement. Once he had gotten his body back under control, he dressed and left the inn in search of some breakfast and today, he was hoping it was a piece of pie.

Lacey cheerily smiled as she watched Tate walk through the foyer, and as he stepped out onto the porch, she commented, "I think someone slept very well." He agreed with his smile. Each day that he stayed in this beach town, he began to come alive even more.

"Restful sleep and rising each new day is something to be thankful for," he commented with sincerity. Credit should be given to Aubrey who appeared so vividly in his thoughts as he jerked himself off because that was the true reason behind his morning satisfied smile. Again, he felt his penis twitch. "Lacey, I'm heading for some breakfast. You want anything?" She shook her head, side to side declining his offer. Tate took a step back and added, "Oh and, Lacey, that guy Levi, the cop, he really likes you. I just thought you should know." Tate planted the seed and wanted to say something since Levi had been helpful and welcoming to him. Her face lit up. Tate didn't require any verbal response from her. Her expressions told him everything, and he would share that in conversation with Levi later tonight.

His morning began with a late start, and the crowd of locals had surely come and gone at the bakery. No line formed outside the door this middle of the week morning. He walked up, knowing in a moment her would see her again. God, he loved just seeing her. If she could only see through his eyes, she would be amazed at the vision he saw within her. Turning the doorknob to enter, he came to an abrupt stop. It didn't turn. No line of locals, no one waiting for a freshly baked item. No one. The bakery wasn't open...The closed sign was still hanging outward. *What is going on? She is regularly open at this time.* He noticed that her car was still parked in the same spot since yesterday. Then it came to him, the obvious reason for her not opening her bakery. It was what he assumed initially. Emerson had her. They must have left together in one vehicle…Emerson's. He hoped they weren't back together. He hoped that hadn't happened.

AUBREY STAYED IN BED LAZILY. She had thought about Tate repeatedly until her eyelids closed last night. She had felt Emerson attempt to have sex with her, but she pretended to sleep. Her mind raced as she was lying in bed with Emerson and thinking about another man. She didn't want to have sex with Emerson. Although Emerson tried to arouse her, he gave up easily when she didn't stir, and he rolled to his side of the bed.

Aubrey was glad he didn't press her for sex so soon. She wanted to make certain it was right to restart their relationship. Last night, they both slept on the opposite sides of the bed. Even when they were living together, she often wished that he would savor sex, take time with it, and lay cuddling after. He liked it a little rough, no foreplay first. He just liked to command; he was in charge. No way was Emerson down with tenderness afterward. After he came, he would leave the bed and walk onto the balcony and often talk on the phone for a half hour.

During the night, she stirred in her sleep and apparently snuggled close to his back thinking of Tate. He inched farther away from her. "Bree, move back on to your side of the bed. It's already too hot in here, even with the ceiling fan going."

She turned to her side of the bed, disappointed as she realized it was Emerson talking to her. Was she glad he was even back in her bed? *"Don't settle."* She remembered the two simple but powerful words Tate offered her in their previous conversation. She repeated the words silently several times as she soon fell off to sleep for another few hours. When she awoke to an empty bed, she hoped again this second time with Emerson that she wasn't settling. Emerson had already left, but a note waited next to her pillow. He told her he was coming back and with all his belongings.

Bree – We should be together. You can't just ask me to stay away again. I went to gather my stuff and will be back soon. I will stop and pick up some fresh coffee for you.

See, that wasn't bad. He was being sweet, remembering a coffee for her until she read the last line of the note. *I knew you couldn't say no to me. Never could.* That made her feel cheap, causing her to bring her knees up to her chest. She felt like he played her, that this was a game to him and he won, landing himself a free pass back in her home. They hadn't even talked about him returning yet. She wanted to set new guidelines so that he knew where she stood on drugs never being brought into her home or presence. *Ever!*

Emerson was gone, probably already throwing all his dirties in a laundry basket for her to clean. She had previously taken great care of him, and she believed that was love.

Lying back and releasing her legs, she ran her fingers over the pillow next to her. What would it be like to wake up in the morning to Tate?

Where did that thought come from? She wondered. Something was in the air, something between them. Shame it wouldn't come to anything; he was not staying long. She slept in today and wanted to take her time to open the bakery anyway. She knew that this was not like her, but she was the boss, and midweek, the traffic for donuts and other pastries was very slow. She pulled herself up from the bed and decided to take a bath.

Taking her time to fill the claw foot tub, she sprinkled one scoop of vanilla scented bath crystals to blend in with the water. She cranked the handle that widely opened the large window pane located above. It appeared to be another beautiful weather day. The curtains in the bathroom blew in and out with each soft push from the warm ocean breeze. When her bath was ready, she added a pinch of cinnamon out of habit. Everyone always thought she smelled like the bakery, but it was her baths that enhanced that scent. She dropped her robe and stood naked. The bathroom mirror held her sight.

She wanted to be elated that she was in love and her man had been by her in bed last night, although her expression that the mirror reflected back at her was sullen. Testing the water and agreeing it felt warm and comforting, she lowered herself into it. Resting her head on the back edge with a tub pillow, she closed her eyes and rethought of every appearance he made into her life since a few days ago. Not

Emerson coming back, but Tate walking in. Walking into her bakery. She didn't want to stare at him, but her eyes couldn't resist. His arms appeared solid and strong. His voice, she loved to hear him speak to her. She liked to make him think she wasn't listening so he would repeat himself again.

Reaching her hand into the water, she located her perfect spot that was located down under. She felt her excitement build with every thought of Tate and each touch from her fingers. The more she envisioned him she found she increased her motion of her fingers on her body. Feeling aroused her body squirmed in the tub water. All four of her fingers pressed harder and maintained circular motions stimulating her even more. She was feeling wonderful. It was Tate that she saw in her mind. She continued pressing even harder, even slipping her one finger into herself. The bath water splashed in the tub. "Tate, bring me there," she said loudly, knowing she was alone and no one but herself could hear.

"Take me there." Again pressing more and more and slipping her own finger further inward. The water helped in slipping her fingers effortlessly into herself. "Oh Tate, just once to be with you...T A T E!" Her body released, rippling the water. She slipped down from the tub pillow under the water and just let herself go with her orgasm. It was one that was brought on by Tate and all the visions she repeated in her head. It felt freaking great and what a way to start a new day.

She and Emerson hadn't slept together in a long time. She couldn't remember the last time that he even satisfied her or took care of her first. That never mattered to him. Emerson was more interested in his release than ever pleasing Aubrey.

TATE WALKED ALL THE WAY to her home on the beach at the opposite side of town. He walked on the street side, not the beach. He was a little worried, but not overly, because she was probably with Emerson. Something in him still made him want to check. It was a long healthy morning walk. He was glad it was a comfortable warm, late summer morning without the heat of midsummer. He remembered her telling him of her home when they talked, and he knew that out of the few that lined that edge of the beach, he would be able to pick hers without looking up her address or her car being there. This had to be hers.

He stood at the edge of the driveway made out of white pebbles that were a huge contrast to the porch wicker furniture that was cushioned with bright colorful fabric patterns. It screamed Aubrey, displaying her home decorating skills similar to her ornamenting a special cake. There was a monogram throw on the one wicker rocker that had a "T" on it, definitely leading him to the correct home. It didn't mean Tate. Her last name was Tanner, which he'd gathered when a customer at the bakery addressed her as Miss Tanner one morning. Her nearest neighbor was a few homes away. It worried him a bit that she was located out on this stretch of sand practically alone.

Tate walked around the side of the porch to see if she

was out by the beach. He pushed at the curtains that he almost tangled himself in. For the age of this home and to have weathered many storms, the wood boards of the porch did not creak at all. It wrapped around the entire house. As he stood there on the side of the house, he saw Emerson's ride. Crap, he was here.

Tate thought he may be, but when he saw no vehicle out front, he was still hopeful that he may have dropped her off. It was so peaceful out this way, no thru driving traffic like the main streets in the town. He was about to make his way back because he didn't want another altercation with Emerson here because he could no longer be the delivery helper of bakery items. That excuse would not fly again.

He heard her voice. Her pretty, innocent, and sexy voice called out, "Take me there." Shit. She was with HIM. Tate knew he had to leave quickly. He felt like he was a creeper as he stood on her side porch. He was about to turn away believing her lovely voice was being shared with another...until he heard her scream loudly. Not the kind that had him breaking down the door, but left him frozen in his tracks. "Oh Tate, just once to be with you, just once..." She hollered his name! His feet didn't move, and he knew this shit was about to turn really bad, knowing she was with Emerson and calling out another man's name. He had to end his unplanned visit and his unknown presence at her home and get himself far away from there quickly.

In another moment, Emerson would be all over her, questioning "Who is TATE?" He picked up his feet to exit the side porch but hesitated. Tate didn't hear her voice anymore or an angry voice of Emerson that he was sure was to follow. He did hear a car pull in over the pebble driveway. The sounds of stones tapping played in the air. A few moments later, he heard a loud man's voice. "Bree, I got you your favorite latte. Hey, were you taking a bath without me?"

"Yes, Emerson, I took a long bath."

Shit, she had been alone, pleasuring herself. Shit, but in a great way. She called out his name. He smiled because he clearly heard her say Tate. She was thinking of him. She liked him. This was all good. However the bad part was, should he even proceed to try to be around her if this guy had already returned to her home?

Tate thought he would leave and figure it all out in the coming days. He still was smiling a big Kool-Aid smile as he thought of her screaming out *his* name in her sweet pleasuring moan. As he walked around front, he saw the piles of clothes in the vehicle that was still running with a guy seated behind the wheel. "Bree, I'll be back in a minute. I want to grab my stuff from Damon's car," Emerson shouted, coming out the front door. Tate realized this day wasn't as great as it first started for him. It turned into SHIT, Emerson was moving back in.

Tate left via the back of the porch onto the beach. From the beach, he noticed how cool her home was. She had a huge porch with steps that led to the beach and an outdoor shower of open half walls. He thought how he would love to play on the beach with her and then stand underneath the shower waters, open to the outside elements. He could stand on the beach viewing her house forever, but wasn't prepared for giving her an explanation as to why he was standing in the middle of the sand directly in front of her home if Aubrey walked out on to her porch.

He picked his feet up and began moving away, quickly distancing himself from where her home stood. He had made it halfway to the inn and had forgotten to take off his shoes. He stopped and removed them. *This sucks. I know I like her. She is in my head every moment lately.* Up ahead on the uncrowded beach, he watched a couple. The guy was spinning his girl around on the wet area of sand. Tate reminded himself that he and Callie were once that happy, playful couple on the beach. When the couple headed toward the other direction away from him, he noticed he was completely alone on the beach.

He was far enough from Aubrey's place and decided to just remain there for a little while. He sat. The sun beating on him felt soothing. It was warming, but not overwhelming. *What am I doing? Chasing a girl, a beautiful girl, but she has a guy, a guy living with her. I am foolish for trying to go this route. I only came here to seek answers. I still have no new information on Callie and no more clean clothes past tomorrow. I need to leave this town and head back to collect my things and return again when I have prepared a well-organized plan. First though, I need to motivate myself to show up at the bar later, put down some local beers, and take Levi up on his invite. Tonight can't come soon enough.*

Chapter Seven

DELUCA'S DEN WAS AN EASY find or it may have been the sounds of the music that had Tate heading in the right direction. When Tate walked in, it was packed. It had a rather large inside with one rectangle bar in the center to serve drinks to every side. In the far back, he could see them racking balls for pool. The bar was four people deep all around.

He thought this must be where the entire town was tonight. Pushing past a few lovely ladies, he paused as he recognized one of them from his work out the other day at the local gym. He smiled and continued to move toward the back end of the bar where he could at least find a standing point by the wall. There was still some open space there. "Tate, hey Tate." That was followed by a strong whistle. He turned and saw a hand in the air. It was Levi's.

"Hey," he hollered back and went in that direction. At the table, he was given a chair and there were buckets of beers chilling. "Thanks, guys." Tate pulled the chair out and sat on it reverse style, leaning his arms on the top.

"Everyone, this is Tate. Tate's into real estate, and he will be here in our town for a short while." Levi led the introduction. All the guys seemed nice enough.

Settling in to a few beers, immediately the conversation loosened and so did Tate. He was enjoying these guys, mostly cops here in town and a few of their friends. If he closed his eyes, he could easily be in Hagerstown in their local pub with Reed and his other fellow police mates. They always bonded so closely. Many little stories passed on each of these guys lips.

They mentioned what went down the other day at *Sweet Treats* and that luckily a good passerby came to help poor Aubrey. Tate found comfort that they were all supporting her as some could be assholes and take the guys side, saying she asked for it or wanted it. He believed that Aubrey never thought that Jackson entering her bakery was to violate her, she liked and trusted that guy. Thank the shit Tate decided to head back over to her bakery one last time that day. He laid his head down slightly and looked at his still bruised knuckles that beat the crap out of that guy. Rubbing them with his fingers, he closed his eyes briefly to wipe that image away. After consuming a few of more beers, if he kept his eyelids closed any longer he would be seeing *her.* Aubrey.

He use to see only Callie, but her images were fading away as Aubrey's were coming in clear and colorful into his mind.

He was again lost in the thought of her pleasuring herself in her home. He must have been standing next to her bathroom from the porch. He had developed a precise visual of her thinking of him in her head and then calling out *his* name. Hearing her want him for just one time, he decided he could do better than that. He would never just do a one-time. He wanted a life time.

"Hey, Lange, drink up." Tate heard the banter of the cops pushing another to drink it down. Loosing count of his own consumption, he felt sorry for the guy, knowing he probably couldn't put another away. Wait, did he just hear the name "Lange"? His eyes opened wide, and he quickly looked around the table. A few guys were putting down another beer. One of them had to be Lange. Tate knew now he had to stay in this town. He knew tonight was not the night to blurt out, "Guys, who is Lange?" He would wait and find out soon enough.

Finding which one was Lange and what he knew about his wife's murder was key. Aubrey's colorful vision in his head faded. Callie's bloodied throat and matted hair became a vibrant visual. Tate swallowed the lump that was forming in his throat. Even a swig of the beer couldn't wash it down.

Tate rose from his chair and went to hit the bathroom. Almost to the bathroom door, he saw a girl making out with a guy. They both definitely needed a room. As he passed, he didn't stare at the girl who was indeed built perfect, but his eye caught the guy she was kissing. If eyes could talk. It was Emerson, and no way was this Aubrey with a short skirt and a halter top with higher than mountain heels. Any guy would be loving her hanging on them, but she was on Emerson. This shit was just so wrong. Emerson's and Tate's eyes remained connected until Tate opened the bathroom door and cut their staring match.

Tate took a hard piss and then went to the sink, hitting his face with water and not liking a feeling that was running through him. A battle emerging. He had distaste brewing in his mouth. This guy was taking full advantage of Aubrey, but he had no right to walk in and throw this news at her. He was going to watch this guy more carefully each and every day. The only time he couldn't was to head home, but he was now certain he would return soon enough.

Lingering in the bathroom, he waited, hoping Emerson would come in and engage him in a fight and give him cause to punch him for being a loser. He never came in. Preparing to glance his way again in the hallway, Tate flung the door open, and Emerson was no longer there. Tate walked a long way around the entire bar and still no sign of him. He knew it was him he saw kissing that girl. He was certain of that. Last Call was sounded, and it had been a fun evening hearing all these guys recap the week's events that cops talk about with other cops.

One cop brought up again, "That was messed up about Aubrey and Jackson coming on to her." Tate's eyebrows rose.

"We're not talking about it here or out of here. That Aubrey is a sweet girl and wants to put it behind her." Pete stopped the conversation there and then.

"Jackson will be punished, but Aubrey has to go back there every day, and I will keep checking on her so nothing like this ever comes close."

In Tate's head, he said to himself, *no, I will be watching over her. I care about her. I want her.* It wasn't the alcohol affecting him because suddenly, he had to adjust himself in his seat. He hoped the others didn't notice.

Tate couldn't sleep. His large body floundered and flipped like a wet seal, sliding all over the bed. It was comfortable before today, but tonight, he was focused deeply on two things. He was going to leave a day earlier than planned, and he needed to thoroughly prepare himself for his return. The sooner he left, the sooner he would return for her. She wasn't even his or anyplace near being his. But he felt so much for her already. He thought of filling in Reed, too, first on Aubrey and next on this Lange guy and then seeing Emerson first hand having a drug exchange.

His mind would not settle. Even though he walked in a slight staggering motion from the bar back to the inn, he made it back to his room. It was very late, and he thought he would fall into a deep sleep quickly. Nope, nothing would let him sleep. He was wide awake in thoughts. Tate supposed he would sleep forever when he died so being awake now wasn't all that bad. To the left of his bed, the brown bags stood—each one with the sweetness that came from Aubrey's hands. Even her hands were amazing, not only in the creation of pastries she made, but when he enfolded hers into his, he felt her tiny fingers holding on to his.

Aubrey dressed quickly as she didn't want to have sex with Emerson. She was already satisfied after taking matters into her own hands. She wanted to remember that exhilarating rush she felt travel through her body that she lacked for such a long period of time. Emerson made several trips to Damon's car and back with his clothes. She didn't offer to help him. She just sat on the stool at the counter in her kitchen drinking the coffee he had just brought her. When Emerson was all moved back in, she heard him holler outside a thanks and that he'd catch up later with Damon.

She didn't question why he didn't just take his own vehicle to collect his belongings, as it was odd that Damon came for him and then brought him back this way. Aubrey had already eaten some oatmeal and sliced fruit by herself. She gathered her purse and told Emerson she needed a lift to her bakery. She needed to arrive there at some point today and prepare for tomorrow's customers.

"Bree, let's go. I am going to drop you off and hit the gym, and later tonight, I will be meeting my brother for beers, so don't wait up for me. Glad we are back together, and I will wake you when I come in." He dropped her off and pulled her head toward his. "Bree we aren't separating again."

She looked at the seriousness cast in his eyes. "No, we aren't. I love you." She did in her heart, but it didn't sound right saying it aloud anymore.

Emerson never responded to her the same. He simply said, "I know you do."

EMERSON HAD EARLIER COMPLETED A few smaller scores with Damon before he returned to Aubrey's home. They had a few appointments scheduled this morning, and

Emerson wanted to make certain that she didn't catch onto any of it again or it would mess up his final plans for his end game.

AUBREY OPENED LATE TODAY AND had lots of catching up in her baking to complete. She knew she would be here well into the evening so it was good for Emerson to be out with his brother. So often he told her he and his brother were hanging out so she had no reason to question him. She thought, too, that Tessa would be home when she returned tonight as she'd told Aubrey she may be in tonight or tomorrow.

Tessa hadn't been upset when Emerson moved in with Aubrey. She and Aubrey talked about it quite a bit before he actually came. He stayed over a lot and thus turned into being there permanently. Aubrey smiled at how close they all had become. Emerson always told her that she had a great roommate, and that was a good thing for people living closely under one roof.

Aubrey took her time with cutting the Red Velvet Fudge pies. She sliced them into very generous pieces. Thinking of Tate and how he would enjoy one, she took a bakery box and sliced him one gigantic slice and also added the loaf of Red Velvet cake just for him. He hadn't come by today, and she wondered if he was out touring all the real estate opportunities the town had to offer.

She busied herself with icing a few racks of cupcakes and made them with extra special designs on the tops. Something was different in her today. Some might think it was her taking back Emerson and feeling loved and in love again, but it was more an anticipation of taking these treats to Tate. Aubrey decided to let all the icing set on her creations. It was well past one in the morning when she left her bakery.

Although hours ago she turned the sign to *closed,* she still was very careful of her surroundings when she left. The street was empty of anyone. The quiet was so peaceful, and she thought she could hear the waves crashing from the beach. Never before had she been overly alert with her surroundings, but since Jackson assaulted her, she wasn't taking any chances. She drove past DeLuca's Den on her way home, which was only four streets out of her way. She did see Emerson's truck parked right up front. She decided to park and head in to see him for a moment and give him a sweet kiss.

She had more sugar and flour on her since she dusted herself twice. It was just still embedded on parts of her clothes. The bar was packed. It was Wednesday night here once again. Aubrey saw a few familiar faces. Levi gave her a wave as she came in, and she walked over to them and gave him and Pete a kiss to the cheek and whispered in their ears, "I have Red Velvet Fudge Pie waiting for you tomorrow." Their eyes both lit up. "Guys, I have to go through all these people. I want to see if I can find Emerson."

Both men commented almost at the same time, "That guy is one lucky man."

Aubrey did a quick once-around, hoping to spot him. She was not successful in finding him. Maybe he left his truck, had too many, and went to his brothers or back home, back to her home now. Anyway, after feeling pushed a few too many times as she stood in one place glancing around, she decided to head home. As she circled the bar, she caught his eyes. He was here.

He observed her finding him here, and a smile lit his face. He was standing directly across from her, but lots of people were separating them. Aubrey didn't break their eye contact and held onto her obvious, direct stare. He kept his eyes focused only on her. No one was surrounding them. A drink went flying as Aubrey ran into the waitress and dumped the tray onto herself. Her eyes dropped in embarrassment, and now she was soaked with alcohol and sticky from the sugar from her shop. *I need to just leave here.*

His hand came and took hers, once again her tiny fingers covered by his large grasp. He pulled her toward the front door. Aubrey didn't hesitate to be led from the craziness of the bar and all those that were savoring their last drinks. She knew the bar wouldn't serve more drinks, but many would stay till dawn.

The air outside was misty from the sea air. She stood next to him, still holding his hand. "Thank you again for saving me." Aubrey tilted her head back toward Tate's eyes.

"SEEMS I ALWAYS RESCUE YOU, but you are the one saving me." He was thinking how he was falling for her and she was saving him from the heartache he carried for so long.

"Me saving you? What could that possibly mean?"

Tate quickly covered, "Oh, the guys wanted me to finish the last round with them, and I think I have had enough."

Their hands were still touching. "Aubrey, I wanted to ask you…"

He was unable to finish. "Bree, Bree!" he heard being called out as Emerson emerged from the side of the building.

Tate simply turned away and felt her fingers slip from his hold. Tate walked back into the foyer of the bar so Emerson would find her and not even know he was there moments before.

AUBREY TURNED TO GLANCE BACK at Tate. "What did you want to ask me?" Her question went unanswered. He already had gone inside.

"Bree, there you are. Someone told me they saw you inside and so I didn't see you and was out here checking the parking lot."

"I'm fine. I just railroaded a waitress with a big order and need to drive home and shower all this mess off me."

"Bree, I am going to go say goodbye to my brother and will be back home to you soon."

Aubrey returned to her car, and Emerson went back into the bar. He never kissed her goodbye, but then no one was present for him to show public affection. Aubrey wondered why Emerson was out in the back lot when clearly, if he came out the door, he would have seen her and Tate. It didn't add up. As she pulled her car from the bar parking lot, she thought she caught a glimpse of a girl standing off in the darkness from the direction Emerson had just come from.

Aubrey thought to herself, *Girl, you need to gather your senses and gain some self-control, because touching a hot man's hand set yourself a flame.* First she was feeling out of control, and next she was losing sight of things in front of her eyes. She was thinking she was seeing things that weren't actually there, and again, she was back to second guessing Emerson.

She focused on the road to arrive home quickly as she reeked of the alcohol that had saturated her clothing.

Chapter Eight

AUBREY HARDLY SLEPT LAST NIGHT. After returning home so late and smelling like a bar cocktail, she laid in the tub to soak off the stench. She waited up for Emerson, but he never showed up. Sleeping very lightly, she waited for him. She knew if he drank too much she would have received a call to come pick him up. The entire night her phone remained silent and the other side of her bed empty.

She was awoken hours later to the ringing of her cell phone. She noticed it was six-thirty in the morning as she was lying facing the wall that the clock hung from. She was certain this was Emerson calling. "Hello," she answered, her voice tired from her just waking.

The caller paused, and she heard some background conversation taking place. She waited to see who this was trying to reach her. "Hey, Aubrey, sorry I kept you holding. I was talking to the supervisor. Listen, I hate to be calling you so early, but my brother was supposed to be at the job site a half hour ago. We got some concrete to pour and wanted to jump on it early this morning," Hayden stated intensely.

"Well, he didn't come back here last night. I saw him at the bar when it closed. He told me he was going back to see you and then he'd be heading here." Aubrey was no longer tired in her response but wide awake, and there was questioning in her tone.

After what seemed to be a long pause and she didn't hear any job orders issued, Hayden returned to the phone and said, "Oh yeah, he did catch up with me. He's probably still crashed on my couch. I never thought to try there. Aubrey, I have to go. The guys are impatiently waiting for their work detail today." He hung up.

Aubrey knew that when someone was caught in a lie there was hesitation in their voice. Hayden had that when she questioned him about his brother. Maybe Emerson was sleeping it off at his place. She needed to be sure, so she paged down through her phone contacts and dialed Emerson. He immediately picked up.

"Hey Bree, before you start getting angry, I didn't come back because I had another round of drinks and went to sleep it off at my brother's. I didn't want to land on your bad side again."

"Well, Emerson, I just got off the phone with Hayden. He called me wondering where you are."

"Bree, I'm here on the site, and he is standing a few feet from me telling me to move my ass and start working. I have to go. I will talk to you later." He hung up.

Could he really have been there on the job site? She had no reason to doubt him. If he didn't want to be with her, he could have never tried to come back, let alone move in.

Aubrey shook her head. She was tired and probably not thinking clearly. As she pulled herself out of the bed to start her day, arms wrapped around her and pulled her back to the bed.

"I'm home. Sorry. Didn't want to scare you," Tessa said as she pulled Aubrey to a hug. "I missed you, Aubrey. What happened while I was away?"

"You didn't scare me. I never heard you come in. Hayden just woke me looking for Emerson, but besides that, girlfriend, you smell like you were drinking all night." Aubrey sat up in the bed her eyes widened as she reacted to what Tessa was wearing.

"Did you just come home from a late night walk of shame? I love your halter top and could your skirt be any shorter?"

Tessa laughed as she removed her clothes, throwing them across the room. She grabbed at Aubrey's pillows and laid herself back in the bed. "I need sleep, I had a long, fun night...morning, I will share details much later. Sleep is calling me. I hope you don't mind me crashing in your bed?" Tessa made herself comfortable. Aubrey lifted her matted blonde bangs that covered her eyes from her face so she could talk to her a few minutes more.

"Tessa, I have to tell you something that's important, and it should come from me before you hear it from the town talkers."

"Hmmm, what do you have to tell me?" Tessa was fighting to keep her eyes open.

"While you were visiting your friends, I had a visitor at

the bakery."

"Oh girl, my eyes are opening. Do tell."

"Well, it wasn't a pleasant visitor, although at first I thought it was."

"Aubrey, spill! Did you meet another man?"

"Oh no, nothing like that. Your cousin Jackson tried to attack me. He tried to…rape me." There. Aubrey said it, no taking it back. She waited.

Tessa lay there searching Aubrey's face for any sign that this was a joke. "For real, he came on to you like at the bakery?"

"No, he attacked me, tried to RAPE me at the bakery. Luckily for me, a guy passing by pulled Jackson from me and beat him up." Aubrey, for the first time since her original breakdown on that afternoon when it happened, lost it again. Her tears poured from her eyes.

"Tessa, I thought he was going to rape me. I fought him hard." Her voice was hesitating in between her words. "I… just…didn't…want…you…to…think…I…led…him…on."

"Aubrey, you would first off never lie. You are like the sunshine here in this town every day. Where is he? I will rip his member from him so he never has a chance to come close to any woman again!"

"Well, they're holding him in a cell until we go to court. I heard from Pete, and he and Levi have no doubt that after we go to court and he is punished that he will ever return to this town. I only hope he hasn't done this to someone previously or ever does it again."

"Come here." Tessa opened her arms to Aubrey and let

her cry hard against her shoulder and her smoke smelling hair. "You know, our family often said something was strange with Jackson, a little too friendly with all the women. Thinking back, I wonder if that's what the family meant. I know he seemed so kind and pleasant…but to try to force you to have sex!"

Aubrey pulled back from the hug that Tessa had her enveloped in and coughed as the tobacco reeked in her roommate's hair and overpowered her senses.

"I know, and I thought Emerson would flip, but he actually didn't, and when it happened, he and I were you know still broken up."

"So where do you and Emerson stand at this moment?"

"He moved his stuff back in yesterday. I guess he has my heart. Doesn't seem perfect at times, but it's better than not having him in my life at all."

"He loves you. I am sure. He just likes to have his macho independence with all his construction coworkers, too."

"So, Tessa, who were you with last night?" Aubrey questioned as she was still shocked to see the outfit she had come home barely wearing.

"Oh, just a guy I have been seeing for some time, but I'm not sure he will commit to me. We are just taking it day by day. You don't know him. He isn't from town." Aubrey hugged her quickly, pulled back, and thanked Tessa for consoling her and went to wipe her face. She needed to open the bakery this morning. She didn't want two days of lateness to become a habit.

✧   ✧   ✧

EMERSON ROLLED OFF THE BED at the Shifting Sands Hotel. He not only rolled off, he fell off. He had a hard time talking with Aubrey as he had to force himself to sound like he was awake and on the construction site, which was pure acting. He remembered checking in here last night. In between kissing her and having his hand up her skirt, he almost lost control in the lobby. The desk clerk knew who he was. Gave him the same room he always did when he checked in late in the night. The innkeeper walked down the hall past that room where Emerson was, and he could hear the sounds of sex happening. Emerson and the girl he brought here went at it for hours until the booze that controlled most of his actions got to the best of him and he crashed down. A few times, he did a line or two that he cut out on the table by the bed to keep him and her going longer. This morning, he was paying the price.

Emerson stood in front of the mirror. Shit, he looked like shit. He set his phone on the sink counter and read the messages as he sat his ass on the toilet for a long while. Double shit. His brother left him several. Luckily for him, he was able to lie his way right through her inquiry from her recent morning call. Emerson had to make an appearance on the site at some point later this morning to make certain he was there and that he would be heading to the florist in town for a fabulous over the top arrangement of roses for Aubrey to calm her doubts.

He dressed and went back to the bed to sit and put on his work boots. He could still smell her in this room. Last night, she took him to places he had never been to with

Aubrey. He knew he couldn't have her with him all the time, not until he pulled off many more deals. He needed her at first to pull off the bigger scores as her beauty captivated the clientele, and that developed into a long client list of repeat buyers.

She flaunted all the goods, dressed in her own sexy style as she delivered the packages. If any of them happened to be undercut or shorter in the contents, the purchasers never took notice. Usually, the clients invited her to stay with them and have a hit or do a line, and she gladly agreed. She worked her way into some of the big pockets in the cities, and he kept supplying them with their needs.

One day, he would be with her when they made a ton of money. Emerson had to settle and keep up a smokescreen that he wanted to be back with Aubrey. He needed Aubrey simply as a cover, remaining with her and keeping her happy. In turn, that kept the town smiling, too, as they loved seeing the two of them together, like a romance story.

He felt rushed yesterday to gather his stuff and return to her home and be back in a relationship with her, because he noticed that the guy at her bakery had that look in his eyes of "I want your girl." Guys saw that shit, and he caught it right away. She was his girl. It didn't matter he had someone else on the side. Aubrey was his.

Again he relived having her back in town with him last night, not Aubrey, but the one who truly had his heart and, more than that, his desire. They almost didn't make it to the bed in this room. Once he opened the door, he immediately pinned her to the wall with her arms above her with his one hand. His other hand tore off her halter that was only held by a tie that was loosely done. His mouth took over her breasts as she tried to squirm from his hold. Emerson smiled. She was perfect, full huge chest, nice ass, and great legs that ran so tall. He remembered seeing her one day long ago in a bathing suit top and shorts, sunning herself in the afternoon out on the balcony at Aubrey's place, and he came totally undone.

It was then that he entered the balcony, not even carefully but told her, "I want you right here." She did not hesitate. In fact, she said she had been thinking about him sexually for weeks. So they had sex there on the balcony that day and then quite often. The only one to see them was the ocean. Emerson laced his work boots. He was ready to go. As he exited, the hotel desk clerk asked him if he had a nice stay. "Always and I will see you next Wednesday, same room. Thank you." Emerson padded his hand with a fifty dollar bill.

WAITING FOR THE TRAIN DEPARTURE out of this town this morning was agony. Tate sat across from *Sweet Treats* hoping Aubrey would come in early, but she never did. His train was scheduled to leave before her bakery opened. He must have looked across the street one hundred times just to see if her car pulled in. Tate decided that he didn't owe her an explanation for why he was leaving town. She was clearly with Emerson, although he knew for certain that they had another moment when they were together outside the bar.

Even just taking her hand in his brought slight excitement to parts of his body. He definitely felt her. His thoughts each night were more and more consumed with how badly he wanted her. Hoping that one night she would be lying in the bed right up next to him. If all they did was lie together, he would settle for that just to be close to her. He was angry that Emerson appeared from the darkness outside the bar. Tate was ready to lead her by hand, to where they could embrace a private moment. A chance when he was going to try to kiss her lips. Looking again at his watch and to her bakery, he noted he still had another twenty minutes before his train pulled in. In a quick panic, he decided to leave her a note. That would work. He asked an awaiting passenger seated at the next bench for a pen and another random person for a sheet of paper. They didn't have paper, but provided him a business envelope. That would do. Back seated on the bench and using his knee to write, he began his message,

Aubrey, I thought I could catch you to tell you I was leaving your lovely town. I don't know what to write you, but I feel I have to write something. I was glad to have met you. Tate paused. It wasn't sounding right. Crossing that out on the envelope, he started on the other side.

Aubrey – you have brought a smile to my face, and I am leaving this town but hope to return very soon. Please be careful in your surroundings. When I return, your bakery will be my first stop. I wanted you to know... Shit, the train was coming early. Tate quickly wrote his name on the bottom and folded it in half. He ran across the street and tucked it in the bakery mailbox slot.

He just made the train and was seated by the window as she finally arrived to open her shop. Beautiful in her pink sundress with little peekaboo cuts outs, her hair was loosely pinned up. He could stare at her forever. He was glad to see her open the mailbox and take all her mail. He knew she would receive his written message. He sat back and rested his head on the seat comfortably. His thoughts were at ease knowing he would be coming back here really soon.

AUBREY JUGGLED HER PURSE AND some new cookie cutters and the mail as she tried to find her key to open the bakery. Once in, she still wasn't officially opened for another hour. She added the mail to her already growing pile on the table in the back room. She really needed to go through that. Maybe this morning, after stocking the cases up front, she would. Her first task, though, was to start brewing the coffee. She needed a large cup this morning.

Once she was with her caffeine fix, she moved quickly and had all her baked items positioned nicely for sale. Moving to the back room opening and sorting the mail was her next task. Pulling a trash can next to her stool she started to sift through the envelopes, separating the bills from the piles of advertisements and junk mail. She started off with a used business envelope that had something written on it, but it was all crossed off. That went into the trash immediately. She didn't need people sticking their trash in her mailbox. It was funny, but the moment she tossed it, her mind thought of Tate.

Aubrey turned the door sign to *open*, and within moments, her bakery was filled. She was busy putting the customers' orders together and shifting her eyes to the door each time the chimes sounded. Tate was who she was hoping would walk in or glance at her from outside through her bakery windows. He never did.

When her day ended, she checked her phone and saw that Emerson left her a text message that he was putting in extra hours and would be back home later. She definitely noticed that he was calling her home his once again. She still felt a flag of uncertainty raise with Emerson, and to clear her head, she thought a nice walk would help. She decided to stopover and visit Lacey at the Hamilton Inn bringing along some bakery items for her and hopeful to catch Tate to deliver his. For some reason, she missed his not being here today even for a minute. She felt the need to see him, even using Lacey as the excuse.

Walking in this town was lovely. Even in season with a flourish of bike riders peddling all over and the streets bustling with tourists, it was beautiful. Today, during the off season, just the sound of silence was wonderful. The inn wasn't far from her bakery for her to walk.

She passed several old Victorian homes that so many owners here maintained very well. There was so much detail in just the trim that ran across the entire front of the homes. Intricate workmanship was displayed in the delicate edges, various design, and swirl cut outs. A lot of upkeep and seasonal painting was required for these homes as the sea air constantly settled over the exteriors.

Aubrey reveled in how each one stood flawless, picture perfect. Perhaps that was why so many came here to vacation in the summer months. It was a popular, comfortable beach town where all the locals took pride in their homes, their rentals, and the beach for the tourists. She hoped her beach home would eventually receive all its necessary repairs and she could view it with the same admiration she was giving to each of these homes.

The Hamilton Inn had been here forever, at least as long back as Aubrey remembered. They, too, were often renovating the rooms and changing the exterior paint colors to keep it fresh and inviting. She felt uneasy as her footsteps brought her closer to the inn. Rarely did she perspire. She didn't even break a sweat when all her ovens were heated and loaded with her baking.

A sudden nervousness traveled through her. Her hand touched her forehead, lifting her bangs, and her skin felt clammy. She attributed that to her intentions of dropping in to see Tate uninvited. She knew it was innocent enough, but she felt different, and she couldn't explain it. If Emerson hadn't called her name in the darkness last night, she would have stood till the sun rose holding onto Tate's hand. In her mind she would have allowed him more than the touch of her hand. She would have liked him to hold her chin, pulling it upward to touch her lips.

With a skip in her step after the last thought of Tate in her mind, she entered the inn. There was no reason she should be tense. Usually Lacey was at the front desk, but a sign was posted: Be back in thirty minutes. Cleaning the rooms. Aubrey went on a quest to find her friend. She couldn't be too far.

On the second floor, she found Lacey finishing up one room and telling Aubrey she was on the last room. "Good, let me help you, that way you will finish quicker and we can have a minute to chat." Aubrey entered the room and immediately saw several of her brown bags with *Sweet Treats* logo on them standing upward on the bedside table. Her thought was that someone liked her bakery. When she went to pull the bed sheets off from that side of the bed, Aubrey saw her name written in ink and a heart surrounding it over and over on the Hamilton Inn notepad. She tore the page off and stuffed it into her pocket. Lacey was shaking out the new fresh sheet to let it drop over the bed, so she hadn't seen Aubrey take the note.

"So, Lacey, I came by not only to catch up, but I brought an order for a guy named Tate who is staying here."

"Well, you can leave it with me. I love your baking."

"I'd rather deliver it to him if I could."

"Well, that's going to be hard."

"Why?" Aubrey asked. How hard would it be for her to leave it for him? Surely they were in his room. She hoped that note in her pocket was his doing.

"Aubrey, he checked out this morning, paid his bill in full, and left me a nice tip. Said he appreciated my hospitality. He also told me Levi liked me."

"He left, just like that? Did he say he would be back?"

"Aubrey, you sound like you liked this guy. Correct me if I am wrong but aren't you with Emerson, the hottest guy this cape has to offer?"

"Yes, I am with Emerson, but I met this guy Tate and promised him some Red Velvet Fudge Pie."

"Well, girlfriend, maybe he will come back one day and try it, but he was more than ready to leave our sleepy town. Doesn't suit him."

Aubrey cut her visit shorter than she planned with Lacey. She wasn't up to small talk, because her head was full of questions. *He's gone. Stop thinking of him, Aubrey. He left this town. Not even a last minute stop for something in the bakery.* Better he left now anyway as she was just beginning to have real feelings for him, and it already hurt. Why would he leave and not say goodbye? There was a connection between her and him. She felt it, and she knew he did, too. Guess her instincts were correct this time. He was just passing through. She left the sweet items all for Lacey and her staff to enjoy. She hugged her goodbye, and they both promised to spend a free night together soon.

"Tessa is back from her visit to her friends so all three of us should plan a girl's night." Aubrey smiled at her suggestion, hopeful it would eventually happen. She watched Lacey wave and return to the inn.

Aubrey walked back to her car parked at her bakery. Something inside her made her tear up. She knew it wasn't her visit with Lacey. She realized she missed Tate already. Tate made her feel safe, alive, and sexy just by staring at her. His eyes fixed on hers made her melt like her chocolate glaze. She knew she would never find that feeling with Emerson, but her life was here. Tate was long gone. Driving the short distance to her home, she again thought of her beach afternoon with Tate. It was easy, comfortable, and she wished then that he would have tried to kiss her.

She wiped her tears on her hoodie sleeve and put on her best 'everything is fine' smile as she entered her house knowing Emerson was already there. Her eyes immediately went to the kitchen, pulled in as there were roses standing tall on the kitchen counter. They were absolutely stunning.

She didn't need to count them, but there were at least three dozen and solid deep red. The smell hit her as soon as she turned her key to open the door. Walking over and placing her nose to the soft petals, she drew in the lovely fragrant scent. Emerson came in from the porch with his swimsuit on. Aubrey took in his insanely toned body and noted he was gorgeous. She could see why the town girls remarked about him and stared at him. "Bree, I was going to take a swim. The ocean water is still warm. Come with me."

"I love the flowers. Thank you, but what did you do wrong? It's not my birthday, nor Valentine's Day or any other special day." She smiled, putting him on the spot.

"Well, it's my thanking you for taking me back day." He pulled her into his chest. She held her breath for one moment. This was not Tate's chest she would be up against but Emerson's, and that was never going to change. "Hey, Bree, go put your suit on. We can hit the beach for this beautiful end of the week day. And if no one is on the beach but us, my day will be even better!"

Emerson released his arms from her and patted her ass to tell her to start moving. Aubrey went and changed into her bikini. No one would ever know how rocking her body was as she mostly dressed with loose clothes or a flowing sundress and an apron on at the bakery. Comfortable in her royal blue bikini, she took down her hair that was pinned up in a simple bun. She began walking toward the balcony. She saw Emerson swimming in the ocean. Down on the sand, she noticed he already spread out a huge blanket. His phone sounded, and although she never answered it, she took a look at the message that was on his screen.

Last night was great! Another reason why I am your partner.
TLU

There was that name, actually initials. Aubrey was definitely going to ask him this time. Playfully, she and Emerson enjoyed their swim.

"Hey, you had a message when I was heading out here. Something about last night being great and this person is your partner? From a TLU?"

Emerson dove under the water to come up with a reply and buy himself a little time. Popping up, he swung his head and said, "Oh are you checking up on me?"

Aubrey was stunned at his reaction. "No, not at all. Should I be?"

"Bree, relax. I met a guy for our construction team, and he is a real worker so last night I introduced him around. He fit right in, so yes, he will be my new partner. You can meet him if you want at the job site."

"You know I can never make it there because I am glued to the bakery most days at the time you are at work."

"Bree, come here. Would I want to tear off your bikini bottoms here in the ocean and have my way with you if I was with anyone else?"

Aubrey felt embarrassed, first for thinking he was doing something wrong and then at his suggestion. He did swim over to her, and her bikini bottoms were removed. They were both out past where the waves break in the ocean standing on a sand bar.

Emerson brought her close to him, concealed in the sea water, and started to finger her. He wanted her very excited so that he could take her from the ocean to the blanket he'd placed on the beach and have her his way. A little rough was Emerson's style. This wasn't a couple making love. It was just sex.

Aubrey was certain her feelings for Emerson had just ended almost as quickly as he came. Their tryst on the beach was hurried. Immediately after, Emerson was pleased with himself. He rolled away from her and then pushed himself up.

"I'm hungry now. Let's see what you can whip up for us to eat. I have to make a few calls, and then I'll see what you have ready." He walked toward the balcony and didn't turn back.

There was no after-sex kissing or cuddling or restarting the heat all over again. She had no appetite, and food was furthest thing from her thoughts. Aubrey sat there alone. She wasn't feeling sorry for herself, but recognizing the closure with Emerson. Her thoughts during the sex were empty and emotionless. She had looked past him to the waves coming in and out, not even feeling a connection to Emerson as he pumped into her steadily.

She didn't regret what just happened with Emerson. The act of sex, it made her realize all she wished was to be with Tate, and not even sexually. She was imagining him being there on the beach, just holding her in his arms. Aubrey carved her emotion into the wet sand. She didn't want that feeling to ever wash away. Written deeply with her fingers was the word LOVE. The waves broke at the surf and thinly crept up so close to her. Then as if she mentally halted the water, the ocean receded.

Chapter Nine

P UTTING THE PIECES TOGETHER IN his mind usually
connected better after a few beers. After the train ride
back to Maryland, Tate entered his apartment, showered,
and welcomed his change of clothes. He had been limited in
his wardrobe the past week. He had to wear the gym tee
shirt back because Aubrey still had the shirt she sat upon in
the sand. He knew he would reclaim it at a later date. Not
that the shirt was that important to him, but seeing her once
again was.

During his train ride he reached out to Reed to see if he
could meet him. He wanted to recap some things with his
friend. Mostly talk with him about seeing what more he
could find on this Emerson dude, and he would probably
have to spill about Aubrey because there was no way his
smile was leaving his face every time he thought of her.

Reed was all for meeting him at the bar after his shift
ended. Reed was more than just a friend. He was truly there
for him like a brother that Tate never had. The night his wife
was murdered, Reed had reached his arm to pull him from
entering the bedroom, the crime scene. Reed's strength was

no match for Tate's, but Tate knew if his friend was trying to keep him out of that area that it had to be really bad. After she was murdered, he had told Reed that he was putting his safety at risk because he could no longer focus on their case load. His emphasis was on his solo mission to find his wife's killer.

Reed was the opposite of Tate. He was the stand back, take in, and see type of guy, and Tate was definitely a walk in and command the room with his strength man. Tate was, though, just a sweetheart, and the person who'd seen the most of that was Callie. Every moment with her was tender. They never fought or argued. It was a relationship that worked perfectly.

Sitting on his chair in his apartment, it felt good to be back here for the moment. Having no real change of his own clothes for the past week was rough. After putting his boots on, he pulled out a large leather travel bag and began to stuff it with more clothes and necessities. He was packing, preparing to head back out of Hagerstown as quickly as he arrived. He had about an hour to kill before catching up with Reed, so he closed his eyes and let his mind go, but before his eyes shut, he focused on the framed photo of him and Callie that was next to his bedside.

He loved her. He'd thought he could never feel again. When she was taken so quickly from his life, his heart was ripped apart, too. He was left completely empty and hollow and very lost. Tate found himself just going through each day with minimal emotions. In conversations with others, he could walk away after the conversation stopped and not remember hearing what others were saying. What he did hear in his head every day were the sympathetic messages from so many after Callie died. His blood pulsed in his temple with each new outreach as someone told him they were sorry for his loss. He almost lost it each time. He knew she was dead. He'd buried her. Worst of all, he hadn't been able to help save her.

He'd broken that day before her coffin like a man never wants to break, especially in front of another man. Reed stayed by the gravesite with him, but gave him his personal space. Tate fell to his knees at the freshly turned dirt pile and wept. He grabbed fists of the dirt and vowed to find who did this to her. He wiped his face with his dirt covered hands, marking his face with a pattern resembling that of a warrior. Reed remained silent from the time Tate rose from the ground till they were back at Tate's home.

"Reed, no way can I stay here ever again. This is no longer my home. My home was taken from me and is in the ground. I'm going to sell it. I don't want to deal with it." They sat parked in the driveway of the home that Tate and Callie were so proud to buy. The Tudor style, single family home fit their wishes. Tate loved the expanded backyard complete with an outdoor kitchen that they used as often as they could to entertain their friends, family members, and Tate's extended police family. As he observed his home from the outside, it appeared to anyone passing by that the lovely manicured home surely contained a perfect couple beyond the front doors, but that was removed. Inside those doors all that remained was pure horror.

Reed, without direction, opened the handle of the car and jumped out. He entered Tate's home that still had yellow tape in certain areas. It took several trips, but he loaded bags of clothes and belongings he gathered from the house, into his car. The seats were packed with Tate's items that were once inside a house filled with love, but now just plastic bags surrounding his grief stricken friend. Tate never wavered from the front seat. His face held a blank stare aimed at the front of his home. After almost an hour, Reed thought he collected most things Tate could function with. His last grab was that of the framed photograph of Tate and Callie.

Tate walked to the table and ran his finger to the side of Callie's face. Beautiful. She was so beautiful. Her long dark hair always tangled in his fingers loosely. He would pull her toward him then let the strands of her hair fall once he had her next to him. Blood filled her hairline, seeping across her entire head, matting down her lovely, soft hair. It flowed and expanded around her face, changing from a delicate healthy skin coloring to a harsh, lifeless white pale tone. Her eyes sealed shut. He only hoped she hadn't seen the knife that took her coming at her. He hoped she didn't suffer in pain. He was told that she bleed out, died within a minute or two, from the cut to her throat. Her lovely neckline that once perfectly displayed the pendant her mother wore.

She wore nothing elaborate or fancy the day they married. What she wore was love and simplicity and a smile that she only gave to Tate. Tate folded the frame gently down onto the table top. He wanted to throw something painfully at the wall in the anger he still felt, even now, so long after, but this was a beautiful memory, the only one he could hang on to. He lost sight of the beauty, and in another moment, he forced himself to shut out the pain. Thinking back to when he left his home that day of the funeral with Reed, he hadn't turned back. He found an apartment soon enough after staying at Reed's place for a number of days. His home sold quickly. He was initially upset when he unpacked his belongings and found this photograph rolled up in his clothes. It was too hard for him to view. In time, it became a pleasant place for his eyes to land. Somehow Reed knew he would want it, and although he never thanked him, he was sure his friend just knew.

With some time still to kill, Tate next cleaned out his refrigerator. Not much food was even in there, mostly take out containers from the previous week. He did know how to cook a good meal, but since his marriage was cut short, he put away making dinner for two and just picked up something for himself on the go. He cleaned up a bit in the apartment and wrote a note to the landlord and stuffed a wad of cash in the envelope before sealing it. He knew he had this month's rent coming due, but he wanted to assure them that even though they didn't see him come and go that they would have next months.

He didn't have much of himself in this apartment. Since the day he moved in, he never made it a home. Nothing decorative hung on the walls. The blinds were all that kept the light out. He never bothered with curtains. Since Callie's death, he hooked up with a few one night stands that offered no attachment, just sex. Nothing emotional developed. No feelings were exchanged. He thought not feeling would lesson his pain he carried, but that didn't work.

His true agony was knowing he would never attach himself to real feelings with any of them or anyone in his lifetime ever again. He never brought anyone back here. The few times that happened, he simply went to their places and always left before they would awaken. It wasn't often, but just enough to keep him believing he was a man. He knew that the loss he suffered would bring demons to him in the night and that he would never feel again, not one beat of what his heart did when Callie was here.

Oddly as it seemed, his heart did beat once more, and he felt it and was surprised by it acting the way it was. Meeting Aubrey was by chance. He was just trying to buy a cup of coffee. It was not the sweet smell of the pastries that made his heart perk up and not the coffee that day. After a simple meeting, his heart came to life.

Never had Tate been nervous with a drug dealer situation and a gun pointed in his direction or when he was trying to impress Callie after initially meeting her. At *Sweet Treats,* he had to admit to himself he almost knocked over his coffee when they touched. His big hand almost dumped the cup right there. Her dainty fingers that were so creative in the treats she made for so many—contacted his skin for a flash, but he had long thought about it. He would normally never go into a bakery. Too often, donuts would fill his desk, and he and his partners would devour each one. Long ago, Tate decided to pass on them. His job was intense enough finding the drug dealers that he didn't need to be further hyped on sugar. Once in a while, he would reach for one, but never seemed to finish it.

Almost time to catch up with Reed, Tate loaded his truck with as much as he could. No telling how long he was staying in the town of Cape May, but he was absolutely heading there again. This time he would have wheels and a change of clothes. He had enough of his clothing for weeks to come considering how full his truck was.

Tate pulled his truck into the side lot of *Dempsey's*. It was a local hang for many in this town, but close for Reed to drive to after his work day ended. He sat only a moment, lost in thoughts of Aubrey patting the sand off his chest. He had been jumping inside, but kept his feet solidly planted on the beach and deep into the sand. He was no way letting his cool down and having her see the effect she had.

A smile came to his face, a big one, and he hoped anyone waking past his truck wouldn't think he was in there pleasuring himself. He jumped high from the seat as a heavy fist hit the side glass of his truck. Damn, it was Reed.

"Hey, guy, you were looking lost in space there." Reed opened his door, and when Tate stepped out, he took him in a hug. "Was worried about you, but then again, I know you are fully able to take care of yourself."

"Hey, thanks for meeting me here. I know it was last minute."

"So what's up with your truck being packed? Are you cleaning house or moving houses?"

"Actually, let's put down some beers. There is a lot I want to cover with you."

Tate and Reed ran a bar tab after they ordered their first round of drinks and food. They knew their conversation would be a lengthy one, and they were sure to sit for a long time. Tate told Reed of the leads he had before. "But there is something in this town of Cape May. This particular lead seems to maybe have been something substantial, although they didn't meet me. I do, though, have a strong feeling in my gut that something *is* there."

"Tate, we have followed every lead thus far, and I will continue to, but we haven't had a break yet. So what news do you have now?"

Tate caught Reed up on his phone conversation with "Lange". He also caught him up on Emerson and seeing a drug deal.

"I can run his name and see what comes up." Reed would always go the extra mile for his man Tate, because that was what true friends, partners did.

"Well, I miss being a cop, I can tell you that, but until I screw my head back on straight, I can't come back."

"Tate, I know that, and the guys do, too. We miss you commanding the show at each stake out." Reed succeeded in letting Tate know he was cared about.

A grin appeared on Tate's face.

"So I know it is not my town, but do you want me to come hang with you in that beach town for a week and see what we dig up?"

"Not just yet." Tate paused. His lips curved into a shit eating grin.

"Oh, there's something you're not telling me here, my

friend. Is there someone in this town you have an eye on?"

"Guess I can't hide shit from you. It's that detective in you every time. I met a girl while I was there, just met her, but I keep thinking of her."

"And you don't want me to come back there with you because she will like me and not you?"

Tate blew out his beer, laughing, "Yeah, something like that. You are the calm one. Me, I walk and talk like Rambo until they actually come to know me."

"Partner—even though you are off on your own case, you are still my partner–seriously, any girl would be happy to know the real you."

"Sounds great, but the Emerson guy I have you checking into, well, he is currently that guy for her. In fact, he just moved back into her place."

"Ouch, that hurts."

"Yep." Tate chugged the rest of his beer. "Can I have another?" He signaled to the bartender.

They polished off some red hot wings and stuffed potato skins and several beers. "I know you're all packed, but I hope you're not heading out of town tonight," Reed stated. "Guess it's going to be like old times…You crashing on my couch."

"Yeah, I am!" Tate was smart enough that he knew when to park his ass and rest from his drinking too much. Tonight was one of those times.

They settled their bar bill. Reed had only matched Tate on every other beer so he easily helped his friend into the front seat of his car and off they went to Reed's for the night.

✧ ✧ ✧

HIS HEAD WAS POUNDING. BLOOD pulsing through his veins made it throb. I want to do this. I have to do this. If I cut the biggest line of this shit and force it in my nose till I can't feel again, it will take the pain away. *Taking the key he held tightly in his hand, he sliced the bag open, and the white powder poured onto the desk. Tate cut it into several large lines. His hand was shaking, and he couldn't steady it. Still covered with dried blood, each line became more jagged.*

He rolled up the one hundred dollar bill he took from the money that was also confiscated. Drug money, it was. All piled in high stacks on the table. They had just brought in some local drug runners and seized all of this from their home.

His nose touched the paper bill as he snorted the powder to his senses. He wanted to be senseless and leave this world. Nothing was worth living for, absolutely nothing, and that was his last thought until he shook his head back letting the powder enter his system. He positioned the money over top to finish the last of the line that remained, and thought he has nothing to live for...except seeking revenge.

After the main portion of the first line hit his nostrils, he shook his head because the amount he snorted. Even after looking at the available firearms in the room he broke down realizing, I can't take my life, as much as I want to be with you, Callie. I would be letting you down not to find who killed you. *He promised in his head that he would be with her again. He stumbled back from the hit he took off the drugs.* I promise you, you have my vow. We took vows…

Reed awoke to Tate calling out in his sleep. As he approached him after coming from his bedroom, he could see he was sleeping in conflict on the sofa. Tossing and mumbling, wiping his nose, shaking his head, yelling about vows. Reed knew the demons of Callies' death had come calling.

"Hey, Tate, hey…wake up." Reed shook him hard on his shoulder until he awoke and flung a fist that nearly clipped Reed's nose. He knew that his friend was still so unsettled.

"Hey, sorry I must have been dreaming."

"No, Tate, it was not dream. You were flopping all over my sofa. Why not try think about this other girl you met from the beach town?" That seemed to work almost instantly, and he could see the calm restoring to Tate's face and mannerisms.

"Yeah, I will try to do that. Sorry I woke you." Reed went to the kitchen to fill a glass with ice and bring Tate some water. When he returned, Tate was fast asleep with a grin and a calm chest, breathing slowly in and out. This girl was still having a lasting impression on him from miles away. Reed watched as Tate's chest rose and fell. He decided to go in and take a chance on falling back to sleep himself. He thought about this girl Tate mentioned, and he knew something was happening in his friends' heart. The look in Tate's eyes told him she was certainly something mighty special. The rest of the late hours were calm. Reed fell back to sleep, and Tate entered a dream state that was peaceful, and he knew this had to be the workings of his mind allowing Aubrey to take up some space.

✧　✧　✧

WITH A HANGOVER FROM TOO many beers, Tate went to Reed's refrigerator and grabbed another. He flipped the top. He learned a long time ago to bite what has bit you. Reed had already put the coffee on. After polishing off a beer, he sat on the bar seat at Reed's counter. Reed's place was a bachelor pad, but at least he had it comfortable. There were a few pictures on the walls that he let a previous girl hang. When it didn't work, she left them, and she did have very good taste. Reed had dated a few girls, but nothing steady. He poured himself into his job, something that Tate knew all about. Tate used to thrive on the next deal they were following. Now he thrived on the next tip that came his way.

"So when do I meet Miss Beach Beauty?"

Tate perked up. "I hope one day. She is just different. She is very pretty but saying what you did makes it sound like she is a beauty queen. To me, she is something special, something deeper than just her looks. Don't get me wrong, she is beautiful. I hope you meet her...soon."

Tate grabbed some breakfast with Reed. He did feel better after he ate several slices of toast and had coffee.

"I'm hitting the road, heading back to that town to see what is going on. See if I can find the person that knew about Callie. And to see Aubrey again." He was feeling life again.

"I will run all the information I can on that guy Emerson. Also, I want to see what I can dig up on that other character you mentioned, Jackson. He sounds too perfect in that community from what you're saying to turn so quickly to the other side. Seems odd if you ask me."

Tate fist bumped Reed and grabbed another coffee for the road. It wasn't too far of a ride from here in Hagerstown to Cape May, and with all the thoughts running through his head, he knew it would go even quicker.

IT HAD ONLY BEEN A few days he wasn't here, but it seemed like he never left. He drove past her bakery on his way to talk with Lacey. He slowed, but all he could see was a lot of patrons. He knew once he unpacked his belongings and settled in that he would reach out to her. Pulling up to the inn with wheels felt a lot better than covering this town on foot. His heavy boots hit the porch steps, and Tate knew if Lacey was at the front deck she would hear the loud footsteps approaching.

"Well, welcome back. You liked us so much you returned!" She was always pleasant in her greetings.

"Actually, I need a place for longer and want to see a few rentals as soon as I can. I thought you could help me with that." He smiled at her. There was something rough about Tate, but when his smile came out, he melted everything in his path.

"Absolutely. Let me give a call to a local realtor that I know, and she'll surely have something that will fit your needs." With a quick phone call and a meeting set up with the realtor in thirty minutes, he hoped to be in a pre-furnished place on the beach soon.

After viewing a few places, Tate filled out the necessary paperwork for a one month stay with the option to continue since it was vacant and off-season. He had to head back to the inn though for the night, and tomorrow, after everything cleared on the real estate office side of things, he could be in that beach house. It was a simple home that had a great view of the beach, but better yet, it was located about ten homes down from Aubrey's. Ten homes sounded close, but actually, they were spaced out pretty well so it wasn't like he could open a window and see her place. It was completely furnished, and he knew once he did a quick walk through that he could see himself in this home. Some of the ones the realtor showed him were over the top. He wanted simple, furnished, on the beach, and definitely this end of town.

After he parked, he walked back in to the inn. Right before he entered the front door, he saw Aubrey driving past. This was a clear route to her home. He wanted to go back down the steps and give a wave. But he figured he had enough of a day so he would rest and go see her soon. Tate stood on the porch of the inn as his eyes watched Aubrey's car till it was out of his sight. Once he was inside the inn, Lacey flashed him a welcoming smile as she straightened out the tourist brochures on the counter.

"So I have to ask you, how do you know that Levi likes me?" Lacey questioned immediately before he headed toward his room.

"He told me so," Tate assured her with a quick wink.

"Oh, I have liked him for a while, too, but I'm not sure how to tell him." Lacey bit her lower lip, obviously wondering if Tate could offer her a suggestion.

"I will tell him. I'm sure I will see him again. I plan to

catch up with him and his friends again as I had a good time with them last week." Lacey was smiling back at him as he proceeded to his room.

When Tate initially entered the room he was staying in, there was a moment of feeling that Aubrey was near. Maybe it was just because he had seen her drive by. He lay back on the bed in this all too familiar setting, he inhaled deeply through his nose and believed he smelled her sweet vanilla scent. He was excited for tomorrow to come, for the chance of seeing Aubrey and to haul all his stuff into his new place.

Chapter Ten

I T TOOK TATE LONGER THAN he planned to set up the rental house. Once he was comfortably moved in, he was on the phone with Reed, following up on things they'd discussed. Interestingly enough, Emerson had a shady past that someone paid to cover up along the way. Many small priors with drugs, always photographed in the back of photos of some of the larger hits but never caught in the acts. Tate knew that he would reach back to Aubrey, but he saw her just the other day kissing Emerson goodbye as he dropped her at her bakery. Tate had been about to pull in for some coffee and saw her, but it was the wrong time. Seeing them together left a sickness in his stomach. He put it off for yet another day and hopefully another stolen moment with her.

The days blended together. Finally situated with cop business, having received what he needed from Reed, he moved forward to try to gain some additional town information and deliver that back to Reed. Perhaps just conversing with locals would shed light on some of them. He decided to head to the bar for the weekly Wednesday guys' night out.

With wheels, he drove the short distance from his rental to the bar. Once inside, it was packed to the walls again. He spotted a few familiar faces from his first time there, and he nodded accordingly. A powerful pat on his back came, and when he turned, Emerson stood at the bar. Tate eyed him up, questioning why he would tap him. Just as he was about to ask, he saw her. Aubrey came from the ladies room. His eyes fixed on her. She was walking a bit carefully, holding onto the stools along the bar. It wasn't so she wouldn't have someone push her aside. He knew she had too much to drink.

When she came around the corner, Pete pulled at Tate. "Hey, I tapped you, and you had to have felt that. Come join us." Good thing Pete had hit him or fists were going to be thrown. He watched Aubrey sit herself up on the stool. Her one sandal fell off and hit the floor. She didn't even notice. It really wasn't his watch to take care of her with her boyfriend here. So he moved to the other side with Pete. Several guys said hello again, and Levi was glad to see him. He thought that perhaps tonight he would listen to see if he heard anyone called Lange. He was still here in the town on the hopes to find someone or a tip to Callie's murder. That was still not settled in his mind.

Emerson lined up another drink in front of Aubrey. From where Tate sat, he could see her. Emerson kissed her on the cheek, and then Tate watched as he left her there and went outside of the bar with a few guys. Two things went through his mind. First, the cop side wanted to see what was going on outside. Second, the man who cared for this girl wanted to make sure no one hassled her at the bar. He walked around the bar to order himself another beer. He moved so she could see him approaching. Her eyes opened wide.

"Hey, I know you. You just roll into town and then out," she accused, pointing her finger at him as he came close to her and pressed himself into the small opening near the bar and infringing on her personal space so he could order a drink.

"Aubrey, are you okay?" He was concerned.

"Why do you care? Like I said, you just roll in and out, kind of like the ocean." She giggled. Clearly, she was drunk as he never saw her like this. Her head dropped down. Tate grabbed her chin and lifted her head slightly. Her eyes were closed.

"Aubrey, let me take you outside for some fresh air." He took her into his arms.

"Tate, I don't feel so good." He knew any moment she could vomit. Quickly, he led her out the side door and helped her sit down on the corner of the porch. The air was calm and had a slight coolness to it. Aubrey seemed to feel slightly better.

"Tate, I am sorry. You always seem to be saving me." Tate sat beside her and held onto her. He knew if she felt that wave of sickness again he would be there to hold her head.

"Tate, I think I am going to…" Tate leaned her from him to vomit, but she turned and kissed him. The moment her lips touched his, he knew it was a drunk messy kiss, but her lips were so soft, and she knew it was him she kissed.

She moaned, "Mmmmm, Tate."

Tate wrapped his arms around her. Her petite body was shielded as they kissed. The music from the bar was gone. The fact that Emerson was somewhere outside exited his thoughts. His lips were fervently on hers. Every inch of his body longed for her, as his mouth passionately tasted the sweetness from her lips. Eagerly his tongue danced with hers, reacting to her hands under his shirt, caressing his chest and heart held within. Tate's kisses held her breathless.

She almost begged for air, but didn't want him to stop. Aubrey pulled from him to catch her breath. Kissing him was beyond amazing. She tucked her head into his chest, her fingers sliding over his, not wanting to leave him, and realizing she enjoyed every second she was with him.

"Tate, I've missed you sooooooo." There was a slurred drunk statement from her. He wasn't sure if she would remember any of this in the morning. He would never take advantage of her, but he wanted to take her mouth to his once more.

EMERSON ENTERED THE BAR, AND the bartender told him he saw Aubrey not looking well and someone took her home. The bartender pointed to the table of the cops, so Emerson was cool with that. Emerson figured she threw up and was crashed on her bed face down till tomorrow morning. From previous experience he knew she couldn't handle drinking a lot so he made certain they drank more and never ate dinner that he promised her. His mind was focused on that text from TLU earlier and it was one he could not resist. He decided to call it a night and he wouldn't be heading to the beach house to check in on Aubrey. Emerson twitched in his pants uncomfortably and knew he needed to make his way to the Shifting Sands Hotel as soon as possible. There, he would surely have her make him come undone the rest of this night.

TIME PASSED, AND TATE AND Aubrey remained cuddled out back. The lights darkened, telling them the bar had closed or was closing. Tate reached to the wooden railing post to lift himself up from where he sat. He felt her hand as she tugged at his shirt, pulling him back down.

"No, Tate, just hold me. I promise I won't throw up on you. It's so good to be right heeeerrrreeee." She dropped her lips to his chest. Through his shirt fabric, he felt her sweet kiss. Each drunk breath she released, he felt the warmth through his tee shirt. He wanted to lift it up and feel her lips on his skin. Tate found himself so uncomfortable with a hard-on that was restricted inside his jeans. He knew he had to sit a bit longer until that calmed. Even with his personal discomfort, he was content as they remained cuddled together for quite some time.

Her breaths quieted, and Aubrey didn't move when Tate lifted her hair to see her face. He tucked it behind her ears and touched them each softly. Still, she didn't stir. She was dead asleep. Tate had heard many cars start and move on out. They had been on the back porch for a long while.

Lifting her up into his arms, he heard the sweetest voice. "Tate, don't let me go…" It made his heart pound. He carried her to his truck and tucked her in delicately. He made a pillow with his jacket that was lying on the seat for her to rest her head on. He was sure when she awoke tomorrow— well, actually later today as it was earlier in the morning— that her head would be pounding. He drove her to her home. When he arrived, there was no sign of Emerson. *How odd. The guy is her boyfriend and doesn't even come to find her or seem to care.*

Tate parked and opened the passenger side of his truck. He hadn't noticed while driving that Aubrey had scooted her body sideways and hiked up the one side of her dress, revealing her lacy thong. Tate started to want her all over again after he tapped down those earlier thoughts to himself to gain control of his own body parts. He touched her dress, lowering it to cover her ass and thigh.

He could have stood there and smiled and stared all night long. He successfully made his way onto her front porch even as she continued squirming in his hold. He let her down and held her to make certain she didn't fall on her face. She pointed her finger at her door.

"Yes, Aubrey, this is your home. I got you home safely." She continued to point. "What are you trying to tell me?"

Lightly, she spoke. "The key is in the flower pot." He steadied her as he reached into the pot and grabbed her door key. *Real obvious spot to hide it,* he thought. He opened the door and let her slowly lead the way; it was either to the toilet to throw up or her bed to pass out. Aubrey led him into her bedroom. Falling into her bed, her sandals slipped to the floor below. She curled up on the one side on top of the bed, never turning it down. Tate wanted her comfortable. He went to pick up a blanket that he saw in the living room on the sofa.

Her place was decorated lovely. Simple but pretty, he would say. Not too girly, just perfect. White washed beach furnishings and a vase with seashells filled to the top. She probably collected them. Several large canvas beach paintings hung on the long main wall. He wondered if she painted them. They were of the ocean, the light house at the end of the beach area, and umbrellas, colorful beach umbrellas.

Tate took hold of the blanket. Worry filled his mind, he knew that at any moment Emerson could walk in. He decided if that confrontation happened that he would go at him, he would lay into him, he didn't care anymore about holding back. Tonight he received confirmation that she liked him in her drunk talking. Most people said their true feelings when they were under the influence and relaxed. Lightly placing the blanket over top of her, he made sure she rested on her side, in case she did vomit. He went to her kitchen to grab some water and find aspirin for her soon-anticipated killer headache. Her kitchen was stunning. Of course, she was a baker. She had double ovens, an industrial refrigerator, and spacious marble counters.

A huge professional knife set, complete with a cleaver, was displayed on her countertop. Each knife was stuck in to the wide, wooden block base. Even though Tate saw that out of the corner of his eye, his body still shook. Every time a knife came in his vision it was bloodied. He paused, closed his eyes, and steadied himself. Now was not the time for the demons to come playing in his head. Shaking his thoughts, he turned back to the set of cabinets with glass front doors, and it was easy to locate a drinking glass for her. He also grabbed a Gatorade that was in the refrigerator. Good to replenish her, for sure. He raided her medicine cabinet, probably a violation for a guy to check that out before he even knew her. He didn't find any aspirin.

He set all the items on the table next to her bedside. He then opened the drawer to her bedside table and, success, he found a bottle of aspirin, but he paused as he stared at the note paper with her name on it that he drew hearts around her while thinking of her at the inn one late night. She had this paper. He wondered how she came across finding it. He was glad to know that she knew that he liked her, and that was all that really mattered. He left the note in its original place hidden in the drawer. After he tossed a few pills to his hand, he capped the aspirin and placed it back in place, covering his heart drawn note, keeping it in her safe place.

He stood at by her bedside, watching Aubrey peacefully sleeping, and he wondered where her dreams were taking her. He dimmed the light to the bedroom and was just a foot out the door when he heard her sweet voice, not slurred, murmur, "Don't leave. Please, Tate, come lie with me and just hold me."

There was no way he'd turn down her sweet request. He took off his boots, set them on the other side of the bed, climbed in behind her, and let her fall back to sleep. He didn't shut his eyes once. He wanted to be alert in case Emerson returned, and he also didn't want to have a nightmare about Callie while lying with Aubrey.

THE FIRST HINT OF DAYLIGHT came through her balcony doors off her bedroom. He barely noticed any signs that Emerson lived here as his eyes panned around the entire bedroom. The room was a soft peach color with grey washed furnishings. She mixed the beach theme with a modern flare. It reminded him of her delicate pastries, a typical donut or bun with a beautiful modern design.

Tate didn't want to move, but he also couldn't stay. He was tired and needed to sleep and didn't want to fall asleep in her bed. Maybe someday, but definitely not today. He slid his arms from her and watched her cling to the blanket instead. She never once removed herself from her bed during the night. She remained asleep in her clothes. He thought to undress her and make her more comfortable, but then again, he didn't want to violate her and lose her respect.

He sat on the large chair across from her and laced up his boots. He knew one thing for sure looking at her sleeping face, the bakery was opening late today, if at all. She was her own boss so she could do that. He walked to the bedroom door and stopped. His feet wouldn't go any farther, only backward to the side of the bed. He knelt beside her. Hoping she could hear him, he whispered, "Aubrey, I hope you rest and don't feel horrible when you awake. It was my pleasure to lie with you all night long. Aubrey, I felt it. There is so much between us. I will check in on you later. I will be here in town for a while. I'm not just passing through where you and I are concerned." He then couldn't resist. He kissed her forehead. He kissed her tip of her nose. He pressed his lips to hers.

He was glad she never hurled last night, but if she had, he would have held her head to the toilet bowl. She was beautiful as she slept. He shook his head. He had it bad for her. Not sure how this was going to turn out, he was not letting her out of his mind. She was the first goodness that continually filled his thoughts…pushing back his horrible memories.

TATE DIDN'T BOTHER TO GLANCE around when he left her house in the morning daylight. Before he left, he twisted the wand on the blinds hanging on French patio doors in her bedroom to darken the room. He wasn't trying to keep that he was there a secret. He was doing no walk of shame. A proud walk, perhaps. He put her key back into her pot, a secret spot obvious as hell for anyone to locate and easily access her home. This was an important matter he would clear with her soon enough, and in the meantime, he would still worry about her. Even with her "boyfriend" Emerson there. Tate learned no woman was ever really safe. He learned that mistake so long ago.

His rental property was just a short drive from her home. Tate pulled in and parked his truck. He sat behind the wheel and remembered the smell of her hair that lingered in his senses. His face had snuggled closely to her neck while she slept for hours. His body rested during the night next to hers, but his mind was going in rapid speed. He thought about being in her bed, and what it would be like to be with her in bed for their first time. Tate wanted to see her face when they made love, to see when she came undone and when it was all his undoing.

One thought in his head was what a beautiful expression took over a woman's face after she was satisfied and comforted. One part of the bed was extremely uncomfortable and a sight he wanted to block out. That was that Emerson shared it with her. It may take time, but Tate was more determined to watch this guy. Let him fuck it up, and Tate would make certain he was there to catch her, hold her, and know that she was loved. WOW, where the hell did that word come from? It wasn't like, or lust, or late. Tate paused at his own front door. The "L" word had just taken over his head. Could he be in love with her already? He knew he felt something. He knew she did, too. Whatever it was, it was certainly worth sticking around for.

Tate hit his bed hard. It had been a long night. A few times, his own body parts fought what he tried to keep stored in his mind. Adjusting his jeans, he'd tried to find comfort with her up against him. He was finding himself hard remembering being right there in her bed, his arms around Aubrey. Her slight movements in her sleep pressed every button in him, almost having him coming completely undone several times. Sleep was on his mind now. That was all he needed so that he could talk to Reed later and see if he had any news for him. *Emerson has to go* was his last thought as he drifted.

THE NEW CARPET WAS INSTALLED in their home months ago. It was a soft light beige color. It still had that new smell to it. Tate knew that if he didn't leave his work boots at the front door that there would be a clear path of dirt from their bedroom to the bathroom. Being married was a change for him, but one he welcomed. Leaving his boots parked at the door each night, he didn't mind at all. Callie wanted the soft color rugs where he would have selected something dark. The light color she chose made their already large bedroom appear more spacious. It had a three panel window that faced out to their tree lined back of their property. He thought about his coming home, leaving his boots at the same place, a little buzzed but taking the stairs carefully.

He had hung out in the evening and had a few beers and words with his partner and some other guys on the force. Callie learned that the night out with the guys that Tate said he would be home early meant early the next morning. He unzipped his jeans in the bathroom light and dropped them to the floor. The belt buckle sounded on the ceramic tile. He looked at their bed, and she didn't stir. His shirt followed. Shutting the light off, he then went to slide naked into their bed to wrap himself with her and the covers. He overestimated the edge of the bed in the darkness and tumbled to the floor, making a loud thud. Cursing under his breath, he knew he had awakened her. He went to rise until a soft hand wrapped around him and pulled him back to the plush carpet.

Callie wanted him. He could feel her need in her touch. She let him lie back on the floor, and she took control, climbing on top of him. Tate could see her lovely naked body above him as the light softly filtered through the arched glass windows from the moon above in the night sky.

Her touch so perfectly matched his needs. Hell, he should have left the guys hours ago if this was what was waiting for him. Callie rode him. He lay back and took it all in. He closed his eyes and he could still see her face, he knew every characteristic of it. He knew she was smiling at the way she was pleasing him. His groans and tender whispers of her name gave her that assurance. She rode him longer than he could remember. He came with everything that he could give his wife. He wanted to return the favor and take care of her, but she snuggled up to his side on the carpet.

He had several beers. That made him exhausted, and his energy was completely wiped out. He lay with her at his side, and he felt her forehead and pushed back her hair one strand at a time. He loved the touch of her skin to his fingers. He drew lightly on her forehead heart motions as he felt her giggle in her movement. He turned to pull her deeper into his chest.

Holy fuck, he could see through the fog in his head. The darkness eventually lifted, peeled back like a painter removing their drop cloth. Tate noticed the carpet was stained. Touching his finger to the wetness on the floor, he noted it was thick like paint. The black and white colors of his dream slowly saturated with color. The spot, wet and pooled with thick liquid, was a dark color, maroon…deep red…BLOOD RED. He kept retreating from the redness that spread in his nightmare until he awoke rigidly backed into the wooden headboard.

Tate shook as he leaned there and reached out to hit the light on and sent it across the floor. He needed to make these visions stop. His breathing was uncontrolled. It was again the night darkness that brought him such unrest. His distaste of the color red was still present, and these nightmares wouldn't stop. He had to put them to rest. *I have focus on something good to rise from this private hell I keep visiting. Aubrey, she is my comfort zone. She is saving me and bringing me back to feeling alive. Red is the color of her beautiful cheeks…Red Velvet is the pie she bakes…Red are the flowers that hang in front of her bakery.* Tate's pulse finally calmed.

Chapter Eleven

A UBREY HAD A CHARM THAT just captured everyone.
The court date was set for Jackson, and finally, he
would be tried and hopefully sentenced a long time for
attempting to rape her. She knew the cops in the town
watched out for her more closely since the occurrence.
Emerson was with her most of the time if she wasn't at her
bakery, but where was Tate hanging out? She must have left
an awful impression on him, seemed he didn't come around
anymore. She knew he was in this town someplace. She'd
seen him so clearly last night.

Even through her mental drunken fog, it was Tate clear
as she remembered him. She also sensed his being near her
in the bar before she actually saw his eyes upon her. She
remembered waking this morning after drinking too much
and feeling horrible. Her head pounded, and her mouth was
dry like a wad of cotton. She squinted her eyes, preparing to
avoid the morning sunlight that poured in from the balcony
door. It didn't appear to be as bright. Perhaps today was a
cloudy start.

Opening her eyes fully, she noticed the blinds were pulled

tightly. Her eyes took in the sight of the items laid out next to her bedside. Tate, he was here last night. He brought her home, she was certain, and this spread for taking away a hangover was his doing. She knew it was no act of kindness from Emerson. She assumed at this early morning hour Emerson was already on the jobsite. Her hand grabbed the aspirin and swallowed it with the blue liquid. Her head hit the pillow again.

She felt him. Tate had stayed with her. She wasn't sure for how long, but she knew he held her if even for a long moment till she passed out. He may have left the moment she slept. She knew he was probably worried Emerson was going to be coming in. She should have worried about that, too, but she didn't seem to at all. Her finger traced her lips. They were chapped and dry, but she knew they were wet last night. Wet with the taste of Tate. Her lips crashed onto his. That wasn't a dream. She knew that had to be real. It felt real. Her lips felt sore and kissed, passionately kissed.

Her cell phone was on the side table face down. She felt like lying just like that in her bed till her head silenced the loud parade noise inside. She turned her phone to see she received a text from Emerson.

Bree, you crashed hard. I am off to work. See you later. Perhaps you should stay home and away from the bakery for a day and rest so you'll feel much better. I made sure you were okay. Tonight, we have a meeting with the guys for the new project. It shouldn't run too late, but don't wait up for me. I'll wake you when I come in.

Normally, the thought of Emerson coming home to her warmed her or it did some time ago. She didn't really think of when he would be coming home to her now. Her thoughts were only on when she would have a chance to see Tate once again. Oh shit! Tate probably wanted nothing to do with her. She was a drunk last night, couldn't stand, and couldn't keep her shoes on. Barely made it from the ladies room to a seat at the bar. The room spun and all she remembered saying was she was going to be sick. She was then carried away.

Tate again rescued her. The fresh air hit her and soothed the feeling of sickness. It didn't take away her drunkenness, though. She was alert enough to know she was seated with Tate by her side. She finally lowered that wall she built up and decided to take that leap, because normally she may never have without the courage that the drinks supplied her. She really wanted to kiss his lips. Even though she tasted of alcohol, she welcomed his lips. Her feelings for him were just as strong even with her being under the influence. Her heart felt him, just as her nipples tightened.

Rolling herself over in her bed, she clenched the pillow that had his head upon it. Tate was there, but she asked herself why would he want her? Clearly, she was living with her boyfriend. He probably was just being kind and making certain she arrived safely home. For a moment, Aubrey closed her eyes and reminisced about his lips, and him kissing her again. There had to be something more. He had to have liked her. She fell back to sleep, and her thoughts were only on Tate. Sleeping peacefully and the aspirin taking effect, her face was calm, and a smile puffed her cheeks. If only what she was dreaming could be there when she awakened.

ANOTHER SLEEPLESS DAY FOR TATE started as he refused to close even one eye after his nightmare this morning. It had him rattled for some time after. They usually passed, but this one was so real. He saw the blood. He even tasted the blood. Actually, he bit his lip so hard during the dream that blood ran from his lower lip to his chin. It was intense this time. The past drew him in and beat him down every time in the sleep zone. He was weak inside, and it tore him apart.

He rose and walked about his place. He knew coffee would settle him. It had the opposite effect on him that others depended on it for. Silence surrounded him. A soft breeze flowed through the windows. A few distant voices he then heard out on the sand. There was a couple walking their dog along the surf. He watched as they tossed a bright green ball ahead of them for their dog to retrieve. He heard splashes as the dog ran into the water after it. The dog emerged from the water with the ball tightly in its mouth and soon caught up to its owners as they continued walking. Tate begged for that moment, when he would be thrown a conclusive tip that exposed Callie's real killer and only then would his mind rest.

His mind all over the place, he thought to reach out to Reed to see if, maybe, he had some good news. He tapped his fingers to his lips while placing the call. She kissed his lips last night. He felt her want him. He knew that he wanted her so badly. He refrained from removing her clothes to make her more comfortable. He resisted skimming more than her breast as she wiggled in the bed. The moment he realized that his finger was next to her breast he froze. God, he wanted so much more, but not like that, with her drunk. He wanted all of her and to see that he could make her happy. He did open his eyes when she first kissed him, not believing that it was actually happening. For Tate, this was real shit. He was feeling again. It felt so damn good.

"Hey, what's up?" Reed said in a clipped tone.

"I wanted to see if you found anything. I know it's soon, but I know you and you are all over looking up detective shit."

"Well, you better be seated. I found out a ton."

Tate sat and reached for a beer from his refrigerator. He knew by Reed's tone he was going to need at least one.

"Well, Emerson is no saint with a few priors that he got off, and this guy has been in the company of several larger dealers in the cities—Philadelphia, Atlantic City, and New York. He is often with a girl, a beautiful blonde. She is working with him as well. Her looks are definitely a diversion for him to have her distract others." Tate thought that must be the blonde he was with in the bar the other time, outside of the ladies room. That girl from the side and back was a stunner.

"Tate, the guys here are onto some of these dealers already. If something goes down and he is with them, he will be taken down, too."

"Reed, you know me. I'm no longer on the force. I will get you to him and you can take him down. One way or another, he is out of this picture with me and Aubrey."

"What, you are already with this girl Aubrey? I missed that."

"I mean what I want with her. Sorry, I jumped ahead of myself there." He grunted. "I know I saw him deal drugs in the daylight to a car a while ago, and that was a small dealing. I think he is sitting pretty in this quaint town with a pile of shit, selling it all over, and mark my word, I will find out. I will sniff it out and be up his ass."

"Tate, he may have nothing to do with Callie's murder. You know that, right?"

"Yeah, but someone tipped me to come here. Something is here for me to find or make right. This girl, Aubrey, she doesn't deserve him. She may not deserve me, either. I am a complete mess, but I want him away from her. That I am sure of. He reeks of bad news, and I don't want her innocently taking a fall for him."

"Well, if you can get to your computer later, I will forward everything I have dug up thus far. Maybe some of the photos I send will show more familiar faces."

Reed and Tate continued to catch up on some of the guys at the force and what they had been up too. Tate acted interested, but his mind kept wandering to lying behind Aubrey in her bed. He couldn't believe that what was a chance meeting in her bakery already progressed to them lying together in her bed. Not that anything happened—well, something sort of did. Tate began falling for her even harder.

Somehow she was filling up his thoughts daily. He didn't mind. Maybe she would push the demons out of his head. He could only hope. A few times, Reed repeated himself because Tate was lost in the conversation, obviously not paying attention. His mind went back to her breasts rising and falling with her breath. She was built very nicely in that area.

HE TURNED ON HIS COMPUTER a while later. It was full of emails. One by one, he went through all the information Reed forwarded him. There were a few familiar faces in the photographs, like a guy named Damon who often appeared with Emerson. Tate was very detailed in his investigation processes, so he created his own files along with all the leads that he previously had that led to nowhere. Perhaps here in this town, someone would be the break he searched for. He knew though that, as much as he cared for Aubrey and that he didn't want to stay away from her, he was going to have to keep some distance until Emerson was brought down. He didn't want her caught in the crossfire of drugs or Emerson catching wind of Tate's watching him, and that Tate would do and closer than a hawk would.

AFTER AN AFTERNOON OF COMPUTER work, a real work out was needed. Tate rose and decided to go put a gym workout in. He hoped he would run into Emerson. He wanted to position himself as close to that guy as he possibly could.

An afternoon workout was perfect. The gym was empty. Seems most people in the town rose early and probably trained first to start their day. Tate didn't have to pause for any of the weights. He did check the door each time he heard someone new arrive. Midway through his workout, Emerson came through the doors. He winked immediately at the desk girl and then kissed a girl on the cheek who was heading out. *What an ass* went through Tate's mind.

Tate and Emerson exchanged glances. "Hey, big guy, didn't know you worked out here, been seeing you everyplace in our town." Emerson stated and reached for the dumbbells to start his adrenaline pumping.

"Yeah, it's a great town. I may just decide to stay for a bit. Got me a rental on the beach."

"Cool, and if you take notice, this town has several attractive girls if you are single."

Tate felt his blood rising. He bit his lip, still feeling the previous sore that he created from biting it hard during his sleep last night, but the pain instantly helped to tap down his rage for this guy. "Well, I will have to meet some of them." Tate forced his reply.

"Cool, man, you seem cool. So are you into anything else besides your workout and girls? I mean, I know where I can score you some great weed or coke if you are interested. The town is dead this time of year, but I can surely supply you with stuff to make it a fun time."

Tate had him, yes he did. He knew this kind who liked to boost about what they did. One day, this kind of guy would fall, trip himself up. Tate would be there to take him down, but he wanted something big to stick on him. Really put his ass away for a long time. He wanted Aubrey to see what he really was like, because somehow Emerson showed her a side that she liked. "Well, I will keep that in mind and reach out to you if I become bored." Tate played it off.

"Seriously, I can find you anything you want...but not my girl. Aubrey is off limits. I see you around her, but I know that she only has eyes for me."

Tate was fuming inside. This guy was so full of himself. If he only knew it was Tate in her bed last night and his lips pressed to hers. It was her taste that hadn't left his mind. Tate refused to respond to him and just grabbed at the weights and began to do another set. Then yet another set.

They both did their own workouts, but when Tate was wrapping up his, Emerson made one last point of pitching a drug sale his way. "Got a big score coming in next month or soon after if you want some, just say the word. I heard you are in town for real estate investments, and you can always throw some money my way for a drug investment if you know what I mean."

Tate put on a sinister smile. "Sure, that sounds like a plan. I will be in touch in the weeks ahead." This guy was a total fuck up, broadcasting his drug dealings, talking to newcomers in the town. Emerson was stupid, it was going to blow up in his face sooner or later, whether it was Tate doing the take down or not.

AUBREY'S DAY DIDN'T BECOME ANY better in the afternoon.

It was a long day of pure day dreaming for her. She did keep the bakery closed, and her eyes, too, throughout most of the hours. Not that she was in pain with a hangover, but pained in the feelings that she had for Tate. They were intense. She remembered his arm folding over her in her bed to keep her safe, his finger graze past her breast as it peaked to a stiff hardness. She wanted to turn back into his arms, but wasn't sure he wanted her. She lay there and remained motionless and felt the heat pool between her thighs, and she kept wanting his lips again, and obviously so much more.

Chapter Twelve

S MALL TOWN PEOPLE TAKE LIFE slowly, but with nothing on the court's agenda, the case against Jackson moved swiftly. Aubrey had to face him later today. Several weeks had passed, and she hadn't even seen Tate. Surely he was avoiding her and so she just kept on with the relationship with Emerson. Even that hadn't progressed further, actually it slowed now that he moved back in. He was always working late or onto another job site and tired when he came home. Her sex life was taking a nose dive, but it wasn't like she was missing it with Emerson. Emerson was back in her home, but not really coming on to her. Perhaps this was better as she was having thoughts about another man.

This morning, she was icing cupcakes and noticed her opposite hand was decorated more than the vanilla cupcake that needed the coloring. She laughed again to herself for drifting in thought of Tate's lips on hers. She came to the bakery early this morning, first hoping to finish all her baking and second to keep her mind off heading to the courthouse this afternoon. She'd asked Emerson to join her for moral support. "You got this, Bree. They will slap his hands, send him to do some time, and it's done." That was not what she wanted to hear, especially from the man that loved her. Aubrey was strong and had been, but to face Jackson again was going to be hard.

She was failing to produce all the baked items she had originally planned, not focusing on her ingredients or missing one here and there. She was just off with her talents today. Deciding to make one last batch of cupcakes and wrap it up, she intently placed all the items into the mixer. With the mixer on, she heard the faint door bells. A patron was entering. Shutting the mixer and wiping her hands to her apron, she walked out to greet them. Her mouth opened, but she didn't speak. Her eyes lit up. Tate stood in the doorway with a dozen roses.

First, this guy didn't seem the flowers type to her. Perhaps she was thinking they were for her and maybe they wouldn't be. Tate walked forward and handed them to her. Aubrey almost jumped happily. Yes, they were for her. She smiled. "Why?"

HE PAUSED, PLEASED IN HER smiling at the flowers and then searching for a vase to fill with water. He wanted her to stand before him so he could take her in, all of her in his arms and heart and sight. He hadn't been in the bakery in weeks. He had driven by several times a day in the hopes of seeing her, but not a chance moment presented itself. "Aubrey, they are to lift your spirits through the rest of this day. Pete mentioned to me the other night when we had some beers that today was Jackson's day in court. I know that this day will be hard, and I wanted to give you something nice to think of while you're stuck in the dreary walls of the courtroom."

"Tate, thank you. I have to head to the courthouse a little later, but this means so much."

He watched her cut the stems and put them in a large pitcher full of water and display them on the corner of her counter. He felt a little saddened they wouldn't be accompanying her home. He knew that would stir questions with Emerson.

"Do you want me to come with you today?" Tate had to offer. He wanted to be there for her. He had in the very beginning and still wanted to do whatever he could for her.

"I don't think so. I appreciate that you want to come, but I need to face him myself and finally put that ordeal behind me. I also don't want you to see me pathetic and breaking down again." Aubrey thought of how many times Tate had seen her crying and drunk and not on her A-game. How was she ever suppose to impress a man that her heart was longing for without being a strong and confident woman? "I don't mind being there, and if you cry, you cry. Not like I haven't seen that side of you already." He smiled, making light of the topic.

"Well, thank you again, but I will be fine." Just as she was about to come from behind the counter, Tate ran to the back of the bakery where smoke was pouring from the one oven. "Aubrey, you may be fine, but your baked goods this morning won't be." He pulled open the door. The racks full of her last batch of cupcakes were dark and not a tasty chocolate but a charcoal burned. They laughed together as he pulled them and tossed them into the sink.

"AUBREY, I WANT YOU TO open the back door. That should quickly remove most of this smoke." Aubrey clearly was dazed. "What you want me more, and right here?" He stared at her, knowing she hadn't heard a word, but that her thoughts were on him. He laughed to himself. It made his heart pulse. She did like him. A second time, he hollered to her but louder and clearer. "Aubrey, we need to open the back door to bring in the fresh outside air."

THAT SHE HEARD CLEARLY AS she was about to move toward his arms, but he was not wanting to reach for her but to wave the smoke down. She took a few steps back and opened the door. This man had her all caught up in him. Even a fire couldn't take her attention away from his body and captivating eyes.

With the back door propped open, the smoke dissipated. Tate dumped all the pans, and Aubrey rinsed and loaded them into the industrial dishwasher for a couple rounds of washing. "That was to be my best batch this morning." She laughed. "I guess I can't be a great baker all the time. They would not have tasted very good."

Tate walked to her and reached for her lips, "They may not have, but I know your lips will."

Aubrey froze as his lips touched hers. She was not drunk this time, and she'd craved his kiss for the past weeks. Now he was kissing her, and it was really happening, and she froze up. Tate pressed on until she parted her lips, and his tongue found the pleasure to roam into her mouth. Her sweet mouth. He thought about her lips and kiss from weeks ago. It had him hard some mornings, but he had the ability to lie back in his beach rental house and let it die down.

Tate picked up Aubrey and set her on the counter top, his hands on both sides of her thighs. His lips still connected with hers. Her delicate fingers wrapped around his throat and fanned through his scalp. What a feeling raced through him. He broke from her lips and lightly kissed her thighs. He wanted to pleasure her right at this moment. He wanted to take care of her and make her feel incredible. She softly moaned as his lips traveled upward on her skin, higher on her leg.

Suddenly, he pulled back, clenching his fists. He couldn't do this. Jackson had wanted her here in this same room, almost in this exact location. Tate remembered the vision of him pounding Jackson, blow by bloody blow.

Aubrey pulled him to her lips again. "Please, Tate, kiss me." He wanted to, but was torn. He lifted her up off the counter and to the floor. He leaned over and pressed her into the pastry case. His mind escaped the vision of Jackson and her. He saw her face, and it was content, beautiful, and he pushed on. Plunging his tongue into her mouth, taking away her breath. Her hands roamed up under his shirt, her fingers clenching his skin with excitement. *Not here*, again the good voice told him in his head. He broke the kiss for the second time. Aubrey looked flushed and confused.

"Not here, Aubrey, not like this. I want you. I really do. Hell, my jeans are packed. I know you can feel that. But you are living with another guy. I can't be that other man. You deserve better."

Aubrey didn't hear all he said, she was so caught up in his lips and feeling his body pressing into her. Feeling his hardness, her legs quivered. All she heard was you deserve better. She was settling with Emerson and just being in a stolen moment like this with Tate. Well, this she wanted and was willing to go for.

The door sounded. Tate had already pulled her from his embrace. "Bree, what the hell are you baking? Smells like smoked pies," Emerson yelled out jokingly.

It didn't take Tate but a moment. He kissed her lips one more time and walked out the opened back door. Emerson came into the back room after helping himself to an éclair from the front counter. "This is really good." He licked his lips to catch the crème filling that he'd spilled. Aubrey turned her attention to Emerson and then back to the rear door. Tate was clear out of sight.

"I overbaked some cupcakes. Can you tell?" Emerson nodded in between the sugar delight that he was consuming. "It was my last batch, too."

Aubrey shrugged her shoulders and went to pull the rear door tightly. The burnt smell lingered, but the air had cleared. She glanced outside, and there was no sign of Tate. The only part that remained was how he felt pressed to her lips moments ago and how he seemed to read her mind because she wanted him to reach up her skirt. His soft kisses to her thighs had her wanting more. She was on fire.

"Bree, your face is really red!" Emerson tucked her hair back behind her ears.

"Oh, probably just from whipping out the pans and waving in the air to keep the smoke tapped down."

"Yeah, you have this hot, sexy tussled way about you today. I like it. Too bad there is no bed in here for us." Months ago, she would have lit up with his mention of sex with her. Not today, maybe not in the days ahead. Her heart was drifting to another.

Emerson didn't linger; he did his usual show of popping in and out on her. His kiss goodbye left her unaffected and didn't linger on her lips as Tate's still did in her mind. Time had escaped her this day as after Emerson left she quickly made some fresh pastries and didn't burn them and stored them for tomorrow. The clock was soon pointing its hands that it was time for her to go face Jackson.

Aubrey quickly freshened herself up in the bathroom off the prep area in the back of the bakery. She kept deodorant and an extra toothbrush and mouthwash in there. She brushed her hair out and pulled it into a loose ponytail. She applied a light peach shine of gloss to her finger and then to her lips. As she viewed her reflection in the mirror and her finger swept across her lower lip, excitement pooled again between her legs because her thoughts were on Tate tasting her lips and moving to taste so much more.

Quickly, she composed herself after that breathtaking thought. She had to push herself to drive over to the courthouse. She had to remain calm and strong, and she would as she thought again of the lovely flowers Tate brought her. The horrible reminders of Jackson holding her mouth, taking her breath away, and threatening her life were the thoughts she didn't want to confront ever again after today. Aubrey locked up the bakery and was on her way.

Finding a close parking spot was a plus this afternoon. She knew that in this town it wasn't like trying to find parking in the city. She took one more glance in the rearview mirror and talked herself down. *Aubrey, you got this. He deserves whatever punishment he is issued.* Giving herself a pep talk, she repeated, "I can do this, put it all behind me." She opened the car door, took a deep breath, and held her head high.

Once in the courtroom, everything changed. Quickly, her head dropped from being held high, and she felt embarrassed as she knew people were looking at her. She was seated nervously next to her attorney in the courtroom, and Jackson appeared. He caught her eyes and smiled lightly to her. She wasn't certain if the smile was genuine or sinister. It didn't matter either way. His presence made her so uneasy. Her thoughts were all over the place. Here was a well-known town man that so many liked, and he was handsome and polite and kind, but he tried to rape her. So extremely opposite of his demeanor.

Then there was Tate, big, strong, obviously handsome, rough voice. She was so scared of him at first, and yet he was the opposite now that she met him. She was in no way comparing these two, but she was just thinking about how her initial impressions of people became the total opposite of what she thought.

Jackson pulled his chair back from the table where he and his lawyer were seated. He did it just enough to gain him inches to have Aubrey in his sight line. She was uncomfortable. Their eyes kept catching each other's. She wanted Tessa here to support her, but she never asked because she felt it would be awkward as Tessa and Jackson were related. She knew her roommate was upset this happened, but Aubrey didn't want to have to make her roommate choose family or friend to support and have any future repercussions.

Aubrey attempted to move her chair in, and it squeaked, loudly scrapping the legs on the floor. "Is there a problem?" one of the court appointed helpers asked her. Aubrey froze as suddenly all eyes were on her. She couldn't do this. The judge hadn't even been announced, and she fled as quickly as she could with tears streaming down her cheeks. She left and went down the corridor to where she saw the restroom sign. In the ladies' room, she faced herself in the mirror. She would be punishing this man today. She wasn't sure she could find the strength to do this. She prayed for courage to appear and couldn't see it. She was defeated.

There was a wait inside the courtroom for her return. Her lawyer approached the judge, who had entered after she left, and he told the judge that she went to the ladies' room and she would be back momentarily.

Aubrey attempted to gather strength. It would all be over in a few hours. She wasn't a fighter. She was unable to even make a tight fist. She was broken, weak, and couldn't go through with this. She couldn't return to that courtroom. She had made her choice, and she would slip out of the bathroom, find someone to message her lawyer, and tell him she was unable to follow through with this. Not today. She had lost herself when she saw Jackson, and it brought back the entire ordeal that she pushed far inside her mind. It was real again and fresh again. He'd tried to rape her, and he would have succeeded if Tate had never come back. Her body shivered remembering.

Washing her hands of this day and drying them with the blower, she was ready to lock herself in her car and drive directly to her home. She pulled the door open, and the corridor was empty. She stepped out, and suddenly, he grabbed her arm. She wanted to scream, to fight him, but this time she could not. She turned into his chest instantly and wept. Tate held her, and his hand comforted her head as he felt her breaths hesitating as she cried. "Aubrey, I know you said don't come here, but you need support. This is hard shit to face a guy that attacked you. I had to be here to help you through this. I asked where you were as I didn't see you in the courtroom. Someone told me to check the ladies' room."

Without awareness of her surroundings, Aubrey pulled her head from his warm body, his comforting hold, and tilted her chin toward him. Her eyes showed her need. Tate would give this girl anything she wanted. His lips took to hers. Her tears had salted her taste, but he let her kiss him back until she pulled from him. She wiped her eyes and pulled both her lips into her mouth and nodded. He knew she was ready to do this, and he was right there with her. He took her hand and kissed the top of her head once more.

"Let's go put this asshole to where he should be." Aubrey tightened her hold to his large hand. She felt Tate give her a reassuring squeeze back.

The courtroom scene played out quicker than what Aubrey had envisioned, or maybe it was her constant reassurance knowing Tate was seated in the back and that kept her mind occupied. It was good that Jackson never followed her line of sight to see Tate sitting back there.

TODAY, TATE SAT LOW IN the chair. He wore a ball cap into the court house, but removed it while he sat in the courtroom. He didn't need Jackson to bring him into this. It would be a swift hearing. Her word to the judge and sentencing of this asshole, clear cut case. It turned out just as Tate knew it would. Aubrey testified against Jackson, and Tate wanted to go up and capture her tears, as he felt her pain in reliving that day with all the questions she faced. She made him proud. Her petite stature rose to the occasion and came through.

As for Jackson, he was found guilty. In the state of New Jersey he was in violation of the Sexual Assault Law, attempting rape with a deadly weapon. That delivered him a hefty fine and up to five years in prison. That was satisfaction for Tate, although several times he found himself ringing his hands when he caught Jackson smiling, because this guy deserved another ass whipping.

AUBREY WAS CONTENT THAT THIS ordeal was finally over. Jackson was still seated across the room in her view. She had noticed that his earlier smile had vanished, since the verdict was announced. Aubrey told her lawyer she couldn't stay here in the court room a moment more. She hugged the lawyer and headed out. Tate discretely followed. He was so happy his girl—well Aubrey—came through. He wanted to pick her up and spin her in the corridor. When he exited, he rushed to join her, his arms waiting to enfold her against his chest until he saw her standing in conversation with a guy.

It was Emerson. He took hold of her hand and walked her outside and down the courthouse building steps. Tate saw the sadness in her eyes, her eyes apologized to him. Tate could see she was not expecting Emerson to have been waiting for her. Aubrey may not have received that spin in his arms on the floor here today, but it was coming. He knew it was all timing. It surprised him Emerson was not here all day, but then again, it probably wasn't convenient. Emerson showed up just to act like the perfect boyfriend. Tate knew he was everything less than that. Tate walked out after several minutes. He smiled in the afternoon sun that this day put away an attempted rapist and that she kissed him. She needed him. His smile was going to stay on his face for many more hours.

Chapter Thirteen

I T SEEMED LIKE TIME PASSED too long in between Tate seeing her again. A few times, he drove to the bakery, but backed out as Emerson was there. If he saw her in a store in town, by the time he went to approach her, Emerson was near. He kept a low profile and was working on a take down every moment. This all was not by protocol, but it was being done by the Tate Manning how to take out drug dealers manual. For him, it was also how to remove Emerson from the likes of Aubrey because now more than ever he was certain that Aubrey didn't love that guy. Tate knew, though, that not seeing her was making him want her more. He knew he liked her already, but for him, it was surely something so much more.

"So what do you have for me, Reed?" Tate was seeking an update. For weeks, they had been looking into Emerson and Damon's lives and coming up with more and more illegal happenings and relationships with others that were not noteworthy.

"Tate, you are dead on with this, dude. Things are being planned. We are seeing the works in place and hearing the buzz on the streets for a big shipment to pass from sleepy town to high town. Perhaps Cape May to New York. We may need you to watch that Damon guy. He seems to be connected with previous dealers. We ran his photo, and he is tied to drugs on the East Coast and for those with deep pockets."

"I am glad you are on board with me on this, Reed. I don't want to jeopardize your job, but know that if you can work with some of the team in Hagerstown to inform the narcotics division in this area then they can surely start to play this into their hands, just like you and I use to. Reed, I miss you, man, and how we worked together."

"Yeah, we did some fine take downs."

Tate did miss him and the life he had. The perfect job for him, great partner, and wonderful married life to a beautiful woman that adored him. He missed it all.

"Where'd you go? I was talking and you went silent," Reed questioned.

"I was here, just thinking this through. So you are going to try to nab him and whoever is with him this month?" Tate was more concerned that this didn't go down at Aubrey's home, her grandmother's home. He didn't want her arrested in the process for just being there.

"We are meeting with the local cops in Cape May next week and will be seeing where they are at with their drug leads and hand over our information to them. Ours will be delivered in person on a platter."

"Sweet and keep me posted. By the way, you can come crash here while you are in town."

"Just like old times only I want your bed and you can move your ass to your sofa." Reed laughed out loud. Tate spent many nights on Reed's sofa.

They hung up, and Tate was still worried that, if this all went down, Aubrey could be a victim of circumstances. He hoped that wouldn't happen. If he found out the timing, he would somehow keep her from it.

AUBREY WONDERED WHY THERE WAS no sign of Tate for days. He hadn't reached out to her or stopped in the bakery. The vase of the flowers he brought to her had died and dried up, but even so, she moved the vase to the back counter by the register and left them there. She wasn't going to part with them...ever. A few times, she spotted him in town, but usually Emerson was with her and she didn't want to be obviously facing Tate's direction. She thought that her last glance to him from the courthouse may have sealed it for him to stay away.

She wanted that day to run up to him when she exited the doors after hearing the verdict and hug and kiss him for his support. She would have never returned and sat next to her lawyer if Tate didn't show up to help her. Her kiss to his lips that day was her needing to confirm all that she felt for him. She was falling in love. In that moment in the hallway, with his lips pressed to hers despite her face streaked with wetness from her tears, she totally lost herself with him. Nothing else surrounded her but him. It was Tate. He clearly had stolen her heart.

Today, she was home preparing to throw a small beach party for tomorrow night. Nothing fancy, just that Emerson had mentioned that it would be nice to have a fun night since all of the Jackson drama had passed. She never thought of it as the drama Emerson mentioned, but more of a live changing occurrence.

Every day since then, she jumped a bit at the bells that sounded on the bakery front door. Most days, she double checked she is locked up before heading back to bake. Many days before the attack, she left the sign displaying closed but the door unlocked in case a local popped in for an end of the day treat. Not since then, as she kept her door secure after hours. Another thing that she changed, too, was she decided there was no need for a hidden key. After that day she woke up from being drunk and Tate had driven her home safely, she knew somehow he would be none too happy at her having her door key right in the front planter for all to see. Her, Tessa, and Emerson all had keys, and that was plenty. Plus if she ever locked herself from her home, anyone in the town would help her.

Preparing for tomorrow evening, she knew Tessa would be around. In fact, Tessa seemed to glow when she mentioned partying with Emerson and some friends coming to hang at the beach. Aubrey was glad that Tessa was happy. Tessa even said to Aubrey, "I like that Emerson more and more." It made Aubrey feel good her roommate did. After all, they were all living under the same roof.

Tessa had left her a note this morning that she wanted to go shopping with Aubrey for some new outfit. The stores were slow on sales this time of year so bargains were to be found. Aubrey knew a day shopping with her roommate would definitely feel good even though they often argued over their different style of wardrobe. Aubrey being more conservative and simple, and Tessa all about the jaw dropping reaction to what she wore.

Aubrey was finishing up at the bakery when Tessa phoned. "Hey, girl, get your running shoes on. We are hitting all the stores. So pack up that cake box and let's head out. I will be there in a few." Before Aubrey could respond anything more than okay, her phoned silenced. Aubrey removed her apron and hung it on the peg on the backroom wall next to the others. She washed off any of the powdered sugar that remained on her forearms from dusting the chocolate brownies. The bells sounded. Aubrey hesitated. She was still open, and Tessa couldn't be here yet.

"I'll be right there," Aubrey shouted sweetly.

A moment later, she came to the front of the bakery, and there stood Tate. "Too late for a cup of coffee?" he asked, never veering from her eyes.

"Well, I was closing a bit early to go shopping with my friend, but I can make you a fresh cup." She was nervous. Perhaps that Tessa might show up and Tate would take his eyes to her beautiful roommate, or perhaps she was scared to be alone with him, knowing her true feelings.

"I actually don't need the coffee. I just felt the need for an excuse to see you." He walked closer toward her.

"Tate, I owe you a huge explanation about the day at the courthouse." Aubrey walked a few steps closer to him.

"You don't owe me that. I figured he would be there. He's your guy, but what you don't understand is I want to be your guy." Tate put it out there, and he felt so good in saying it. Her face lit up. Her cheeks reddened, and her lips waited to seal the deal on the words he just dropped on her.

Tate leaned close to her face and swept his finger across her cheek, gently removing a trace of powdered sugar that remained. The door bells rang.

"Hey, you ready to go or what? Put the closed sign up. And who are you?" Tessa took a complete once over of Tate from top to bottom. She was very impressed. She actually licked her lips, tilted her head, and said, "Hmmmm."

"Hi, I am just a guy wanting a cup of coffee."

"Well, Aubrey, hurry up and brew this handsome man a cup of Joe so we can go!"

Aubrey appeared embarrassed and didn't feel the need to tell Tessa who Tate was. After all, to Tessa, he was just a patron. Aubrey didn't want to introduce Tessa any further to Tate because he clearly had stolen her heart and she was going to protect that.

Aubrey turned and went to the coffee pot. There was still half a pot, and the coffee station hadn't been turned off yet.

Tate moved to the counter. "That will be fine. I don't mind coffee you've had just as long as it is warm."

Aubrey knew he was just being nice. As he waited for her to pour it, he glanced back at Tessa. She was focused on her cellphone texting someone. Tessa sensed his watching her. Aubrey caught their interaction, and it unsettled her to where she over poured the coffee and burned herself. "Ouch!"

Aubrey immediately ran her hand under cold water.

Tate jumped behind the counter, took her hand in his, and held it under the water stream. "I am sorry," he whispered.

Tessa still clearly engaged in a texting session never noticed what happened. "Don't be, please. Don't you ever apologize, you have done nothing but been good to me."

"So are you two about ready to wrap up the coffee cup thing and let me take her shopping?" Tessa chimed in.

Clearly, she missed their touch. Aubrey felt it when he grabbed and caressed her hand, beneath the coolness of the water. Her moment of insecurity passed. He did care about her, but she loved him and wasn't at all sure he could ever love her.

Tate grabbed the coffee and poured out the extra, placed a lid on it, walked out, and thanked her politely for making it for him.

When he was far enough past the bakery, he tossed it into the first trash bin he came to. He climbed into his truck, and his fists hit the steering wheel hard. He wasn't angered by the fact her friend interrupted them. It was that her friend was the girl kissing Emerson outside the bathroom that night he saw Emerson at the bar. If he told Aubrey, she wouldn't believe him, and surely this girl would deny it.

Something was going on in the small town, and he was going to go inch by inch and uncover every sand granule to see what it was. Tate remained in his truck, taking in one more sight of his girl. Yes, he was certain that day was coming soon that she would be his. He had his fix of her as she walked out with her friend. His eyes never wavered from the girl in the pink flip flops and printed pink and white sundress to the girl in the short denim mini skirt with heels and too much makeup. Tonight, when he hit the bed, he would dream of springtime with the pastel colors that remained in his thoughts from his vision of Aubrey.

Aubrey and Tessa were off hitting store after store. Aubrey was excited when she came across a black cotton eyelet dress. It had little cap sleeves and flared out just a bit from the waist. She never wore black, but putting it on, she felt sexier and thought that Tate would love her in this. Then she remembered her buying an outfit was for her house party and that Emerson was her boyfriend and he would see her in this dress.

"OMG, that outfit is unbelievable!" Aubrey could say no more. Tessa had on a tight halter sundress that hugged her every curve and barely held a breast, let alone both of them. Aubrey knew that Tessa would knock them out at the beach party. She just wasn't sure which guy friends of Emerson's from his work would be there. Damon had noticed Tessa, but still never made a move. Aubrey was sure any available man would move on this after seeing her.

"So you think I should get this? Coral isn't my color at all, but it does fit me perfectly." Tessa fixed herself again in the mirror and did the duck lip face, acting like she was taking a selfie. Aubrey just nodded in agreement to her in the reflection. Aubrey smoothed out the dress she was holding. It was nothing like that one Tessa was displaying, but Aubrey liked her selection. A simple dress was plenty for

Aubrey. It was shorter than what she usually wore, but she figured she would be fine at her own home for the party. If she was uncomfortable, she could go to her bedroom and change it out.

"So now let's go for shoes," Tessa suggested. Aubrey rolled her eyes. It was a beach party so shoes were optional.

She knew Tessa would enter the room, though, with high heels just to impress those spinning their heads her way.

"By the way, I wanted to give you a big hug for handling yourself in the courtroom with my cousin. That had to be hard. I haven't brought it up, just wanted it to die away for you."

Aubrey smiled at Tessa and appreciated that from her. It had appeared to go away, only so did Tate, which that made her sad. Today, she was close to spending time with him, but that was ruined when Tessa walked in. Perhaps it was better that way. Aubrey still hadn't given Emerson the words to vacate her home. In fact, they had sex yesterday, and although Emerson groaned and said it was great, Aubrey just went through the motions. It wasn't anything great for her, unless it was Tate's arms touching her, his lips kissing her, and him deep, so deep inside of her. Aubrey was really off in thought. "Hey, Aubrey, lets hit the shoes..." Tessa pulled her arm and off to another sale at another shop they went.

THE LAST THING TATE WANTED to do this evening was think of what to have for dinner. He decided to stop at the popular fish taco hang he heard about and grab some to go.

Dining alone had become a habit of his for a long time. He couldn't even remember when he last had a meal with a female, a real dinner. He entered and was aware of the line to place the orders, so this place must be as good as they say. By the time he reached the front to place his order, they told him it would be a twenty minute wait. Tate decided to have it served to him and eat in. He went to the bar and took a seat and ordered a beer. Each sip went down smoothly. He finished it and asked for another just as his order arrived.

Picking at his food and taking a sip of his beer, he suddenly didn't miss her presence. He turned, and there was Aubrey placing her to-go order. She was hesitating and biting her lower lip to decide her final selection.

"Just pick," Tate said to her.

"Oh, I pick you," Aubrey replied without hesitation and then quickly covered with, "I meant I came to pick up food."

He smiled. Tate knew exactly what she said, and he knew she meant it. His heart tapped inside his chest at her words. Time would tell if she picked him.

"So can I join you here till my order is ready?" she asked politely.

"Aubrey, you can join me anyplace, anytime. You need not ever ask that. I think you know how I feel about..."

He was stopped short. A waitress popped her nosey head in between them and said, "How do you feel about the tacos?"

"Good, they are really good," Tate said and hadn't even taken a bite. Aubrey blushed, and Tate had to touch her. He was trying so hard to refrain, but wanted to just feel her touch.

"Do you want a beer while you wait?" He offered her a sip of his only to touch his hand to hers as she took hold of the glass.

Aubrey took a tiny sip and then remarked, "Sure, why not." She chose a cider beer.

When the bartender set it in front of Tate, his fingers wrapped around the neck of the bottle and he slid it closer to Aubrey. When her hand went to it, she laid it over his. He touched her again and came undone. He pulled his hand and signaled with his hand to the bartender for his attention to bring her a glass. He couldn't have her touch him here like this. He needed more. He knew what she tasted like and felt like. He was falling and falling fast for her.

"Thank you for requesting the glass." She happily caught his eyes. She was so lost, so far gone over this man. It was amazing how lately her everyday thoughts were so full of Tate that a few times she almost slipped and called Emerson by Tate's name. She knew that she was not feeling it for Emerson anymore, but she also was guarded and not wanting to end her relationship with Emerson if this dream man by her side on the bar stool was going to leave town in a moment's notice once again. She needed stability in her life. Her life was here, and that wasn't going to change. She needed a man here for her. She could, though, dream about his deep eyes and that he could be hers one day. She could dream.

"Aubrey, your order is up," the waitress hollered to her.

Aubrey leaned over to her and asked that she wrap half of it. Then she turned to Tate and asked, "Do you mind if I stay and eat my dinner with you?" Aubrey had no idea when Emerson would be home tonight. He messaged her earlier that something came up and he was tied up later than normal, and so that was why she was just picking up something simple this evening for dinner. Even Tessa rushed off after receiving a text while they were out shopping. Changing their plans, all she told Aubrey was, "I got to go meet my new man." She gave no details, but left Aubrey high and dry so quickly. It was when her stomach made itself known to her while driving home that she pulled into here for tacos. Once in the parking spot, she also noticed his truck, Tate's truck, was here as well. She spent about fifteen minutes in the car mirror adjusting her hair since it was messy from trying on clothes, and she added some blush to her cheeks and a sweep of gloss to shine her lips. She hoped he would see her.

"I would love for you to join me. Is this considered a dinner date? Because there is no other girl I would rather dine with in this town or any other." Tate waited for an answer. She just shook her head and was amused that since the first time he caught her eye, he hadn't given up on making her feel special.

They both ate and shared a few beers. Their conversation was in a low tone heard between just them as music was playing in the bar. Aubrey jumped up. "I hope you're not leaving just yet?" Tate was disappointed. He didn't want her to leave.

"Oh, no, but I do have to go pee." She smiled and walked toward the ladies room, and Tate never let his eyes waiver from the edge of her dress and thinking of what it would be like to lift that delicate pink dress up over her head and become totally lost inside her. If the patrons at the bar turned in his direction and caught his smile, they would believe he thought that the tacos were the best here. However, Aubrey was the one that lit up his heart every time he saw her.

When she came back, Tate had already paid for his check and hers, including her take home container for Emerson. It was the least he could do. After all, he would be taking this girl from him. He knew that for certain.

"Let's head out of here, sound good?" Tate leaned in close to her and awaited her response.

Nervously, she said, "Yes, let me take care of my bill."

Tate took her hand from her wallet. "Already done." He held her hand and didn't care who saw them. He walked boldly from the bar to the sidewalk out front. He opened his passenger side door. Aubrey never hesitated. She climbed up and tucked her dress under her tightly. She was in this truck before, she vaguely remembered. It was the night she drank too much, and Tate came to her rescue and took her home to her bed. The night he stayed and lay with her. Just up against her, but so closely that she could feel his blood pulsing.

Aubrey send a text to Emerson as soon as Tate walked around to the driver's side. She wanted to check what time he would arrive home. His response was quick that he would be really late, he was sorry, and he would remind her tomorrow what she meant to him. Aubrey shut her phone. She was glad Emerson was tied up for several more hours. Tate missed her texting, and she was glad of that. She didn't want to be sneaky, but wanted to spend more time with him.

"Well, I guess what they say is true," Tate admitted as he climbed in behind the steering wheel. "This place has the best tacos and more." Licking his lips, he shot her a wink purely for her. It melted her. She adjusted herself in the seat. This man was having her come undone with just a simple glance. With his eyes on the road but his heart set on her next to him, he drove where he knew she would love to go—the remote end of the beach line far away from the town people and any distractions.

Parking up on the beach as the curb line was low, his truck clearly made its way over it. Darkness surrounded them when he killed the truck lights. The ocean water had a slight glow from the moon light as they both heard the soft crashing of the waves. "Aubrey, may I kiss you?" He was holding back with every ounce of restraint, but wanted to be a perfect gentleman. This was about her, making certain she was comfortable. Tate wanted every moment to be about her.

She eyed out the window, didn't give him her response. Pausing for a long quiet period, she eventually faced him. Without words, her hands softly held his chin as her lips agreeably covered his. Her lips sealed the answer in his heart. He felt like a teenager again, parking near the water, secluded, and with a beautiful girl. Only this girl brought him more than just wanting to have her sexually here. He wouldn't do that. Not here, not yet. Even though his heart was racing and his dick was throbbing, he wanted her slowly and passionately and when she was no longer living with Emerson. He would wait for that time. He could do that. He would be here for her then when that time came.

He and Aubrey kissed for hours. Their surroundings escaped, and she was leaning in his arms, gazing at the tiny little ripples that danced across the ocean. *To forget where you are and nothing but who you are with*, Tate was thinking, *is pure bliss.* A few times during their kisses, he felt her hand skirt past his dick on his jeans, and he repositioned himself in his seat. Again, she found the precise spot that touched him, and he told her, "Not here…you could have me explode in a moment, but I want to be with you when the timing is right…for us."

She totally respected that. Unfortunately, she still had a boyfriend. She did let Tate lift the edges of her dress and touch his finger to her thigh. A chill ran through her, and wanting more followed right behind.

They didn't want to end their time together, but the faint smell of the taco order bagged on the truck floor reminded them she needed to return home to Emerson. Tate hoped she would end that relationship soon, but didn't want to press her. She needed to do it. Tate reached to start the engine, and Aubrey adjusted her dress. Tate took his finger and lifted her chin to his lips one more time. After taking her lips into a passionate, savoring kiss, he said, "Aubrey, right here and now is where I always want to start again with you." She kissed him quickly, her too knowing she wanted this, all of this, whatever he had to offer, even if stolen moments like they just shared.

Tate maintained every last bit of willpower he could find and took her back to her car at the bar. He kissed her again before she jumped down from his truck. He kissed her lips, her nose, then to her forehead before taking a last breath of her hair. He needed to remember every moment with her, as something extraordinary was happening between them.

Seated in her car, she clicked the seatbelt into place. Her fingers rolled over her lips again and again. He could see her hesitating. He hoped she wasn't second guessing the time they just shared. It was then she pursed her lips to her fingertips and freed them, displaying a blown kiss in his direction. His hand went into the air. He caught it then brought it to his chest and his heart as she smiled.

He stood and watched her drive off until her car lights darkened. He missed her already. He hoped he would sleep peacefully this night with her in his heart. One thing he needed to do first, though, was rid himself of one demon, and that was the tacos she forgot in his truck that were for Emerson. Tate made a point to toss them in the first street trash can he passed on the way to his beach house rental.

Chapter Fourteen

R EED SHOWED UP AT TATE'S door step as promised and
let himself in. Tate never locked his doors, especially
here in this town. Reed made his way to the main bedroom
and dropped his bag on the floor. He lay back in the large
king bed. This was nice. He could grow to love it, especially
with a wide expanse of the beach just beyond. No wonder
Tate wasn't budging from here.

Actually, Reed knew it was the girl. It was Aubrey that
Tate couldn't stop mentioning every time he and Reed
spoke. Reed hoped, staying briefly with Tate, that he would
have the chance to meet her. The main reason he was here,
though, was to assist the Cape May Police department with
his drug expertise. Previously, they all spoke and scheduled
his week to put their plans in place. Lately, too much activity
had been brewing about a huge deal going down. If Reed,
Tate, and local cops had any say, it would be the drug dealers
taken down. Even though it was the middle of the day,
listening to the recurring sounds of the water crashing
outside, Reed drifted.

Tate parked his truck in the driveway, and he caught the

sight of his own smile in the rear view mirror. He had a great workout which was satisfying, but this smile was carried over from spending time with Aubrey last night. He noticed that Reed had arrived while he was at the gym. Entering the house without even calling his name, he immediately saw Reeds his feet hung over the side of the bed. If his friend was claiming the bed for his visit, he was welcome to it. No argument would come from Tate. Reed had helped to give Tate a life back, and he owed him so much for that. Glad that Reed was here, tired from his work out, Tate fell into the living room chair and threw back a cold beer. He was just about finished when Reed came out to join him.

"So I heard no complaints about me taking over your main bedroom," Reed joked and swapped out Tate's empty beer for another cold one.

"None from me. Welcome to my new place, not too bad." Tate looked outward.

"Feels like paradise. I may become very used to this. First, there is a girl that is perfect in your eyes and now this scenery. I think I may have to move here, too."

"You are welcome here anytime. I don't know how long I will remain after we clean this town up. Have to wait and see how this all plays out." Tate clinked his beer to Reed's.

"We have received a solid tip that the drug deal is going to take place next week and at your girl's house. A few highly connected guys are heading into town and already made their reservations at a local inn. They don't travel to where there isn't any action."

"I have to make certain she's not there. I *do not* want her involved in this."

"I understand, but we can't guarantee she won't be at her own house."

"Reed, if you give me word when it's about to happen, I will personally distract her away from there."

"I will keep you informed every step of the way, just as we have done in our past takedowns. Nothing has changed, just this one has better scenery for sure," Reed commented, staring out the window along the beach. "Hey, Tate, look at this INCREDIBLE VIEW!" Reed's focus concentrated as his eyes opened wide.

Tate's interest peeked from the excitement in Reed's voice. Joining him to see outside, they watched two girls walking past his beach rental. One was so beautiful. She had on a black sundress and was carrying her sandals. The other was not even a second glance to him. Aubrey and her friend from the bakery were a nice vision, walking down the beach. He was not going to miss this opportunity. He went out on the balcony and hollered to her, "Hey, Beautiful!"

Reed followed him out. "Do you know them?"

"Well, the prettiest one is Aubrey."

Reed didn't have to be a detective to know exactly which girl. Tate couldn't contain his expression that matched the petite girl with the biggest smile.

"So what brings you girls up this way?" Tate asked.

"Actually, we are having an end of the season party at our place tonight. If you both want to come, there is plenty of food and alcohol to be had." Tessa smiled sexily at Reed.

In a quiet tone, Tate told Reed, "Watch that one. I will

fill you in later as I guess we are attending a party tonight."

"We will catch you later, ladies. Thanks for the invite."

AUBREY TURNED TO WALK DOWN the beach. Aubrey felt so happy; she finally knew which house he was renting. She didn't want to stalk him. She heard he was down this way. Usually, when she passed the house from the front, his truck wasn't around, so she was guessing it was one of at least seven homes he could be renting. Often she would drive by a few times, but never saw his truck. Today, after finishing most of the preparations for the beach party, she suggested to take a walk with Tessa like they often did for girl talk. She hoped to see Tate or catch a glimpse of him maybe from the beachside to which home he was at.

She was feeling very confident and pretty in her new dress and glad if even for a moment that he saw what she was wearing. Now with Tessa inviting these two guys and a few that were in another house along their walk, the party was expanding in size. It usually did when they're the hosts.

Good thing Aubrey knew Levi and Pete well, that way they would warn her if the party was loud rather than issue her a citation. Since it was off-season in the town, she doubted anyone would be affected. Emerson was the one that led some previous parties to becoming outrageous. He would bring in many of his construction workers, and they would drink till they passed out on the beach. Tonight should be very interesting. Aubrey hoped Tate would make an appearance.

✧   ✧   ✧

"WELL, SHE IS DEFINITELY INTO you. Did you see her face light up?" Reed was teasing Tate.

"Yeah, but she lives with her boyfriend. Small obstacle, I would say. Hey tonight you can run interference. And by the way, that friend with her, I think she is already sleeping with Aubrey's guy. I saw her with him at the bar quite a while ago. No doubt in my mind on that."

"Well, I will steer clear of her and work on what I can gather on Emerson. This could be enjoyable work time."

Tate hit the shower first while Reed was talking on the phone with Levi, going over some further details of their sting. Levi of all people, Tate shook his head. Mr. All American Cop was now going to be knee deep in a huge drug bust here in quiet Cape May.

Tate let the water run over his body. He had held onto restraint with Aubrey earlier, and tonight, just seeing her in the late day sun on the beach, he wanted to lift her up and carry her here to his place. He leaned his head under the water and let it flow. For a long time, he used to stand just like this, thinking it would wash away the demons that attached to him. Finally today, it seemed to lift them some. As long as nightfall wasn't upon him where he had to sleep, he should be okay. It was the nightmares that haunted him so. Those he couldn't shake.

Reed pounded on the door. "Hey, Prima Donna, keep some hot water for me." Tate laughed, taking in a mouth full of the water.

✧ ✧ ✧

AUBREY DIDN'T WANT TO DRINK heavily this evening. She wanted to enjoy her invited friends, and finally, she was to have some time with Emerson as he had been awfully busy with work as of late. She wasn't sure which projects he was constructing, and he didn't know what bakery orders she was filling. Since getting back together they passed each other emotionally detached, often only sharing a kiss here, a hug, and one tryst in the bathroom, it was very quick in case Tessa awoke.

Other than brief simple moments with Emerson, Aubrey spent all her other time thinking of Tate whom she was feeling more romantically attached to. Even in the bakery as she iced cupcakes, she wore more icing than went to the cake top when she thought of him. Walking the beach line earlier with Tessa was fun as they caught up on a lot of girl talk, but the one thing Tessa didn't reveal was who this mystery man was she was seeing. Too many nights she came in late and smiled all day. Her heavily made up face also wore a satisfied expression that she had fallen for one guy. It was something she couldn't hide.

Aubrey took in the gorgeous view of the beach homes that lined the shore. She supposed she, too, displayed that air about her, only she knew it was for Tate, disguising it well in Emerson's presence. Her lips had smiled when her eyes connected with the guy standing out on the balcony, very handsome guy for sure. It was Tate. Then to her surprise, another handsome man stepped outside, joining him. She smiled pleasantly at the other guy but she was so excited inside that Tate saw her in her new dress. She hoped he liked it. Aubrey wanted to twirl around in it for him, thinking how nice it would be to have him come down from the balcony and pick her up, spinning her playfully over the salt water. Instead, he hollered down and never took his eyes from her.

She did check out his body. His dark shorts hung low and he was shirtless with color across his chest and on the one arm. It was beautiful, like a canvas of powerful roses and a dedication of such. Yes, his tattoo was definitely dedicated to someone, perhaps his mother. Aubrey's eyes followed the lines on his skin intently until she heard Tessa invite them to the party. Oh shit. How was this going to work out? Aubrey and Emerson there and in walks the ever amazing Tate. Her heart skipped in its sequence. She rolled her lips, tucking them in, holding them inward. She was nervous, but more notably excited. Tate always made her feel that way.

When she turned to walk with Tessa back to her home, she never returned a glance at the men. Tessa did and said, "Yep, they are both staring this way." Both girls enjoyed their time on the beach, and once back to the house, they busied with the final pre-party tasks. Emerson was in charge of the alcohol, and Tessa was preparing some finger foods in the kitchen. Aubrey stayed on the beach area, putting together table arrangements of sand and flowers. She was thrilled the weather lately had remained unseasonably warm even as the early autumn days had arrived. She would have thought to set up the party indoors if the evening temperature was too cool outside, but the past few weeks a warm front hung over the east coast, and summer weather lingered which wasn't a bad thing. In the glass jars, she first poured blue dyed beach sand. Then she pressed a white tea light candle firmly in place. Setting several of the jars together, her final touch was loosely scattering yellow and white roses around them. A simple decorative design, it pulled the yellow color of the chairs' fabric all together.

Glancing up through the open balcony doors viewing the kitchen, she spotted Tessa and Emerson exchanging cheerful smiles. It was surely going to be a fun evening. Aubrey was glad that her roommate and guy were good friends. Aubrey knew that if she kept things on the path with Tate that she was going to have to let Emerson loose and kick him out of her home again. He hadn't been living there too long this time, but it was always feeling off, not like when they first moved in together. Aubrey felt she would know the timing of when to talk with Emerson. Right now wasn't it. It was party time.

Cutting the last of the white and yellow roses, she almost slashed her finger. She caught a moment between Emerson and Tessa. He was admiring her outfit as she assertively modeled in front of him. Next, he was cheering her along as she proceeded to dance seductively to the music that played loudly. Aubrey watched Emerson join her moves. He danced very close to her body, never touching her, but it seemed intimate. Oh, it had to be just friendly. Aubrey couldn't be jealous. Her feelings were drifting farther away from Emerson like the sand and the waves of an outward tide.

Aubrey distracted herself from staring at them, positioning the final flowers and cleaning up the excess greens from the tables. She touched the delicate rose petal and felt its softness. It was how Tate first kissed her lips, sweeping across them delicately. Tate had tested the waters with her. Then, when he full out kissed her lips, she went breathless. Never in all the kisses in her life had she gone winded. She lost her breath when Emerson kissed her too hard and fast, but not like the lips crossing over hers as Tate's did, slowly, passionately, and she wanted them to remain right on hers.

"Do you need help?" Tessa was at Aubrey's side, and Aubrey never sensed her coming up close to her.

"No, actually, I think I can handle them both, I mean, these." Aubrey blushed. Tessa moved over to the chairs and fluffed the pillows on them. The whole atmosphere and evening weather were perfect. Aubrey never understood the whole fluff the pillows thing. They never moved or deflated, but whatever. At least Tessa moved over there and missed her verbal slipup.

TATE TOOK A FRIENDLY HIT from Reed as he punched his shoulder after they jumped into the truck, "Are you ready for this?" Reed probed as Tate appeared worried. "Yeah and no, I like her a lot, but she is with this guy we need to take down so it's love of our job and love of her...Wait, did I just say I love her?" Tate shook his head.

"I think I heard you loud and clear." Reed laughed. "How many beers did you have? Wait, it was only two so you know what you are talking about."

When they pulled up to the curb line of Aubrey's beach

home, Tate parked and waited. He was observing some of the people who were just arriving. "We should run all these tags on these cars and see if anything comes up as well," Tate commented and knew Reed was on it, as he instantly took photos on his phone without the flash. With their watchful eyes, Tate and Reed made sure no one saw them checking out the vehicles as they leisurely approached the front door.

The front door was open and welcoming to everyone. Emerson was on the far side of the living room. Tate remembered the layout of the house from the time he brought Aubrey home and put her to bed. He remembered carrying her down the hall and laying her onto her bed, her arm reaching out to him to stay with her.

He respected her enough to not take her in her own home while she was with another man living under her roof. It was becoming increasingly risky, though, as his feelings were growing beyond his heart radius, and he was slipping and saying he loved her already.

WOW. She came in from outside, and the wind had blown her hair and slightly lifted her dress. It was a very short dress, and again Tate was dazed and captivated with her remarkable beauty. Several strands of her hair were out of place like the night he laid her head to her pillow. He remembered tucking it into lay behind her ears. His eyes could not stop roving from her black gem sandals to her thighs. She was showing a lot of skin on them this evening. Her dress even had little holes in the fabric allowing him a peek at her skin underneath. He wanted her so badly.

Tate tilted his head in awe at her smile, and her eyes shined from her cheeks. He had her. She was charmed by him. There could be no one else in this room because, at this moment, it was just her and him. Reed handed him a cold beer, severing his concentration. Tate took a big swig from the bottle. It tasted so good. He then returned his focus toward Aubrey because that was better. Tessa tugged Aubrey's arm, leading her to the kitchen for help with plating up more food. Tate switched his sight to Emerson, who was staring, too, and why wouldn't he be? Aubrey was lovely. Although Emerson's eyes were focused directly on the right and that was where Tessa was positioned near the kitchen counter.

Reed and Tate worked the room, talking with a few people here and there, and they fit in perfectly. Emerson caught Tate's eye and walked over toward him. "Hey, who invited you guys? I am kidding with you two, but if you want more than beer, you know I am good for that." Emerson was boldly and openly offering drugs.

"We received invites from a beautiful blonde haired girl that hollered up to us when she and Aubrey were walking on the beach earlier. Reed and I were enjoying beers on the balcony, and they happened past." Tate emphasized beautiful blonde, recalling seeing Emerson and her kissing before. Reed nodded in agreement to Tate's recap.

"Just messing with you. Tessa is our roommate, Aubrey and mine, and had I seen you at the gym today, I would have told you come on by." Emerson looked at Reed. "I already met Tate, and you are?"

"Reed. I used to work with Tate until he became a big real estate tycoon. Buying land and building everyplace."

"That's what I hear, the town is buzzing he is here to do big business." Emerson offered again, "Gentlemen, I have the connections to make your stay even finer. From drink to drugs, you name it, I have it or will acquire it." Emerson was then pulled by his friend.

From the photos that Reed and Tate had, he was Damon. Damon whispered something in his ear, and they both headed down the hall like they were going to the bathroom together, only men never did that shit. They entered a room that was before Aubrey's bedroom and closed the door. Tate was certain they were doing drugs. It was his time to have a second, or at least five seconds, with Aubrey.

He entered the kitchen as she was cutting up more veggies to plate. The large knife set him back a moment. Taking a deep breath, he went over and grabbed her hand. "Aubrey, tuck your fingers in when you cut these, like this."

He had her hand in his and showed her so she wouldn't slice her fingers. The intensity ran through both of them. Tessa had left the kitchen when Tate was entering it, and she gave him a wink. She seemed set to talk to Reed. Tate was assured Reed would talk with her, but he wasn't bringing her back to Tate's tonight or any night. Tate could see Reed with someone like Lacey. He did notice Lacey out by the beach from his view off the balcony. He hoped Levi would show up and possibly make his feelings known to her. If he didn't, Reed would be all over a nice girl like her.

Tate pressed Aubrey into the center island of the kitchen.

His body behind her and hard as he pressed farther for her to feel him. He smiled, outwardly still helping her cut the veggies. Aubrey took her hand to her side, pretending to wipe it on the dishtowel, and grabbed Tate's ass and pulled him tightly to her. She wanted him right there. It was a good thing the food was out doors under a canvas overhang and they were the only two here in the kitchen.

Tate took his hand up under her dress slowly. Still keeping her body innocently pressed forward and out of view with the island, his fingers trailed up her thigh. Fuck him now, all the blood just raced to one place on his body, and he was rock hard. He just touched her panties, and they weren't panties. It was a thin string. She was wearing a thong. He was completely undone. He trailed the edge of the thong with his finger. She groaned lightly. He felt her squirm. He knew this was the wrong place for them, but he couldn't force the arousal of his hard on to subside.

Aubrey added fuel to it, taking her hand from his ass and holding it over his hand to lead his finger closer to her entrance. Her soft groans grew heated, her smile larger on her lips, and her face reddening. His finger tip touched the entrance. Wet. He dipped it into her several times as she let out light breaths with a tiny noise escaping her throat that he could hear even with the music going on. Fuck him, he needed to gain control. One of them did. He pulled his finger from under her dress and brought it to his nose. Her scent. He had her scent on him. He would remember that all evening long because he couldn't be this close to her any more.

There was a plan to take Emerson down, and it needed to be carried out. Tate couldn't let Aubrey know, because if she let it out to Emerson, it could be all over. Tate moved from her and leaned over to the sink and ran cold water on his hands. He also patted his face with the wetness. That probably wouldn't help, but it would take him down a bit from the moment.

Aubrey pulled herself together and tucked her fingers in and chopped hard at the celery stalks. Reed was positioned at the kitchen door. He let his friend take that moment. Hell, he would have, too. Aubrey was lovely. He was happy that his friend had found someone. He knew when he saw Tate throw water on his face that he was undone and trying to gain control. No one entered the kitchen. Reed stood guard, taking charge and directing people away from the kitchen area toward the location of the food and drinks. His watchful eye for his friend kept the kitchen unoccupied of others.

Tate couldn't leave her like that, though. He walked over, adjusting his jeans. He leaned to her neck from behind. "You and me, we will have our time together. I want you to know that those five-point-three seconds we just had were pure bliss to me and will carry me for a long time. In case you haven't realized, I am falling for you hard, girl." He lifted her hair and placed a gentle, lingering kiss to her neck. He wasn't concerned if anyone noticed. He wanted her to understand that he deeply cared for her and would wait to be with her.

The knife slicing through the veggies silenced. She embraced each tender touch from his lips that trailed along the nape of her neck traveling toward her ear. Softly, he whispered, "I get so lost in you."

"I KNOW. I FEEL THE same," Aubrey said lightly. She tingled with pleasure when he announced he was falling for her. She already had felt his hardness and the effect she had on him. She calmed herself and her thoughts of him whisking her up into his arms, carrying her away in his hold to somewhere private. She would cherish his words that they would be together. She also believed that time was not far off.

TATE DROPPED THE REST OF her hair to her shoulder. He adjusted himself again before emerging from behind the kitchen island. Her giving him confirmation of her feelings was all he needed. He could enjoy this party across from her the rest of the night, even if Emerson had his arm around her or kissed her. Tate knew she was his—well, not yet, but one day. In his heart, she was already taking over space to be his.

As he left the kitchen, he observed the hallway that led to the bedrooms. Emerson emerged from one of the bedrooms. Oddly, though, Tate saw him lock the door. He wondered if Aubrey knew he locked doors in her home. Why would he secure a door? Reed had seen it, too, and went to see what was going on in there. Tate needed the bathroom to relieve himself is a grand way. Both guys walked in the hallway. "So you guys ready to really party?" Emerson reopened the door, and there—exposed on the table—were bricks of cocaine and money spread all over.

This guy was dealing and not just some tiny eight ball or dime bag. It was a large shipment. Reed noticed the storage tote next to it that he probably stored it in when not showing off his goods. Come to think of it, earlier a few men stayed very briefly at the party that stood out, they were out of place for a beach party. They were clearly carrying big money in their high end suits, trying too hard to fit in. It was obvious to Reed. Who wears a pricey suit to a beach party?

Reed's eyes widened. Hell, they could take Emerson down tonight on his deals locked inside the one bedroom. He knew, though, this was the tip of much more, and in the days ahead, when the law did intervene, it would certainly be a record bust.

"I have to hit the toilet," Tate spoke to remove himself from the room. He needed to get his remaining hard-on under control. The blood was slowly finding its way back to other parts of his body.

"You want any?" Emerson prompted Reed, waving his hand to display his goods.

"In a bit, I'll come back. Let me enjoy another beer or two first. Plus, there is a girl I was about to move on, so let me get back there."

"Always a girl that will sway you. I have my own nice girl, if you catch what I'm saying, and I also have another that is the perfect girl for me. I keep them close, but secretly separated. Eventually, I will end up tossing away the nice one. Nice is purely a temporary means for me." His tone was arrogant, his mannerisms cocky—this guy was too proud of himself. If he could have patted himself on his back, he would have. Reed agreed with Tate. This guy was bad news, scum that needed to be removed.

Reed knew without a doubt he was speaking of Tessa and Aubrey, and there was no confusing the "nice" one. He was glad Tate didn't hear their conversation, or he would have already flattened Emerson to the floor. Many times, Reed saw Tate stand alone in the faces of the drug dealers before their backup arrived. Reed knew this situation could be even more dangerous because still seeded in Tate's mind was his loss of Callie. That's shit that was never forgotten. Emerson could easily have set Tate off tonight with his comments.

When Tate came back from the bathroom, Reed was back at the corner of the living room, taking in all the scenery and watching the party unfold. Mentally noting, if this was where they would be taking Emerson down, how the rooms were laid out. Tate knew exactly what was running through his friend's head. What was running through Tate's was that moment he was able to touch her, to feel her, and his desire craved to taste her.

She stood several feet across the room from him, remaining the courteous hostess. He knew under her dress was a thong. His fingers had traveled its thin hold. Tate had to look away for a distraction so he didn't get hard again. Tessa brushed closely past him in the hallway, he assumed heading to the bathroom. He was wrong. Emerson appeared and pulled her into his chest. They privately entered the bedroom, Aubrey's bedroom. The door shut behind them. This fucking guy was bold. He didn't care who he hurt. His girl was in the living room being kind to the guests, and he was in her bedroom with her roommate.

Tate stood next to Reed, quietly explaining what just unfolded. The last thing he wanted was Aubrey heading to her
bedroom. Reed thought he would be good diversion so he
approached her and introduced himself as Tate's friend and
asked about the lovely town. Always a topic Aubrey boasted
about, they sat on the sofa, and she smiled, talking with him
and playing tour guide from her home. Tate grabbed some
fresh beers and walked over and handed one to Reed, but
left them in conversation. Aubrey didn't break her words,
but her eyes followed Tate's and smiled brightly.

A short time later, Tessa staggered a bit in her walk from
the bedroom, fixing herself. Emerson walked behind her,
but then unlocked the side room and escaped into there for
a long time. Tessa went up to Reed and Aubrey and
squeezed herself into the sofa space and the conversation.

Tate was flipping inside. This girl just had sex with Emerson in Aubrey's bedroom. He was certain of it. How
damaging was this going to be to Aubrey? He hoped she
would leave Emerson and fall completely for him. That,
though, sometimes seemed like total fiction. Still Tate
remained hopeful for that day they would have their own
love story.

The night closed with a bang and beautifully displayed
fireworks. Had there been that loud popping sound without
the announcement of the fireworks beginning, both Tate
and Reed would have been seeing who was first to reach the
truck for their guns. It was the end of the season party, but
not an end of anything for Tate. He watched and wished on

the lights as they shot in the sky to someday lie with Aubrey and watch them together.

The party ended, and soon dawn would be awakened. Tate and Reed had left late in the morning, too many beers and too many yoyo times of Tate having a hard-on and then it reoccurring again, especially when Aubrey bent over in the kitchen to tie up the trash. It was a simple act that showed a peek of her ass and the black thong that was in place underneath. He had the chance earlier to touch that thong, but more he had touched her…right there. *Oh, don't go there again, Tate.* Yet another hard-on was developing. He could torture himself no more.

They said their good byes. He hugged her, but all he could say softly in her ear was, "Girl, you have me." Emerson came across the room to say his goodbyes to them, too. He walked out with them. Knowing Aubrey was clear out of hearing his conversation, he said. "I want to be honest with you guys. I have some good shit coming in here in about a week. It's a heavy deal that we are cutting up for a lot of our connections. I could use some help if you want to help me, and you can take some stash for yourselves as well. Think on it and let me know. I got a good vibe with you guys. You are cut just like me. One thing, don't share any of this with my girl. She is clueless. I like her that way. I have another that is smarter and keeps me coming back for more if you know what I mean." Emerson arrogantly boosted openly. "Guys, thanks for dropping in, time for me to go back in and play nice with my Bree."

Reed pushed back Tate with all he could with just the

force of his hand. Tate saw his own fireworks. He wanted to take Emerson down to the fucking ground and have him eating fists of the pebbles on the driveway. Emerson saw no reaction from Tate, as he had turned and was headed back into the house. With that, he and Reed hit the street to head up to Tate's place numerous beach houses away. Once back at Tate's place, Reed shouted, "Night." He headed to Tate's bedroom. Looks like Tate was taking on the sofa tonight. It was fine. The images of Aubrey in his head would clearly stay with him till morning.

Chapter Fifteen

C ONSUMING ALCOHOL COULD CONTRIBUTE TO altering people's thoughts and moods. Early this morning as everyone slept from the party that just concluded, others heads were spinning out of control. Tate's mind was reeling over Emerson's words. Fussing on the sofa and unable to sleep, Tate punched his pillow to tap down his upset. His head later fell back, comforted by the fluffy cushion. He finally drifted because the beers took over and her beautiful face appeared. Aubrey was lovely. He turned on his side, knowing the hardness was not the pillow being uncomfortable, but his body reacting to his thoughts.

Patience, Tate, he told himself, *that fucker is coming down, and she will be yours. She is yours already in mind and touch. One day you will have her, all of her, and no fucked up guy like Emerson will have a moment in her presence.* He would have a second chance to be there for a person he loved.

He was brought here for a reason. It had changed from the original course, but everything from the day he stepped off the train here in this Cape May had pulled him in her direction. Like a magnet, he was drawn to Aubrey, and when it's right, they would be together. His smile expanded on his face as his pants did below. He drifted off and was not even thinking of any demons from the past making their way into his head. She was his for this evening. Remembering her black dress and—oh, how could he forget—her thong underneath, he'd made her wet and squirming at his touch. He, too, was now moving in his sleep. It took quite some time for him to let out a relaxed breath, and he was at rest. Deep asleep.

WHEN THE FIREWORKS LAUNCHED EARLIER, the vengeance ignited within Tessa. The loud noises that exploded in the night sky brought her back to a moment when she lost someone she loved. The crackling and popping display of color reminded her of the sound of bullets that ripped through her brother. She lay in her room knowing that just down the hall was the man that held her heart now. He had joined with her long ago in pushing drugs, and when he learned her brother was taken out in a job gone wrong, he loved her and told her they would seek revenge.

It was easy to find out who was behind her brother's loss of life. A wealthy old man in Hagerstown ran drugs and didn't keep it too much of a secret. Apparently, Tessa's brother became hungry for more work and drop-offs, and when he asked the old man for more, he was told he was greedy and thus the old guy slowed down his need for his usefulness. What happened, though, was Tessa's brother Bryan was in over his head.

He worked a bit with their cousin Jackson on some real estate deals—some of which were on the up and up and some shady. Bryan also tried to skim drugs and money from the old man, and he caught wind of it. One evening, Bryan and the old man exchanged harsh words. It concluded with Bryan being dismissed from working for the man. During their talk Bryan's eyes traveled the room, there was something threatening in the old man's tone that made him nervous. He caught sight of a photo of the old guy and a young, beautiful girl. He had known the guy had a daughter.

When the old man went to take a piss, Bryan took the photo from the frame and folded it in his jacket pocket. He thought possibly one day that photo would be useful. The old guy returned from the bathroom and shouted some final words to someone on the phone. He then escorted Bryan to the front door without any further conversation. When he left the old guy's place, he knew he was being tailed. He wasn't too far down the road, and a car tapped his bumper hard from behind. Thinking quickly, Bryan was about to floor his vehicle and maneuver distance away from them, but his window glass shattered as bullets fired, never giving him that chance.

Tessa received the call from the authorities to come to Hagerstown to identify her brother. The police said it was a random shooting. They found no drugs on him or anything. They did find a photograph that they kept for evidence. They knew the photo was of a local guy and his daughter. At the hospital, Tessa was comforted by a police officer for her loss, and he shared with her the photo her brother had on him. She asked in a nonintrusive manner who the guy and his daughter were. She obtained a name, and that was all she needed. She would return to Hagerstown another day, and this old guy would suffer a loss like she had felt.

Tessa turned in her bed. She yearned for Emerson's precise touch that made her body explode. Earlier in the night, he made her come, but that time was too rushed. All the hotel romps that they met up for were often too quick as well. He promised her that after this next huge deal that finally they both were taking off from sleepy town to the beaches of Costa Rica, where he was already setting up their future living accommodations. That they would be able to rise and fall in each other's arms every waking day. He needed this cover with Aubrey a little bit longer. He told Tessa that, lately, he and Aubrey didn't have sex much. He wanted to keep his little perfect girl happy. He knew she was busy at the bakery, and that was all that consumed her life.

Tessa didn't feel one ounce of remorse in befriending Aubrey. She was too easy to have become her friend. One evening at Deacon's Den, Tessa sat next to Aubrey. Tessa had stares from all the men in the bar. Aubrey asked her, "How do you do it? They all like you." Tessa knew then to have Emerson, the hottest guy in town, hook into Aubrey and give her attention, and they could use her lovely home out at the edge of the beach for all their dealings in the quiet town, totally unsuspected.

That night at the bar, Tessa faked tears, telling Aubrey the guys may like her but she needed to have a real girlfriend to be a true friend to her. She told Aubrey that she recently lost her brother and she couldn't bear to live in the apartment they once shared one beach town over. She told Aubrey her cousin Jackson handled real estate and he was searching the Cape May area for a place for her but hadn't been successful.

Aubrey had been sucked in. She gave Tessa her napkin to wipe her fake tears and said, "Actually, I need a roommate to help me with half the expenses, and I have a nice beach home at the far end of town. Very quiet but lovely views. I know who your cousin is. He is so nice to everyone in town. Perhaps you would like to room with me?"

In between her fake tears, Tessa smiled inside and shook her head lightly in agreement. Now here, she lies in bed alone. A few years have come and passed. Steps down the hall from her was her lover, who was still stringing along her set up bestie. It's almost game time, though. A big deal, a lot of cash, a place already set up for them from monies that Emerson had been skimming from deals and his family's business. It was all falling into place perfectly.

Tessa needed a drink of water as her drinking tonight had left her parched. She rose from her bed, only wearing a tee shirt, and wished Emerson would find her in the kitchen and also quench her sexual desire.

In the darkness, her wishes became true. Emerson couldn't sleep. He had done too many lines that messed his head up this evening and kept his heart racing. He was sitting on a stool at the counter when she came into the dark kitchen. She knew her way to the refrigerator with just the light of the moon peeking in the balcony doors. She reached in and grabbed a cold water bottle. Suddenly, he grabbed her. He wrapped his arms around her and brought her to stand in front of him. He lifted her tee shirt over her head.

Emerson grabbed at her breasts and sucked hardly. He liked it rough. They had to be quiet. If Aubrey heard a moan or odd noise, she would be out here. At least the master bedroom was located a distance away, and the waves were crashing to the shoreline loudly this evening. Emerson positioned their master bedroom balcony doors wide open for the fresh air and to stifle his groans while having sex with Tessa. He didn't stop with her breasts.

He rose from the stool, bent her naked body over the granite counter, and dove inside her. He gave it to her hard. He had wanted her all night long, but for appearance's sake, he stood with his hand resting on the shoulder of Aubrey and a painted smile. His earlier tryst with Tessa in his and Aubrey's bedroom was just an appetizer. He wanted her to quiver not from the coolness of the tiled floor to her bare feet or her arms holding her balance on the cold granite surface, but he wanted her to shake from him pounding her. Emerson loved her and wanted her and pretending all this time with Aubrey was taking a toll on him.

Their plan was derailed once when Aubrey caught Emerson with a heavy load of drugs and told him to leave her home. That ended the ease of Emerson and Tessa screwing whenever Aubrey was away from the house. With his recent return back to Aubrey's home, he acquired free range again. Taking advantage of that, he was at this moment shaking his release deep inside Tessa, giving her every ounce of his built up tension from this evening watching her in her sexy outfit as she worked the party crowd. He also saw his own friend Damon checking out Tessa this evening. Damon knew Emerson saw another person besides Aubrey, but didn't know it was Tessa. Emerson thought about that as he was plunging her harder and harder again. He wanted to make her know she was his. Only his.

Tessa bit her lip tightly as he pulled out and then thrust powerfully back into her. She came with fireworks exploding in her mind. Yes this is just what she needed to allow her to sleep well through the morning's light.

Tessa thought she heard Emerson moan "Mine" as he came inside her. They only remained in the kitchen a bit longer. He walked her down the hallway, kissed her lips, left her, and headed toward the master bedroom. He was becoming possessive, just as she had always been, and it almost tripped them up to being caught by the law long ago.

In her room, she took the water bottle and rubbed it to her throat to cool herself down. Emerson had her in flames. Her feet pattered across the tiles in her room. She climbed in bed. Tessa drank the water and set the empty bottle on the side table. She touched her throat again and remembered his touch as her eyes tired. Deep into her sleep, nightmares paid her a visit. Her blissful sleep of being sexually satisfied was marred with her standing with a blood drenched knife.

It was to be an easy hit. Their intent was to rob the house and tie up the daughter—Callie was her name, and she was a beautiful girl. They would take photos of Callie and then send them to the old guy and demand money, a plan that

Tessa and Emerson worked through in their heads and planned for a long time. Not that money would bring Tessa her brother back, but they would demand this old fuck pay and dearly. Plus if they roughed up the daughter a bit it would be icing on the cake.

When they entered the house, they heard the girl on the phone speaking to another that she thought someone entered the house. Tessa knew their time was limited now and they had to move swiftly. She gathered some things of value and tossed them in a duffle downstairs and then would join Emerson who was already heading to contain Callie. Upstairs, Emerson pulled his gun on her and placed a single finger to his lips for her to remain silent.

Callie stood several feet from him, silent and frozen. The only movement in the room was the bulge growing in his pants and his eyes considering this lovely girl in her short nightgown. Nervously, her phone slipped from her hand and fell to the carpet toward him. Slowly, he retrieved her phone. She stood motionless and frightened, at his mercy. Emerson gradually walked backwards, taking several steps and keeping his attention focused forward on her. He took aim and tossed her phone, landing it in the master bathroom toilet. He stepped a few slow paces back and lowered the toilet lid, and pulled the bathroom door shut. He was relieved that was silenced. The next sound that filled the air was only of Tessa footsteps approaching on the stairs. He told the terrified girl no one would hurt her. They wanted to rob her of what her father took from them.

"Wow, she is fucking beautiful!" Emerson exclaimed

when Tessa entered the bedroom.

Tessa watched Emerson closely and saw something that still today haunted her. His expression was excited and aroused. He wanted to do this girl. She could sense he was tempted. Something raged in her. Maybe it was that this girl's father took her brother from her and that could never be replaced. Tessa walked over toward Callie. She was stunning. Tessa studied Emerson, noticing his eyes fixed with desire for this girl.

"So do you want to fuck her before we leave here? Do you? Do you want to have her while I watch or have both of us together?" Emerson was silent, but his eager smile and hard-on both grew. "Emerson, I really want you to enjoy this…because that is NOT going to happen!" Tessa reached up and, not according to any of their plans, slashed Callie's throat and let her fall to the carpeted floor below.

Emerson stood shocked. "Why…why did you do that?"

"I saw how she excited you. I deserve to be desired by you, not her! Her father took my brother from me, and she was not taking you, too. A life for a life." They gathered more valuables, making it appear like a random robbery. Their original plan to capture a photo of Callie alive held against her will in exchange for money was altered. She was dead so there wasn't any money to be had.

Emerson loved Tessa and eventually came around to the fact that, if someone took a family member from him, he would kill, too. He knew he didn't want Callie, but she sure was pleasing to the eyes. That too set Tessa in a frenzy. To this day, they followed up on if the police in Hagerstown ever found who murdered Callie. No one had been found or connected in the past few years, only a few random leads that led to no place. Most of the talk was that it was because of the old man that his wife and daughter were murdered.

Tessa and Emerson did make off with a lot of cash and belongings from the home that night. On the way out, Tessa noticed a lovely wedding photograph displayed across the room. The man in the photo was handsome as far as she could see, very handsome. She smirked at the frame vengefully, pleased with herself knowing the husband would soon find his lovely wife gone, just like her brother's life that was taken from her. It wasn't planned this way, but Tessa single handily took out her own justice.

Emerson had thought about climbing into bed with the old guy for business, but Emerson was pretty well connected with several drug dealers and he liked to keep his control. Knowing that old guy took out Tessa's brother defenselessly in cold blood boiled in him, and he wanted revenge as he knew Bryan and he was in love with his sister. In the end, Tessa took the old man out as she took away the last love he had. His daughter. It was agreed that Tessa and Emerson would never speak of Hagerstown or what happened on the evening Tessa's jealousy and revenge escalated out of control.

They made it look like a burglary, exiting the home via the rear door and smashing that window from the outside. Earlier, Emerson was skillful in disabling the alarm to gain entrance. He knew it would gain them some time, but not certain how much. Emerson and Tessa were assured no one saw them enter or exit the home.

THE BRILLIANT LIGHTS DANCED IN the night sky, and her eyes roamed to catch his as the sparkles cascaded downward. Aubrey gave every glance to him. Tate caught each one until the finale of the fireworks concluded. She lay in bed wondering if Emerson was going to try to have sex with her this evening. She pulled the sheet around her snuggly like a barrier. She had brushed her teeth and rinsed her mouth and stumbled into her own bed. She drank a lot here and there this evening in between her talking with friends, and she did grab a few bites of food to fill her belly, which let her drink some more. She drank to keep her thoughts of Tate tapped down.

The crab stack that she made of crabmeat and avocado with tortilla chip triangles filled her belly, and a later snack of some flatbread pizza soaked up some more of her drinks she consumed. When Tate hugged her goodbye, she didn't want to let him go. She saw Emerson engaged in a serious conversation with Damon, a guy who always creeped her out a bit.

She did, though, smile good night to Reed, and he made her feel very at ease. He was warm and friendly, and she liked he sat with her and actually listened to her talk about this small beach town. She was sure she was boring him, but she had his complete attention, which was kind. Her petite arms wrapped partially around Tate's waist. She felt how solid and fit his body was as she lightly hugged him in a friendly manner, but didn't want to release her hold. She wanted him to take her to bed. Not fuck her like she felt Emerson did, but make love to her, to every inch of her.

Her hands and wishes slipped away in a flash as he pulled back and thanked her for the party. "Good night, Aubrey." Her name was held safe again within his lips. She tossed later in bed, uneasy that Emerson was back here and not certain how that was going to play out. She felt the bed dip as Emerson climbed into his side. He moved up behind her. She pretended to sleep. His fingertip trailed along her shoulder that wasn't covered with the bed sheet. She didn't budge. She felt him turn in the bed to face the opposite way. She let out a soft breath of thankfulness. She thought well into the night about Tate. Her mind exhausted and her body tired, she slept.

REED STRETCHED HIS ARMS. HE slept great in this king bed all by himself and not one care about his friend on the sofa. He rose and saw that Tate was hanging over the edge of the sofa, apparently distressed in his sleeping. Another night of bad dreams were surely haunting his partner. He still called him that, and he would always be that to him. Working with the locals here in Cape May on this drug case was like working with Tate all over again, and no one would he want by his side more than this man. This man put everyone before himself. This morning after stealing his big bed, Reed felt a bit guilty and would put this man in a good waking mood as he prepared some breakfast and fresh coffee.

It was nice to rise to someone taking care of him, even if it was Reed. They actually both managed to have a good time at the beach party, but even better was the opportunity for a view of Emerson's stash. That pile in the one bedroom that he shared freely to so many during the night was huge. Tate and Reed agreed he was sitting on something coming up soon that was much larger and would involve big connections.

"Aubrey sure is lovely." Reed broke their morning silence.

"That she is my friend," Tate confirmed. "And that is why I hope to keep her far removed from this, very far removed."

Reed knew that the plans were to take out Emerson at the end of the week. He hoped Tate would stay out of it so that the police could handle it from here. He hoped Aubrey wasn't around, and he could use Tate to hopefully deter her from her home when the raid occurred. This was all if everything played out perfectly.

They were handed Emerson on a platter. Coming to this town on a dead-end tip at least would rid a nice place of scum and drugs. That was a perk for him being here. Plus, he was gaining a wonderful girl he could fall in love with. Hell, he was already in love with her. He had been from the first cup of coffee. She stopped his heart. She started it again, and from the moment he met her, he couldn't stop thinking of her. He was thinking less of Callie and her being gone so brutally and more of Aubrey and just the way her smile warmed him. "Hey, you have it bad. I say her name, and you go all lost in space on me." Reed grabbed his stomach and laughed. Tate was right there with him because he had launched into love just a short time ago.

✧   ✧   ✧

REED PICKED UP THE LAST piece of bacon and dipped it into his runny egg yolk on his plate. He tossed back a mouthful of coffee and finished his breakfast. He piled his dishes in the sink for Tate to clean. That's what friends were for. He told Tate he was meeting with the local cops. He told Tate to lay low. "Think about the end game and winning the girl."

Tate knew that Reed saw in her last night what he was describing. When Reed left, Tate couldn't sit tight. He drove down past the bakery even though his stomach was full, but would have lied to tell her that he was hungry for a pastry. It was closed. He even stopped and parked his truck and peered in the window to see if she was in the back baking. No sign of her. He knew she was probably home, cleaning up or sleeping the night party off. He hoped it was one of those two scenarios and not the third one of her lying in Emerson's arms.

To put his head back on straight, he decided to hit the gym and maybe stop in and say hello to Lacey. Last night, he stayed inside the house for most of the party, never having the chance to talk with her in person. Lacey hung out down on the beach, but he did extend a sociable wave from the balcony toward her down below. He wished that Lacey was Aubrey's roommate. He knew Tessa was Aubrey's friend, but it shocked him at the house last night to hear they were roommates. It boiled inside him that this girl that Aubrey looked up to and probably compared herself to was screwing Emerson. Well, that helped him at least to know he was dead on about this guy being a loser. He didn't want Aubrey hurt.

They were who she lived with. All this was wrong. All so very wrong.

After a workout, he drove by the Hamilton Inn to catch Lacey, knowing she was surely there. Sure enough she was. "You want to come stay here again? I thought you took up in the beach house down the way."

"No, and I did. I love the house there. I just wanted to say hello to you as I didn't quite have the chance to last night. So did you enjoy the party?"

"I did, but I can't stand Tessa. She is all full of herself. Last night, she was all nice in front of Aubrey, and then I heard her putting her down in a conversation, saying she couldn't see why Emerson was with a girl like that." Lacey read Tate's face as it tensed, fearing she may have said too much. "I wanted to defend Aubrey, but she hurt my feelings long ago when she chose Tessa to move in with her and not me. We have since patched our relationship, but really Aubrey is such a better person than Tessa will ever be, and if it's purely she needs the rent money, I'd help to rid her of that girl and find another to help her with expenses. Tessa is not the friend she thinks she is."

"Well, now I have a clear picture of where you stand on her roommate. I will let you in on a little secret, too. I think she is a little trashy and Aubrey shines with class."

Lacey smiled knowing it was okay what she just spilled out of her mouth.

"In fact, I stopped here for a reason. I wanted to see if you and Levi have connected? I haven't seen him to ask him. My friend is in town, Reed, and I did see him glancing your way last night."

Lacey blushed. "Actually, Levi has approached me. He said he is working on something really important at work. For this small town, that has to be something big. But he would love to take me to a movie in the weeks ahead."

That was all Tate needed to hear to not bring Reed into the mix. He was also glad he stopped here to say hello and gain an earful of girl gossip that confirmed his stance on Tessa. He thought the whole roomie relationship of Aubrey and Tessa was so odd it seemed scripted. Maybe he was thinking too much into this, but it seemed that not only was Emerson using Aubrey to make him appear squeaky clean, but maybe Tessa had something to hide behind her confident demeanor. Thanking Lacey for the conversation, Tate left, and he smiled as he walked out the foyer of the inn. He felt Lacey starring at his ass the entire time.

Grinning as he climbed into his truck, he was happy that Levi approached her. Levi was a local cop with good morals, and they seemed like a nicely suited pair. He hoped that when he rid Aubrey from Emerson that him and her would do dinner or plans with Lacey and Levi if they blossomed into a couple. Time would tell how all this romantic beach saga would end.

ARRIVING BACK TO HIS BEACH house rental after not once but three more drives past the bakery in case Aubrey opened late, Tate saw Reed loading up his truck. "Going back so soon?"

Reed nodded. "Yeah, I'm still scheduled for a few days on regular duty, but the end of the week, I'll be back here to embark upon this towns drug dealers." Tate wanted the details. He craved them when they were close to a bust, but Reed told him very little. Maybe it was best so he didn't dive in and disrupt what the police were putting in place. His job was done. He'd led them to Emerson, also to others dealing drugs from this town to the cities. Tate would let them do their job, the one he walked away from, and he would do his of watching out for Aubrey. He thought his position was key to guard her heart.

"So I will be back here Friday. It looks like that is the D-day for your boy Emerson."

Tate could take that. He could take another week of staying away from her. His time to be with her wasn't long from his reach. He knew in his heart, too, that she felt the same. After last night, it was more a certainty. Giving Tate a man hug, Reed then left. Tate watched his closest friend, such a good man drive away. He knew this guy would be in his life forever. He hoped he, too, would find a wonderful girl. Perhaps this town had many lovely ladies when the tourist season became prime. If he was still here in town, he would hang with Reed and find him a nice girl.

With his beach rental now quieted and him alone, he decided to hit the shower, eat something, kick back, and try to stay out of the plans for Emerson…that was a task that was going to require a lot of restraint. He had to do this. It had to go by the book and with him out of it. It was happening. All the pieces were in place, and this guy was going to be caught and put away. Also, Tate knew that he and Aubrey fit together so well. Last night, a hurricane couldn't have pried their bodies from that kitchen island. It was a good thing it hid what the lower half of their bodies were doing as they smiled forwardly to anyone passing from the other room. Behind them, only the appliances observed their actions and they would never tell.

Chapter Sixteen

SOMETIMES ANTICIPATION SEEMED TO MAKE time stand still. Often, Tate felt this way before a drug bust or when they were involved in a timely stake out. For Tate, the days this past week were the longest that he could ever remember. He did go by her bakery often, but most times were not for him to stop. Tate's timing seemed to be off. Emerson was there, or his truck was, so Tate kept driving. He busied himself with hitting the gym and never caught a chance meeting with Emerson, even when he varied his work out times and hit the gym twice daily.

Something was going down, he could feel it brewing. To not run casually into Emerson meant something big was happening. Tate was patient and waited. The days were numbered and counted down quickly. One more day remained. It was already Thursday evening, and tomorrow was slated for the takedown.

He hadn't heard from Reed all week, except that Reed was busy with too many details to share but would be coming to see Tate when it all concluded. He would fill him in on every detail including the look on Emerson's smug

face when they carted his ass off to jail. Reed did share that
he hoped this was an easier bust than some they did. Having
previously been shot twice in the past, one to his chest and
another that grazed his head, Reed was scared from those
brushes with death and didn't want another to come whirling
in his direction.

Tate was not going to be there to back him, take charge
in front of him, but Reed assured Tate they had plenty of
support and backup. All he did leak to Tate was this was
much larger than any of them ever thought. Tate's brows
rose. Interesting. He knew his partner wouldn't lie to him so
he was anxious to hear all the details soon if he wouldn't
share now.

He trusted Reed to let him in when he could be brought
in to things. Reed often shared as much as he could on
Callie's murder even if it meant he could lose his job. Tate
grabbed himself a beer and advanced to the back porch of
the beach house. It was much larger than the balcony above
and filled with overstuffed furniture. The night air was very
warm for this time in the season. Usually, it was a little
cooler, but he was feeling heated. Tate pulled off his shirt
and undid the top snap of his jeans. With no one to impress,
he made himself comfortable. Polishing off his beer in a
short time, he slowly relaxed, slipping back into the chair
and cushioned by the priceless view. Expanding before him
was the sun setting. In a matter of minutes, it changed
quickly from a full fiery ball to suddenly half a circle and,
soon after, appeared to have sunk into the water, only
leaving brilliant streaks of red and orange across the early

evening sky.

Tate had showered earlier and fixed himself a thick steak he smeared with ketchup and a large potato loaded with sour cream and chives. He was good on his own in the kitchen and lately found himself buying groceries once more and preparing a meal for one and hoping it would double in the days ahead. His days of takeout were dwindling. He would pass the fast food or easy stops to carry out a meal and instead think about what he was going to cook. After his meal and settling back in to the chair on the porch in the night darkness, he listened to the waves approaching and busting at the sand's edge. It was a dark night, no moon light shining down, and a quiet dark space for him to lie and think about all that had happened in these past months. That would keep his mind occupied as tomorrow was the day that Emerson was being brought to justice.

HAVING STAYED AT THE BAKERY all day, although Aubrey told Emerson she wouldn't be home until late, she was actually heading there hours earlier than planned. He didn't pick up her incoming call nor did he answer her text. She thought he was still working or having a beer and didn't hear her call come over. Maybe he was in the shower cleaning up from a hard work day in the sun. She was thinking how to handle tonight. Emerson said he wanted a special evening with her soon, and she wanted a night to tell him that she was falling out of love with him. She wondered if he meant special as in a proposal. She hoped that wasn't it.

As she grabbed the box of iced cream cheese carrot cake muffins that Tessa loved and also a double chocolate muffin for Emerson, she smiled, knowing if they were both home they would love her treats. She would never be anything but sweet to him, as he had been with her for over two years, give or take their brief break. She knew, though, what she had to do, and soon she had to confront Emerson about her mixed feelings.

Pulling into her pebbled driveway, she saw that both Emerson and Tessa's vehicles were there. She could hear music playing loudly through the open windows. Nice to have a fun night with them both. That was a treat for her to have activity in the house at night. Besides their recent party, most recently Tessa stayed out all hours with some guy who was certainly making her smile and Emerson he was over-loaded with work and concrete pours to have on the ground before the season changed. He explained to her if they were successful in pouring the concrete foundations in before winter they had work to keep them inside building all winter long. It sounded legit. She never doubted him.

As she entered the house, the door was unlocked. It usu-ally wasn't because she was the only one home. She saw the bottle of wine half empty on the counter and some shot glasses, too, with limes cut near them. Aubrey was guessing that Tessa had her man here and was celebrating with him or Emerson was drinking early preparing to take her to bed the moment she came in as he did long ago. She wasn't certain of how she felt about that last thought as she hadn't slept with him all week. The last man that touched her was Tate as he dipped his finger into her. That thought kept her licking her lips all week, and it wasn't over the icing she was making every day…it was his touch.

Hearing moans, heavy moans, oh shit, she was in the kitchen by the refrigerator and could see a couple on the balcony having sex. She hoped Emerson was crashed on their bed as Tessa was definitely having a pleasant romp. She could see Tessa's completely naked back and heard her gasp, "Take me hard. You love me, tell me."

Aubrey started to walk away to head to her bedroom to tuck herself in there till her friend climaxed and redressed, and she stopped dead. "I love you Tessa, you are mine forever," the guy stated.

WOW, Tessa actually found a guy to truly love her. Tessa moaned again so loudly. "All these months I texted you, my love. Every day I told you. TLU. Tessa Loves You!" Aubrey stumbled over her own footing. TLU? She saw that on Emerson's phone several times. It couldn't be…then she replayed the words professing the guy's love to Tessa…that was Emerson's voice. She was sure of it.

Putting her feet in motion, she hurried to the bedroom, dropping the box of treats in the trash can as shock seemed to hit her and she stumbled to hold herself up. Opening her closed bedroom door, the bedroom revealed an empty bed. On to the master bathroom, clear. No Emerson showering, not even a trace of water on the floor. Moving hesitantly back through the hall, she saw both spare bedrooms doors were ajar with tightly made beds and no one present.

The hall bathroom had a light on. She calmed herself that

Emerson was probably in there taking a crap, not using their master bath, and her mind hearing his voice was playing tricks on her. Opening the handle slowly, it was empty except Tessa's cell phone on the bathroom vanity. She entered the bathroom and sat on the toilet, trying to silence the rapid beating of her heart. Should she invade Tessa's privacy and read her friend's messages? What if Emerson was out with his brother and Tessa was here on the balcony having a good time with her man that Aubrey has yet to meet?

Aubrey opened the lock screen and started to go through the texts. So many were to him, how she loved him, wanted him, enjoyed the hotel time with him. Couldn't wait to be out in the open with him. *Perhaps this man is married,* Aubrey thought. *Maybe that is why she hasn't revealed him.* Aubrey continued her detective work or invasion of privacy on her friend. The messages were endless. She stopped at one that broke her heart. Her face paled.

My Love, drop went as planned as they usually do. You and I, we got this. We have conned them all. I am coming back from the city with a ton of money for us, and for our forever together that's almost near. Emerson, Tessa Loves You.

O-M-G, there it was on the screen. Tessa loved Emerson. Aubrey had been played for so long. Her heart sank at the feeling of how betrayed she was. The hurt of a friend, of a boyfriend that she had loved. Hell, she loved Tessa, too. It was when she went to the photos that she couldn't stop from feeling sick and shaking. There were photos of Aubrey sleeping on the lounge on the balcony and Tessa messaged Emerson – *I will meet you in my room in 15 seconds. She is sound asleep. TLU*

Or others that said, *she just left for her sweet little bakery to play make the cakes today, so come in my room. My legs are spread, waiting. TLU*

One message after another, Aubrey scrolled through. She saw the ones that Emerson wrote back, of his love for Tessa, what he sexually wanted to do with her, or commenting on what they just had done. He pointed out in a few messages how their plan was almost interrupted with Aubrey asking him to move out. He also said he was simply going through the motions with Aubrey for these next few weeks till their plan unfolded.

Tessa wrote a message that she was upset when her cousin Jackson couldn't keep his pants zipped up. It upset her that she had to play nice to Aubrey and try to be sympathetic. That was never part of any plan. In fact, that was something Jackson just up and did. Aubrey now understood why Emerson reacted calmly and wasn't upset about it as much as she thought he would have. Hell, Tate was fuming and beat the crap out of Jackson. Emerson sort of swept it under the rug. It was probably because he didn't want a spotlight shining on Aubrey or in their direction.

Tessa vented in a text message to Emerson saying she had been more than sympathetic with this entire arrangement for the past few years of letting the guy she loved curl into bed with her roommate that she never ever cared about. It was all about the perfect house location at the edge of the beach, a place to store drugs safely out of the way and traffic them for huge amounts of cash so this sleepy town would never suspect. Never in a million years would anyone think that it was all coming from sweet little bakery girl Aubrey's home. Aubrey reread Tessa's words...it had been years of set up. She pulled herself up from the toilet and steadied her legs on the floor. Her eyes were building up tears, pooling in them but not falling yet.

Her mind told her she couldn't stay here in her own home. She couldn't confront them, though she realized they used her...Aubrey didn't know where to go and what to do, only she had to leave and leave now. Exiting the house almost as quickly as she had come, she didn't realize until she was in her car that she took Tessa's phone. She drove down the street and then veered off to a side street where she pulled over and broke down crying.

This street was mostly for the summer rentals and had no activity so her moment would go unnoticed by anyone in the town. Her tears fell hard. She had, too. Being a good person all her life, these two set her up and carried out a plan for years. That word 'years' just rang over and over in her mind. She wasn't certain how long she cried and wiped her face and started to compose herself and cried again. It was, though, hours. She knew they wouldn't miss her coming in on them and catching them because she originally said she would be baking late into the night.

She left her car. It felt like it was closing in on her. She needed to get air, be free and breathe. At the entrance to the beach from the side street, she removed her sandals and looped the straps together and flung them over her shoulder. She found herself walking on the beach, alone in the darkness. A few times, she stumbled in the sand at the lumps she misjudged with her footing and came up sandy. Dusting herself off as best as she could, she didn't really care about sand attaching to her. She cared about fake people attaching themselves to her life. She had lost track of time. She left her watch near the sink at her bakery when she was washing her hands before she left. She meant to grab it but didn't want to drive back just for that. It would still be where she left it tomorrow.

Several houses stood in total darkness, not rented for the season. She walked a bit more carefully in the sand, afraid of walking upon a broken glass bottle or flip top that remained after the tourist season as the beaches are cleaned often during then. Her feet came to a stop. She dug her toes deep in the coolness of the sands floor. Standing before her was a beach house with lights on inside. She knew where she was. Nervously, she came around from the beach to the entrance on the side. She wiped the sand off her feet as best as she could. Her tap to the screen door was light. The inner door was half open. She could see she was definitely at the right house. She could see him in just his jeans, his incredible bare chest full of color, walking into the kitchen and holding a beer by its neck.

Aubrey explored every inch of him from his shaved hair to his bare feet. She wanted and needed his comfort, his touch. Her initial tap to his outer door was gentle and timid. Aubrey's first try was not answered. He hadn't heard her approach. Tightening her fingers, making a fist, she banged harder.

Tate heard the sound and knew he had someone paying him a visit. From the kitchen light to the darkness beyond the door frame, he could see it was her. Her tiny frame only filled a portion of the door. Why was she here? Did they change plans and the deal was happening earlier than planned? A million thoughts hit his head as he made the twenty foot walk to reach the door, welcoming her inside.

"Tate, I am sorry to come here like this." He clearly saw distress in her eyes, and they had been crying. He saw sand all over her and wondered what in the hell happened. She was startled and dazed like she was lost in the woods for a period of time.

"What happened?" He wanted to comfort her, but he stood waiting for her to move to him.

"Emerson has betrayed me. Tessa has betrayed me." Tate stood, and Aubrey came closer. "I have only been thinking of you since you came into my bakery long ago. Tonight, with you on my mind, I went home to confront Emerson about my feelings that I don't have for him anymore."

Tate tensed. "Did he hurt you? Is that what happened?"

"He hurt me, but not physically. I walked in to him and Tessa having sex on my balcony. They thought I was coming home late from a full night of baking." Aubrey paused, taking in a breath, and also feeling stupid for coming here to dump this on Tate. She turned to walk away.

"Aubrey, I am glad you came to me."

She dumped her sandals from her shoulder like a cinder

block weight. She felt relieved he said that. She fell into his arms. Aubrey freed her one arm that was hugging him and pulled out the phone from her pocket. "Tate, it's all here. They are both involved in drugs, serious drugs, and they have been in love for years…years, they planned this."

Tate held her tightly. She was safe in his arms. He was glad he could offer her this much. He was relieved she was not in the midst of what was going down tomorrow. To-night, she was his, and he knew tomorrow and each day after now she would be always.

Tate held her, comforted her. He led her to his sofa. She sat but was still dusting off sand. "I am sorry. In my upset, I stumbled a few times on the beach in the darkness. It is black out there tonight, no moonlight to lead me here." She smiled, her eyes still clearly saddened.

Tate went to the bathroom and brought her a towel to wipe off the sand. "Better yet if you want to take a quick shower and change, I can offer you some sweatpants and a tee shirt." A shower to him sounded perfect if he could shower with her…perhaps someday.

He was stunned when she said, "Sure." He led her to the bathroom and laid her out towels. He told he would give her privacy and gather clothes for her and lay them out, too. He was nervous, though. Tate wanted to have her in his arms, and she was finally here. He went through his dresser drawer to find something to fit her. He knew his sweats would be at least a foot of a trip hazard for her. Already having her fall over her feet on the beach, he wasn't risking that here in his place. He found scissors and cut the bottoms off a pair of gray sweats with a drawstring that he knew had to be pulled to its tightest to hold them up on her. Then he found a tee shirt that would do. One that was the tightest on him but would be so roomy on her.

He opened the bathroom door and was hit with the heat blast of steam. Glad she was immersed in the shower, he placed the clothes on the edge of the sink, shut the door, and went to find a wine opener in one of the kitchen drawers. He could offer her a glass to relax her and let her tell her story of everything that happened earlier.

Although beer was his beverage of choice, he'd grabbed a few bottles of wine when he stocked the house. He thought maybe one evening he could entice her here for a drink…just maybe. Tonight, he did not lure her or invite her, but she came. She was in his freaking shower. He was amazed at the turn of events. He reached out to Reed to assure him Aubrey was out of harm, and safely with him. He decided to leave a text. Simply, he wrote:

Reed, I got Aubrey. I will keep her safe. Not letting her leave here tonight. Good luck tomorrow, partner, and I want every detail.

Finishing his text, he looked up at the petite, wet headed, beautiful girl before him. She really did take a full shower. She said rinsing herself under that warm water was like washing away Emerson and Tessa from her skin. She towel dried her hair and placed the towel on the floor next to her as she sat right up next to him. Tate took the comb from her hand and gently combed her hair. Already, it was air drying.

She was a low maintenance girl. When he was done, he placed it on the towel. Tate tucked a wet strand behind her ear, trailing his hand along her chin. Her face was lovely, freshly cleaned as she removed her smudged makeup. "Aubrey, you are so beautiful. I told you that when I met you, and you thought it was a line. I am telling you it's a fact. Believe me, it's no line."

She licked her lower lip slowly and bent her lip inward and held it.

"Aubrey, all this time that I have known you, when I closed my eyes at night, I saw only you. When I opened them, I always missed you."

She couldn't hold back the tears, not for what saddened her earlier in the night, but over the intense love she felt for this man. A love that had her humming at the bakery, gazing out the window often, and hoping to see him day after day.

"Please stop biting your lip. I want you to kiss mine." Tate leaned toward her face and brought her lips to connect with his. Her taste was exactly as he remembered. A glass of wine he poured for her was untouched. She needed nothing to relax her. It felt right here. He felt perfect. Everything else faded away. They lost themselves in their kisses. Tate felt like he was taking advantage and finally broke their lips. "Do you want anything? Dinner? I'm sure you haven't eaten and not sure you feel like eating. What can I bring you?"

There was a long pause, very long. She was thinking. *Hmmmm.* She moaned lightly, rethinking the question. What did she want? "Well, there is something I would like...I want you to make love to me."

Spoken sweetly and with certainty. Tate knew he wanted her and hearing her confirmation she wanted him was another one of those counted moments. No one was coming to interrupt them. She was far out of danger from the take down tomorrow. She was rid of Emerson…it was finally their time. He led her to his bedroom. Tonight, he was going to sleep in his own bed instead of his sofa.

Tate felt funny removing his clothes from her. She was dressed like a mini Tate. He laughed and made light of it as he removed his tee shirt over her head. She had put her underwear back on after her shower, and he left that in place for the moment. The pretty pink bra was such her style. He undid the drawstring of his sweatpants that swam on her body. Matching pink panties revealed themselves. She was absolutely beautiful lying in the center of his bed, her petite body lost on the vast king-size comforter. Tate backed off the bed and removed his jeans and dropped them to the floor. No underwear followed as none were under his jeans. He lay next to Aubrey naked, completely exposed to her.

Aubrey followed the color lines of Tate's tattoos. She ended her finger with an abrupt stop on a knife dripping with blood piercing a heart. Not a tattoo of a girly heart but a beating heart. Clearly written through the blood was VOW. She was about to question this, and she knew he felt her pause.

"So I guess you want to know their meaning? My tattoos." He didn't flinch. He took her fingers in his and traced over the tattoo as he told the story and reassured her it was fine to touch them. "My wife was murdered." Aubrey remained silent, saddened by this for him but awaited him to continue. "Drug dealers took her life, I believe, and made it appear like a random burglary. I vowed to find who did it. When she was taken selfishly and tragically from me, I died, too. Aubrey, you have awakened my heart. It pumps life again."

"Tate I am so sorry." Her eyes glazed over, searching the sadness in his.

"Don't be sorry. You have brought to me what I never could have imagined." He brought his lips to her finger and then took it to his chest. He then brought his lips to the top of her head. Her hair dried, but smelled like his shampoo. He rested there, inhaling. Taking this in, this moment, her…telling her his secret, his loss, his scars. He lay there next to her, his weaknesses fully exposed. The softness of her pink undies matched her lips and the color in her cheeks. He wanted this, her softness, her…all of her.

Making love to a beautiful woman was something he never thought he would have again. He meant not only physically beautiful but inside as well. This girl tugged at his heart and expanded his lower member. Tate wiped back her bangs. "Aubrey, I don't play around, sleep around. I am a one woman guy. I want to be your guy. I want you to be my woman."

Aubrey sat up again. Tears took to the very corners of her eyes. She took off her bra and let her full breasts fall, her large mounds exposed to him. She leaned against Tate, skin to skin. There was no holding him back tonight. He was going to make love to her the entire night long. Then he was going to hold her again in his arms and hope when his eyes closed he would have peace.

Taking her breast to his lips excited her, and she squirmed her panties off. He would have loved the act of removing them slowly, but they were off, and he couldn't complain. His mouth was full of her nipple, and it hardened, letting him know she was ready and right there with him, prepared to take the fall.

Every moment he touched her, caressed her, filled her, and came undone in her was heaven to him. He didn't compare her to any other sex he had in the past. He just embraced the deepest feelings and emotions that rose within him. He didn't want to be a sap, but he told her, "This, us, it was amazing. Aubrey, you have no idea how much I feel for you." The "L" word was there, but it wasn't the timing for that, not just yet, one baby step at a time.

This, though, was not a baby step. Their coming together in his bed was one hundred steps forward, a race in the sand, a huge hurdle. They crossed it together. He heard her moan. He heard her call his name like she did while he was on the porch, although that was something that he chose never to reveal to her. He wanted her to trust him and not think of him as a creeper.

Tonight, he held her in his arms the entire night. He felt his eyes go heavy, and when he couldn't fight it any longer, he let them fall. When he opened them, he wasn't scared or in night sweats. He was in love, holding his love tightly to him. He actually drifted a few times and wasn't visited by the darker side. During the night, they rose and fell again several times. Each was as incredible as the very first.

Awakening after a blissful sexual encounter should be serene. No demons entered is head, and Tate was relieved and no longer nervous. He actually made love to her perfectly and satisfied her as she did him, lying with her an entire night in the dark and awakening feeling wonderful. Aubrey squirmed from him and his hold under the blanket, and he watched as her beautiful naked body walked across the room and entered the bathroom.

Chapter Seventeen

T HE MORNING OPENED TO A day full of brilliant sunny
rays dancing off the waters. Tessa's heart raced for the
incredible night of sex with Emerson that never seemed to
stop from the balcony to the kitchen to her bedroom.
Sometime late in the night, Emerson slipped into the
bedroom he and Aubrey shared only to receive a call from
Damon. He had to leave the beach house, but assured Tessa
everything was going according to their plans. The biggest
score was coming in tonight, and in the morning, they would
cut it all out for delivery once Aubrey had gone to her
bakery.

It hadn't worried Emerson that Aubrey wasn't home yet.
Sometimes she would stay and play with her sugars until the
wee morning hours. He left her a note on the pillow that he
went to help out Damon. He was actually glad he missed
her. It was amazing with Tessa here in this house for
countless hours. They christened so many new areas.
Tomorrow after the delivery and the cash was received, he
and Tessa would roll out of here, make their final deliveries
in the city, collect the funds, and then follow their detailed

plan to its final payout. Passports in hand, they would leave together and head to Costa Rica.

Emerson kissed Tessa, and she lifted from the bed to cling to his lips even more. She loved this man and would kill for him, die for him. She had killed, it was in a rage of loss from her brother's murder that jealousy ripped through her when Emerson commented on that girl being lovely. She killed her a few years back. That was in their past, Tessa felt her lips swollen from all the kissing her and Emerson shared this evening. Some of his kisses were forceful and intense. She had him forever, he was hers and they had an incredible future planned together.

She lay back in her bed, wondering how sex was between him and Aubrey when they were together just feet from her room. She never heard Aubrey moan or call out his name. She supposed she just lay there and let him take her and then rolled over to sleep. Well, she need not worry anymore about them having sex. No more images of Aubrey and Emerson would cross her mind. Tomorrow, they were out of here. Tessa and Emerson planned to leave a note to salt the wound. *Thank you for the stay. We fell in love. Bye.* Simple and to the point. They doubted she would ever search for them, probably curl up in a ball and cry her eyes out.

The hours passed, and it was odd that Emerson hadn't contacted Tessa. She fell into a sound sleep, satisfied from all their sex and dreaming of what lay ahead.

AUBREY WAS IN THE BATHROOM when the phone on the

table sounded. Tate reached over to read the text coming in from Emerson to Tessa. He told her he was okay and received the entire drop. It was the motherfucking load. They had hit the top. He said he was going to his family's bar to put down a few with Damon, and then they would be back. He would not wake her until after the sugar princess had left for her bakery. He knew Aubrey would be out early and so they scheduled all the pickups close to nine in the morning. It was on. He told Tessa that he would be banging her before the first dealer banged on the door for their pickup.

Tate read it over and over. He reached for his phone to contact Reed. Again no answer. It went to voice mail, but he did forward him a lengthy detailed text. He was thankful that he had confirmation of it happening and, most importantly, that Aubrey was here safe in his home.

She came out with her eyes tired, and she slipped the tee shirt over her head that last night fell to the floor. Quietly, she climbed back under the covers. Wrapping her body around his, she felt secure, happy, loved, and this was a new day, a beginning like no other for her life and to be with Tate openly and honestly.

He felt her wrap her body to his, and he loved it. He pretended to sleep, not wanting her to be alerted by the calls. In fact, he silenced her girlfriend's phone and placed it face down. His girl had seen enough on that phone screen. Yes, he was thinking last night confirmed she was his girl. They both drifted off to sleep for a little while longer.

✧   ✧   ✧

THE SIRENS WERE SILENCED. THE entire team was in place. On the beach, a couple walking in shorts and tee shirt held hands displaying they were in love. They were both narcotics officers. The old fisherman a home down at the beach casting a line to the sea with nothing attached was waiting to catch drug dealers, not fish. He, too, was a narcotics officer. The entire corner of the street surrounding Aubrey's home was marked off with unmarked cars ready to move in.

At approximately eight o'clock in the morning, Emerson emerged from his bedroom. He slept soundly when he came in because he had too many beers and shots. He wasn't even certain if Aubrey was next to him in the bed. He saw a box with her *Sweet Treats* label on it in the trash can so at some point she came in the night and left already. Good for him and great for the deal about to be served up for breakfast. Without a knock to her bedroom door, Emerson made good on his texted promise. He climbed in bed behind a sleeping Tessa and took her.

She awoke smiling, so glad today began with sex and that they were leaving this town. After Emerson removed himself from Tessa, she went to shower and dress before the first haul was to be picked up. That was all happening in less than a half hour. After she dressed and Emerson jumped in for a quick dip in the shower, he joined her at the counter in the kitchen. They had the gigantic load all cut out and separated. At nine o'clock sharp, three different cars pulled into the beach house in a quick manner. Each person jumped out and peered about cautiously, checking if the area appeared all clear, before going into the house.

Emerson had wanted Damon here today as back up to watch from the outside. He and Damon put down quite a bit of liquor last night, but Damon assured him he would be there. When Emerson texted him after his shower, Damon replied – I'm on it. Emerson knew he could always count on Damon. He had backed him up on so many deals that they lost count.

Damon, though, didn't proceed too far. Coming out of his apartment, he was immediately apprehended by two officers. They caught a glimpse of a weapon on him. They weren't taking chances with this guy. They moved swiftly, taking him into their hold and leaving him unable to reach for his weapon. They removed his gun and also the several bags of white powder that was in his jacket. Seems like he was going to have a party of his own or surely sell some on the side today. Now the officers had his phone in their possession, and if Emerson reached out via text for anything else, these two officers would surely answer back the perfect answers.

They smiled at the ease in taking this guy into the squad car. Guess there wasn't going to be anyone watching out for Emerson this morning. It wasn't long before a text came through on Damon's phone. It was from Emerson confirming with Damon to keep a good watchful eye, as they were cutting through all the stash and smoothly dealing and hoped to be packed up and out of there before noon when Aubrey would be heading home for a break in her day. Emerson also promised Damon a nice cut of the shipment and a nice sum of money for his help.

The first three men were serious when they came in, taking huge shipments and forking over wads of cash, stacks of bills. Emerson need not count them all. It was piling up nicely. Tessa was already fanning herself with several stacks of bills, keeping herself cool until it was time for them to leave the beach house together...forever.

She was never nervous until today. This was the first time in all the drug dealings that she felt anxious. She kept watching the clock, wishing the numbers passed and it was time to take off. Off to paradise and her and Emerson finally being together...forever. She laughed in her head at the thought of Aubrey finding out all along that Tessa was Emerson's love. It didn't bother her at all the scam they were doing, playing house for so long as her roommates.

Success brought a smile to Emerson's face, and he grabbed Tessa's neck toward him. He plunged his tongue into her mouth and kissed her hard. "That was easy. Hope the rest moves just as quickly." He was examining the dwindling pile of cocaine. He couldn't help himself. He cut two large lines, one for him and the other for Tessa, to begin their own private party.

As the first three men left, they turned around in the driveway and began to head out, each in a different direction in case anyone was onto them. Each of them were apprehended just a few blocks away. It followed with the next half a dozen dealers dropping in for their cut. As the hours ticked by, it was almost time to pack up and bail out of here.

Their plan had worked, and they were tying up the loose ends. Emerson went to the bedroom to leave the note that he and Tessa fell in love on the pillow for Aubrey to see when she came home. Tessa was packing up in the kitchen. Emerson heard some noise from the kitchen that sounded like she was slamming items as she packed. He knew she was frustrated for living here and playing house as a roommate for so long, but it totally paid off. They were set for a long, long time. "Ready, Tessa? Let's blow this beach house." When he returned to the living room, he didn't hear her talk back. He turned to the kitchen and saw her seated on the counter chair with her mouth taped and a gun pointed at her. It was Reed, the guy he met at the party the other night.

"LET HER GO!" Emerson jumped toward Reed to save Tessa and was stopped in his flight by two other officers. None of these men had he ever seen in this town's local line up of cops.

"Sorry we taped her mouth, but we weren't having her tip you off. You are going down my man." Reed smirked at Emerson, his hands struggling in the cuffs while he was lying face down on the floor. Several more narcotics officers arrived and began to package up all the drugs and the money and search the rooms for anything else. Reed pulled the tape from Tessa's mouth. She tried to spit at him but missed.

"Your plan didn't work. Emerson, you failed me. It didn't work!" Tessa began to cry fake tears. The officers weren't buying her sobs one bit.

Emerson fired back, "I didn't fail you. You did this! You invited a fucking cop into our home! You invited him to the party!"

Tessa screamed back, "You're right. I did do that. I have

failed you now, but I am not sorry for taking that girl out long ago. You betrayed me. I saw the way you wanted her. In all the time I have been with you, I have never come to see that look from your eyes for me. You wanted that rich old drug guy's little darling girl. If I hadn't come up to that bedroom, you would have taken her. I stopped that. So you can blame me if you want for bringing a cop here, but I blame you for the blood on my hands and making me take a life."

The other officers in the room weren't hearing every word that she just spoke. They were taking it as a lovers' quarrel, but Reed froze when he realized their conversation was about Callie. Everything suddenly fell perfectly into place from the ties they had to Hagerstown and Tate's father-in-law. Reed knew he had to tell Tate everything. They'd vowed to never hold anything back. This town led Tate here on a tip that his wife's murderer was here, and she was. If what she was spilling from her mouth held truth, she murdered Callie. Here was the murderer sitting before Reed, bound in cuffs in the beach home and waiting to be taken away and processed for drugs.

The murder would be reinvestigated and if she was proven guilty or tied to it in anyway, that would be additional sentencing for her as well. The murderer of his partner's wife was the roommate of the woman his partner fell in love with in this town. Reed knew a text of all this was not going to happen. He would clear out of this house and deliver all the news in person—first, the great news of the take down of nine drug dealers and then the main distributors running the drugs. He'd received confirmation that the narcotics officers were already heading back to the station with Damon in their vehicle.

HE TAPPED HIS FINGER SOFTLY to her nose to awaken her lovely face. She squinted in the bright room. Tate shaded her eyes and told her how lovely it was to wake up next to her. He hoped there were no regrets, and when she took his finger to her lips, that was all the reassurance he required. "So I was thinking, how about I make you some breakfast? Yes, I can cook, and you can shower or do you prefer we shower and we make breakfast?"

Aubrey was still sleepy so she said she would shower and then join him for coffee, definitely coffee. He was in agreement with whatever she requested. He watched her naked ass move from the bed again to the correct door. He heard the shower water release. He looked at his messages. Reed left him a voicemail.

It went as planned, arrested and taken down. They are all in custody. I will recap with you later. No guns fired, a huge bust, though. Thanks, man, you were instrumental in this even if you weren't there this morning. The locals are also very happy with you as I slipped to Levi who you really were. He said he knew who you were, but didn't know you were involved previously in the narcotics division. Not sure what's up with that. You will have to figure that one out with him, but he and the force here are grateful this morning that they are rid of a dozen drug dealers. Maybe more as they are following the tips to those in the city that were to have drop offs later today. Thanks, man.

Tate was happy it was done, and more importantly, that she was safe here. She had been in his arms, in his bed, in his home, and now his life. Reed was unscathed, too, and the town would no longer be marred by the drugs or bad press. Since it was off-season, it would keep the news a bit quieter. Tate removed another pair of sweats from his dresser and a clean tee shirt. He again trimmed them to size to fit her petite legs. He placed them in the bathroom and didn't disturb her showering. Happy at the news, Tate pulled on some gym shorts and went to start the coffee brewing and the bacon frying. What a wonderful day and perfect breakfast he was beginning to make.

AUBREY TOOK LONGER IN THE shower than normal. Her feelings were bursting from her. All her life, she had never felt this loved. Even though Tate hadn't said it, he showed her love last night. He made her feel wanted like her parents did when they were alive. She touched her breasts as the water sprayed over her. They were sensitive, and she welcomed that because Tate's lips were on there for a lengthy amount of time. She washed her neck and felt his lips trailing down from her ear each time, sending a tingling sensation through her body. She washed her body and remembered him entering her. He'd slowly penetrated to make certain she was okay with him going farther. He stopped and asked for her permission.

She'd wanted him for the past few months, and no words could escape her mouth but yes. He filled her completely. Aubrey, knowing she was a petite girl, was afraid that Tate's size would hurt her. She took all of him in her, and the original tightness escaped her thoughts as soon as her body pooled with wetness. Tate slid in and out with ease. She couldn't stop smiling in the shower.

Aubrey finished her shower and dressed in yet another set of clothes that he laid for her by the sink. She would have to remember to buy him new sweatpants for the two pairs he custom cut to fit her.

TATE HAD BREAKFAST ALL SET up. All he needed was Aubrey to walk her fine ass and beautiful face into the morning light that sprayed across the kitchen. He opened the balcony doors to smell the ocean just beyond. A perfect scenario. He envisioned after breakfast taking her back to his bed and forgetting the time of day as he became lost inside her.

Tate heard her steps coming and poured a coffee for her. He was about to present it to her when he saw it was Reed. "Partner, it was perfect. You should have seen Emerson's face. He blamed his girl Tessa for inviting us to the party. He was shocked to see me with all the other cops."

Tate wanted details. He thrived on this.

"So you got them all? How many in total?"

Reed was excited talking. His voice raised, "Partner, it was a fine morning for our narcotics division and the locals. We got at least nine drug dealers, Emerson, Tessa, and their guy Damon that was still at his place. Two officers picked him up."

"Wow and the drug load?" Tate was fired up.

"It was HUGE! As Emerson texted, the motherfucking load!"

Tate and Reed clinked the coffee cups. "I want to hear all these details over again. I came to this town on a different lead, I meet the girl whose guy is a dealer, and we take him down…WE TOOK HIM DOWN!"

Reed was pleased. "How did you make certain she wasn't there when this happened? I mean, how did you make certain Aubrey stayed here?" They both stopped and stared at Aubrey, who made her entrance to the corner of the kitchen.

"He didn't have to keep me here. Actually, I came here because I trusted him. From what I just heard, congratulations are in order, *partner*?" Aubrey looked at Tate and didn't sway from her stance of being highly upset. She continued staring directly at him. "I don't know who you are, but I do know that you set me up!"

"Aubrey, wait…" Tate stumbled for what to say. She was turning to the door, and he didn't want to grab her to scare her. "Wait, I can explain everything, and so can Reed. We are the good guys…" With her sandals in hand, she reached the table and snatched her car keys from where she left them last night. She walked to the porch.

BAREFOOT AND DISTRAUGHT, TEARS NOT falling yet but making their presence known, she was defeated. Everyone set her up. Who could she trust?

Without turning back, knowing he was at the door, she asked, "Please don't come after me. Please just leave town and leave me alone." The tears came falling. She walked down the beach in the morning sun, squinting. The sting of the tears was far less than the pain in her heart. Tate didn't a move an inch to come after her. He stood shocked with his arms fixed solidly on the door frame. Under his breath, he said, "I vow to you, I won't give us up."

TATE'S VISION BLURRED AS HER figure became less and less clear. This entire day turned for the worse in a minute. She had heard the entire conversation he and Reed shared. She heard Reed call him partner. Surely she was confused and thought the worst. Tate would give her a moment to cry and to be alone as she wished. It tugged at his heart not to run after her and crumble before her, but he knew once she heard the entire story she would forgive him for not telling her he knew of the set up. She would hopefully understand that really he was a former narcotics agent and he wasn't in real estate.

Tate realized how she must have felt hearing Reed and his words. He knew she doubted that he actually had feelings for her if he held back things from her and lied to her about who he really was. Tate pounded the frame of the door once she was out of sight, although the echo was heard in the air. When he turned, Reed had left and was rapidly taking the steps two at a time from the balcony to the beach. He knew his friend surely went to patch this.

REED HAD TO SPRINT ON the beach to catch up with her. Aubrey's petite legs moved quickly to place herself far away from Tate. "Aubrey, wait up, please give me just one second. If you don't, I will talk anyway. You need to hear this."

"Don't!" Aubrey didn't want to hear Tate's friend tell her more lies. They were happy and high fiving their coffee cups for their drug bust. Her insides came apart, her heart torn open. "I don't think you know this and I want you to know that I needed Tate once, he helped me, he actually saved me and it appears I helped you both, so consider us even. We are even, so that means I NEVER have to see him again...EVER." From this moment on, Aubrey was not going to be a victim anymore. Aubrey picked up her pace. She didn't stumble in the sand at all in the daylight. She walked till she veered off the beach to the main street to find her car.

TATE STOOD ON THE BALCONY watching Reed return. He had hoped he would have Aubrey with him. Tate wanted to explain it was a huge misunderstanding. That didn't happen. He could see Reed approaching slowly and alone. Tate sat on the balcony of the beach house already with a beer in hand and tried to let the first sip take the lump from within his throat.

THE NEWS BLEW THROUGH THE town quite quickly and, by

midday, almost all the locals had heard of the drug arrest that happened early in the morning. They felt shocked at first that it happened in their town and then safer that there were multiple arrests. Tate was on another beer, not sure the number. Reed was there matching him. The day that started wonderfully ended so horribly. Reed told him that somehow he would win her back. Tate brushed it off. "I will try, but if she seriously doesn't want me, I will have to respect that." His mind was saying the right things even with several beers in him, but his heart was telling him to never let her go.

A NEW DAY SOMETIMES BROUGHT a new vision. Aubrey awoke in her bed the next morning. Even though her heart hurt and her eyes were still delicate to the morning light, she was determined make his day productive and accomplish something. Her first item on her agenda was that she needed to clean out Tessa's room and then throw out all Emerson's stuff in her home. Tessa and Emerson were gone, and she wanted to rid them from her home. If it wasn't her grandmother's home, she would have left here. Instead, she was taking it back. She felt tossing all their items would bring satisfaction back that she had some control in her life even if it was just in regards to her home.

Forcefully, she boxed up their stuff and dragged it to the curb, which took her hours. She never went in to her bakery. She found the simple note that Emerson left on her pillow that he and Tessa fell in love. Aubrey laughed under her tears. *Well, I hope you both stay in love in your jail cells.* When she thought about the jail cells, she thought, *Tate is Reed's partner. He is a cop. He never told me. That is why he protected me at the bakery from Jackson; that is why he didn't want to become involved.*

She was mostly upset, though, that if he truly cared for her he could have told her. He could have shared with her that Emerson was in love with another. Tate had to have known about Tessa and Emerson. Cops knew that shit.

She wondered from the start why Tate took to her so quickly. He listened to her. She wondered if it was all just to gain information to do their big drug bust. Again, the vision of the two cops clinking their coffee mugs filled her head. She had nothing to celebrate anymore. In that shower, in his place, she was on top of the world. She was already celebrating the new day with Tate and their relationship that was very real, intensely deep, confirmed by the most incredible sex and emotion she ever experienced. If Aubrey had to sum it up, they truly made unbelievable love.

Lately, her biggest celebration was cleaning her home, airing it out, and throwing out every reminder that Emerson and Tessa were parts of her life here. The police did a great job of sweeping her house and removing all the items for the case they needed. They took computers, Emerson's phone, and all the drugs and money. Today, her cleaning busied her, and the day was already over, and maybe tomorrow, she would head to the bakery. Maybe not…

TATE DROVE BY THE BAKERY all day. Never did the closed sign open. Tate went by her home and sat several homes away in his truck, watching her haul out box after box and pile items curbside for the trash. Ringing his hands tightly, he wanted to help her, but knew she wouldn't want his help. Watching her through his windshield, she finally took a break. As she sat on the bottom step of her front porch, her head dipped, and her hands covered her face. She was breaking apart.

He fisted the steering wheel. Upset and disheartened, Tate had to make this right. Only he wasn't certain how. There was one person that he thought he could talk to who would listen, perhaps be in a position to help him. Quietly, he drove his truck from his point near Aubrey's and hoped he could lean on this person.

He parked, and his boots announced his arrival as he crossed the porch. He entered and saw Lacey in her normal spot ready to greet a guest, although he knew she surely heard him coming. He knew he looked like a train wreck, but saw that she still offered a smile and didn't question him. "Lacey, do you have a few minutes I can talk to you privately?" She nodded yes to him. He explained to her his involvement in this morning's bust.

"Tate I heard a lot already from Levi, and he told me he was glad you came to our town."

Tate was happy she and Levi were talking, but he came here because his heart was breaking over Aubrey. He hoped her friend could help. Maybe he was grasping at straws, but he had to try.

Lacey led Tate to the porch on the other side of the inn, normally bustling with visitors but today empty. The windows were open to display the view. Tate couldn't hold it back. His already saddened eyes teared. "I care about her, Lacey. I really do. I couldn't tell her who I really was. It would have blown the entire bust wide open. I tried to keep her far away from what was going down."

"Tate, I know she truly cares about you. When you first left town, she came here to visit me, but I know it was to see you. She brought red velvet fudge pie, and she knows I don't eat that. It was obvious when I told her you checked out that her face drained. I never did really like Emerson. He was full of himself, but he was the town catch. At first, I envied her having him and for taking in Tessa, but I love Aubrey as my friend. I think you are genuine, and I don't know how I can help, but I will try."

Tate told Lacey more about moments he and Aubrey shared and spilled to her his feelings. It felt good because, when he lost Callie, he shut down and never expressed himself. He ate it all and kept it inside.

They ended their conversation with a comfortable hug, and Lacey agreed to talk to her and figure out where Aubrey's feelings for Tate stood. If she was successful and Aubrey admitted she missed him and cared for him, Lacey would reach back to him with that information. She knew she could find him at the beach house or the gym.

LATER THAT DAY, TATE WENT back to his rented beach house and said good bye to Reed, who had to return to Hagerstown. "I will hopefully find a way back to her," Tate told his partner.

"I am hoping you will."

Reed left, and the silence filled the house that last night was full of emotion and heartfelt tenderness. Tate lay to rest on the sofa. Each day that followed for the next two weeks were the same. Aubrey took no calls from Lacey and didn't answer her door at home. Aubrey only went to the bakery two days each week and closed quickly. She did see Tate parked across the street, and after he paused for a car passing by before walking across, he looked up and she had turned the sign to *closed*. He really did need to respect her and leave this town. In fact, with no word from Lacey, he figured another chance with Aubrey was over.

AT LEAST THIS TIME WHEN he left the town, he was driving his own truck, not waiting on the train. He packed up the beach house rental tightly and left it clean like he found it. He told the realtor he would drop off the money and key on his way out of town. As he pulled in to the real estate office, he noticed the police station was just next door. Pete was entering the station and gave a wave. Tate nodded.

After dropping the key and money he had in an envelope through the office slot because they were closed on Sunday, he headed back to his truck. Levi had pulled in and hollered over, "Got a minute, Tate?"

Sure, he did. He had no place to be. Tate and Levi entered the station and took up in a conference room for quite some time. When they broke their conversation and Tate stood to leave, he now knew that the "Lange" that gave him the tip to come to this town was Officer Levi Lange. He thanked him for bringing him here. It was a tip that may have led him to his wife's killer.

Levi stood, too, and thanked Tate for his help. "I think, Tate, you may want to sit back down. I have two more things to go over with you. One is breaking news and the other an offer."

Tate could barely digest the first item. Could it be that Tessa was the killer of his wife? They were still investigating it thoroughly, but her confession seemed to have validity. The offer, well, he would just have to sit on that for a while. His life was not at all together, so he told Levi he would give him a decision, hopefully soon. He was heading back home to Hagerstown today. As he left town, he gave it one more ride past the bakery, and even today, a Sunday when people like to have a treat after breakfast, the bakery wasn't open. There was no sweet breakfast deal awaiting him.

Chapter Eighteen

A S TATE DROVE, THE SCENIC roadway flashed past him in a complete blur. He didn't even know how he arrived at his destination safely because his head had been so far removed from concentrating on the road. Tate pulled into his apartment. He was back home. He had returned, and no one was there to greet him. Why should there be? His life was empty and lifeless once more.

Opening the door to his place was not met with the rush of the ocean breeze that seemed to breathe life back into him. The soft patter of her feet he heard in his head silenced. The sudden realization of complete emptiness took hold of him as he stood in his living room.

He switched on one light and could see the sofa still had a pillow and blanket on it where he always slept, when he could sleep. Being in the bedroom didn't feel right as his nightmares came there to visit too often. Placing the items he'd stopped and bought at the grocery away in the refrigerator and the cabinets, he was back and all moved in.

There were no sounds of the waves crashing just beyond. He had come to find that rise and fall of the surf soothed him. He put the television on just for noise, but that didn't compare. He dropped his clothes at the entrance to his bedroom. Having just returned to his place, too soon the walls began closing in. There was a place he thought he should go, that maybe just sitting there for a while would calm him.

Leaving almost as soon as he arrived, he headed down the road. The neighboring bar was brilliantly lit and posted the evening's specials. Few cars filled the large blacktop lot. Tate passed it by. He continued to drive several miles, noting a few more local bars lined the roadside. Finally, he came to where he wanted to be. He pulled into the cemetery and followed a road that was two dirt lined paths.

The early evening sky was filled with colorful hues of yellow and orange. He parked and, on auto pilot, he by-passed all the head stones till he came to hers. Callie Sana Manning. Yes, her taking his last name was a highlight of his life. He use to roll it off his tongue. *You are my Callie Manning, my CALLIE MANNING.* He loved her so. Seated next to her on the ground, he lost control of his emotions. His eyes suddenly filled with a rush of painful tears.

No one could hear him as he cried out, "I messed up. I couldn't protect you, and I thought I was offered another chance at happiness, but I have lost Aubrey." Tate sobbed, a big guy breaking to the core. The sorrow that built up inside of him made it difficult to swallow, his throat restricted, almost impossible to clear, and he tried several times.

Darkness filled the night sky. His fatigued body was banked up against Callie's headstone, just as if he was seated in his bed leaning on the headboard. He didn't want to leave her, but he knew he couldn't just stay here all night. Surely, the morning caretakers would call the police, thinking he was a drunk or homeless. Tate rose and caught his last tears as they formed from his eyes. Surrounded by only the silence of the night, he thought he heard a gentle whisper, "It will be okay." His mind was playing with him. Those words carried softly into the night air because he wanted them to come true.

Pulling himself together, he headed back to his truck. Before reaching for the door handle, he took his hand to his lips and released a kiss in the air, hoping it would land where Callie rested. Seated behind the wheel of his truck, he lowered the windows to hear the crickets making noise as he watched intermittent fireflies shine tiny spotlights over the head stones.

Feeling lost, he pressed the radio buttons for a music distraction. The first song that played was sad. Tate said to himself, *Yeah, that about sums up my life.* Steering his truck back onto the main road, the song selections changed. He turned up the radio really loud, as high as it would go. It was playing a hopeful song about life taking you on a path to someone who loved you. He smiled as it was a railway that led him straight to her, to that town, and to meeting Aubrey.

His mind wondered what was she was doing at this moment. His heart pumped again just thinking of her beautiful face. There was no injustice in his thoughts for Aubrey. Tate realized his wife would have wanted him to move on. Never did he think he would, or could, until Aubrey. Tonight, he hoped his visit to the cemetery would give him some peace, and perhaps he could fall asleep once he returned to his apartment.

Holding his steering wheel firmly, his truck kept him straight as he passed the local bar, now packed with vehicles. Tonight, he didn't stop. He only needed the company of himself, which he had grown accustomed to for the past two years.

TATE SMILED AS HE SAW her again. Her colorful sundress fitted her perfectly and her bangs blew softly in the ocean air. In her hands were her flip flops as she dug her toes into the sand. Her eyes warmed him, and she had him with just the tiniest smile from her lips. He had gone so long without seeing her. Could this be real?

He turned from his beach chair slightly. He thought that if he lay several hours a day that eventually she would walk past. Today, she did. He lay and watched her walk closer to him. She was coming in his direction; she saw him. Tate thought about what the first words would be that he would say to her. It had been far too long in seeing her. His chest was doing its own flip flops, unlike hers she was holding. If he lay here, in a moment, she would be blocking his light. She would, he hoped, kneel in the sand and place her lips to his.

She walked up and was within inches from his chair. Still not knowing what to say to her first, he waited for her touch. Her hand reached out to his, and when he went to take it, he fell from the beach chair. Tate shook his head and opened his eyes. He was so far removed from the beach. He had fallen from his sofa. "Oh fuck!"

In his dreams, he saw her. At least this was better than seeing the blood and death of Callie over and over. This dream, though, hurt just as bad. His heart pained. Once again, he was faced with another restless night. Turning to the television, he hit the remote to give him again just some room noise.

AUBREY COULDN'T SLEEP. SHE LEFT the lights on in the kitchen to give her home some illumination in the dark night. It was odd that suddenly her home contained only her and no one else. Tessa and Emerson had been here and made it fun for the past few years. Shutting that thought down quickly, she reminded herself they betrayed her and she would rather be alone, and that she was. She heard Tate rode out of town, and that news came to her after Lacey tracked her down.

It was nice to talk to Lacey and pour her heart out to another. Too much was bottled up inside her. One thing she knew was she loved Tate. It wasn't something she would forget or toss away like a badly baked dozen cupcakes, but someday, hopefully, she would put him behind her, too. Tonight, though, she just wanted to remember him one more time.

Pouring a glass of wine she hoped would make her tired, she wanted to remember Tate touching her, feeling him, and loving him. She was on the verge of saying those words to him after she came from the morning shower. She wanted to put that "L" word to him and see his response. She had gained enough confidence and clarification that he was the guy she wanted. Her heart was ready to take that leap.

As she turned the corner of her hallway with her wine, it fell to the floor. It crashed and shattered. It was just like her turning the corner to Reed and Tate's conversation that made her and Tate come apart...far apart. She was here, and he was back in his town. Back to his life and probably without a thought of her, even though Lacey seemed to think that he cared very deeply for her friend. Lacey tried to tell Aubrey that he seemed so genuine and caring. That the look in his eyes was sincerity, and yes, Lacey said she saw the passion he had when he said Aubrey's name. It seemed to her that it was love or definitely close to it.

After sweeping up the glass and wiping up the mess, Aubrey thought to herself what a mess she was. Tomorrow, she would move on and go back to baking tons of treats for the town and keep herself busy just like she had when she asked Emerson to move out. She could do this. It would take time, but eventually, Tate would fade from her heart and mind like each summer season eventually does.

TATE ROSE FROM THE FLOOR after his brief fall from his dream. He was uncomfortable and thought that he would try to lie in his bed. At least on the spacious king sized bed, he wouldn't fall off. He hit the pillow. He really messed it up with Aubrey. He was back here in his own place and needed to busy himself and keep his mind occupied so it didn't venture back to her. She didn't want him or he would have heard different. Tomorrow, he would go see Reed, catch up on all that went down, and maybe ask for his spot back on the force.

After visiting Callie this evening, he knew he had to move onward. He would take a step forward even if it didn't turn out favorably. Tate considered himself blessed in his lifetime to have been able to love two women. He had fallen in love with Aubrey. He wanted to tell her that night they spent together but was afraid his true feelings would scare her so early on. He knew, though, when she came into the kitchen after her shower, the moment his lips met hers to wish her a good morning, he would have said, "Good Morning, my love." That would be the first slip of his intentions and surely the real words would fly from his mouth by mid-morning or later in the afternoon. As he rolled over he said a silent goodnight and final goodbye to Callie. His eyes tired and heavy…he saw Aubrey and her smile. "Aubrey, I do love you. I fucking love you." He slept.

Awakening in his own roomy bed, Tate was confused at first as to where he finally fell to rest. He sat up, reaching his arms toward the ceiling. He stretched and moaned. Morning felt so good to him. Luckily for him, the nighttime hours ticked by and delivered him a sound sleep. He reached for his phone and called Reed. They agreed breakfast was in order to catch up. Tate could be there in fifteen minutes.

Tate loved breakfast and having it with Reed was good

but not as good as that breakfast he had been whipping up for Aubrey that saddened day. Before taking another mouthful of his pancake stack, Reed pressed him. "So partner, when are you going to make it official? You're back here now. Settled into your apartment again, living, returning to the gym and your routine, so why not get reinstated and reclaim your badge?"

That was the only thing left for Tate to do. "You know I was just thinking about that last night. I need to make some firm decisions, and requesting to be back with you and the guys may be the biggest step."

Reed would be happy to have him back, working every day on the force. Time had healed Tate. It had appeared it never would, but lately, he seemed in a better frame of mind, like the good old Tate that Reed knew for so long had surfaced from within.

Their morning breakfast ended with a fight, though, over who would pick up the check as it always did, but the waitress would be pleasantly surprised as she was paid double and double tips. Neither backed down this morning as to who would pay.

After a stop at the gym for them both to work out and then parting, Tate headed back to his apartment. Just as he pulled in his cell phone sounded. It was a call from Levi. He hoped it was news on the case. "Hey, what's up?"

"Tate, glad I caught you. Don't mean to press, but our budgets are being approved, and we need to know your answer soon if you want to be on the force with us. We would sure like to have you."

"Levi, I was just thinking of my options today at breakfast. Can you give me another week?"

"Sure, but don't take too much time. We have a pile of crime building up here that needs tending to."

Tate laughed knowing that was far from the truth. He liked this guy Levi, and he liked the beach town, and he still loved her.

After hitting the shower and relaxing in front of his television with a cold beer, he reflected on the decisions he had to make. Obviously, he was a good narcotics cop. His previous chief said he was the best. He had loyal friends. Hell, he and Reed were more like brothers than friends. They'd passed the friend mark a long time ago. So he had two offers and both great, only he wasn't sure he could take Levi up on his. He knew returning to Cape May would break his heart if he passed Aubrey and couldn't have her as his.

His mind was all over the place, but he did know something he truly wanted to put into motion and something that would make a great mark on a lot of people. He made a few calls, first to some construction companies and then to his bank, informing them ahead of time that he would be withdrawing a large amount of money over the next several weeks. This sounded like he was leaving town. Far from that, he would be bringing those funds to a town. After being on the phone most of the day that turned to night, he felt everything was moving in the right direction.

Sometimes, just one day could make all the difference in the course of a life. For some reason, as Tate hit his pillow to sleep in his bed and slept comfortably, he knew time was healing him. He knew, somehow, life would direct him. Tomorrow would awaken him to the unknown. He still hadn't answered Levi on his offer, which Levi requested his response soon. Tate also hadn't given confirmation to Reed to partner up again with him. As sleep took his body over, he knew he needed make a choice, and somehow he would find out where he was meant to be.

Chapter Nineteen

T ATE AWOKE REFRESHED. FOR FAR too long he suffered, lacking any restful sleep, but lately, the past few months, he was making progress. He rose and showered and didn't know what lay ahead of him for this new day. Nothing appeared different this morning. The sun rose the same time, and his apartment still needed a cleaning. He still wasn't working and just surviving day to day, month to month. Something didn't set with him, this particular morning his mood was overly optimistic which was unusual. After all the setbacks he encountered, he was finally sensing a break was coming. Not sure when it would arrive, he believed it was close.

After pouring a fresh cup of coffee, Tate sat at his kitchen table and cleared a spot to open all his mail that had piled up. His rent and important bills he always paid, the rest of the mail that came in he piled to sort through...whenever. He was never one to stay on top of that. Going through the huge pile, he came across a recently dated envelope from the Hamilton Inn. He was certain he paid Lacey for everything that was due for his accommodations last season. It was probably just a springtime advertisement for their new rates to previous customers. When he opened it, his heart began pounding in his chest.

Dear Tate,

I hope I am not intruding on your life that you have returned to, but I feel you would want me to tell you what's been happening here in town. Specifically, what's been occurring with Aubrey. It took quite some time as she shut everyone out but finally we spoke and that progressed with her opening up to me. She loves you. She hasn't said it, but there is no denying what she feels. Your name brings a reaction to her eyes.

I have spent these past months with her, and our relationship is so much closer than it ever was. I am thankful for your help with our town's drug problems, but I think you need to come back here to Aubrey. Try to make it right again. So much time has passed, and she understands what went down. I think it was a lot for her to handle. From losing her parents long ago to Tessa and Emerson conspiring behind her back, the final straw was you, the one person she wanted and was falling for, not telling her the truth.

I am taking her out today for some spring shopping, and I think it will make her smile. I know she will not reach out to you. Aubrey would never do that, but if you come back to our beach town, I just know if you see her and she sees you that you both will somehow move back on track together.

Tate, she does nothing but think of you all the time. I even see her eyes follow a truck that looks like yours down the road. Go to her. I am certain she feels for you exactly what you feel for her.

Also, thank you for your intervention with Levi. He and I are doing just fine. You played cupid for us, so please, please do the same for yourself and Aubrey.

Again, sorry if I am stepping out of line in sending this to you,

especially after so long, but I just thought you should know. Hope to
see you coming back through our town one day real soon.

~Lacey

He closed his eyes and reread the words of the letter. Aubrey loved him. What great news to finally hear. It was amazing that the winter months passed so quickly and he never selected either job offer. He worked out and just laid low maintaining a simple life with himself, occasionally reached out for some nights with Reed and the guys at a local bar. He wasn't into meeting any girl that looked his way, his thoughts still remained on *her*...Aubrey everyday. The letter confirmed she loved him. Tate had hoped she did, but time had passed, and he'd thought her feelings may have waivered. He knew he had to go there. Go to *her.* Without hesitation, he packed some things and was on the highway in no time. He hadn't a plan, but he did make one stop, a very important stop to a local friend who could maybe help him with winning her back.

JUST ANOTHER LOVELY SPRING DAY unfolded in Cape May, New Jersey. Early tryouts were happening on the beach for the new lifeguards as the summer season was approaching. They were pulling their boats from the ocean after rowing out over the waves. Next Tate watched as they began their lengthy run down the beach and back again. He remembered long ago this regimen when he was a lifeguard. He didn't linger too long at the beach. He paused his truck there to compose himself before he went to see Aubrey. The store-fronts were placing their items outside and sale signs in their windows. Aubrey was about to turn bakery sign to open, but didn't. She stopped as she saw Tate pull in. It was his truck. It was him. He was really here. She had thought of him in her head for so long. She had even wanted to reach out to him right after she left his beach house, but the hurt had been too overwhelming.

He couldn't have really wanted to hurt her that way. He couldn't have used her. She believed in him. She didn't want to give up, even though she was the one that walked out on him. She'd heard his plea but never turned back. She remembered how she broke. Thank god she had Lacey to lean on these past months.

His eyes, she could see his eyes through the storefront glass. Everything inside her wanted to run out and embrace him. Aubrey couldn't do that. She remembered Reed's words, how it was perfect in the way Tate set up Emerson. Did he really use her to do that? She still wondered. Even with the misplaced thoughts, she was smiling inside already but wondering why he was showing up at this time. She remained calm, but inside, she was bursting with happiness to see him. She hadn't removed him out of her head nor her heart.

Tate walked up from the side of his truck, not aware that inside the bakery she was shaking her head in amazement that no man should look that good. His visits to her bakery were missed. She'd permanently etched his likeness in her mind. Even in the darkness that one night, she mentally traced his body to store in her thoughts, which she remembered vividly these past months. The sign remained *closed*.

Aubrey unlocked the front door and let him enter. "I am not open for business yet." Her feet padded across the floor, keeping a safe distance between them.

"I can see that, but I just stopped on the chance I could get something." He hoped that didn't sound wrong. He didn't want to upset her.

"Well, since you are here, what would you like?"

He answered her without hesitation. "I would like to say that I came in for coffee, but that is not true. I would like to say I would love one of your sweet baked treats from the counter, but that isn't true, either. Actually, I would like to take you for a short drive from here where we can then take a walk together. It will just be for a little while, and I promise to have you back here soon. I promise."

Aubrey answered, peering downward at the floor like she was searching for something and keeping her voice steady, "That would mean I will be late in opening."

"Well, Aubrey, I don't see any line outside yet." Tate smiled after stating his observation.

Her eyes widened as she lifted her head, and she almost broke a smile, too. "Why do you want me to walk with you?"

"Aubrey, I have something to talk to you about. And a walk on the beach would be a much better atmosphere." Tate tilted his head, asking her to come with him with his eyes.

Aubrey couldn't resist this guy. She tried to even after he used her for the drug bust. She had no idea what his talk was going to be, but she knew the days he wasn't here crushed her. He reached for her hand. She didn't reach to his. Time had passed over the months, and she had come to the decision in her mind that he was a onetime happening.

Tate moved towards the door. "Aubrey, please come for just an hour?"

Aubrey turned from his eyes. Without a response, she moved to the back of her bakery. She was back there a long time, hoping Tate felt a little nervous that she'd slipped out the back. Aubrey took her time shutting down the oven. She also had to finish one important pie and package that up.

As she moved around, she spotted his shirt, the one they'd once sat on. She had cleaned it and gone to take it to him, but he had long checked out of the rental. Several times, she would hold it in her hands and relive that one night that he made love to her. She laid the shirt back down on her counter in the back of the bakery. She wasn't ready to part with that one last piece she clung to that reminded her of him.

Why did he stay away? Why didn't he try to fight for her? Aubrey said for him to stay away and leave her alone, but deep down she really wanted him to fight for her, explain what happened to her. If he hadn't meant to harm her, then why wasn't he honest from the beginning? She wanted him to come back and hold her shoulders and tell her his words of what she meant to him. Tate never did. He had simply left town. She regained her composure.

WHEN HE HEARD HER FEET hitting the floor, his breathing calmed. She was coming back to the front of the bakery. Aubrey had a large brown bag in her hold. Tate figured it may be to drop off to one of the elderly locals, as that would be something Aubrey would do. He didn't question it. His mind was on her.

Tate helped her up into his truck. She let him. He stole a moment looking at her legs and thighs as her navy sundress rose slightly as she situated herself. He tucked her dress carefully under the side of her thigh, making certain to touch her skin to his hand. She was actually seated in his truck.

Tate was trying to read her. It was a blank stare. He had hopes that there would be a welcoming smile, and that wasn't there. He thought a hug. That connection didn't come. Maybe he was wrong for being here.

He thought of the letter from Lacey. "Tate, she does nothing but think of you all the time. I even see her eyes follow a truck that looks like yours down the road. Go to her. I am certain she feels for you exactly what you feel for her." His eyes focused on the hood of his truck as he sat there, Aubrey still silent.

As Tate turned the key, he had to keep in his mind that this girl loved him. Her actions were completely opposite. "So a new season is already here." He tried to make small talk.

Tate didn't push her for more conversation, noting her watching the scenery pass by along the road the entire short drive to the end of the beach line where they first sat one afternoon that seemed so long ago. It was there that he knew they had a connection even before their bodies ever came together. He only heard silence while he spoke to her and then finally she spoke, "Yep."

Aubrey couldn't say more, her heart was exploding once more. Just his voice sent tingles through her body. It was a long, cold sleepy winter in the town, and with the new season awakening, what a beautiful new day it was for him to return. Aubrey couldn't believe he was really here once more. He was within inches of her touch.

WHEN THEY ARRIVED AT THE far end of town, Tate parked his truck. Through the windshield, they could see the stretch of beach had several trucks parked there and workers in a flurry of activity. Aubrey perked up. "What's happening here?"

"Seems like they are renovating this area," he responded with a smirk.

"Well, it needed to be cleaned up, but...wow! It cleaned up beautifully. I can't believe I didn't know this was being done here." Her eyes opened wider.

The beach area that was once high dunes and overgrown sea grass was flattened and clean of debris. There was a large sand box play park being installed for children to enjoy and an eatery area and new wrapped chairs and umbrellas that were coming off the trucks. The workers gave a wave. Tate knew in his mind this area would also be a perfect location if Aubrey ever wanted to open a second bakery. "I never thought this town would renovate this area. I stopped coming here. Tate, isn't this lovely?" Her voice had excitement and wonder in it as she searched from one area to another. Still with her interest in the cleanup of the beach area, she didn't turn to him to smile. She only displayed it to the windshield.

Tate's heart filled with anticipation of her reaction, knowing this was only the beginning. He released the handle and jumped down from his truck. He went around to help her out. He knew she would let him help her as the truck was high for her petite legs. Again, his thought went to the sight of her legs. He had seen every inch of her. He wanted that again, forever.

"Hey, Mr. Manning…Coming along nicely, isn't it?"

"Certainly is." Tate downplayed the contractor.

"Wait, how does he know you?" Aubrey scrutinized Tate's eyes, still not certain if he was going to pull something over on her once again.

"Aubrey, walk with me. There is so much for me to explain…please let me have that chance." She gave him her hand and let him lift her down. She took off her sandals and began to walk ahead of him to see all the progress on the beach. Tate remained at the truck, removing his boots. He set them on the ground outside his truck, knowing no one would take them. Once she took in the view of all the construction, she began to walk along the waters' edge with Tate moving up closer to her.

"Aubrey, thank you for coming here with me. I wanted to tell you many things, but first, the most important is that you are seeing me and giving me the chance to tell you how sorry I am that everything that was so incredibly wonderful fell apart for us so quickly. I have thought about you a lot." Tate's eyes glistened as he rethought his past few years. Aubrey fixated on the sand as she walked a step ahead of him. "You know my wife was murdered, but actually, I came to this town on a tip to find who murdered my wife. I was married until someone slit her throat."

Aubrey stopped immediately, and her eyes filled with intense sadness.

"My wife left behind a sizable amount of money for me to do something good with, and I knew that this area meant something special to you. One of my projects over the past months was to put this into motion. I think many will enjoy this expanse of the beach far better with all the improvements. Aubrey, you need to know that I never found the person I was to meet that first day. I didn't intend to meet you. You changed my life. Something changed in my heart. I never told you because I was facing too many demons of my own that I never wanted to burden you with."

He watched as she played with her toes in the sand; that seemed to distract her momentarily. Then he caught her eyes and saw the warmth and concern and knew she was listening to his every word. Tate continued. "After we met, I carried an uneasy feeling with Emerson, and I have to admit I wanted to take him out of the picture several times, but I left you to follow your heart." They started to walk slowly again and her hand lightly touched his forearm. It was a start. Tate felt her. "Aubrey, the night we were together was unbelievable." He watched her eyes travel away, looking out at the water as she remained silent. They both kept their feet marking the sand and proceeded farther down the beach.

Tate was nervous. Never did he feel his palms sweat like this, not even in the gym working out. Her silence was confusing him. He wasn't sure it was right that he came back. Well away from the renovations, they came to a stop, and Tate told her how he thought of her over this time that they were apart. "Aubrey, I know we didn't work out before, so I am certain that I will not mislead the next girl that has my heart and gives me a night like we shared. I will give her all of me and hope to gain all her trust."

THIS WAS NOT GOING WELL as Aubrey didn't like the sound of what he just said. It sounded like he was over her or moving on. She needed to focus on something to not start crying. Her eyes came upon a seashell poking up from the sand. It appeared as if it was reaching up for someone to take hold of, and that was what she needed, too. She traced the detail in the edges of the shell. Years back, she would have picked it up to add to her collection, but she had far too many displayed throughout her beach home. Lifting her head up, having kept her tears at bay, she saw Tate had walked several steps away from her and had his back to her. She had no idea what to say to him. She felt like next he was just going to tell her to walk back, and he was going to take her to her bakery.

He approached her and reached for her hand. "Please know I am so sorry." "Give me your hand." He took her right hand into his and held it gently.

Here it comes. She felt the goodbye. He didn't pull her closer. In fact, he turned her and led her by the hand, and they began the walk back to the truck. Then he stopped and gazed out at the ocean. His voice hesitated. "Aubrey, what we had was real, and I will never forget it." His hand released hers from his hold. Tate put his hands into his pockets of his jeans.

The tears pooled in her eyelids. It was the most real love she had ever felt in her lifetime. She didn't want him to leave, but she could never beg him to stay in this quiet town. She wanted to touch him once more, but the signals he was giving showed he was backing away.

Standing before her, he saw in her eyes pure love staring back. Overcome with emotion, he choked up. Momentarily, he appeared disappointed, unable to pronounce his devotion. Loudly, he attempted to clear his throat. He swallowed freely and then finally spoke. Aubrey waited, thinking he was going to deliver a final goodbye.

Tate continued to look at her. A long moment passed, and he spoke softly, "Give me your other hand…" He pulled out a beautiful blue diamond solitaire ring—as perfect, flawless, and unique as she was—from inside his pocket. A local jeweler helped him in the selection just hours before he came here.

"Aubrey, I love you. I have for some time. I want you to be with me and hope your heart loves me, too. I want you to trust me going forward. Do you think you can do that?" Her head nodded in answer to both his questions. "More importantly, I felt something the very first time we touched that awakened my heart. Will you take this ring? Will you *take me?*"

HE WASN'T CERTAIN OF HER long pause, worsened by the sudden release of her hand from his. Instantly, she focused in the direction of where all the vehicles were parked on the sand. Her feet began running toward his truck. He thought he scared her off, that this was too much for her to deal with, but then he saw her coming back as quickly as she left. She brought back the brown bag she had left on his truck seat. His first thoughts were confused, but perhaps she was returning his shirt to him that she kept long ago.

When he opened the bag, the smile on his face said it all. He set the bag to the sand, picking her up just as a wave came in and wet her to her thighs. He lowered her to the dry sand and slid the ring perfectly onto her finger. The brown bag was washed up and opened in the process. The seagulls were already circling…sensing food from miles away. In the bag was a red velvet fudge pie. The still visible icing on top read, I love you! That was all the confirmation he needed. He didn't care if the seagulls dove in and took off with the pie, piece by piece. He had her, all of her sweetness, entirely in his hold.

While her smile beamed more than the sunlight to the beach, he cleared his throat to tell her more. "Aubrey, besides the proposal, I wanted to tell you that I wouldn't have been leaving this town anytime soon."

She scanned his eyes, pressing her brows together and

questioning, "Why? Did they bring you back for the case against Emerson?"

"Well, sort of." Tate tightened his hand around hers, seeing the ring peeking from below. "Aubrey, actually, I have taken a job."

She could only ask, "Where?"

"Well, I personally think that you will like this job I have accepted. I will be working with Levi and Pete."

Her excitement was conveyed by the hoarseness of her voice. "You are going to work here on our police force?"

He nodded like she had earlier then nudged her to start walking again. A short time later, they came to a heart drawn in the morning sand. The water had not yet reached it to wash it clear.

"Aubrey, I need to hear the word 'yes' from you. Aubrey, I love you."

He was going to be here, stay here, and be with her. He was all hers now. Aubrey's mind was racing. Before she could give him her verbal yes, she had to explain a few things. "Tate, I thought of you a few times, too." She admitted to herself it was every single day, not a few times. He smiled, and she saw that he knew the truth. Aubrey began to cry. She couldn't hold it back. All this was rushing at her in amazement.

"Tate, if you could see through my eyes, you would be amazed at the vision of you that stands before me." Aubrey wiped her eyes and continued, "I am so happy in this moment. I have loved you in my heart, in my daydreams, and since the first time you came to my rescue. I felt my heart come to life the first time I touched your hand."

With that, Tate placed his lips against the beautiful ring on her hand. It sparkled in the morning sunshine. "Aubrey, I love you. Say yes. Give me that one word from your lips. Let me keep this ring in place forever." He knelt down and waited.

Aubrey looked down to the sand and then to his eyes. Tate was still kneeling in the sand as Aubrey brought her lips to his. Knocking him to the ground in surprise, they lay in one another's arms, their lips not breaking contact. Aubrey broke their kiss. "Yes!" Tate recaptured her lips and wasn't going to let her leave his arms. The ring slipped a bit forward on her tiny fingers, but luckily, the ring never left her finger. He pushed it in place as they fell backwards onto the soft, cushioned sand.

Epilogue

THE SPRING LONG PASSED, AND as another summer season ended Aubrey was brought closure as the rulings were handed down for Tessa, Emerson, Damon, and others that would put them away for some time. Tate still had no final closure due to lack of evidence of Tessa or one of them murdering his first wife Callie, but he was certain they had a hand in what went down. That was enough for him.

Reed shared with him plenty of information, showing Emerson in Hagerstown with Damon and also a photograph of Emerson with Tate's ex-father-in-law. That put an unpleasant taste in Tate's mouth but a smile on his face, knowing they were all going to serve a lengthy amount of time. Surely they wouldn't return to this favorable town if and when they were released.

The tourists loaded their cars and vans full of their belongings. Bikes were fastened tightly to the back of their vehicles. *Sweet Treats* was closed today, though many visitors would have been taking snacks for their road trips home. Aubrey didn't even think for a second about losing any money at the bakery. Instead, she was gaining something worth so much more.

She walked out onto the balcony of her beach home, a home she shared with Tate since he proposed to her. The steps from the balcony to the beach were lined with beautifully colored flowers in potted planters, similar to the ones Aubrey recalled her grandmother once grew. On the beach below her, the sand was raked and rose petals formed a large heart for her to stand within by Tate's side in a few moments. Tate stood their already. He was the perfect guy. When he moved in with her, he had fixed the leaks and anything else that was wrong with the house. Today, it stood with character and curb appeal as Aubrey once wished it would. When it rained the home remained dry inside. Tate installed, new sink fixtures, new windows, new doors, a double lock system, an alarm system, and a state of the art barbeque. They hired a local painter, who made the exterior vibrant once again, and he even added the expensive decorative scrolled trim across the top of the house as a surprise for Aubrey. Tate and Aubrey together made this house such a wonderful place for them to call their home.

Tate stood tall beside the minister, who was there waiting for her arrival. Both the minister and Tate glanced upward to the balcony doors often. Lacey rushed up behind her to smooth out her white sundress and tucking one piece of her hair back into the loose-pinned bun. Slipping her feet from her white flower flip flops, she made her way down the steps to the sand.

Tate stood proudly with Reed to his side. Aubrey surpassed beautiful. She was radiant as she came to stand in front of Tate. Before the minister was to proceed, Aubrey asked for a moment. Lacey's mouth dropped open. Reed glared questionably at Tate. Tate glanced toward Aubrey. Her feet backed away from the sand carved heart. Everyone held their breath nervously, awaiting what was to come. She walked a good distance away to where her words could not be heard if she spoke softly. Tate followed.

"TATE, BEFORE WE DO THIS, I need to know you are all in." Her words were whispered to his ears. "All in."

"I am totally all in with you, forever. I love not only you but who I become having you as mine, so why would you doubt that?"

Tears pooled in her eyes, about to form the drops to fall. She tilted her head up to him. "Because I have something to tell you."

"Tell me. You can tell me anything." He waited.

"You and I, I mean I…Tate, we're pregnant!" She presented a sweet forced smile. It was a smile similar to someone yelling out "Surprise" at a party. Hoping the recipient isn't upset but rather happy for the amazement.

Tate stood composed, and a sudden calm passed over him. It was a wonderful feeling. Aubrey searched his face for a response or reaction. In his sexy, rough voice, he simply stated, "Aubrey, I fell in love with you, and I love to make you smile, but every time you smile, you glow, and I fall more in love with you. This is one of those times."

✧　✧　✧

WITH THAT, THERE WAS NEVER a more joyous of a ceremony to be had. In Tate's heart, he was already celebrating. He pulled her to him, taking her lips and tears to his mouth and sealing the love he felt for her at this moment. Lost in her, lost in this moment.

"I don't think we pronounced you man and wife, yet. Should we begin?" A voice was heard that made them laugh with their lips connected. Oh yes, there was a wedding to be performed. Tate broke their kiss and announced, loud enough for anyone to hear even as the waves crashed down, "Aubrey, you have made me the happiest man. I love you today and every day that I awake to find you next to me. Your sweetness has filled my heart, oh yes, and my stomach." He laughed.

"Tate, I never thought I could feel loved, truly loved. I lost that feeling when my parents died, but you bring a smile to my heart every day." Tate and Aubrey continued with professing their love to one another as they embraced several feet away from the minister, Lacey, and Reed as they were carrying out their very own private ceremony. They sealed their promises to one another with a long kiss. Tate took her hand and led her back into the heart in the sand.

"Okay, minister, let's legally make us married," Tate stated with a wink.

"I believe you both have professed your love and jumped to the kiss. I pronounce you man and wife." Their private moment and ceremony was enough for them. She was stunning as he watched her thank the minster and hug Lacey and Reed. They had forgotten the rings that Reed was holding, so it was another simple placement of those eternal symbols to his and her fingers to complete the day. She was his wife, he her husband, and he was going to be a father. One moment, stopping in this town, had changed his life for the better, forever. He would never forget that he had loved Callie. She was part of his life that was once happy, and it was her memory that had brought him to this town.

AS THE SEASONS CHANGED QUICKLY, the following spring brought a busy schedule of parking tickets and traffic violations to Tate, and Aubrey had brought on Lacey to work with her full time at the bakery. Aubrey was busy with preparing for the opening of her second bakery, *More Sweet Treats,* at the other end of town. Lacey had never wanted to stay at the inn. She just went there long ago when Aubrey was friends with Tessa.

Their spring ended with a big celebration, that of their son Tanner's arrival. There was no indecision in choosing their baby boy's name. Tanner was Aubrey's last name, which would honor her fallen family members, and their child was proudly given that birth name to carry forward.

REFLECTING BACK ON THE MANY seasons that passed since then, they had each been more wonderful and fulfilling. Today, Aubrey told Lacey she was heading out early in the afternoon. She trusted Lacey with every aspect of her business. She was so glad her and Lacey's friendship had grown, which should have happened long ago. Tate pulled in the front spot of the original *Sweet Treats* with the large black SUV that he purchased after trading in his truck.

They were about to take a ride to their favorite destination, but any place he traveled with her was breathtaking, he continuously had her right next to him. Aubrey's eyes lit up and sparkled beautifully, as if watching fireworks in the night sky. She focused on the only man that held her heart safely and then to Tanner, who won her heart the day he was born. He was a clone of his daddy, destined to one day be a heart throb. It was his eyes.

She kissed his tiny nose and beheld his impressive baby blue eyes as Tanner smiled back at her playfully. It was a life she never pictured for herself. They were heading to the sand park area, the one that Tate put into motion and the town raved about. When they arrived there, Tate knew Tanner's favorite sandbox, and he lowered Tanner carefully into the one that was a train caboose. So often Aubrey and Tate ended their days together and headed to this area of the beach to reconnect their hearts and just to remember where their life together had started. Although some days their lives busied, they knew they would never become derailed from this love they share with one another.

The End

My track thus far

Life takes us all astray, but those who are eternally in our hearts are never far.

Thank you to my loving husband Michael, my family, my friends, photographer Werner Tedesco for the amazing photo gracing the cover of this book, Jacy Mackin for editing this storyline (I know my original manuscripts are usually quite challenging), my awesome personal assistant Amy Hemp, my street team The Vivacious Vixens with their leading lady Rachel, and my cats Nyah and Cody who hold me in their hearts as they meow to be fed.

I want to make a special mention of one author that I have crossed paths with while on my writing journey. Our dreams and passions in the writing world have brought us so close, and she has been a truly supportive person to me. Her heart is too big for her chest. We have plans for the future together that will surprise the writing world and readers. Andrea to me, A.L. Wood to everyone else, I send you a virtual hug.

To all those who have brought smiles to my face, to those who have come from the past so long ago to the present as well, it is a breath of fresh air to have you in my life. Sometimes my smile is so big my cheeks hurt. It has been my pleasure to have shared memories and great moments with you all. Excitedly, I focus forward to the next crossroad and choosing the direction to take, whether I actually head that way or get *Derailed*.

More Romance by Author Renee Lee Fisher

The Heartbeat Series:

Rock Notes (Chapter One Sample to follow)

Love Notes

Music Notes

Coming Soon:

First Beat

First Bass

First Taste

The Crossing Series:

The Knot Hole (Chapter One Sample to follow)

The Passage

The Muse

Follow
Author Renee Lee Fisher

Website:

www.reneeleefisher.com

Email:

author@reneeleefisher.com

Facebook:

www.facebook.com/reneeleefisherauthor

Twitter:

twitter.com/ReneeLeeFisher

Excerpt from Rock Notes

Chapter One – Meeting

I AM IN A NEW *part of my life, driving through an early spring day, air thick with falling petals swirling about. I think back to where I was months ago and I remember my marriage ending. It was a horrible cycle of emotions for me, first came so many tears and pain. Then I had so many questions as to why was I suddenly replaced with a woman that he hired to work in his office. I thought we had a solid and secure relationship. His walking away from me was staggering. I then suffered loss of self esteem and later I found anger which was hard for me to release, I kept so much inside. I still carry with me a self-doubt. I'm not sure I can rely on my judgment enough to trust any future partner. My husband ending our marriage knocked me down, but each new road I travel, I will get stronger. I turn on the radio to hear something to sway my mood. The music immediately takes me away on a journey as I travel briefly from traffic light to traffic light through town. Seems like the changing of the light pattern is in a sequence of musical themes like the chorus repeating over and over, red – yellow – green. Go – it is now time for me to go and begin my journey writing*

about the band. Conveying through my words their passion, their singing, and their playing to becoming seasoned musicians. I follow all the traffic to the concert this evening.

This is my story **Rock Notes**.

"MAX, MAX, MAX RAND EXCUSE me, do you have a moment to talk to me?" I closed in on the far corner of the stage. I had purchased a front row ticket to this evening's local concert to take in tunes and set myself up for the possibility of conversation. "I know you don't know who I am so let me introduce myself. I am Madison Tierney, call me Madison or Maddy. I am a freelance creative writer, once a columnist and now I'm writing a book titled, "Rock Notes" which I follow a band in depth, and I'd like that to be your band "Rolling Isaac's." I didn't want to intrude on his time, so I simply said, "I know you have so many young ladies wanting you to sign autographs and their bodies," I smiled and continued to talk in a confident manner, "but I just wanted to give you my business card in case we can speak in the near future or have your band representation contact me."

Looking up at Max and his combination of youthful and mature yet awesome, truly awesome good looks, I shouted out "Oh and I thought the show was great." I beamed about it trying to remain calm, as I was more mature, rather than getting all flustered by a mere young band playing.

Max looked me over from his vantage point above and smiled a kind brim and nodded. I drank in all his chiseled features and his dark chocolate, delicious hair that had tousled all over during the concert, looking very sexy like he had been rolling in bed for hours. It was then that he turned slightly to jump down and he placed his stunning, well built arms on the edge of the stage and the tattoo under his sleeve peeked briefly through. He was wearing a tight white long sleeve tee pushed up onto his forearms, and he was completely soaked with his sweet sweat from singing to the crowd. I wasn't certain what was inked on him but I knew it drew me in. It was colorful and his tee shirt sleeve was stuck to him. I could see his firm, fit stomach also as the tee clung to his torso. I looked up, startled to see he was now standing in front of me and still smiling tenderly. He took my hand gently and slightly slid his finger over my fingertip as sensation ran through me, it was only for him to take the business card but it left me sort of out of breath, scattered my thoughts for a moment. His eyes pulled me in like an inviting Caribbean ocean, they were a deep tropical blue and his dark eyelashes swept over them. I had to rethink and tell my body to blink as I was captivated. I thanked him and hoped to hear from him and as he walked back I stood and stared at his tall frame and truly awesome body…he did not turn around. I went to finally leave when my feet would allow me to move them and I glanced back to take in the entire empty, darkened stage only to see him leaning on the far side and sending a smile and wink my way. I looked around to see if it was meant for someone else and then back to him where he laughed and nodded his head to me.

I walked to my car and thought about Max Rand and our brief meeting and I was concerned about my attire for some odd reason…as it took me hours to decide earlier what to put together which was very unlike me. It was like taking time to prep for a date. I kept reselecting pieces from my closet to make me look a bit more hip and trendy. Finally I had chosen simple jeans, black boots and a black top with open shoulder areas. The appliqué on the shirt was a striking detailed cross with hearts that seemed to dance across the top and wrap to the back, almost like a hug, I added a black gem belt. Checking my look in the mirror, I was content and headed to the concert. I was just about to take hold of the car handle when my cell phone sounded, its timing making me think I set off my car alarm. I reached into my pocket and was surprised to read:

I watched your nervous smile, and caught a glimpse of the top you wore, one of my inks looks like it. I sing yes, but I am also believe it or not, involved in the band's representation…can we continue our conversation at a quiet space tomorrow? Max Rand

I fumbled for a reply to him, could this actually be happening, he was contacting me in mere moments? I sent him a voice text as a reply –

Yes, sure. Under my breath I said absolutely.

That was so stupid of me, an adult to say yes, sure, and he probably heard me say absolutely…what was I thinking, I had to be in control of this proposal for my writing and I should not feel like a school girl, shy and nervous, my phone sounded again.

I can meet you in Philly. There's a coffee house there. It's the 2ⁿᵈ Street Coffee Café. I began in the biz there and I hang out there upstairs. Meet you at two o'clock. The address is the name. I got the first cup.

Wow was this really happening, I decided to take control of my life for once and go after the stories I wanted to write and now I was going to possibly have my foot in the door per se. I replied:

Sounds great...I'll be there

Of course I would be there. That is all that I could say to him without sounding too over anxious. I smiled to myself and opened my car and positioned myself behind the wheel ready to start to take control of my life.

I drove out of the city skyline to my townhouse. I had just begun to make it my new home over the past few months. The collapse of my marriage was devastating. My husband of ten years, Thomas, came to an epiphany that he just wasn't in love with me anymore. He had taken me to bed and poured his heart out about how we were soul mates and destined to be together in the end, but there was something missing for him. As we made love that evening trying, I thought, to save or recapture what he felt he was lacking, I was unaware that this was his goodbye to me. He held me in his arms until dawn, but when I awoke he had left and moved out. I broke down and since I was always the one in the shadows of him, I had no real confidence to stand alone or walk tall. I was lost and lacked all confidence in my ability to love another. I didn't find out right away, but the dark, ugly truth eventually made it out into the open. The fact was that Thomas found someone else, but apparently did not want to come right out and tell me that himself.

We met in college, as I was deciding to be an English Major to write or do something like that with my degree; he had all his ducks in a row and set goals and was heading for the big business world. He had followed in his family's steps and was soon interning with a leading financial company and heading for the top. Great pay, high-rise condo in the city, convertible automobile of the latest year and me as his wing person, just along for the ride and always in the shadows. He loved me I know but I always felt he could do better with someone showier, someone that wanted the life that he sought after. For me hanging in sweatpants and cami tops all day and writing different poems and stories was pure satisfaction. We had been in love and enjoyed so many memories together for ten years. He kept striving for the top so we put off any plans of starting a family and I was content with that as I had come from a slightly dysfunctional family that the peace and calm of just him and I was perfect.

We had a beautiful over the top wedding with all the trimmings. Thomas's family planned it all and the only say I got was that I loved crème tea roses with dark pink edges and so on my wedding day the only thing I remember smiling at was that there were a few of my favorite flowers. I really just wanted it simple but he wanted to show the world that he was getting married, only for me to find out later that the company he was working for wanted their employees married to show a secure status and responsibility. Now I wonder if he was really in love with me or was it a business tactic.

Pulling into my driveway, I was finally reaching a comfort level in my life that took so long to get to after my breakdown. My townhome was quite comfortable with several extra rooms. One of the rooms held my desk and all my writings strewn about and another was filled with music for me to enjoy as I wrote. It also contained various art pieces, treasures I carefully selected. These rooms became a source of comfort for me, it became my tiny slice of heaven, a safety net for me to be in and feel secure.

I threw my keys on the table in the entranceway and entered my bedroom and saw all the clothing choices I picked through earlier for the evening all over the floor. I laughed at my mess and climbed up onto my bed. I reached for my notebook, tucked my knees comfortably and began to write a handwritten note for Max Rand.

Max Rand:

As I sat this evening in the front row of your Philadelphia Concert, I was all too captivated by you. I am not certain in my lifetime that you will ever read this, my first love letter to you, nor have the opportunity to read my words as I write them. I just knew that something touched me deep inside as I sat below the stage and watched you and the band begin to perform. As the show progressed I could not take my eyes from you, not in a star struck way, but I felt I was pulled in by some force to you. I know this is crazy as I had just met you but I felt I knew you for such a long time.

My heart is not in a good place right now, I still

feel something tugging inside and I knew that you started that pull. Let me tell you that your blue eyes are so warming, they searched the crowd and landed on mine and I felt them envelope me. So many fans were on their feet tonight dancing and singing all the words to your songs. I sat firmly in my seat, mostly because I felt if I stood that my legs might weaken mainly due to how your passion was coming through in your music and it made me crumble.

Max, as I handed you my business card I wondered how I could love you and fall for you. It was almost love at first sight. I guess this is pretty sappy for me writing about you like this, and it feels as though I am gushing with my first never to be read love letter. This will be added to my Love Notes and be like my secret diary. For now I will await our next encounter and see what feeling comes to me at the sight of your face or the sound of your voice.

Maddy xo

My eyes tired from writing and I drifted into thought. I am not sure if I'm still awake daydreaming or if I have actually fallen asleep. I was again at the concert from this evening and as they announced the band, Rolling Isaac's I was looking and searching to connect with Max's eyes and there they were. He sought me out and winked and never took his deep blue eyes from me…he reached out on one song, his hand stretching toward me and almost touching me as I reached toward him. Wanting that touch, wanting that feeling…wanting a brief passing of his igniting sensation. He got on his knees and his hands were clasped around the microphone as if in prayer. He was deep in a ballad and pouring his heart into it. He looked at me and I sank, it was so very crushing, it tore at my heart.

I was all wrapped up in the sheets and woke to music coming from my programmed ring tone on my cell phone, a tune from Tenth Avenue North called *Love is Here*. I exhaled and for that moment in my dream, love was there. I was still in my clothes from the concert, twisting in the sheets. Who was calling me now, and what time was it? I glanced at the clock it was already after eight in the morning. I slept through and Jillian called. I missed meeting up with her at eight to head to the gym. I reached out and dialed her back, and told her I was so tired and slept in but would meet her later in the week.

Jillian had become my rock over the past months. She was the first to enter the door to the high rise condo my husband and I shared after he left me. She had to pick me up, carry me and take care of me for many days. She taught me to lean on myself and take control and never be so dependent on another that I would lose myself. We shared so many girl talks and girl days together. My phone now sounded with a text that she would catch me later and hoped my tiredness was because I met someone and had fun and a late night. Although she knew that had not happened over all these months and she knew that I was not seeking that she asked anyway. I had been so deeply hurt that I didn't think I could go that route ever again.

Now that I was up I stripped down and decided to take a shower and see what was ahead of me for today as I had to meet Max Rand. Just then while in thought for the afternoon my phone sounded and a text came through. I thought Jillian was reaching out again to make the gym a little later but it was from Max.

Good morning Madison, hope you're free later tonight. I have rehearsal and if our conversation goes well, you can come meet the band. It'll give them a chance to decide about you writing about us. Hope you slept well.

Wow, I stood there, completely nude, reading this and the water in the shower continued to run, if only he knew how great I slept. I dreamt of him. This was chilling to my naked body, but in such a good way.

The rest of the morning seemed to drag; it is always like this when you want to be someplace. I caught up on cleaning since my clothes were all over and also prepared an outline for my writings in hopes my project was approved.

Soon it was time for me to leave to meet him. As I was driving into the city it took me back to Thomas and me living there before. I was happy and in love then. Thomas still lived downtown, and still almost like it was written on his calendar, would call me and leave a message of how he was thinking of me each month that has passed since he left and since the divorce. Each time he would leave in the message that he knew that we would be back together sometime in the future but he needed time to find himself, or he'd say he wasn't there yet. He never admitted to me that he left me for another woman. I heard he moved on real quickly with a new office intern, that he handpicked for the position but I heard it wasn't all that wonderful lately and there was trouble early on in their new paradise. I never took his calls because as angry as I felt inside, I admit I was weak and I would have broken down and taken him back. I would have liked closure, to hear him tell me his side of what happened. After all the time that has passed, I still felt something for him for all those years together as man and wife. We all make mistakes or wrong decisions and I always believe in second chances. I think he may have been convincing and I would have crumbled.

I was going round and round on the city streets hoping to park close to the coffee shop, but luck was not on my side for parking. I finally managed to take a spot as someone was leaving but several streets over, so my afternoon arrival time was delayed by about fifteen minutes. When I arrived I walked in and was greeted by the employee behind the counter in a very friendly manner. Before I could tell him I was meeting someone he told me that Max was upstairs already. Upward I went and smiled at the idea that Max already alerted the coffee staff of my impending arrival.

Max was deep in thought and writing in a journal as I approached. He wore cool looking silver rimmed reading glasses that he had not worn on stage and a hat that snuggled down covering his ears. He looked so everyday, average, but still very breathtaking in his normalcy. I was surprised as he seemed reserved and not exposed as when he was up the stage last evening with screaming girls surrounding him. He looked simple, still drop dead good looking but he camouflaged it this afternoon with not having a tight tee, tight jeans or the cuff bracelet. He had worn a leather cuff bracelet last evening that he had kissed before raising his hand to the crowd at the end of the show. I wanted to ask him about that gesture but figured I would in time if I saw him do it again in concert. Today, if I didn't know I was meeting him, the same Max Rand from last night, I would have passed this guy by on a street. His attire was toned down, plain loose black tee with an open buttoned shirt over top, loose and worn and torn jeans and it appeared work boots. I pulled out the chair across from him as he looked up; he was really lost in thought there for the moment.

He paused and then complimented the color of my shirt. I felt the heat as he was staring at my chest. "Madison, wow, you look so warm."

"I'm not warm, I feel fine."

"No, I mean your shirt color highlights your dark hair and sends a warm glow. I guess I am stumbling here for something nice to say. But you look good. You're good looking and you remind me of the warmer days coming." He also sniffed in the air and said, "You smell good, really good."

"I guess thank you and thank you, you may make me blush."

Wow, did he just floor me with a compliment, and he actually smelled my Light Blue fragrance, even though I only applied a trace of it. I felt shifted in my thoughts. I had to gain composure and so I blurted out nervously, "Glad you could meet me so soon." I spoke in a professional manner trying to sound more and more confident.

He smirked and simply replied "Yeah, sure absolutely." Sounding just like me last night. He asked how I liked my coffee and took the liberty of ordering some lunch selections since if this went well, he wanted me to head to meet the band so there wasn't time for food until much later.

We began talking and I explained to him that I was following my dream of writing and had certain pieces that I wanted to complete and put together in a collection. One was to get in depth with a band. Why his band? Well I had heard them play a tune months back called *Missing Ash* and during the lowest time in my life, I had downloaded it and played it too often as I wrote at home in my writing room. I dared not tell him that, all I said was, "I have heard great chatter about the Rolling Isaac's." Also, since they were a local band from Philly. I could easily attend a lot of their shows and perhaps get stories from them to write about.

I drifted in thought for a moment; here I was trying to start a conversation and hearing Thomas in my head telling me that my writings were good, although he never really cared to read them. They weren't making him the big bucks in the corporate world so he just seemed to pass me over. But I had been so in love with him, perhaps I should have ignored my passion of writing and been more in tune with him.

"Madison, hey come back"…Max was seeking my reply. I jumped as he lightly touched my hand as it lay near my untouched coffee. It felt comfortable, safe and he kept fingers on top of my hand.

"You zoned on me, where did you just go?" He asked. I apologized to him as I slid my hand out and took a sip of coffee. I told him that I drift often into thoughts that take me away for a moment but not thoughts I want to stay in.

I started the conversation explaining that if I wasn't going to be an intrusion or bother tagging along with them, I wanted to cover them and get some real raw, natural experiences of the band. The talent, their hopes, and what they gave up to have their dreams. I told him it could be for a few months or longer but that would depend on if it became bothersome for me to be with them. I knew they played in Philly often but knew they traveled about as well. I told him the travel wouldn't be a problem and would be at my own expense. In between my speaking with him I managed to take in some bites of food, but I was still nervous. I felt like I was on a first date. I was trying to settle myself and continued to tell him some of my story.

My husband Thomas made a lot of money and he thought to leave me a nice divorce settlement. He did this despite saying that we would never be over. I guess his leaving me for someone else helped him to not have the guilt of carrying on an affair and staying married. I think he felt that he could try out this new woman and if it didn't work then he would have me in the wings. I lived a simple life so the monetary agreement would surely carry me far. But I didn't tell Max any of this, I just looked into the dark blue eyes that I had dreamt of and was stunned that they were the same blue as in my dream. I told him I was in a position to do my own travel and would not be any burden to them. I did then produce for him several pieces of writing that I published in the past from being a column writer for years at the city paper and then to a few books that were out on the shelves of several bookstores. None were best sellers, but to me, humble accomplishments. I had so many confidence steps to climb in my life now but I think I was feeling like I was on the second step.

Max glanced at the portfolio of items I brought supporting my occupation and smiled. He said, "I know exactly who you are, I followed your weekly column. You wrote the editorial piece a few years ago supporting bands. It highlighted a new, up and coming band, our band the Rolling Isaac's." Max continues "I still have the clipped article someplace back on **The Wall.** That's what we call it where we rehearse and where the band tacks up our memorabilia. You should see this wall it's freaking awesome!" He flashed me a devilish smile and said. "Slapped all over are new items about us, photos of our loved ones, and many we have loved and left the next day."

I shook at that last statement; I had been drawn in by his keepsake of the article, but then stunned by the morning after thought. Thomas had left me the morning after, left me after ten years. I had been so caught up in him that I lost me.

I could feel his eyes, warmth focused in on me and I moved around in my seat. As we talked I couldn't help thinking about the other girls. I was trying to convince him to let me follow the band, but I knew I was different from them. I knew that I was about eight years older than Max

Rand. Nothing that he said or did made me feel old, but that was just one way I was different than the rest of his followers.

"What the hell, a pretty, smart lady asks to write about me and the band, I say yes, and you can start by calling me Rand. I'm done with hearing the girls scream "Max". I tune them out. You though Madison I would listen to. It also gets confusing with me being Max and my Uncle Maxwell. Rand makes it easier. So I say, it's a go," Max said.

"Then Rand it is, thank you." I cheerfully sounded, and I nodded to agree.

After a few more bites of food from Rand's lunch selections, I started to ramble a bit. I paused only when he would eat as I followed the food to the edges of his lips. I was getting easily distracted, but then I calmed myself and told Rand a little about why I was pursuing this project now. I explained that I'd been through a painful divorce and I was beginning a new chapter in my life. I offered little in the way of details, hoping to make it clear I didn't want to revisit this subject. I needed to take a moment in my life to recapture my dream and goals and was hopeful that he could help me with that. I talked innocently to him about losing love and wanting to fill my days now with work and keep busy – that love wasn't something for me anymore. Rand looked and closed his eyes for a moment and there was something else that appeared in the blue when he reopened them, something in his thoughts but I didn't press. He knew I sought out approval for this venture with them, so he again said it was no problem.

Rand said, "Madison, all of us hurt and have been cut deep. We look for a new start, if we can ever find it." I wasn't sure where that part of our conversation was heading but he smiled warmly at me.

"Ready? Let's go" he said and grabbed my hand and tucked his journal under his other arm. I felt his fingers just hold the edges of my first three fingers lightly. He never paid a tab, but left a large bill under my unfinished coffee cup. He led me down the steps, waved goodbye to the staff, and we walked out to the black Hummer parked in the very front space. He released my fingers very slowly, in a way that made me shiver. I reached in my portfolio case and pulled out my voice recorder and hit record. I began to say with excitement in my voice, "This is the start of my writing Rock Notes." He opened the door for me, as he walked to the other side, in my whisper voice that began to shake on my recorder; I added "OMG!"

We drove about forty five minutes to where they had their space to rehearse. It was out in the suburbs of the city, in Bucks County. As we pulled up onto the location I stared at the oversized, completely redone barn. It was a sight to take in. I had seen many old barns, but this has a modern twist to its exterior. The architecture was beautifully done, not where I expected a band would rehearse. There were several acres of cleared, rolling green property that surrounded it and there was a custom built home off in the corner. It was such an awesome home; it looked like something from that television show on HGTV would have built. I wondered if their rehearsals were a nuisance to the neighbors. When I questioned him on it, he simply replied that he knows the owner and the owner never complains. We had exchanged brief conversation in the car, mostly about how much mileage does the Hummer get, weather and stupid, yes stupid, conversation topics from me. I had blundered through the conversation, but most of the unspoken communication came from Rand. He often glanced over at me and smiled, just simply smiled. I put music on and when it was their music on his playlist I said stupidly, "This is a great tune." Again, Rand flashed me his simple smile, not telling me how dumb I was coming across.

When we pulled into the open area to park in front of the barn, he told me to wait. He came around and opened the Hummer door for me. Thomas had not done this in years; I always let myself out of my side. It was such a nice gesture from Rand and the start of our business together and I hoped that the band would be as comfortable and welcoming to me.

Where do I begin? The band, all too charming, and hot looking, not as charming as Rand, and definitely not the heat of Rand's looks, but they were like a band of brothers to one another. Don't get me wrong, they talked up their stories of the girls they won and tossed. Yes tossed, and their words pitted in my stomach but I knew I had to suppress that and be calm. Rand even said, "Madison, good luck with us, you may not like us, other days you may, but don't fall for any of us, we're dysfunctional."

"Who's not functional?" was shouted by one of the band members from behind us. That gave us all cause to laugh and then I then began to meet each of the band members.

Introductions began with none other than Isaac; the person the band was named after. He was a local to the Philly area, and from what I had seen one incredible guitar player. I was introduced to him as *my front row*.

I asked, "Why was I named that?"

"Rand saw you in the front row of our show and he never took his eyes off you." Isaac's answer tugged at my heart.

Isaac seemed to be the loudest of the members and oh so ready to party. He already had a few girls waiting for him. Hoping for a kiss and that he might stay with them. I'm not sure if he needed this attention as he was a confident guy. My first take on Isaac was he was the life of any party.

I was talking with him about what I do for a living, and Rand came and tugged at him for a moment. Rand said something to him and then Isaac replied, "Hell yes, to the front row chick." Just like that, I was approved to follow along with them.

The other members then came over and were introduced to me. Next I spoke with Raeford who played the drums. He was from the Midwest, Decatur, Illinois. He was the silent one of the band I was told, and he looked so much like Usher. Rand had filled me in that Raeford brought the funk and soul to some of their songs. To me, he seemed mysterious, quiet but when I saw him on the drums the evening before he went off, so I knew he had another side.

I was introduced to Ron and Kent last. Ron was their keyboard player, wearing sunglasses indoors – in the evening. I wasn't sure what that was about but he was very friendly. Ron welcomed me aboard and told me he was from the south. He had a slight southern drawl and was very kind. Kent was from upstate in Pennsylvania, from a small town called Clarkes Summit and he was the bass player. He was the most muscular, or should I say overly muscular, he would intimidate any person at a gym. He was very solid and fit and had a shaved head and a few piercings. He said he was destined for the military until he met up with these guys and music took over. As Kent approached me, he did not hesitate to pick me up and twirl me about and then he planted, yes planted, solidly a kiss right on my lips. I was shocked for the moment and they all laughed and he released me. The only one who seemed annoyed was Rand. He shook his head "no" to Kent and then Kent smirked at him as he simmered in his joyous greeting.

Rand told the rest of the band that I was going to write about them and to be themselves and pretend I wasn't there so I could capture them raw and real as much as possible. Rand then took me over to an area that was the loft of the barn, completely furnished with sofas and chairs and a bar that overlooked their practice stage area. As he left to head down to practice he said "Madison there's beer, help yourself and get writing. I believe it will be very interesting."

I pulled out my voice recorder and spoke into it a lot of my initial thoughts. I also pulled out my portfolio and laptop and began to type and type. The title read alone on a full page – *Rock Notes*. The band practiced for several hours, I periodically got up and stretched. I turned away and decided to help myself to a beer, well a few in the timeframe and then I walked over behind the sofa area to see **The Wall** up close and personal. This was amazing; it was huge and had a backdrop on it like a brick wall. I scanned over all the contents and in the center was the band's name, Rolling Isaac's and in each area of the wall a band member had a large area of their name and keepsakes. I saw Rand's area and there were photos of him with many, many young girls. So many photos of him with his microphone, on his knees singing and it looked like he was on the verge of crying. Next to one of these photos was a beautiful photo of a girl, so model like in looks. She had dark hair similar to his in color and shoulder length like his. She also had the most beautiful blue eyes. Next to this picture, were words signed by Rand, it read, *I will forever love you Ashley*. It took my breath away for a moment and I thought that perhaps this was the love of his life. Maybe it went bad, or perhaps they were still together, although I wasn't about to ask.

I saw many newspaper clippings and articles about all of them posted all over **The Wall**. I searched to see if my column was there and it was. I reread what I had written several years ago and I was surprised at the end of the article to see a circle around my name. Yes, just below my column photo, there was a definite circle around just my name, *Freelance Columnist – Madison Tierney*.

It was a good piece of writing if I say myself and it brought the band a lot of attention. I had done research on different bands in the city and had listened to their earlier music and critiqued it and wrote a piece about their sound and their following, although I never met them. So here I was now after meeting them, and I smiled that here I was a piece of their famous **Wall**.

Throughout their rehearsal I caught many moments of Rand staring at me. He was singing and it felt as if he was driving his voice right through me. I was always a fan of Rock music and when Rand began to sing a slow ballad, I was unable to move, I felt weak as it tore me up. It was about love lost and the emptiness you undergo and time spent on love that was gone in a moment. I wasn't sure if he had glanced my way then to see the tears in my eyes but I hoped he hadn't because I didn't want him to think I was that pathetic. Love lost was definitely where I was. He glanced up to me in the loft as soon as he finished the final melody, adding another verse without anyone playing the music. It was then that I turned away with tear filled eyes and I walked over to choke down another beer hoping to dissolve the lump in my throat.

As their evening rehearsal, or should I say early morning rehearsal came to a close, he headed up to me in the loft area. Some of the band guys had earlier invited some of their friends which were girls, to come hang out near the stage during their rehearsal. I stayed up in the loft the entire time away from them putting some of my thoughts to notes. I was watching Rand as he had stopped, yet again, to kiss another pretty young girl and patted her on the ass.

When he reached me I said, "So are you spreading the love?"

He replied, "Madison, I have no love, I just make them feel good. Actually, I feel nothing." He said, "I lost love for anything long ago." I felt bad for starting this conversation and told him I was sorry for the intrusion into his personal life. I had a few too many beers and I know I tend to get all curious and weepy when I drink. I gathered my belongings and then he pulled my hand toward him but I wasn't certain where we were going. I thought we'd go back to get my car in the city, but then he said, "Madison, come with me," in a serious, sexy tone. A few girls were hooking up with some of the band members. Isaac was loud in shouting out to two girls that they were both for him this morning. Rand never said goodbye to them, he just waved a hand up and we walked from the loft to outside into the morning darkness and then down the path toward the house just beyond.

As we walked I asked him if we were going to wake anyone at this house. I also suggested to him that I only lived out by the National Park, only about a half hour away so if it wouldn't be a problem he could just take me home instead of all the way to the city for my car. He did not answer; he simply took hold of my hand and led me closer to the grand front door. When we got in front he removed a key and opened the door to a beautiful, lavish wooden foyer. Rand then spoke. "I've had too many beers and you look beat, I say we get your car when the sun comes up." He then said as he brushed past my ear tucking a fine wisp of hair behind my ear, "Madison, make yourself comfortable in my home. You can crash down in any of the rooms upstairs. There are plenty of boxes of the band's tee shirts if you want to change, help yourself. He continued with, "You're now part of our band" and his eyes sparkled and he smiled and then he headed toward the kitchen.

"Madison what can I get you?" he asked with an intriguing tone.

While what I really preferred is to spend more time with him, even at this late hour, I replied, "I don't need anything but thank you, all I really need is some sleep." He laughed and replied, "I'm getting cases of Red Bull for you to keep up with us on the road."

"Don't worry I will keep up, today was just a long introduction."

"Madison we have only just begun, but sleep well."

It really had been a very long afternoon and evening, and I was mentally exhausted trying to process all that had happened today. I headed toward the upper level and went in the very first room to crash. I laid my body on the first bed I saw not bothering with my clothes. Since it was spring and the evening weather was nice, I had worn a crème colored lace cami top with a floral sweater over it and jeans, but I barely recall slipping the sweater over my head.

Once my eyes closed, my thoughts turned to Rand, lost soul, lost love, so similar to me but then on stage he was so confident and sure of himself and his place in the world. That confidence was something that I lacked. He attacked the stage and all his charm and stunning looks dissolved those that set their eyes or minds on him. My mind kept trailing over and over about him. His deep blue eyes, his messy dark hair that just swept over his shoulder, his towering height, his hidden inks. I could think of nothing but him.

I tensed for a moment when I felt someone hovering over me. I felt a breath and caught the scent of Rand fresh from a shower. I was lying on my side and I slightly opened my eyes. I knew I was seeing him, not dreaming. I could see him getting closer and I shut my eyes, remaining so very still. He reached down, took his curved fingers down my cheek, so slowly and tenderly and then he leaned in and kissed me on the forehead. Trailing his mouth down from my forehead he placed a soft kiss on the side of my neck and then moved upward to the tip of my shoulder and he lightly bit at my cami strap. I was so completely shocked and although I wanted to reach around and tell him I was awake, I couldn't move. I had hopes that in the darkness he didn't see me see peak out at him moments earlier. He then whispered, "Night Madison" and he tugged off my boots and pulled a light blanket over me.

When the sun appeared in the bedroom I awoke all nervous, I got up and went to the bathroom. I had to search my purse for items to make myself presentable. It had only been about four hours that I slept. I gathered my boots and put my sweater back on and went downstairs to find Rand already wide awake and in the kitchen making us some breakfast.

"I'm starving," he said looking at me like he was ready to devour me. "Madison what are you hungry for?"

He made me hesitate to answer him, I was definitely hungry for him. "I think I could eat something." My stomach was excited and jumping inside just from seeing him so relaxed and cooking.

"Your phone has been vibrating all morning."

"What's vibrating?" I was too focused on his body and didn't hear his words.

"Your phone, you left it on the steps last night with your computer."

"Oh, okay that's what was vibrating." I was still watching his body in motion, and was thinking of how I would like him to make me stir. He caught me staring at him and I looked away and then I remembered I had silenced my phone during their practice and then powered it up when we walked over to the house. I had to pull myself together so I went to retrieve my phone and I looked at all the missed messages, they were from Jillian. I hollered back, "Rand, I just need a few minutes to check my messages." I went into his main front room and dialed her back.

"Where the hell are you?" Jillian yelled. She was so worried that I hadn't called her and she stopped by my place having her own key and I was no where to be found. It took some effort to calm her but I told her briefly what had happened since the concert.

"Jillian can you take me to Philly today to get my car? I don't want to put Rand out anymore. I'll just see if he can bring me back to my house."

"I'll agree only on one condition, I want every single detail, don't leave anything out, I want all of them!" I had to put my hand over the phone as she said this. She was so loud and I hoped Rand did not hear any of this.

"Hey, I should go, I don't want to be rude, he is making me breakfast," I whispered to her.

"No I bet you're his breakfast…but I'll come get you at noon. You can tell me then how great this sexy man is."

I didn't get to comment, as she hung up too quickly. Rand flashed me a sexy smile when I returned to the kitchen, I wasn't sure if he heard any of our conversation. I did look up at the high ceiling in his house and knew each word spoken echoed.

"Wow this smells and looks so good," I commented but wanted to say you look and smell so good.

"Madison, take notes, you can write this too, I can cook and I am very good." Again that sexy smile pursed on his lips.

Before me was a breakfast feast. There were berry filled pancakes, sliced fruit, fresh squeezed orange juice and turkey sausage links and of course coffee made just like he had ordered for me at the coffee shop and it was in a large to go cup that read 2nd Street Coffee Café. I bet he had tons of these to go cups, he said he was a regular there.

As we sat at breakfast Rand was still writing something in his journal.

"Rand, this tastes delicious, thank you."

"Madison you seem so easy to please."

"I am a simple person, but I want to know about you, can I ask you a question?"

"Ask away Madison."

"Well this is a lovely home" I began and "well did you always live here? Was it your parents'? How did you and the band meet? Who inspired your music?"

Rand began, "Hey slow down, you said a question" he

paused, "and that's several questions. But, yes, this is my home; built the year after our band got our big break. I figured since my mother, Angela had passed away from cancer right before then and she left me money I would do something good. I had the recording studio built for our rehearsals. It honored her as I continued with my passion for music."

I looked at him and smiled tenderly and then wrote some notes. He continued to answer my numerous questions. "My inspiration was my grandfather Archer, he taught me music from as far back. He was great but he left this world before my mother." Rand continued, "If I ever have a son he will be called Archer after my grandfather." And there was a smile on Rand's face like a child at an amusement park for the first time. I held his look of pure love that he displayed as he mentioned his mom and grandfather, it was so endearing and then doing what I do best, I blurted out, "What about your father is he proud of you?"

"Well," Rand replied in a serious tone, "not someone I want to discuss, to me he is Paul and right now dead to me. He never really acted like a father. When my mom got ill, he couldn't handle it, he left. He hated I played music. Hated I was the singer in a band. He hated that Ashley was my biggest cheerleader. I'm young, I stayed out late, I drank and he told me I lacked responsibility and purpose. He told me to get a real job in the business world, but not be a singer in a band."

I looked at him as he answered and mouthed silently that I was sorry. I was sorry to hear about his mother passing and his dad's desertion. I saw his eyes swell but not break, perhaps this was his love lost.

I wanted to change the subject and said, "Rand, I have lost too, most recently, my husband, Thomas. We were married ten years. He just one day up and left me, for someone at his office. The one good memory that I have from my wedding was the flowers. They were my favorite – delicate crème roses with dark pink edging. I don't want to bore you but Thomas had become my life and world for a long time. As for my family life, it's only me. I was an only child. It was lonely. I guess that is why I love Jillian so."

I never stopped. Once I got started, I kept right on going. "And, to make my life crazier, my mother, Grace left my father, John and I for my father's younger brother Jake. She and my uncle moved off to Galveston, Texas. I haven't heard from her since."

Rand responded, "Wow your mom leaving with your uncle that's hard."

"It was, and I found myself swamped with the memories of her abandoning us, of how it felt and how I knew that I'd never truly understand relationships again."

"Do you miss her?"

"I do, she is my mother, but I never knew how to reach out to her. Since I was still with my father, I didn't want to add to his sorrow of her departure. The only saving grace, per se, for my father during that awful time was that he didn't need to raise me as I was already a teenager."

"So tell me about your father."

"Well, he was a police officer; he was a little tough on me

since I was his only child. He recently retired but back during his days on the beat, he was strong like a Robocop. Everyone looked up to him. His fellow officers called him Mick, but everyone else called him Mr. McCormick out of respect. He was a very strong man but her leaving us really broke him I lived it and witnessed it."

"I miss my mother and uncle being part of my life. My mother was a true romantic and very creative so I think I have her to thank for my writing traits. But the romance part I no longer have. I hope I am not boring you with my story?"

Rand looked happy that I was sharing stories with him, "Madison not at all, I like when you talk to me, you're very…interesting."

I decided to continue and told him how I met Thomas after which I took a deep breath and then let out.

"My father adores him, and when we divorced my father blamed it on me. He told me that I didn't try hard enough to love and stay with Thomas. I haven't had the chance to repair this relationship with my father, if there is any to fix. Even now my father and Thomas talk and get together, that hurts me."

"I'm sure he adores you, what's not to like." Rand took my hand into his and began to stoke his thumb over my knuckles. "Maybe in time you and your father will reconnect." Rand could see me pushing through this with pained eyes so he changed the family topic rant of mine to geography. I was immediately grateful for his attempt to distract me and got lost in Rand's story as he kept hold of my hand with his soothing light touch.

He began to tell me that he always lived in the city and loved the vibe. He also explained how his music career all began by singing at the 2nd Street Coffee Café. Later, he ran into some other musicians and it was Isaac that shouted one drunken night for them to form a band. They all agreed to pursue this venture and their dreams of making their music together. It allowed them to combine their individual musical talents. They all fell into it quite nicely and the band in turn took off from local venues to now statewide venues. They decided together to name themselves *Rolling Isaac's* as Isaac always rolled into the practice sessions late. They didn't have a demanding schedule since they tried to stay grounded in normal life, but they did have a manager to oversee their schedules and travel and bookings.

Rand told me about his Uncle Maxwell, who had been hired to be the band's manager. He was Rand's mother's brother who took a special interest in Rand after is mother died and his father left. Maxwell was very good at the finances and the other business aspects of music. Rand's Uncle Maxwell had never had any children and never married. He had built himself a nice bank account from working in the music industry early and no one to share with, except his nephew Rand. Maxwell took care of all the schedules and arrangements from the band's equipment, to venue. He kept all the big things that went into a performance with the band low key. Maxwell took care of his guys and wanted them to focus on the music. Maxwell let them do what they did well; create their tunes while he ran around behind the scenes.

Rand continued to tell me that he had been named after his uncle and always felt a strong bond with him. His uncle always encouraged Rand to write his own songs. He was very proud and never disappointed in the career path Rand chose. He believed Rand had such talent and his music was a true art form.

The knowledge of his losses pained me since I too knew that feeling of loss. Rand then started on an upbeat note to change the tempo of our conversation. "This book is going to be great! You're a good luck charm to our band when you write about us. Plus this time I'm looking forward to hanging with you." I got up to help him with the dishes and he said, "Madison, leave it, go crash in the sunroom. I know you only slept a few hours." I wasn't about to disagree. I turned to head to the other room, as we were standing very close, he brought up his hand to the side of my cheek and touched me gently. Just as he did while I lay pretending to sleep last night. I gushed inside, I could not wait to share this with Jillian, but then I stopped. If he could not love then what was this? Just to make me feel good like he had with kissing those girls last night and many other nights in the past? I was confused and so I walked out into the stunning, bright sunroom.

The décor was masculine but eclectic. Several music themed items were in there and the rays of sunshine warmed the room as I curled up in the taupe colored leather loveseat looking outdoors and taking in the property from this view. My eyelids got heavy and I drifted.

My phone sounded and I jumped up. It was Jillian heading to my house already. Rand was lying at the other edge of the loveseat with me, leaving only about eight inches of separation between us and he was writing in his journal.

"Can I bother you? I need to get home Jillian is coming to take me to get my car. I left it parked on 5th Street yesterday."

"No bother Madison, I can take you all the way to your car."

"No, Jillian is heading to my house anyway and she lives in the city so it's not out of her way."

"Oh, that's right you have a story to tell her, she wants to hear all about us." He started to laugh.

"Oh, I guess you heard our conversation." I was blushing.

I diverted that topic and said. "I just bought a new white Audi. I just didn't want to leave it in the city too long."

"Hey don't worry I'll get you back and I'll meet Jillian." He laughed and then said, "If I don't get you to her soon your phone will never stop ringing."

Jillian was already in my driveway when we arrived. Just like so many others, she knew who Max Rand was, but she's never met him. When he jumped out and came to open my door, her eyes got large. And then, when he took my computer and belongings into his arm, she smiled brightly. When he walked up to my door and met with her, he took her hand lightly and introduced himself, and she melted. He had that way with all the girls and lately the grown women as well.

"Rand thank you so much for the ride and the writing opportunity. I will talk to you later to go over your travel schedule." I gave him a quick hug and started to move away.

He pulled me close and said, "Madison, we leave in the morning. It's going to be a packed schedule, first Florida, and then we come back to Philly for a few weeks. Then we have Atlanta, Texas and back here to Philly to regroup." He then moved one hand to touch the side of my face as his lips lingered on my cheek what seemed a very long moment. I nervously pulled my face away, and then Rand said, "I spoke with my Uncle Maxwell and all arrangements are done. We will be by around ten tomorrow morning, so you better get packing!"

He pulled me in for a hug and smiled to Jillian who was standing behind me. When he released me, I was still leaning toward him even after he had left and driven off.

Jillian whispered, voice quivering "Holy Shit!"

Excerpt from The Knot Hole

Chapter One

"I HATE THIS OLD WOOD paneling," Taryn said aloud as she poured more Liquid Gold onto the soft cloth, continuing to rub new life back into the old wood. She had been doing this job for years now. Actually, since she had been a little girl.

Some people had a favorite picture, piece of jewelry or even a special tree. Her mother had a favorite room, this sewing room, with its four wood paneled walls. It couldn't be the kind of paneling which required only a quick wipe with a damp cloth, no, for her mother it had to be real wood, the actual smell from the wood carried through the room and you felt like you just walked into a home design store.

Each year since her mother's death five years earlier, Taryn had threatened to tear out this paneling, or paint it . . .

or something, but she never did. Taryn would curse and give the wooden walls stern glances. It would seem almost sacrilegious to remove it though. As a child, this wood paneling was at the center of their family. Her father had sanded and stained each panel to perfection, and then added the final coat of finish to make it as smooth and shiny as glass.

It had taken her father many evenings and weekends to complete the room making it as her mother had dreamed it should be. Her room in which she could sew, read, relax, and escape to her dreams. When her mother was in this room with the door closed, everyone respected her need to be alone. When the door was open anyone could wander in and out.

Taryn recalled these memories of her early childhood as she continued to restore the life back into the paneling. Those memories seemed to surround her in this room, and they appeared like a play in three acts. First there was the joy and love her parents shared during the timeframe that it took to complete the walls. She recalled the renovation party her mother had arranged when it was completed. It was almost as though they were welcoming a new member into the family.

The next several months had been spent in finding just the right things to go into the room. Soft shades of yellow were the dominant colors, with beautiful tan thick pile carpeting. Each frame on the walls displayed a picture or painting that held special meaning to her mother. A vision only she could "see" as she created it.

The third act occurred every summer. When school was finished for the year, her mother would bring out three cans of Liquid Gold and a bag of soft cloths she'd been accumulating for the past year. She'd hand a can and several cloths to me and to my sister, Carolyn, and we would begin a week long project of rubbing new life into mother's precious wood paneling. An annual ceremony.

It was an almost solemn experience, such was the reverence we were taught in the care of mother's wood. We worked together for several hours a day, and as we worked, my mother would tell us stories. Each one so descriptive that they gave us a visual we still carry in our minds. We knew she made up the stories and they were very good, we could hang on her words for the entire time. Each year she repeated some of our favorites from earlier years, as well as adding new ones.

As I recall some of the stories, I still find them amazing and timeless. They weren't fairy tales. They seemed real, just as though mother were telling us about a friend of hers and the experiences this friend had; conversations that had taken place. Mother loved to dream, and apparently dreamed so vividly that she was able to tell us such beautiful and seemingly real stories.

Taryn raised herself up from her knees and stretched her sore back, rubbing her tight arm muscles and rotating her head to release the kinks. Again she said aloud, "I hate this wood paneling, now that I have to do it by myself, now that there are no more stories." Taryn stood with her shoulders slumped and felt defeated by this chore. Despite this, to remove it or change it in any way would cause her mother's spirit to become restless, of this she was sure.

She could always feel her mother's love, her essence, in this room. Taryn wondered if indeed a tiny piece of her mother's soul had remained in this room to enjoy it, in peace, throughout eternity. Taryn knew she could never change the wood walls in her mother's dream room. "Well, that's enough R & R for one afternoon. Reminiscing and Rubbing!" She threw the towel into the bucket making the statement that she was done for this day.

Taryn let the water from the shower spray over her body for a long period of time. She felt the soothing sensations of the warm water refresh her from being hunched into the corner polishing the baseboards earlier. Next she quickly dressed as food was needed in her home and the weekly grocery shopping was next, along with several other stops along the way. This was always her busiest week of the year. She was determined to keep to the schedule of devoting several hours each day, in order to finish with the wood panel cleaning in one week's time.

The next afternoon Taryn was back at work, continuing to restore the shine to the walls of the sewing room. As a child she had always been amazed at the many patterns the grains in the wood contained. As she sat back in her mother's favorite chair taking a much needed break, feet propped up and drinking a glass of iced tea, she followed some of the patterns in the wood. Her hazel colored eyes came to rest on the *dream spot*. To anyone else it appeared as a flaw in the otherwise beautifully patterned wood. She remembered asking about the one dark spot on the wood, and her mother's smiling reply. With love in her eyes, she'd said she and her father had searched through many pieces of wood paneling to find the perfect circle that would be her dream spot.

It was a perfect six inch circle, darker in color than the rest of the panel. Taryn learned when she was older that it really was just a knot hole. Her mother told the story of how rough that spot had been when she'd found it, and that her father had worked sanding it by hand with very fine sandpaper to make it perfectly smooth. Once, when asked where she got all of her beautiful stories, her mother smiled that twinkle-eyed smile and told them the stories all came from her dream spot.

The first year they'd polished the wood, she noticed her mother took great care to polish the panel particularly around this area. The second year she'd told Taryn she could have the honor of polishing that panel. The third year the honor went to Carolyn. And so it went year after year, each taking a turn polishing that distinctive area. Taryn returned her attention to polishing, in order to finish the last panel for this summer's ritual cleaning. The last panel was always the one with the knot hole. Another half hour and finally it would be done.

As Taryn rubbed the familiarly scented cloth up and down with the grain of the wood, her cloth passed over the knot hole. She experienced a moment of shock as she thought it felt hot beneath the cloth. "What the hell!" she said aloud. She rubbed over the same spot again, and yes, it did feel heated. She transferred the cloth to her left hand placing her palm over the dream spot. Several things happened at the same moment. Her hand pushed easily through the knot hole, all the way to her elbow. Her body became rigid so she couldn't move.

Panic and fear immediately set in. However, she seemed unable to move, to react physically to the situation. All she could see before her was the wall and her arm from the elbow up. The rest of her lower arm and hand had disappeared into the wall . . . without a hole to disappear into! In her panic, Taryn thought this must be what it felt like to be confined in a strait jacket, fully conscious, but unable to move a muscle in her body.

"Okay, Taryn. Get a grip," she said, "breathe, in and out slowly." The fear receded a bit, as she concentrated on breathing. She'd always been the very practical member of the family. Now was the perfect time to be realistic. "Get real here, Taryn. It is impossible that what you think you see is real. Right? Right! My arm is not stuck in a wall with no hole in it."

She couldn't move her arm. Screaming for help would do no good, since no one was close enough to her home to hear her. A strangled laugh emerged from her very tight throat as she said a silent thank you that no one could see her, or she would certainly be deemed crazy. She slowly became aware of the feeling developing in her missing hand and arm. There was warmth on the skin of her hand . . . no, heat on her hand. No, her hand was *enfolded* in heat.

"Of course," she said, "my hand is outside and the sun is

shining on my hand. Right, Taryn. You stuck your hand through the wall and it's dangling outside. Where is the blood?" She concentrated on her hand and the heat and felt suddenly calmed. How could she feel so calm when her . . . "Taryn" . . . a long silence followed but she was sure she had just heard her name spoken. If someone called her name then . . . "Oh, my God. Someone IS outside. They see my hand."

"Taryn." She heard it again. She seemed to recognize the voice, but couldn't identify it.

"Taryn, don't be afraid. It's only me it's your mother."

"Mother!" Taryn screeched, "Mother?"

"Yes, Taryn, it's me. Really." Her mother's voice responded. "I've been waiting for you to find the secret of my dream spot. I knew you would. Do you feel my hands on yours, Taryn?"

"I feel the heat, yes." Taryn answered.

"I'm holding your hand, Taryn."

"Mother, this isn't real. It's impossible."

"No, Taryn, it isn't real. It's a dream experience. Do you remember the stories I used to tell you when you were little?"

"Of course, Mother. I could never forget your stories."

"Those stories were my own experiences, Taryn. I knew you children would be frightened if I told you the secret of this room and the knot hole, so I never did. I knew someday you would discover the surprise on your own, in your own time. And now you have."

"Mother, my arm can't be stuck in a hole that's not there.

Nor can I be talking to you. You aren't there either. I must be stressed out and don't know it. I'm hallucinating!"

"No, Taryn. You are perfectly healthy and in your right mind. It's only that your mind cannot accept what it's seeing and hearing. It's a totally foreign concept to your mind. I have been allowed to remain nearby until you discovered this, just as I knew you would. Now that you have found it, my dear child, I can continue with my own journey. Your father has been waiting for me for a long time now, so I will join him. Together, we are off to more adventures. Have a wonderful life my dear Taryn, and enjoy the dream spot. It's now yours. It will provide adventures you cannot imagine. Remember my stories, Taryn. They were my adventures. I must go now, dear. Remember always that I love you."

Taryn was stunned. She couldn't speak. She felt her muscles begin to relax and saw her arm and hand slowly emerge from the wall. She stumbled over to her mother's favorite comfortable chair and collapsed into it, totally drained and exhausted. She fell immediately into a very deep and dreamless sleep.

Taryn awakened feeling happy and refreshed. Then she remembered her experience . . . or . . . had she dreamed it while she slept? If it had really happened, it wasn't real anyway. Her mother had said it wasn't real, that it was a dream. A waking dream?

Still feeling confused, Taryn busied herself and gathered the cleaning supplies together, she quickly realized the can of Liquid Gold was on the floor in front of the last panel. The cloth was on the floor as well, just where she must have dropped it . . . if what she thought she'd experienced really had happened?

✧ ✧ ✧

TARYN SLEPT UNTIL ALMOST NOON the next day. The long nap the afternoon before had kept her awake until the early hours of the morning. In order not to think about the afternoon's experience, she read well into the middle of her latest paperback. The heroine's troubles kept her mind well occupied until sleep finally came.

She heated a cup of water in the microwave, added a tea bag and took it out to the deck to enjoy the warm summer sun. All was well with the world that spread out before her eyes, BUT, she wondered, was all well within herself, with her life, with her future? She had a good life, an easy life, a contented life. Then why am I so restless lately, she wondered. She swept back her bangs from her forehead and played lightly with her hair deep in thought.

Last night was a perfect example. She enjoyed Brandon's company and felt comfortable with him. She had been dating Brandon on occasion for about a year, but that's all it was. It was comfortable. She routinely attended fund raising events for various causes. It was always more enjoyable for her to attend with Brandon, than alone. He wasn't the great love in her life, and she knew he wouldn't be. The love that she knew would be hers someday was not there, not like the love her parents shared. She knew she wouldn't settle for less in her mate, but then, she wasn't really anxious to get married right now either. She was only twenty-four and felt she had plenty of time. He did serve a purpose aside from good company. His presence seemed to keep others from being as blatant as they might have otherwise been about their expectations of her. Taryn enjoyed a relatively easy life. She had a comfortable income, and most of her peers knew she didn't have to work for it. As a result, they had expectations that she give to each and every cause. Taryn would have done it anyway, but their attitude soured the experience for her.

She had a number of friends, but they weren't close as she and her friend Ashlee were. Ashlee had moved to the west coast when a great job offer came her way a year ago. She had met Ashlee the first day on campus as a freshman, and it was "like" at first sight. They had roomed together for the next four years. Ashlee had been her source of strength when her mother died so suddenly in her third year at State. Sadly she earlier lost her father who had died while she was still in high school. Her sister, Carolyn, had married during her senior year in college and now traveled from post to post with her career Navy husband. She had only seen Carolyn twice since her mother's funeral.

Taryn was therefore alone when she graduated from college. Ashlee accepted the invitation to come to Virginia with her, to get a job in the area and share Taryn's home. And so it had been, until Ashlee received a reply to a resume she'd sent to the west coast. It was the job she'd wanted, in order to get started in her Hollywood career as a costumer. She'd moved to California a year ago.

It was funny. Just the other day she had been rushing

around with so much to do. All busy work! I really don't have anything important to do, and I'm still not sure what kind of a future I want, she thought. I don't have a burning desire for a husband or children. I'm a writer, but I don't have a fiery aspiration to write, I just do it as it comes to me. There is no strong yearning to find that grand, passionate relationship right now or if I ever will encounter that in my lifetime. Mentioning lifetime, hers had taken a very different turn on one particular day a while back.

THE SUMMER AFTER GRADUATING FROM college, she and Ashlee had started out early one Sunday morning to spend the day at the shore. They'd stopped at a mini-market to fill their cooler with drinks and to buy some beach snacks. They'd also bought one lottery ticket with the change from their purchases. A few days later they found themselves with the *winning* ticket. They both already had what they considered comfortable incomes, but now they were guaranteed a very sizable check once a year, for the next twenty years. That's when Ashlee decided she could pursue her dream of living in California and began sending out resumes. Ashlee would definitely fit into the California lifestyle. She was a beautiful girl with long blonde hair and built very nice as well as already having the look of one of those female Baywatch lifeguards. Her eyes always captivated the people she met. They were a bright blue and she was often asked if she enhanced them with color contacts. Her smile too was not to be missed, it was a great asset and would be a plus to get her into the doors of the Hollywood scene.

Taryn had resigned from her job to chart a new course. She started that journey by buying out her sister's half of the house their mother had left to them to share. She had to consider that this was, at least in part, the problem. She couldn't help but wonder if it was because she didn't have to work, that the need to work was missing. During the year she'd worked as a writer for the Sun Times, she had enjoyed it. But when she no longer needed the income, it had been so easy to leave the job and take some time to decide what she wanted to do with her skills that might be a little more exciting, more rewarding somehow.

"What are you waiting for, Taryn?" She asked herself aloud. "Where is your new venture? Writing a few articles now and then? Spending long research hours at the library for the Pulitzer Prize novel you plan to write someday? Waiting for love to come and find you?" *Enough already!*

Taryn made it to Wednesday without giving into the nagging thoughts of the dream experience with her mother. She also pushed back her thoughts of what her path in life should be. She had not entered the sewing room since last Saturday afternoon. She knew she was no longer afraid of what might or might not have occurred in that room, but still she hadn't been ready to go back in and face her questions.

Taryn entered the room and walked around slowly, lightly sweeping her fingertips over the sewing machine, the love seat, the picture of a beautiful thoroughbred horse, the lamp her mother sat beside to do her delicate hand work. She stopped and turned. Slowly, she walked to the distinctive panel across the room. She thought, once again, about her hand and arm being IN the wall, of her mother's touch on her hand, and her mother's voice. Slowly, she raised her right hand and touched the knot hole delicately with her fingertips. It was cool to the touch, not hot. She hesitated a moment, then placed the palm of her hand completely over the spot. It was still cool to her touch. She waited, with her hand still on the wall. No movement. The wall remained the same.

Almost relieved that nothing had occurred, she released the breath she had been holding and turned to walk over to her mother's favorite chair. She glanced at the door as if it had spoken to her, wondering if her mother had her dreams when the door was closed and the family gave her privacy. She walked over and slowly closed the door.

She returned to the chair and sat down, tucking her legs under her body. Feeling comfortable now, Taryn wondered how her mother had used the dream spot when she'd been sitting in this chair. Feeling very foolish, but too curious not to follow her thoughts, she spoke aloud in a sarcastic tone. "Mother said you belong to me now, dream spot, and that you will show me adventures I couldn't begin to imagine. Do you have an adventure to share with me?"

Taryn kept her eyes on the knot hole, holding in her mind the memory of her mother's warm hands holding her own, as she had the other day. Taryn didn't believe that anything would occur, but the dream spot began moving slowly, as she continued to watch it and concentrate on it. It gradually increased its counter clockwise movement until it was spinning so fast it was a blur to her wide open eyes.

There was a whirring sound, like a top spinning. It was coming across the room towards her. The faster it spun, the louder it sounded, and the closer it appeared to her. The sound seemed to slam hard into her solar plexus and she gasped for breath. It hit her like when the floor moves with a loud clap of thunder during a storm. She then began to spin, faster and faster and in a split second it stopped, she stopped, and there was total silence.

Taryn was aware she had squeezed her eyes tightly shut and now hesitated opening them. She didn't know what she might see, or if she really was being given an adventure. This is silly, this is impossible, she thought. Open your eyes, Taryn! You'll see there is no adventure, only the sewing room. Right! Okay! Here goes!

As she relaxed in order to open her eyes, she became aware of a smell. Quickly she squeezed the lids tight shut again. Smell. What do I smell? Fresh air. Sunshine. Grass. Flowers. I hear water running. I hear birds singing. I'm outside, not in my sewing room.

Slowly she opened her eyes again. Very slowly, so she could shut them quickly again if she had to. Silly, silly, Taryn. Eyes open or eyes closed, I swear you are outside, so you might as well look.

She peeked through narrow slits between her eyelids, and sure enough she was outside. Her eyes opened wide now in surprise. She was standing in a meadow filled with all kinds of wildflowers. Some she recognized, such as beautiful purple liatris, stargazer lilies, and black eyed susans'. . . others she had not seen before and therefore could not identify but their colors were all so incredibly vibrant. She could smell the light fragrances, and combined they reminded her of a bowl filled with potpourri.

She found that she was standing beside a stream. The scent was of a cool crisp rain that just passed over. The water was slowly flowing past her, lazily washing around large stones breaking the surface. The stream was very clean and clear, allowing her to see the pebbles on the very bottom.

Taryn began walking, following the direction of the water. It seemed so silent, and yet there were many sounds. The birds, the leaves rustling in the trees, the sound of the water washing around the stones. She felt very peaceful even though there were many questions hovering just out of reach of her mind. She could only feel. Calm, relaxed, peaceful. It didn't seem important, at the moment, how she had gotten here or even where "here" was.

The stream appeared to end just up ahead of where she was walking. As she got closer, she realized it was taking a sharp turn to the right. She followed around the turn and saw a wooden footbridge crossing over the water a little further ahead. The footbridge wasn't new, but it looked very sturdy. Maybe someone took special care of it as she did with her mother's wood paneling.

She walked part way across the small bridge and decided to sit down. Dangling her legs over the edge of the bridge, Taryn watched the water flow towards her and then pass beneath her. Adventure! The water was having an adventure and so was she. A career, a family, a passion for living and creating a course to follow in her life seemed very far away now, and totally unimportant.

Suddenly, she felt more than alone when she saw a movement off to her right. She turned her head and saw a man walking toward the footbridge from the opposite bank. As he came closer he raised his hand in greeting and said, "Good Afternoon." Taryn could feel him speaking to her, but it felt like he was speaking directly into her head. She knew it was crazy, but she heard him even though she was not really hearing his voice. She wondered if he was a ghost or spirit. She could see him and feel a presence but he wasn't real. She thought if she put out her had to shake his that his would pass right through hers. Taryn returned his greeting and began to stand, but he raised his hand again indicating for her to stay seated.

"May I join you for a few minutes?" He asked.

"Yes." He had nice eyes, smiling eyes, and she felt that he was a gentle man. He was tall and very lean, his skin was pale but his eyes told the story. They were gray in color and looked so deep and endless. She asked, "Are you the owner of this beautiful meadow?"

"No I'm only the caretaker or one who oversees things that occur."

"I feel like I'm trespassing. Is it okay that I'm here?" Taryn asked concerned.

"Of course, Dear. You are most welcome to be here. Are you enjoying your first adventure?"

Taryn was stunned and sure that her face registered the surprise she felt that he should know about her adventure. She asked, "How did you know why I am here?"

"Well, Dear, I've been the caretaker here for an endless amount of time, and I have dubbed this place The Passage."

"It sounds like the name of a secret place," she replied.

"Not a secret at all but for select individuals to experience." He smiled at her to put her at ease.

"I think it will be fun. Am a little nervous as you can see. Do many people come here for an adventure?" She asked.

"Oh, my, yes," he answered. "Many people have come here for their first adventure. Many people who decide to try a dream adventure have questions and doubts as to whether it's real. You might say it's a sort of the training ground for future dream adventures."

"Have you talked with many of these people?" she asked.

"Yes, that's my job. I welcome new visitors and make sure they feel comfortable. Some have expressed great anxiety over their visit here and make the choice of not having any more dream adventures."

"My mother seemed to enjoy hers long ago. She told us such wonderful stories about them. Of course I didn't find out they were real occurrences until just a few days ago. I always thought she was just a very good storyteller."

"Did you ever wonder how so many writers could write so many books and articles, and all have a different story to tell?"

Again surprise registered on her face. "You mean some authors really are writing about their adventures?" Taryn asked.

He nodded his head methodically in response to her question.

"Are you saying this place is a starting point for would-be writers?" she continued.

"Not at all. I would describe this place more as a starting point for a creative person to explore and expand their imaginative powers, no matter what their talent. However, don't limit your thoughts to that idea, for this place is far more than that."

"My mother was a very creative person in her passion for making clothing. She was a seamstress, but she only produced clothing for me, my sister and herself. And she took great care in creating her sewing room. Is that how she came to visit here?"

"Yes. In one sense. Her creativity had no boundaries. She loved to work with fabrics, textures and colors. However, she placed being a mother and wife above a career, so she never allowed her artistic ideas to reach out into the world of fashion, where, I might add, she could have been very successful. Because she was so very inventive, she extended that ability into creating a perfect room for herself. Her innovative essence was still not satisfied and that's what led her to discover the dream adventure. Many times I told your mother she should publish her stories so other people could appreciate them. She always said they were only for her children to enjoy. It was her boundaries that caused her to decide that she couldn't take a chance on becoming a known author. In her mind, that would take her away from her family and home."

"I've thought about publishing some of her stories. But mother was so against the idea, I haven't dared to do so . . . as of yet." Taryn smiled back.

"You may do so if you like, for they are now your stories. Your mother gave them to you as she gave you the dream spot to explore if you choose to do so."

"So you know about that?" Taryn questioned.

"Yes. We keep track of our visitors and their progress."

"Somehow through that knot hole I got here, but . . . how do I get back?" Taryn questioned as she wrinkled her brow.

"Well, as soon as you have decided your dream adventure is completed you will find yourself comfortably back in your chair in the sewing room."

"Is it always that quick and easy?" Taryn voiced.

"No, Dear. Not always. Sometimes you'll find that you're not finished with your dream adventure, but that you go back anyway."

"How? Why?" Taryn was confused.

"For any number of reasons. Your body may require a meal, the phone may ring, someone may come to your door, or you may have an appointment to keep."

"You mean I can never get stuck in an adventure and not return home?"

"You, Dear, will never get stuck anywhere. You will always return home. Your mother always returned. It wouldn't be considered an adventure if you stayed in it forever. It would create a crisis in your world". He stood up. "I'll continue my walk now. Enjoy your adventures." He smiled and raised his hand in farewell. Taryn curved her lips into a soft closed lipped smile and raised her hand, offering the same gesture. Within moments Taryn heard a distant whirring sound and before she could locate its source, she was leaning back in her chair in the sewing room.

Her first thought was to wonder how long she might have been gone. She checked the light on her answering machine, but there had been no calls. She turned on the TV and flipped to The Weather Channel. It was still the same date and no more than a half hour could have passed. Funny, it seemed like hours must have passed during her adventure.

24796326R00211

Made in the USA
Middletown, DE
07 October 2015